The strange History
of suzanne Lafleshe

THE WOMEN'S STORIES PROJECT
Susan Koppelman, editor

Between Mothers and Daughters:
Stories Across a Generation

The Strange History of Suzanne LaFleshe
and Other Stories of Women and Fatness

The Other Woman:
Stories of Two Women and a Man

The strange History of suzanne Lafleshe

and other stories of women
and fatness

Edited by Susan Koppelman

Foreword by Alix Kates Shulman

THE FEMINIST PRESS
AT THE CITY UNIVERSITY OF NEW YORK
New York

Published by the Feminist Press at the City University of New York
The Graduate Center, 365 Fifth Avenue
New York, NY 10016, www.feministpress.org

First Feminist Press edition, 2003

09 08 07 06 05 04 03   5 4 3 2 1

This publication was made possible, in part, by public funds from the New York State Council
on the Arts.

State of the Arts

NYSCA

The Feminist Press would also like to thank Jan Constantine, Dorothy O. Helly, and Nancy
Hoffman, for their support of this book.

Library of Congress Cataloging-in-Publication Data

The strange history of Suzanne LaFleshe and other stories of women and fatness / edited by
Susan Koppelman ; foreword by Alix Kates Shulman.— 1st Feminist Press ed.
    p. cm.
    ISBN 1-55861-451-6 (pbk. : alk. paper) — ISBN 1-55861-450-8 (library
cloth : alk. paper)
    1. Women—Fiction. 2. Body image—Fiction. 3. Overweight
women—Fiction. 4. Short stories, American—Women authors. I.
Koppelman, Susan.
    PS648.W6S87 2003
    813'.01083522—dc22
                                                                      2003018681

Cover art: *Doing the Lambada* by Beryl Cook © 2000. First published in Beryl Cook's *Cruising*,
Victor Gonzalez Publishers, London. Reproduced by permission of the artist c/o Rogers,
Coleridge & White Ltd., 20 Powis Mews, London W11 1JN.
Text design by Dayna Navaro
Printed in Canada on acid-free paper by Transcontinental Printing

◇

To My Beloved Granddaughters,
Jasmine Grace Cornillon and
Sarah Jade Cornillon
Perfect at Any Size

◇

Many of the most virulent stereotypes about women in general have not been discarded but merely transferred, so that negative qualities once attributed to all women are now considered the sole province of fat women.
—W. Charisse Goodman, *The Invisible Woman: Confronting Weight Prejudice in America*

The challenge we face is to change patterns of exclusion, rejection, privilege, harassment, discrimination, and violence that are everywhere in this society. . . . Large numbers of people have sat on the sidelines and seen themselves as neither part of the problem nor the solution. . . . Their silence and invisibility allow the trouble to continue.
—Allan G. Johnson, *Privilege, Power, and Difference*

It is not easy to become beautiful. It requires hard work, patience, and attention to detail. It also takes a certain firmness of purpose. Beauty is in the eye of the beholder, and it may be necessary from time to time to give a stupid or misinformed beholder a black eye.
—Miss Piggy, *Miss Piggy's Guide to Life*

The meanings attributed to extraordinary bodies reside not in inherent physical flaws, but in social relationships in which one group is legitimated by possessing valued physical characteristics and maintains its ascendancy and its self-identity by systematically imposing the role of cultural or corporeal inferiority on others.
—Rosemarie Garland Thomson, *Extraordinary Bodies: Figuring Physical Disability in American Culture and Literature*

I used the word fat. I used that word because that's what fat people are. They're fat. They're not large; they're not stout, chunky, hefty, or plump. And they're not big-boned. Dinosaurs are big-boned. These people are not necessarily obese, either. Obese is a medical term. And they're not overweight. Overweight implies there is some correct weight. There is no correct weight. Heavy is also a misleading term. An aircraft carrier is heavy; it's not fat. Only people are fat, and that's what fat people are. They're fat. I offer no apologies for this. It is not intended as a criticism or insult. It is simply descriptive language. I don't like euphemisms. Euphemisms are a form of lying. Fat people are not gravitationally disadvantaged. They're fat. I prefer seeing things the way they are, not the way some people wish they were.

—George Carlin, *Brain Droppings*

At the Cooper Institute, two separate studies—one following 9,925 women and another tracking 25,000 men—found that fitness level is a much stronger indicator against early death than weight. Being thin offers no protection, in and of itself.

In other words, the death rate for men and women who are thin but unfit is at least twice as high as those who are obese and fit, the Cooper Clinic found. Better to be large and exercise than thin and a couch potato.

None of this is news to Deb Lemire of Cuyahoga Falls, Ohio. Yes, she's overweight. But, no, she's not unhealthy. "The diet industry isn't interested in our health," Lemire said. "It's interested in our money."

—Tracy Wheeler, *The Modesto Bee*, July 23, 2003

Some code words have multiple meanings. "I'm so fat" is a common lament with at least three separate translations. When I first started meeting with girls, middle-class students complained constantly of peers who overused the phrase. In fact, in a study called "Fat Talk," researchers noted that most girls who said "I'm so fat" weren't fat at all.

First, "I'm so fat" is used as a tool of indirect one-upping. "Girls ask each other if they are fat, and that is a way of competing with each other," an eighth grader explained to me. "If they are skinny and ask themselves if they are fat, what does that say about me? It's a passive aggressive way of saying the other person's not skinny." In "Fat Talk," girls described "how their friends practically 'accused' them of being thin, 'as if it were my fault of something.'"

"I'm so fat" is also used as a roundabout way to seek positive reinforcement from a peer. "I'm so fat is fishing for compliments," thirteen-year old Nicole said. . . . When they say that it's because they want attention.

Finally, girls use "I'm so fat" to short-circuit the possibility of getting labeled "all that." The researchers found that if a girl didn't say she thought she was fat, she would imply that she was perfect. "In other words, saying she doesn't need to diet would be an admission that she didn't need to work on herself—that she was satisfied." Instead, they found, the "good girl" must put herself down, and so wind her way to the compliment she is seeking.

—Rachel Simmons, *Odd Girl Out: The Hidden Culture of Aggression in Girls*

Anyone who discusses dieting at dinner is unspeakably rude and should not be hired as an academic or accepted as a friend. It is boring and it is gauche.

—Emily Toth, *Ms. Mentor's Impeccable Advice for Academic Women*

CONTENTS

ACKNOWLEDGMENTS

On April 13, 1973 at 9 A.M. at the Atkinson Hotel in Indianapolis, Indiana, I stood before a room filled with people, announced, "I am fat," and slowly peeled the wrapping off of a giant Baby Ruth candy bar and took a bite. This act was the taboo-breaking climax of a multimedia presentation called "To Be Fat: The Uses of Obesity in Advertising," co-presented with Beth Mahan on a panel entitled "Images of Women in Advertising" at the third National Meeting of the Popular Culture Association.

Of the eighty-four panels at the conference, eleven focused on various aspects of women's studies. Of the remaining seventy-four panels, ten more of the panels had at least one presentation that represented a women's studies perspective. A quick skimming of the program from that 1973 conference reveals the names of many of the women who became known as the pioneer mothers of feminist thought and pedagogy. Under the auspices of the Popular Culture Association, we held what I believe was the first national gathering of women's studies pioneer scholars.

Over the years I have attended almost all of the annual conferences, anticipating them with excitement, participating in them with enthusiasm, and remembering them with pleasure.

On April 17, 2003, at 10:30 A.M. at the New Orleans Marriott Hotel, I presented a preliminary paper on what has become the afterword to this book. I recalled the session thirty-three years earlier in Indianapolis and noted that things have gotten much worse for fat people over these three decades. But I noted also, with great joy, the growth of both the fat liberation movement and the size acceptance movement and the founding in 1977 of the National Women's Studies Association, the second organization to which I gave my wholehearted loyalty and love.

I want to thank Ray B. Browne and Pat Browne, founders (along with several others) of the Popular Culture Association and organizers and shepherds of thirty-three annual conferences. With wisdom and grace, they welcomed us all, making room at these conferences for every kind of intellectual, cultural, theoretical inquiry. Ray was my mentor and my dissertation director.

Ray and Pat were my first publishers, enabling me to bring *Images of Women in Fiction: Feminist Perspectives* into the world in 1972. When I was looking for a doctoral program in which I would be allowed to pursue the course of study I was already engaged in, a study of the history of U.S. women through literature, law, popular culture, psychology, and sociology, Ray welcomed me to Bowling Green State University in 1970 with his characteristic twinkle, saying, "Why not here?" When I announced that I wanted to do a dissertation on feminist literary criticism, Ray said, "Why not?" When I asked Ray and Pat if it would be all right to invite all the women's studies scholars I could locate to the conference in 1972 they answered, "Why not?" When I proposed talking about fat women they said, "Why not?"

Emily Toth, Robert Penn Warren Professor of English and Women's Studies, Louisiana State University, channeller of Ms. Mentor, Kate Chopin biographer, women's studies and popular culture pioneer, was on the panel on images of women in advertising in 1973 speaking about "The Fouler Sex: Women's Bodies in Advertising." In 2003 she shared the podium with me to speak about "Women of Substance and Good Eating in New Orleans." Emily has been my dear friend for thirty-four years and we have egged each other on to increasing splendor, applauding each other, cheering for each other, creating a world in which we might survive with our belief in ourselves intact. She has always been there to read, reread, and make suggestions about my work, and to encourage me and to laugh with me.

Cheri Erdman, Ed.D., started the journey towards fat acceptance with me in Bowling Green, Ohio, in 1973. She was one of the most vital participants in a fat women's consciousness-raising group and she has gone on to write, lecture, and teach about size acceptance in the intervening years with wit, wisdom, and dignity.

I am grateful to the authors of the stories, especially Susan Stinson, Elana Dykewomon, Lesléa Newman, Wanda Coleman, Roz Warren, and Elena Diaz Bjorkquist, each of whom was generous enough to talk about her work with me and answer my questions about her stories, and all the others whose work provides us with credible and incredible visions of what was, what is, what ought to be, and what is on its way. Without them, of course, there would be no book.

Jean Casella, the publisher and director of the Feminist Press, invited me to bring my ideas for short story collections to her and responded to me with such warmth and enthusiasm that I felt emboldened to begin my work again after a six-year hiatus in which I have been totally focused on family health problems.

Elissa Fox of the Feminist Press put in many hours working with me on permissions and other questions relating to the material included in this book, and always maintained a cheerful and kind demeanor. She also offered some fine ideas for improving the book.

Lieutenant Matthew Ryan, brilliant linguist, compassionate, funny, raconteur in the honorable tradition of his dear parents, Jim and Jeanne Ryan, and beloved friend, paid for that grilled chicken sandwich.

Michelle Ennis Hinkebein, my beloved play-daughter-in-law, passed on to me the wisdom of her father, Arthur Ennis: "Only a dog likes a bone."

Alison Franks (folklorist and fabric artist), Sarah Port (registered nurse), Elizabeth Dane (social worker and teacher), Merrill Joan Gerber (writer and teacher), Alan Goldberg, Psy.D., ABPP, J.D. (neuropsychologist and attorney), Louise Bernikow (writer and feminist activist), Gaye Lewis (businesswoman, first cousin, and couturier), Dorothy Taber (M.A., C.R.C.), Eva Shaderowfsky (photographer and writer), Barbara Harman (artist and writer), Harold Smith (artist and teacher), Bette Tallen, Ph.D. (coordinator of diversity training at the University of Central Florida, diversity trainer/educator, and political theorist), Linda Wagner Martin, Ph.D. (scholar, writer, and teacher), Martha Baker (writer and editor), and Dan Chaon (writer and teacher) each read and commented on portions of this work at various points in the process of my writing and shared with me insights and information based on their professional training, research, experience, and personal wisdom. Every one of these dear people encouraged me in this work.

Alix Kates Shulman, one of the most important philosopher-novelists to be nurtured and to nurture the women's liberation movement, wrote her generous and erudite foreword to this book.

Edward Cumella, Ph.D., the Director of Research, Education, and Quality at Remuda Ranch in Arizona, a respected in-patient facility that treats about 700 women with eating disorders each year, has shared both wisdom and facts with me with grace and generosity.

Seth Montes helped me unravel the mysteries of the term *skanky*.

Barbara Temkin, Ph.D., psychologist, introduced me to a wide variety of useful books and articles that not only broadened my thinking but provided me with several of the epigraphs.

Gaye Lewis and Lorraine Linden, owners of the wonderful Manassas, Virginia BBW (big beautiful women) boutique CLASSIX (www.classicsboutique.com), have been teaching me about beautiful clothes, terrific accessories, and self-esteem for many years.

Mary and Tom Hanson joined me in my search for images of BBWs in art, took me to Nogales, Sonora, Mexico to show me the work of one of Mary's favorite artists who loves to paint women like us, and shared many works of art via the internet as I searched for a cover for this book.

Dr. Rosemarie Garland Thomson, disability studies pioneer scholar, provided me with material that helped me find ways to talk about fat women and disability rights.

Sheila Tobias, devoted feminist activist, educator, and writer, has supported and encouraged my work for three decades; in 1980 she gave me the great gift of Marcia Millman's *Such a Pretty Face,* and almost a quarter of a century later gave me the great gift of Susan Bordo's *Unbearable Weight.*

My son, Edward Nathan Koppelman Cornillon, and my daughter-in-law, Ellen Kathleen Cornillon, shared with me their insights and perspectives in important conversations we had about this book. And in the midst of all of this, Nathan, computer maven, bought me a new computer, got me hooked up to Broadband, installed XP, and generally mentors me not only in computer matters but in logic.

Alma Arminta provides us with desperately needed help in managing our domestic life, and brings into our home and our lives, to give us joy, her wonderful daughters Ponchetta, Suzanna, and Victoria.

Jenene Bowman, massage therapist extraordinaire, helped keep me mobile and pain-free enough to complete this work.

Ann Elizabeth (Beth) Younger of Louisiana State University, introduced to me by Emily Toth, helped with story research and brought several stories to my attention, most particularly "Goodbye, Old Laura" by Lucile Vaughan Payne and "Primos" by Connie Porter.

Nicole Francis Davis and the students in Emily Toth's spring 2003 class Women Writers at Louisiana State University, Baton Rouge, "field tested" some of the stories.

Nova Smith and the students in Andrea Lapin's spring 2003 section of Women and Society, the introductory women's studies course at the University of Pittsburgh, also "field tested" some of the stories.

Our butterscotch cat, Riff Raff, now almost seventeen years old, supervised the entire process, often while sitting across my shoulders. He suffered a life-threatening illness this summer of 2003 and we are grateful that he survived.

And, finally, *sine qua non,* my thanks to Dennis Mills, my husband, and Frances Koppelman, my mother, who, as always, read all the stories and talked about them with me and then read many versions and revisions of the introduction, afterword, and epigraphs. They also provided me with diversion when I needed it, protected space and time when I needed it, love to nurture my soul, and many yummy meals to nurture my body—and my soul, too, because food is love.

Susan Koppelman
Tucson, Arizona
September 2003

FOREWORD

KOPPELMAN'S TREASURE

It is a well-established fact of literary history that women writers pioneered the English novel, women playwrights were among the most popular on London's Restoration stage, women fiction writers participated in the creation of the American short story and brought it to new heights of popularity. But no matter how original, popular, or appreciated they may have been in their own time, women writers have usually faded into oblivion soon after death. Peruse any recent roster of writers past—from course syllabi to publishers' backlists—and even after decades of active feminism you will see a depressing gender imbalance. With a few iconic exceptions, women's works are soon forgotten, robbing us of insight and pleasure, and skewing our understanding of the past—until a feminist resurgence produces the hunger and scholarship that lead to their rediscovery and return to print.

The Second Wave of U.S. feminism was profoundly lucky to have in Susan Koppelman just such a hungry, committed, and very independent scholar to lead this work of recovery. Even before there were university women's studies departments, she began her feminist scholarship, editing what is probably the first collection of Second Wave criticism, *Images of Women in Fiction: Feminist Perspectives,* published in 1972. At about the same time, she launched her ambitious life-project: to pan the archives for forgotten (and undervalued) nuggets of women's literature. A passionate reader and devotee of the short story, Koppelman gradually became one of the country's leading authorities on U.S. short fiction by women.

Her persistent search has yielded up a treasure of thousands of women's stories, many of which might otherwise have remained lost in the stacks. She maintains a personal archive of more than 3,500 and estimates that she has read more than 25,000. The earliest come from early nineteenth-century gift books and annuals; the most recent from contemporary "literary" and genre (science fiction, mystery, and romance) magazines and anthologies; and some come from feminist publications of both the women's suffrage and women's liberation movements. At least half of the treasure Koppelman uncovered in long-defunct nineteenth- and early twentieth-century popular illustrated magazines—in their time often the only, and usually the most remunerative, outlet for publication of even the finest literature by women.

So far, she has published seven thematic anthologies of women's stories, on subjects of crucial concern to women, with more on the way. And although these books include but a small portion of the total treasure in Koppelman's collection, her anthologies have provided the reading public with invaluable views of life in this country, past and present, as seen through women's eyes. By organizing her anthologies thematically, placing smack in the middle of her books' titles the devalued subject matter and concerns that have historically marked women's lives and literature, Koppelman has defied that devaluation. With such titles as *Old Maids, Between Mothers and Daughters, The Other Woman,* and *Women's Friendships,* and collections on the themes of nineteenth-century lesbians (*Two Friends*), battering and resistance (*Women in the Trees*), and women and fatness (*The Strange History of Suzanne LaFleshe*), these anthologies lead the reader deep into the complexities that underlie the tragedies and triumphs, the sufferings and joys of more than one and a half centuries of diverse and varied women's lives. By de-fragmenting a single complex theme before our eyes through a carefully selected range of stories of different eras, different angles, and different styles, Koppelman invites us to compare and contrast—and thereby to begin to comprehend. Out of a handful of disparate yarns she magically knits a multicolored garment of enduring substance.

Many unexpected aesthetic delights await Koppelman's readers. Here are stories alternately, and sometimes simultaneously, gripping, poignant, sly, funny, disturbing, surprising, brave, and always illuminating. As an early advocate of the importance of popular culture (a field still unnamed while she was earning her doctorate in literature), Koppelman has smartly side-stepped the issue of "quality" by which the literary establishment has traditionally devalued the writings and interests of women as trivial, transitory, or dull. Like the largely female audience who always valued stories by women no matter what their origin or what the critics said, without apology Koppelman takes women's work seriously, finding it every bit as important as men's contributions to the ongoing project of consciousness that is literature. Through a process of distillation, she has selected from thousands of possibilities artfully balanced collections that span time, region, faith, class, race, ethnicity, sexuality, dis/ability, generation, age, and experience. The stories in these anthologies range from the first short story ever published in the United States by an African American (the 1859 "The Two Offers" by Frances Ellen Watkins Harper), through ethnic fiction by early twentieth-century Jewish writer Martha Wolfenstein and Hispanic writer Maria Cristina Mena, to once best-selling novelists like Susan Glaspell, Kate Chopin, and Dorothy Canfield, to fiction by such recently acknowledged masters of the form as Zora Neale Hurston, Sandra Cisneros, and Joanna Russ. Each of the anthologies can shock us out of complacency; taken together they help to correct a biased history. And many of the individual stories can deepen our understanding of ourselves—such is the power of literature.

This tireless work of search-and-preserve—a lifelong labor of love—is Koppelman's gift to us. To ensure that her gift endures (for such are the vicissitudes of publishing and gender politics that already some of Koppelman's anthologies are hard to come by), the Feminist Press has launched an exciting and ambitious program, the Women's Stories Project, which will appropriately begin with the publication of several Koppelman anthologies, including a new collection as well as important reprint volumes. The project also plans to establish an online catalogue of hundreds more stories by U.S. women writers, selected under Koppelman's expert supervision. In this way, a new generation of creative artists, feminist seekers, specialized scholars, teachers, and ordinary readers alike will have easy access to a nineteenth- and twentieth-century literary heritage that, for all its fragility and incompleteness, is indispensable to us.

Alix Kates Shulman
New York City
April 2003

INTRODUCTION

Not too long ago I was invited to lunch at a popular restaurant with my husband and three other people, two of whom I hadn't met before. The event had been arranged by Matthew, a man we all knew and loved, to celebrate a recent personal success. My husband and I looked forward to the event because we love Matthew, whom we had known since he was a baby. We expected to like his friends and anticipated having fun.

I chose among the mouthwatering offerings with difficulty. Finally, as the fashionably slender server finished taking the fourth order and turned to me, I decided on the spicy chicken sandwich. The description of the grilled chicken breast with melted provolone cheese, red pepper mayonnaise, and caramelized red onions on ciabatta bread sounded scrumptious. But the server, instead of writing my order down on her pad, protested: "That's very rich. It's delicious, but it's *very* rich."

I asked, "Is it as good as the description says?"

"Oh, it's wonderful," she said. "In fact, it's one of our most popular items."

"Well, then, "I said, "that's a good recommendation. That's what I'll have."

"But," she continued to caution, "It's very, very rich."

"What's wrong with that?" I asked, knowing full well what she meant. I was being simultaneously cautioned and reprimanded, reminded that because I am fat, I should always be on a diet, reminded that as a fat person I am not supposed to *ever* eat without apology in public.

She stopped cold. I repeated, acting as if I thought perhaps she hadn't heard it or understood it, "What's wrong with it being very rich?"

Meanwhile, all conversation at our table had stopped. The couple I had just met began to look embarrassed. My husband and our friend, who had "gotten" the exchange, looked at the server.

"Well," she finally stammered, "I just mean that many times people can't even finish it."

"Oh," I said, "I'm not worried about that. I'm sure you have take-home boxes."

"It's just," she said again, "it's so rich."

"Well," I said, laughing, "I'm an American. And we like riches. Isn't that why all our parents or grandparents or great-grandparents came to this great land? To get a share of the riches? To partake of the fat of the land? I believe in the American Dream of riches. I'm a patriot. So bring me that so-rich sandwich."

Everyone laughed, even the server. But underneath my laughter, I was boiling mad. And I still am.

I often wonder why we fat folk don't lose our tempers more often when we are confronted by the arrogance and insensitivity of fatophobes. All our immensity must surely be good for something besides the pleasure our lovers feel when they touch our sensual bodies. We fat people are usually stronger than most people. Our muscles are constantly being exercised and developed by carrying all that weight around. So why don't we throw that weight around more often? Why don't we just beat up people who attempt to humiliate us?

I don't know why, but we don't. Maybe we should. Maybe, just maybe, the best way to stop the constant abuse, humiliation, condescension, social exclusions, refusal of jobs and health insurance, and physical threats heaped on fat people, is to *stomp them out*—if not literally, through physical violence, then figuratively, through our words, our votes, our organized activism.

Unfortunately, though, many of us have swallowed the propaganda of the body fascists and think we don't deserve better treatment. Many of us believe that we are all they say we are—ugly, stupid, lazy, out of control, and undeserving of love. Many of us hate ourselves. Many of us spend our summers hiding in black raincoats instead of celebrating the sunshine in bright bikinis. But fat-hatred is not about truth; it is simple, old-fashioned, and culturally condoned prejudice.[1] Sizeism is oppression.[2]

But what and who exactly *is* a fat person? And what constitutes fat? It depends on who's judging, and when. In the early twenty-first century in the United States, even slender women have learned to think of themselves as fat and to hate their own flesh.[3]

When does a person become fat? As you read through these stories, where no specific weight is mentioned for the supposedly fat person, try and figure out how much that woman actually weighs. Can you do that?

In the thirty-one years that I have been searching for, collecting, and thinking about U.S. women's short stories, I have accumulated 167 stories in which a woman's body has been judged too fat. Sometimes the judge has been the woman herself, a woman who is fat or thinks herself or feels fat. But just as frequently it has been someone else imposing the judgment. The feelings associated with the judgment that a woman is fat, whether the judge is the woman herself or someone else, have mostly been negative. However, it is evident, over the period of one hundred years covered by the stories in this selection from the 167, that the hatred attached to the bodies of fat women is a social judgment rather than an objective observation or a scientific "diagnosis." One indication of this is simply the fluidity and range of what is judged to be a fat body and how that judgment differs from one historical period to another.

We like our salaries to be enormous, our orgasms to be monumental, our successes gargantuan. We want our SUVs huge, our king-sized beds massive, our TV screens gigantic. We want our horizons to be vast, our experiences to be immense, our fast food meals super-sized. We buy ourselves colossal breasts and want our male lovers (if we want them at all) to have mammoth penises. But we are supposed to want, our female bodies to be small, tiny, wispy, featureless, infinitesimal, waiflike puffs of smoke on the verge of disappearing. And many of us do want just that.

The more education some of us get, the more wealth, the more success, the smaller we think our bodies have to be. We can never be small enough (without dying) and we are always ashamed about how big we are.

Who profits from our shame about our bodies? Whose interests are served? How did we learn to feel such profound distaste for our own flesh? What are we distracted from when we worry about the sizes of our various parts? What might we feel guilty about if we didn't feel guilty about eating? What could women accomplish, how powerful might we become, if all the energy we turn toward our own bodies were released onto the world?

In a world full of war, famine, pollution, and disease, why do we constantly hear about an "epidemic of obesity?"[4] There seem to be more newspaper stories and TV news features about this "epidemic of obesity" than there are about any other threat to the health of our population.

Any *other* threat to our health? Who says fatness is a threat to our health? Fat is not a terminal disease.[5] The oppression heaped upon fat people is the primary cause of the early deaths of some fat people.[6] High blood pressure, cardiovascular disease, suicide—all these ailments are common to those who live under the constant stress of oppression. They are also common consequences of yo-yo dieting[7]. And many of the most serious health problems of fat people result from our unwillingness to go a doctor when we have a medical problem. We ignore the problem, or try to cure it alone, because we are reluctant to repeat our past experiences of humiliation by doctors, of condescending dismissal of our complaints, patient blaming, and general unkindness from medical personnel. Health issues that might have been easily treated early on become life-threatening and, sometimes, life-ending.

On the other hand, not all fat people die young. Look around you. Don't you see all the fat old ladies out there? Some of them in their eighties are still being counseled to count their calories! The ones I know just laugh at that advice.

But the broadcasts continue. We are told that our out-of-control, blossoming, burgeoning, and beautifully abundant flesh is not only a threat to the health of those of us who are larger than we are "supposed" to be (according to doctors and insurance actuaries), but a threat so serious to the economics of the health care system that we fatties, all by ourselves, might bring the entire system crashing down on the heads of our under-cared-for population.

The talented actor Camryn Manheim lashes back at this attitude in her memoir:

> Kathy Smith is a fitness guru, who took it upon herself to write about my acceptance speech at the Emmy Awards in a newspaper column headlined "If Fat Becomes Hip, We Are In Extreme Trouble." Really? How so? What kind of trouble? I'm just trying to figure out what kind of chaos the world would be thrown into if fat became hip and hips became fat. Would there be chocolate rationing? Would Wall Street buckle under heavier brokers? Would all the pork in the federal budget actually be appropriated for pork? It's hard to imagine exactly what this "extreme trouble" might be."[8]

Our big round bellies and bountiful bouncy bosoms, our meaty thighs and chubby calves, our fat cheeks, top and bottom, our jiggley upper arms and pudgy ankles are such a threat to our great democracy that patriotic citizens take it upon themselves, without prodding or invitation, without special training or promised rewards, to accost those of us who threaten the safety of the United States in this fat way and to remind us of our patriotic duty to diet for the sake of the nation. Some of the comments, the attitudes, the public rhetoric on fat people seems to brand us as treasonous, or even as sinners.

In her book *Real Gorgeous*, Kaz Cooke writes, "According to diet lore, 'indulging' or 'giving in to temptation' is a 'sin.' Strangling a few people is a sin. Invading East Timor is a sin. Ethnic cleansing is a sin. Testing nuclear weapons in the Pacific is a sin. I'm sorry, but eating doesn't quite make the grade." [9]

What might we fervently wish for if we weren't wishing to make ourselves smaller? Where might we go with our energy and ambition if we weren't walking nowhere on treadmills? What other kinds of calculations might we occupy ourselves with if we weren't counting calories and grams of carbohydrates and figuring out just how many sit-ups we had to do to "pay for" that slice of banana cream pie? Who is getting away with what while we are watching our bathroom scales instead of our elected officials? What kind of courage would it take for us to stop hating how we look? What kind of self control would we need to really enjoy a meal without ambivalence? What might women want— or demand—if we weren't kept busy always wanting to be thinner?

So much useless, frivolous sorrow—and yet the suffering is as real as if it all really mattered. The suicides, the self-mutilations, the despair, the desperation, the grief, the shame—grand opera emotions about trivial and evanescent matters of the flesh.

In the stories in this collection, women from more than one hundred years of American history and diverse parts of American culture struggle with the loathing we have been taught to feel for our own bodies and with the contempt that others feel for our bodies. Fat children's lives are made hellish and the cruelties inflicted on them are seldom disrupted by adults.[10] Women are divided from each other, friendships ended or never begun, and family relationships distorted.[11]

But things do finally start to change—fat women realize that other fat women experience what they do; they discover themselves as a group of people being treated badly. Friendships begin to develop among fat women and between fat women and not-fat women. Like oppressed racial or ethnic groups, fat women begin to find their pride, their rage, their self-esteem, their love for each other, their determination to create social change, to take charge of naming their own reality, and, finally, an assertion of self-love.

Many adult fat women have come to consciousness of themselves as oppressed women and joined in the creation of a social justice movement. We are finding our voices in short stories that express defiance, joy, celebration, rage, and sisterhood. However, at the same time, a new set of stories about adolescent body angst has also appeared. A generation of very young women, whose bodies are the least "fat" of all the bodies found in these stories, seems to suffer more profoundly about their weight than any women before them. How can these young women be saved before they starve themselves to death?[12] Perhaps by women of all sizes and body types joining in a common cause, across generations, to end sizeism.

Wanna hear a joke about a fat woman?

No!

And, by the way, the spicy chicken sandwich was, indeed, delicious.

NOTES

1. "There's a certain gleefulness with which many of us greet news of our compatriots' flabbiness. It's an opportunity to feel superior to those, we imagine, with poor self-restraint and worse taste, eating their way to an early grave on Big Macs and Chee*tos." Nina Shapiro, "Epidemic or Exaggeration? The alarmist rhetoric on fat is a little flabby," *Seattle Weekly* , July 18–24, 2002.

2. Check out "Sizing Up Weight-Based Discrimination," May 3, 2002, on *www.tolerance.org* for an excellent summary of the ways in which the impact of anti-fat bias is experienced in the lives of fat people. Tolerance.org is a web project of the Southern Poverty Law Center, leaders in education and advocacy against organized racism and hate crimes. According to a personal communication from Bette Tallen, Ph.D., Coordinator of Diversity Training at the University of Central Florida, diversity trainer/educator and political theorist, July 14, 2003, the bias is not "just" prejudice, not "just" discrimination, it is oppression: "The problem here is that fighting back against prejudice is only part of the deal. To

deal with fat oppression means to respond with the same type of strategies that we do to any system of oppression. We are not only talking about personal pain. We are talking about a society that benefits in specific ways by the oppression of fat women—it reinforces sexism by not only teaching women to not take up space, but to be smaller, and less powerful than men—to deny them of some of the very same tools we need to survive (self-defense, personal senses of integrity and self love). Sizeism is integrally connected to other systems of oppression. . . . Anti-fat hatred is not just an accidental thing: Powerful institutions—such as the medical system, media, corporations who benefit from it have systematically incorporated it into every aspect of life."

3. "Many psychological studies have concluded consistently that many women simply do not like their own appearance. This conclusion was drawn by Judith Rodin et al. (1985), who coined the term 'normative discontent' to describe the 'norm,' if not the 'normal.' SED, or 'subliminal eating disorder,' has been coined to characterize those who are neither overweight nor underweight but are obsessively and excessively concerned with their weight. The woman who never thinks about her weight might be considered 'abnormal.'" Janice S. Lieberman, Ph.D., "On Looking and Being Looked At" in *The Round Robin: Newsletter of Section I, Psychologist-Psychoanalyst Practitioners, Division of Psychoanalysis (39), American Psychological Association*, 18:1 (Spring 2003), 10.

4. The world's media have become too "fixated" on obesity, according to the man leading World Health Organization attempts to improve global eating habits. Derek Yach, executive director for non-communicable diseases and mental health at the WHO, said the excessive focus on obesity stigmatized the obese and ignored the fact that thin people were not necessarily healthy. Adam Jones and Frances Williams in Geneva and and Neil Buckley, "WHO warns against media obsession with obesity," *New York Financial Times*, June 24, 2003.

5. The evidence that fat is not the danger it is advertised to be is wide-ranging, multi-disciplinary, well-known in the sciences by those who care to know it, and easily accessed. I will not summarize it here but interested readers who are unaware of the fact that dieting is dangerous and fat is not, that inactivity and depression are dangerous and fat is not, that the stress of oppression and internalized self-hatred are dangerous and fat is not, are welcome to consult the various fat acceptance sites and books listed in the bibliography for information.

6. "The root word of the word 'oppression' is the element 'pressed.' The press of the crowd; pressed into military service; to press a pair of pants; printing press; press the button. Presses are used to mold things or flatten them or reduce them in bulk, sometimes to reduce them by pressing out the gasses or liquids in them. Something pressed is caught between or among forces and barriers that are so related to each other that jointly they restrain, restrict or prevent the thing's motion or mobility. Mold. Immobilize. Reduce." Excerpt from Marilyn Frye's essay "Oppression," included in her book *The Politics of Reality: Essays in Feminist Theory* (Trumasburg, NY: Crossing Press, 1983) 2.

7. "There are stronger and more consistent links between body weight variability and negative health outcomes, particularly all-cause mortality and mortality from coronary heart disease. Weight cycling may also have negative psychological and behavioral consequences; studies have reported increased risk for psychopathology, life dissatisfaction, and binge eating. The bulk of epidemiologic research shows an association of weight variability with morbidity and mortality." Kelly Brownell and Judith Rodin. "Medical, Metabolic and Psychological Effects of Weight Cycling." *Arch Intern Med* 154 (1994), 1325–1330.

8. Camryn Manheim, *Wake Up, I'm Fat!* (New York: Broadway Books, 1999). Manheim, an actor, writer, producer, and social activist, describes her own journey to self-acceptance in this book.

9. Kaz Cooke, *Real Gorgeous: The Truth About Body and Beauty* (New York: W.W. Norton & Company, 1996).

10. According to a report compiled by the National Education Association, students who are overweight face almost constant harassment, discouragement and even discrimination at school. They are often ostracized by their peers and denied places on sports teams and cheerleading squads. Such treatment can result in low self-esteem and limited horizons, the report states. Sometimes, the consequences are extreme. In 2002, a twelve-year-old Florida boy killed himself when the teasing about his weight became unbearable. A number of studies indicate that children who are overweight pay a high price socially. Dr. Jeffery Sobal of Cornell University says that kids who are shown pictures of other children with a variety of physical attributes—including excess weight, facial disfigurement and missing limbs—pick their overweight peers last when asked whom they would like to play with. And the effects of discrimination can last a lifetime. "All kinds of tests have been done," says Sobal. "Submitting virtually identical applications to colleges, for example, with photographs of overweight or average weight people, produces strikingly different acceptance rates. The same goes for job applications—write '260 pounds' in the weight column rather than '160,' or send testers in with similar résumés for interviews, and the results point to a strong correlation between obesity and rejection."

According to Sobal, people tend to stigmatize the overweight because of the perception that obesity is self-inflicted, and that it represents some essential character flaw. "Today, the youth culture identifies health with thinness. It follows that people who are overweight are not in control, not self-disciplined." In actuality, he says, there is increasing evidence that obesity is as much a matter of genetics as of personal habits. From David Aronson, "No Laughing Matter." See the full article at www.tolerance.org.

11. "I wished that my mother had accepted me as beautiful in my entirety, including my body. In [my daughter] Veronica's mind, there was no question that her mommy was beautiful. In my mother's mind, I would be beautiful only if I lost weight." From Diane M. Ceja, "Mothers and Daughters: Healing the Patterns of Generations," *Radiance*, Fall 1992.

12. "The mortality rate among people with anorexia has been estimated at 0.56 percent per year, or approximately 5.6 percent per decade, which is about 12 times higher than the annual death rate due to all causes of death among females ages 15–24 in the general population." Mental Health Research Association www.miraresearch.org.

However, the mortality rates associated with anorexia are much debated for a variety of ideological reasons. The best summary of the issues I have found is at www.polisci.ucla.edu in "Anorexia Statistics" by Berry O'Neill, an Associate Professor at the Yale School of Management, 1966. The issues surrounding the anorexia mortality rates are the same issues debated in regards to the "fat" mortality rates. Death certificates list immediate cause of death, not the mental/emotional/social circumstances that led to the death.

JUANITA
Kate Chopin

Till early in this century, Venus was almost always drawn in the guise of an endomorph: moon-faced, pear-shaped, and well fleshed out. And the aesthetic ideal was not far removed from the living reality: Pound for pound and millimeter for millimeter, women have always been fatter than men.
    —Anne Scott Beller, *Fat and Thin: A Natural History of Obesity*

To all appearances and according to all accounts, Juanita is a character who does not reflect credit upon her family or her native town of Rock Springs. I first met her there three years ago in the little back room behind her father's store. She seemed very shy, and inclined to efface herself; a heroic feat to attempt, considering the narrow confines of the room; and a hopeless one, in view of her five-feet-ten, and more than two-hundred pounds of substantial flesh, which, on that occasion, and every subsequent one when I saw her, was clad in a soiled calico "Mother Hubbard."

Her face, and particularly her mouth has a certain fresh and sensuous beauty, though I would rather not say "beauty" if I might say anything else.

I often saw Juanita that summer, simply because it was so difficult for the poor thing not to be seen. She usually sat in some obscure corner of their small garden, or behind an angle of the house, preparing vegetables for dinner or sorting her mother's flower-seed.

It was even at that day said, with some amusement, that Juanita was not so unattractive to men as her appearance might indicate; that she had more than one admirer, and great hopes of marrying well if not brilliantly.

Upon my return to the "Springs" this summer, in asking news of the various persons who had interested me three years ago, Juanita came naturally to my mind, and her name to my lips. There were many ready to tell me of Juanita's career since I had seen her.

The father had died and she and the mother had had ups and downs, but still continued to keep the store. Whatever else happened, however, Juanita had never ceased to attract admirers, young and old. They hung on her fence at all hours; they met her in the lanes; they penetrated to the store and back to the living-room. It was even talked about that a gentleman in a plaid suit had come all the way from the city by train for no other purpose than to call upon her. It is not astonishing, in face of these persistent attentions, that speculation grew rife in Rock Springs as to whom and what Juanita would marry in the end.

For a while she was said to be engaged to a wealthy South Missouri farmer, though no one could guess when or where she had met him. Then it was learned that the man of her choice was a Texas millionaire who possessed a hundred white horses, one of which spirited animals Juanita began to drive about that time.

But in the midst of speculation and counter speculation on the subject of Juanita and her lovers, there suddenly appeared upon the scene a one-legged man; a very poor and shabby, and decidedly one-legged man. He first became known to the public through Juanita's soliciting subscriptions towards buying the unhappy individual a cork-leg.

Her interest in the one-legged man continued to show itself in various ways, not always apparent to a curious public; as was proven one morning when Juanita became the mother of a baby, whose father, she announced, was her husband, the one-legged man. The story of a wandering preacher was told; a secret marriage in the State of Illinois; and a lost certificate.

However that may be, Juanita has turned her broad back upon the whole race of masculine bipeds, and lavishes the wealth of her undivided affections upon the one-legged man.

I caught a glimpse of the curious couple when I was in the village. Juanita had mounted her husband upon a dejected looking pony which she herself was apparently leading by the bridle, and they were moving up the lane towards the woods, whither, I am told, they often wander in this manner. The picture which they presented was a singular one; she with a man's big straw hat shading her inflamed moon-face, and the breeze bellying her soiled "Mother Hubbard" into monstrous proportions. He puny, helpless, but apparently content with his fate which had not even vouchsafed him the coveted cork-leg.

They go off thus to the woods together where they may love each other away from all prying eyes save those of the birds and squirrels. But what do the squirrels care!

For my part I never expected Juanita to be more respectable than a squirrel; and I don't see how any one else could have expected it.

THE STOUT MISS HOPKINS'S BICYCLE
Octave Thanet

The desire to be slim is not simply a result of fashion. It must be understood in terms of a confluence of movements in the sciences and in dance, in home economics and political economy, in medical technology and food marketing, in evangelical religion and life insurance. Our sense of the body, of its heft and momentum, is shaped . . . by the theater of our lives. . . . Our furniture, our toys, our architecture, our etiquette are designed for, or impel . . . us towards, a certain kind of body and a certain feeling of weight. Each epoch has had different tolerances for weight and for fat-ness. Since the 1880s, those tolerances have grown especially narrow, especially demanding. We take for granted now a constant personal vigil against overweight and obesity.

. . . People liked being fat a century ago; now they like being thin. . . . Given more than a century of failed diets. . . . [of] so many disappointments, people might have looked . . . back and taken . . . stock.

—Hillel Schwartz, *Never Satisfied: A Cultural History of Diets, Fantasies & Fat*

Frances Willard, head of the Women's Christian Temperance Union and a leader of the women's rights movement, learned to ride a bicycle at the age of fifty-four. She became convinced that cycling could be one of the keys to women's freedom. In 1895, Willard wrote, "We saw that the physical development of humanity's mother-half would be wonderfully advanced by that universal introduction of the bicycle sure to come. . . .

Susan B. Anthony was also convinced that bicycling did "more to emancipate women than anything else in the world." A woman on a bicycle, according to Anthony, was "the picture of free, un-trammeled womanhood."

—Elaine Reynolds, "Racing with a Butterfly"

There was a skeleton in Mrs. Margaret Ellis's closet; the same skeleton abode also in the closet of Miss Lorania Hopkins.

The skeleton—which really does not seem a proper word—was the dread of growing stout. They were more afraid of flesh than of sin. Yet they were both good women. Mrs. Ellis regularly attended church, and could always be depended on to show hospitality to convention delegates, whether clerical or lay; she was a liberal subscriber to every good work; she was almost the only woman in the church aid society that never lost her temper at the soul-vexing time of the church fair; and she had a larger clientele of regular pensioners than any one in town, unless it were her friend Miss Hopkins, who was "so good to the poor" that never a tramp slighted her kitchen. Miss Hopkins was as amiable as Mrs. Ellis, and always put her name under that of Mrs. Ellis, with exactly the same amount, on the subscription papers. She could have given more, for she had the larger income; but she had no desire to outshine her friend, whom she admired as the most charming of women.

Mrs. Ellis, indeed, was agreeable as well as good, and a pretty woman to the bargain, if she did not choose to be weighed before people. Miss Hopkins often told her that she was not really stout; she merely had a plump, trig little figure. Miss Hopkins, alas! was really stout. The two waged a warfare against the flesh equal to the apostle's in vigor, although so much less deserving of praise.

Mrs. Ellis drove her cook to distraction with divers dieting systems, from Banting's and Dr. Salisbury's to the latest exhortations of some unknown newspaper prophet. She bought elaborate gymnastic appliances, and swung dumb-bells and rode imaginary horses and propelled imaginary boats. She ran races with a professional trainer, and she studied the principles of Delsarte, and solemnly whirled on one foot and swayed her body and rolled her head and hopped and kicked and genuflected in company with eleven other stout and earnest matrons and one slim and giggling girl who almost choked at every lesson. In all these exercises Miss Hopkins faithfully kept her company, which was the easier as Miss Hopkins lived in the next house, a conscientious Colonial mansion with all the modern conveniences hidden beneath the old-fashioned pomp.

And yet, despite these struggles and self-denials, it must be told that Margaret Ellis and Lorania Hopkins were little thinner for their warfare. Still, as Shuey Cardigan, the trainer, told Mrs. Ellis, there was no knowing what they might have weighed had they not struggled.

"It ain't only the fat that's *on* ye, moind ye," says Shuey, with a confidential sympathy of mien; "it's what ye'd naturally be getting in addition. And first ye've got to peel off that, and then ye come down to the other."

Shuey was so much the most successful of Mrs. Ellis's reducers that his words were weighty. And when at last Shuey said, "I got what you need," Mrs. Ellis listened. "You need a bike, no less," says Shuey.

"But I never could ride one!" said Margaret, opening her pretty brown eyes and wrinkling her Grecian forehead.

"You'd ride in six lessons."

"But how would I *look*, Cardigan?"

"You'd look noble, ma'am!"

"What do you consider the best wheel, Cardigan?"

The advertising rules of magazines prevent my giving Cardigan's answer; it is enough that the wheel glittered at Mrs. Ellis's door the very next week. He went on to Miss Hopkins's, and delivered the twin of the box, with a similar yellow printed card bearing the impress of the same great firm on the inside of the box cover.

For Margaret had hied her to Lorania Hopkins the instant Shuey was gone. She presented herself breathless, a little to the embarrassment of Lorania, who was sitting with her niece before a large box of cracker-jack.

"It's a new kind of candy; I was just *tasting* it, Maggie," faltered she, while the niece, a girl of nineteen, with the inhuman spirits of her age, laughed aloud.

"You needn't mind me," said Mrs. Ellis, cheerfully; "I'm eating potatoes now!"

"Oh, Maggie!" Miss Hopkins breathed the words between envy and disapproval.

Mrs. Ellis tossed her brown head arily, not a whit abashed. "And I had beer for luncheon, and I'm going to have champagne for dinner."

"Maggie, how do you dare? Did they—did they taste good?"

"They tasted *heavenly*, Lorania. Pass me the candy. I am going to try something new—the thinningest thing there is. I read in the paper of one woman who lost forty pounds in three months, and is losing still!"

"If it is obesity pills, I—"

"It isn't; it's a bicycle. Lorania, you and I must ride! Sibyl Hopkins, you heartless child, what are you laughing at?"

Lorania rose; in the glass over the mantel her figure returned her gaze. There was no mistake (except that, as is often the case with stout people, *that* glass always increased her size), she was a stout lady. She was taller than the average of women, and well proportioned, and still light on her feet; but she could not blink away the records; she was heavy on the scales. Did she stand looking at herself squarely, her form was shapely enough, although larger than she could wish; but the full force of the revelation fell when she allowed herself a profile view, she having what is called "a round waist," and being almost as large one way as another. Yet Lorania was only thirty-three years old, and was of no mind to retire from society, and have a special phaeton built for her use, and hear from her mother's friends how much her mother weighed before her death.

"How should *I* look on a wheel?" she asked, even as Mrs. Ellis had asked before; and Mrs. Ellis stoutly answered, "You'd look *noble!*"

"Shuey will teach us," she went on, "and we can have a track made in your pasture, where nobody can see us learning. Lorania, there's nothing like it. Let me bring you the bicycle edition of *Harper's Bazaar*."

Miss Hopkins capitulated at once, and sat down to order her costume, while Sibyl, the niece, reveled silently in visions of a new bicycle which should presently revert to her. "For it's ridiculous, auntie's thinking of riding!" Miss Sibyl considered. "She would be a figure of fun on a wheel; besides, she can never learn in this world!"

Yet Sibyl was attached to her aunt, and enjoyed visiting Hopkins Manor, as Lorania had named her new house, into which she moved on the same day that she joined the Colonial Dames, by right of her ancestor the great and good divine commemorated by Mrs. Stowe. Lorania's friends were all fond of her, she was so good-natured and tolerant, with a touch of dry humor in her vision of things, and not the least a Puritan in her frank enjoyment of ease and luxury. Nevertheless, Lorania had a good, able-bodied, New England conscience, capable of staying awake nights without flinching; and perhaps from her stanch old Puritan forefathers she inherited her simple integrity so that she neither lied nor cheated—even in the small, white-washed manner of her sex—and valued loyalty above most of the virtues. She had an innocent pride in her godly and martial ancestry, which was quite on the surface, and led people who did not know her to consider her haughty.

For fifteen years she had been an orphan, the mistress of a very large estate. No doubt she had been sought often in marriage, but never until lately had Lorania seriously thought of marrying. Sibyl said that she was too unsentimental to marry. Really she was too romantic. She had a longing to be loved, not in the quiet, matter-of-fact manner of her suitors, but with the passion of the poets. Therefore the presence of another skeleton in Mrs. Ellis's closet, because she knew about a certain handsome Italian marquis who at this period was conducting an impassioned wooing by mail. Margaret did not fancy the marquis. He was not an American. He would take Lorania away. She thought his very virtue florid, and suspected that he had learned his love-making in a bad school. She dropped dark hints that frightened Lorania, who would sometimes piteously demand, "Don't you think he *could* care for me—for—for myself?" Margaret knew that she had an overwhelming distrust of her own appearance. How many tears she shed first and last over her unhappy plumpness it would be hard to reckon. She made no account of her satin skin, or her glossy black hair, or her lustrous violet eyes with their long, black lashes, or her flashing white teeth; she glanced dismally at her shape and scornfully at her features, good, honest, irregular American features, that might not satisfy a Greek critic, but suited each other and pleased her countrymen. And then she would sigh heavily over her figure. Her friend had not the heart to impute the marquis's beautiful, artless compliments to mercenary motives. After all, the Italian was a good fellow, according to the point of view of his own race, if he did intend to live on his wife's money, and had a very varied assortment of memories of women.

But Margaret dreaded and disliked him all the more for his good qualities. Today this secret apprehension flung a cloud over the bicycle enthusiasm. She could not help wondering whether at this moment Lorania was not thinking of the marquis, who rode a wheel and a horse admirably.

"Aunt Lorania," said Sibyl, "there comes Mr. Winslow. Shall I run out and ask him about those cloth-of-gold roses? The aphides are eating them all up."

"Yes, to be sure, dear; but don't let Ferguson suspect what you are talking of; he might feel hurt."

Ferguson was the gardener. Miss Hopkins left her note to go to the window. Below she saw a mettled horse, with tossing head and silken skin, restlessly fretting on his bit and pawing the dust in front of the fence, while his rider, hat in hand, talked with the young girl. He was a little man, a very little man, in a gray business suit of the best cut and material. An air of careful and dainty neatness was diffused about both horse and rider. He bent towards Miss Sibyl's charming person a thin, alert, fair face. His head was finely shaped, the brown hair worn away a little on the temples. He smiled gravely at intervals; the smile told that he had a dimple in his cheek.

"I wonder," said Mrs. Ellis, "whether Mr. Winslow can have a penchant for Sibyl?"

Lorania opened her eyes. At this moment Mr. Winslow had caught sight of her at the window, and he bowed almost to his saddle-bow; Sibyl was saying something at which she laughed, and he visibly reddened. It was a peculiarity of his that his color turned easily. In a second his hat was on his head and his horse bounded half across the road.

"Hardly, I think," said Lorania. "How well he rides! I never knew any one ride better—in this country."

"I suppose Sibyl would ridicule such a thing," said Mrs. Ellis, continuing her own train of thought, and yet vaguely disturbed by the last sentence.

"Why should she?"

"Well, he is so little, for one thing, and she is so tall. And then Sibyl thinks a great deal of social position."

"He is a Winslow," said Lorania, arching her neck unconsciously—"a lineal descendant from Kenelm Winslow, who came over in the *May*—"

"But his mother—"

"I don't know anything about his mother before she came here. Oh, of course I know the gossip that she was a niece of the overseer at a village poorhouse, and that her husband quarreled with all his family and married her in the poor-house, and I know that when he died here she would not take a cent from the Winslows, nor let them have the boy. She is the meekest-looking little woman, but she must have an iron streak in her somewhere, for she was left without enough money to pay the funeral expenses, and she educated the boy and accumulated money enough to pay for this place they have.

"She used to run a laundry, and made money; but when Cyril got a place in the bank she sold out the laundry and went into chickens and vegetables; she told somebody that it wasn't so profitable as the laundry, but it was more genteel, and Cyril being now in a position of trust at the bank, she must consider *him*. Cyril swept out the bank. People laughed about it, but, do you know, I rather liked Mrs. Winslow for it. She isn't in the least an assertive woman. How long have we been up here, Maggie? Isn't it four years? And they have been our next-door neighbors, and she has never been inside the house. Nor he either, for that matter, except once when it took fire, you know, and he came in with that funny little chemical engine tucked under his arm, and took off his hat in the same prim, polite way that he takes it off when he talks to Sibyl, and said, 'If you'll excuse me offering advice, Miss Hopkins, it is not necessary to move anything; it mars furniture very much to move it at a fire. I think, if you will allow me, I can extinguish this.' And he did, too, didn't he, as neatly and as coolly as if it were only adding up a column of figures. And offered me the engine as a souvenir."

"Lorania, you never told me that!"

"It seemed like making fun of him, when he had been so kind. I declined as civilly as I could. I hope I didn't hurt his feelings. I meant to pay a visit to his mother and ask them to dinner, but you know I went to England that week, and somehow when I came back it was difficult. It seemed a little cold we never have seen more of the Winslows, but I fancy they don't want either to intrude or be intruded on. But he is certainly very obliging about the garden. Think of all the slips and flowers he has given us, and the advice—"

"All passed over the fence. It is funny our neighborly good offices which we render at arm's-length. How long have you known him?"

"Oh, a long time. He is cashier of my bank, you know. First he was teller, then assistant cashier, and now for five years he has been cashier. The president wants to resign and let him be president, but he hardly has enough stock for that. But Oliver says" (Oliver was Miss Hopkins's brother) "that there isn't a shrewder or straighter banker in the state. Oliver knows him. He says he is a sandy little fellow."

"Well, he is," assented Mrs. Ellis. "It isn't many cashiers would let robbers stab them and shoot them and leave them for dead rather than give up the combination of the safe!"

"He wouldn't take a cent for it, either, and he saved ever so many thousand dollars. Yes, he *is* brave. I went to the same school with him once, and saw him fight a big boy twice his size—such a nasty boy, who called me 'Fatty,' and made a kissing noise with his lips just to scare me—and poor little Cyril Winslow got awfully beaten, and when I saw him on the ground, with his nose bleeding and that big brute pounding him, I ran to the water-bucket, and poured the whole bucket on that big, bullying boy and stopped the fight, just as the teacher got on the scene. I cried over little Cyril Winslow. He was crying himself. 'I ain't crying because he hurt me,' he sobbed; 'I'm crying because I'm so mad I didn't lick him!' I wonder if he remembers that episode?"

"Perhaps," said Mrs. Ellis.

"Maggie, what makes you think he is falling in love with Sibyl?"

Mrs. Ellis laughed. "I dare say he *isn't* in love with Sibyl," said she. "I think the main reason was his always riding by here instead of taking the shorter road down the other street."

"Does he always ride by here? I hadn't noticed."

"Always!" said Mrs. Ellis. "*I* have noticed."

"I am sorry for him," said Lorania, musingly. "I think Sibyl is very much taken with that young Captain Carr at the Arsenal. Young girls always affect the army. He is a nice fellow, but I don't think he is the man Winslow is. Now, Maggie, advise me about the suit. I don't want to look like the escaped fat lady of a museum."

Lorania thought no more of Sibyl's love-affairs. If she thought of the Winslows, it was to wish that Mrs. Winslow would sell or rent her pasture, which, in addition to her own and Mrs. Ellis's pastures thrown into one, would make such a delightful bicycle-track.

The Winslow house was very different from the two villas that were the pride of Fairport. A little story-and-a-half cottage peeped out on the road behind the tall maples that were planted when Winslow was a boy. But there was a wonderful green velvet lawn, and the tulips and sweet-peas and pansies that blazed softly nearer the house were as beautiful as those over which Miss Lorania's gardener toiled and worried.

Mrs. Winslow was a little woman who showed the fierce struggle of her early life only in the deeper lines between her delicate eyebrows and the expression of melancholy patience in her brown eyes.

She always wore a widow's cap and a black gown. In the mornings she donned a blue figured apron of stout and serviceable stuff; in the afternoon an apron of that sheer white lawn used by bishops and smart waitresses. Of an afternoon, in warm weather, she was accustomed to sit on the eastern piazza, next to the Hopkins place, and rock as she sewed. She was thus sitting and sewing when she beheld an extraordinary procession cross the Hopkins lawn. First marched the tall trainer, Shuey Cardigan, who worked by day in the Lossing furniture-factory, and gave bicycle lessons at the armory evenings. He was clad in a white sweater and buff leggings, and was wheeling a lady's bicycle. Behind him walked Miss Hopkins in a gray suit, the skirt of which only came to her ankles—she always so dignified in her toilets.

"Land's sakes!" gasped Mrs. Winslow, "if she ain't going to ride a bike! Well, what next?"

What really happened next was the sneaking (for no other word does justice to the cautious and circuitous movements of her) of Mrs. Winslow to the stable, which had one window facing the Hopkins pasture. All around the grassy plateau twinkled a broad brownish-yellow track. At one side of this track a bench had been placed, and a table, pleasing to the eye, with jugs and glasses. Mrs. Ellis, in a suit of the same undignified brevity and ease as Miss Hopkins's, sat on the bench supporting her own wheel. Shuey Cardigan was drawn up to his full six feet of strength, and, one arm in the air, was explaining the theory of the balance of power. It was an uncanny moment to Lorania. She eyed the glistening, restless thing that slipped beneath her hand, and her fingers trembled. If she could have fled in secret she would. But since flight was not possible, she assumed a firm expression. Mrs. Ellis wore a smile of studied and sickly cheerfulness.

"Don't you think it very *high*?" said Lorania. "I can *never* get up on it!"

"It will be by the block at first," said Shuey, in the soothing tones of a jockey to a nervous horse; "it's easy by the block. And I'll be steadying it, of course."

"Don't they have any with larger saddles? It is a *very* small saddle."

"They're all of a size. It wouldn't look sporty larger; it would look like a special make. Yous wouldn't want a special make."

Lorania thought that she would be thankful for a special make, but she suppressed the unsportsmanlike thought. "The pedals are very small too, Cardigan. Are you *sure* they can hold me?"

"They would hold two of ye, Miss Hopkins. Now sit aisy and graceful as ye would on your chair at home, hold the shoulders back, and toe in a bit on the pedals—ye won't be skinning your ankles so much then—and hold your foot up ready to get the other pedal. Hold light on the steering-bar. Push off hard. '*Now!*'"

"Will you hold me? I am going—Oh it's like riding an earthquake!"

Here Shuey made a run, letting the wheel have its own wild way—to reach the balance. "Keep the front wheel under you!" he cried, cheerfully. "Niver mind *where* you go. Keep a-pedalling; whatever you do, keep a-pedalling!"

But I haven't got but one pedal!" gasped the rider.

"Ye lost it?"

"No; I *never had* but one! Oh, don't let me fall!"

"Oh, ye lost it in the beginning; now, then, I'll hold it steady, and you get both feet right. Here we go!"

Swaying frightfully from side to side, and wrenched from capsizing in the wheel by the full exercise of Shuey's great muscles, Miss Hopkins reeled over the track. At short intervals she lost her pedals, and her feet, for some strange reason, instead of seeking the lost, simply curled up as if afraid of being hit. She gripped the steering-handles with an iron grasp, and her turns were such as an engine makes. Nonetheless, Shuey got her up the track for some hundred feet, and then by a Herculean sweep turned her round and rolled her back to the block. It was at this painful moment, when her whole being was concentrated on the effort to keep from toppling against Shuey, and even more to keep from toppling away from him, that Lorania's strained gaze suddenly fell on the frightened and sympathetic face of Mrs. Winslow. The good woman saw no fun in the spectacle, but rather an awful risk to life and limb. Their eyes met. Not a change passed over Miss Hopkins's features; but she looked up as soon as she was safe on the ground, and smiled. In a moment, before Mrs. Winslow could decide whether to run or stand her ground, she saw the cyclist approaching—on foot.

"Won't you come in and sit down?" she said smiling. "We are trying our new wheels."

And because she did not know how to refuse, Mrs. Winslow suffered herself to be handed over the fence. She sat on the bench beside Miss Hopkins in the prim attitude which had pertained to gentility in her youth, her hands loosely clasping each other, her feet crossed at the ankles.

"It's an awful sight, ain't it?" she breathed, "those shiny things; I don't see how you ever git on them."

"I don't get on them," said Miss Hopkins. "The only way I shall ever learn is to start off without the pedals. Does your son ride, Mrs. Winslow?"

"No, ma'am," said Mrs. Winslow; "but he knows how. When he was a boy nothing would do but he must have a bicycle, one of those things most as big as a mill wheel, and if you fell off you broke yourself somewhere, sure. I always expected he'd be brought home in pieces. So I don't think he'd have any manner of difficulty. Why, look at your friend; she's 'most riding alone!"

"She could always do everything better than I," cried Lorania, with ungrudging admiration. "See how she jumps off! Now I can't jump off any more than I can jump on. It seems so ridiculous to be told to press hard on the pedal on the side where you want to jump, and swing your further leg over first, and cut a kind of figure eight with your legs, and turn your wheel the way you don't want to go—all at once. While I'm trying to think of all those directions I always fall off. I got that wheel only yesterday, and fell before I even got away from the block. One of my arms looks like a Persian ribbon."

Mrs. Winslow cried out in unfeigned sympathy. She wished Miss Hopkins would use her liniment that she used for Cyril when he was hurt by the burglars at the bank; he was bruised "terrible."

"That must have been an awful time to you," said Lorania, looking with more interest than she had ever felt on the meek little woman; and she noticed the tremble in the decorously clasped hands.

"Yes, ma'am," was all she said.

"I've often looked over at you on the piazza, and thought how cosey you looked. Mr. Winslow always seemed to be at home evenings.

"Yes ma'am. We sit a great deal on the piazza. Cyril's a good boy; he wa'n't nine when his father died; and he's been like a man helping me. There never was a boy had such willing little feet. And he'd set right there on the steps and pat my slipper and say what he'd git me when he got to earning money; and he's got me every last thing, foolish and all, that he said. There's that black satin gown, a sin and a shame for a plain body like me, but he would git it. Cyrils' got a beautiful disposition too, jest like his pa's, and he's a handy man about the house, and prompt at his meals. I wonder sometimes if Cyril was to git married if his wife would mind his running over now and then and setting with me awhile."

She was speaking more rapidly, and her eyes strayed wistfully over to the Hopkins piazza, where Sibyl was sitting with the young soldier. Lorania looked at her pityingly.

"Why, surely," said she.

"Mothers have kinder selfish feelings," said Mrs. Winslow, moistening her lips and drawing a quick breath, still watching the girl on the piazza. "It's so sweet and peaceful for them, they forget their sons may want something more. But it's kinder hard giving all your little comforts up once when you've had him right with you so long, and could cook just what he liked, and go right into his room nights if he coughed. It's all right, all right, but it's kinder hard. And beautiful young ladies that have had everything all their lives might—might not understand that a homespun old mother isn't wanting to force herself on them at all when they have company, and they have no call to fear it."

There was no doubt, however obscure the words seemed, that Mrs. Winslow had a clear purpose in her mind, nor that she was tremendously in earnest. Little blotches of red dabbled her cheeks, her breath came more quickly, and she swallowed between her words. Lorania could see the quiver in the muscles of her throat. She clasped her hands tight lest they should shake. "He's in love with Sibyl," thought Lorania. "The poor woman!" She felt sorry for her, and she spoke gently and reassuringly:

"No girl with a good heart can help feeling tenderly toward her husband's mother."

Mrs. Winslow nodded. "You're real comforting," said she. She was silent a moment, and then said, in a different tone: "You ain't got a large enough track. Wouldn't you like to have our pasture too?"

Lorania expressed her gratitude, and invited the Winslows to see the practice.

"My niece will come out to-morrow," she said graciously.

"Yes? She's a real fine-appearing young lady," said Mrs. Winslow.

Both the cyclists exulted. Neither of them, however, was prepared to behold the track made and the fence down the very next morning when they came out, about ten o'clock, to the west side of Miss Hopkins's boundaries.

"As sure as you live, Maggie," exclaimed Lorania, eagerly, "he's got it all done! Now that is something like a lover. I only hope his heart won't be bruised as black and blue as I am with the wheel!"

"Shuey says the only harm your falls do you is to take away your confidence," said Mrs. Ellis.

"He wouldn't say so if he could see my *knees!*" retorted Miss Hopkins.

Mrs. Ellis, it will be observed, sheered away from the love-affairs of Mr. Cyril Winslow. She had not yet made up her mind. And Mrs. Ellis, who had been married, did not jump at conclusions regarding the heart of man so rapidly as her spinster friend. She preferred to talk of the bicycle. Nor did Miss Hopkins refuse the subject. To her at this moment the most important object on the globe was the shining machine which she would allow no hand but hers to oil and dust. Both Mrs. Ellis and she were simply prostrated (as to their mental powers) by this new sport. They could not think nor talk nor read of anything but *the wheel*. This is a peculiarity of the bicyclist. No other sport appears to make such havoc with the mind.

One can learn to swim without describing his sensations to every casual acquaintance or hunting up the natatorial columns in the newspapers. One may enjoy riding a horse and yet go about his ordinary business with an equal mind. One learns to play golf and still remains a peaceful citizen who can discuss politics with interest. But the cyclist, man or woman, is soaked in every pore with the delight and the perils of wheeling. He talks of it (as he thinks of it) incessantly. For this fatuous passion there is one excuse. Other sports have the fearful delight of danger and the pleasure of the consciousness of dexterity and the dogged Anglo-Saxon joy of combat and victory; but no other sport restores to middle age the pure, exultant, muscular intoxication of childhood. Only on the wheel can an elderly woman feel as she felt when she ran and leaped and frolicked amid the flowers as a child.

Lorania, of course, no longer jumped or ran; she kicked in the Delsarte exercises, but it was a measured, calculated, one may say cold-blooded kick, which limbered her muscles but did not restore her youthful glow of soul. Her legs and not her spirits pranced. The same thing may be said for Margaret Ellis. Now, between their accidents, they obtained glimpses of an exquisite exhilaration. And there was also to be counted the approval of their consciences, for they felt that no Turkish bath could wring out moisture from their systems like half an hour's pumping at the bicycle treadles. Lorania during the month had ridden through one bottle of liniment and two of witch-hazel, and by the end of the second bottle could ride a short distance alone. But Lorania could not yet dismount unassisted, and several times she had felled poor Winslow to the earth when he rashly adventured to stop her. Captain Carr had a peculiar, graceful fling of the arm, catching the saddle-bar with one hand while he steadied the handles with the other. He did not hesitate in the least to grab Lorania's belt if necessary. But poor modest Winslow, who fell upon the wheel and dared not touch the hem of a lady's bicycle skirt, was as one in the path of a cyclone, and appeared daily in a fresh pair of white trousers.

"Yous have now," Shuey remarked, impressively, one day—"yous have now arrived at the most difficult and dangerous period in learning the wheel. It's similar to a baby when it's first learned to walk but 'ain't yet got sense in walking. When it was little it would stay put wherever ye put it, and it didn't know enough to go by itself, which is similar to you. When I was holding ye you couldn't fall, but now you're off alone dependent on yourself, object-struck by every tree, taking most of the pasture to turn in, and not able to git off save by falling—"

"Oh, couldn't you go with her somehow?" exclaimed Mrs. Winslow, appalled at the picture. "Wouldn't a rope around her be some help? I used to put it round Cyril when he was learning to walk."

"Well, no, ma'am," said Shuey, patiently. "Don't you be scared; the riding will come; she's getting on grandly. And ye should see Mr. Winslow. 'Tis a pleasure to teach him. He rode in one lesson. I ain't learning him nothing but tricks now."

"But, Mr. Winslow, why don't you ride here—with us?" said Sibyl, with her coquettish and flattering smile. "We're always hearing of your beautiful riding. Are we never to see it?"

"I think Mr. Winslow is waiting for that swell English cycle suit that I hear about," said the captain, grinning; and Winslow grew red to his eyelids.

Lorania gave an indignant side glance at Sibyl. Why need the girl make game of an honest man who loved her? Sibyl was biting her lips and darting side glances at the captain. She called the pasture practice slow, but she seemed, nevertheless, to enjoy herself sitting on the bench, the captain on one side and Winslow on the other, rattling off her girlish jokes, while her aunt and Mrs. Ellis, with the anxious, set faces of the beginner, were pedalling frantically after Cardigan. Lorania began to pity Winslow, for it was growing plain to her that Sibyl and the captain understood each other. She thought that even if Sibyl did care for the soldier, she need not be so careless of Winslow's feelings. She talked with the cashier herself, trying to make amends for Sibyl's absorption in the other man, and she admired the fortitude that concealed the pain that he must feel. It became quite the expected thing for the Winslows to be present at the practice; but Winslow had not yet appeared on his wheel. He used to bring a box of candy with him, or rather three boxes—one for each lady, he said—and a box of peppermints for his mother. He was always very attentive to his mother.

"And fancy, Aunt Margaret," laughed Sibyl, "he has asked both auntie and me to the theatre. He is not going to compromise himself by singling one of us out. He's a careful soul. By the way, Aunt Margaret, Mrs. Winslow was telling me yesterday that I am the image of auntie at my age. Am I? Do I look like her? Was she as slender as I?"

"Almost," said Mrs. Ellis, who was not so inflexibly truthful as her friend.

"No, Sibyl," said Lorania, with a deep, deep sigh, "I was always plump; I was a chubby *child*! And oh, what do you think I heard in the crowd at Manly's once? One woman said to another, 'Miss Hopkins has got a wheel.' 'Miss Sibyl?' said the other. 'No; the stout Miss Hopkins,' said the first creature; and the second—" Lorania groaned.

"What *did* she say to make you feel that way?"

"She said—she said, 'Oh my!'" answered Lorania, with a dying look.

"Well, she was horrid," said Mrs. Ellis; "but you know you have grown thin. Come on; let's ride!"

"I shall never be able to ride," said Lorania, gloomily. "I can get on, but I can't get off. And they've taken off the brake, so I can't stop. And I'm object-struck by everything I look at. Someday I shall look down-hill. Well, my will's in the lower drawer of the mahogany desk."

Perhaps Lorania had an occult inkling of the future. For this is what happened: That evening Winslow rode onto the track in his new English bicycle suit, which had just come. He hoped that he didn't look like a fool in those queer clothes. But the instant he entered the pasture he saw something that drove everything else out of his head, and made him bend over the steering-bar and race madly across the green; Miss Hopkins's bicycle was running away down-hill! Cardigan, on foot, was pelting obliquely, in the hopeless thought to intercept her, while Mrs. Ellis, who was reeling over the ground with her own bicycle, wheeled as rapidly as she could to the brow of the hill, where she tumbled off, and abandoning the wheel, rushed on foot to her friend's rescue.

She was only in time to see a flash of silver and ebony and a streak of brown dart before her vision and swim down the hill like a bird. Lorania was still in the saddle, pedalling from sheer force of habit, and clinging to the handle bars. Below the hill was a stone wall, and farther was a creek. There was a narrow opening in the wall where the cattle went down to drink; if she could steer through that she would have nothing worse than soft water and mud; but there was not one chance in a thousand that she could pass that narrow space. Mrs. Winslow, horror-stricken, watched the rescuer, who evidently was cutting across to catch the bicycle.

"He's riding out of sight!" thought Shuey, in the rear. He himself did not slacken his speed, although he could not be in time for the catastrophe. Suddenly he stiffened; Winslow was close to the runaway wheel.

"Grab her!" yelled Shuey. "Grab her by the belt! *Oh Lord!*"

The exclamation exploded like the groan of a shell. For while Winslow's bicycling was all that could be wished, and he flung himself in the path of the on-coming wheel with marvelous celerity and precision, he had not the power to withstand the never yet revealed number of pounds carried by Miss Lorania, impelled by the rapid descent and gathering momentum at every whirl. They met; he caught her; but instantly he was rolling down the steep incline and she was doubled up on the grass. He crashed sickeningly against the stone wall; she lay stunned and still on the sod; and their friends, with beating hearts, slid down to them. Mrs. Winslow was on the brow of the hill. She blesses Shuey to this day for the shout he sent up, "Nobody killed, and I guess no bones broken."

When Margaret went home that evening, having seen her friend safely in bed, not much the worse for her fall, she was told that Cardigan wished to see her. Shuey produced something from his pocket, saying: "I picked this up on the hill, ma'am, after the accident. It maybe belongs to him, or it maybe belongs to her; I'm thinking the safest way is to just give it to you." He handed Mrs. Ellis a tiny gold-framed miniature of Lorania in a red leather case.

The morning was a sparkling June morning, dewy and fragrant, and the sunlight burnished handle and pedal of the friends' bicycles standing on the piazza unheeded. It was the hour for morning practice, but Miss Hopkins slept in her chamber, and Mrs. Ellis sat in the little parlor adjoining, and thought.

She did not look surprised at the maid's announcement that Mrs. Winslow begged to see her for a few moments. Mrs. Winslow was pale. She was a good sketch of discomfort on the very edge of her chair, clad in the black silk which she wore Sundays, her head crowned with bonnet of state, and her hands stiff in a pair of new gloves.

"I hope you'll excuse me not sending up a card," she began. "Cyril got me some going on a year ago, and I *thought* I could lay my hand right on 'em, but I'm so nervous this morning I hunted all over, and they wasn't anywhere. I won't keep you. I just wanted to ask if you picked up anything—a little red Russia-leather case—"

"Was it a miniature—a miniature of my friend Miss Hopkins?"

"I thought it all over, and I came to explain. You no doubt think it strange; and I can assure you that my son never let any human being look at that picture. I never knew about it myself till it was lost and he got out of his bed—he ain't hardly able to walk—and staggered over here to look for it, and I followed him; and so he *had* to tell me. He had it painted from a picture that came out in the papers. He felt it was an awful liberty. But—you don't now how my boy feels, Mrs. Ellis; he has worshipped that woman for years. He 'ain't never had a thought of anybody but her since they was children in school; and yet he's been so modest and so shy of pushing himself forward that he didn't do a thing until I put him on to help you with this bicycle."

Margaret Ellis did not know what to say. She thought of the marquis; and Mrs. Winslow poured out her story: "He 'ain't never said a word to me till this morning. But don't I *know*? Don't I know who looked out so careful for her investments? Don't I know who was always looking out for her interest, silent, and always keeping himself in the background? Why, she couldn't even buy a cow that he wa'n't looking round to see that she got a good one! 'Twas him saw the gardener, and kept him from buying that cow with tuberculosis, 'cause he knew about the herd. He knew by finding out. He worshipped the very cows she owned, you may say, and I've seen him patting and feeding up her dogs; it's to our house that big mastiff always goes every night. Mrs. Ellis, it ain't often that a woman gits love such as my son is offering, only he da'sn't offer it, and it ain't often a woman is loved by such a good man as my son. He 'ain't got any bad habits; he'll die before he wrongs anybody; and he has got the sweetest temper you ever see; and he's the tidiest man about the house you could ask, and the promptest about the meals."

Mrs. Ellis looked at her flushed face, and sent another flood of color into it, for she said, "Mrs. Winslow, I don't know how much good I may be able to do, but I am on your side."

Her eyes followed the little black figure when it crossed the lawn. She wondered whether her advice was good, for she had counseled that Winslow come over in the evening.

"Maggie," said a voice. Lorania was in the doorway. "Maggie," she said, "I ought to tell you that I heard every word."

"Then *I* can tell *you*," cried Mrs. Ellis, "that he is fifty times more of a man than the marquis, and loves you fifty thousand times better!"

Lorania made no answer, not even by a look. What she felt, Mrs. Ellis could not guess. Nor was she any wiser when Winslow appeared at her gate, just as the sun was setting.

"I didn't think I would better intrude on Miss Hopkins," said he, " but perhaps you could tell me how she is this evening. My mother told me how kind you were, and perhaps you—you would advise me if I might venture to send Miss Hopkins some flowers."

Out of the kindness of her heart Mrs. Ellis averted her eyes from his face; thus she was able to perceive Lorania saunter out of the Hopkins gate. So changed was she by the bicycle practice that, wrapped in her niece's shawl, she made Margaret think of the girl. An inspiration flashed to her; she knew the cashier's dependence on his eye-glasses, and he was not wearing them.

"If you want to know how Miss Hopkins is, why not speak to her niece now?" said she.

He started. He saw Miss Sibyl, as he supposed, and he went swiftly down the street. "Miss Sibyl?" he began, "may I ask how is your aunt?"—and then she turned.

She blushed, then she laughed aloud. "Has the bicycle done so much for me?" said she.

"The bicycle didn't need to do *anything* for you!" he cried, warmly.

Mrs. Ellis, a little distance in the rear, heard, turned, and walked thoughtfully away. "They're off," said she—she had acquired a sporting tinge of thought from Shuey Cardigan. "If with that start he can't make the running, it's a wonder."

"I have invited Mr. Winslow and his mother to dinner," said Miss Hopkins, in the morning. "Will you come too, Maggie?"

"I'll back him against the marquis," thought Margaret, gleefully.

A week later Lorania said: "I really think I must be getting thinner. Fancy Mr. Winslow, who is so clear-sighted, mistaking me for Sibyl! He says—I told him how I had suffered from my figure—he says it can't be what he has suffered from his. Do you think him so very short, Maggie? Of course he isn't tall, but he has an elegant figure, I think, and I never saw anywhere such a rider!"

Mrs. Ellis answered, heartily, "He isn't very small, and he is a beautiful figure on the wheel!" And added to herself, "I know what was in that letter she sent yesterday to the marquis! But to think of its all being due to the bicycle!"

THE HOMELY HEROINE
Edna Ferber

Women are everywhere proclaimed and praised to be the beautiful sex; this is one of the most effective and encompassing of sexual stereotypes. Yet the underside of that apparent compliment is a most unflattering fixation on female appearance and a fear and hatred of all that can be construed as ugly in a woman. Such ugliness, we are repeatedly told, is depressing, distressing and even socially dangerous. . . . This taboo governing female appearance is most emphatic in the symbolic worlds of celebrity, fashion, pornography, film and television. There, "beautiful" women are accorded the awe of a fetish, while the "ugly" are blatantly subjected to what Gaye Tuchman has termed "symbolic annihilation"—the trivialization or condemnation of a group accomplished by its systematic exclusion in the imagery of the mass media. . . .

The obsession with female appearance and resultant standards of beauty (with thinness as a prime example) have as much to do with fascism as with fashion—that is, with politics as well as aesthetics. . . . Yet no one is born with some innate sense of what constitutes good looks, bodily perfection or who should have these in the greatest measure. Instead, these are acquired tastes; they shift through time, are learned through socialization, and are precisely political.

—Jane E. Caputi, "Beauty Secrets: Tabooing the Ugly Woman"

◇

Millie Whitcomb, of the fancy goods and notions, beckoned me with her finger. I had been standing at Kate O'Malley's counter, pretending to admire her new basket-weave suitings; but in reality reveling in her droll account of how, in the train coming up from Chicago, Mrs. Judge Porterfield had worn the negro porter's coat over her chilly shoulders in mistake for her husband's. Kate O'Malley can tell a funny story in a way to make the after-dinner pleasantries of a Washington diplomat sound like the clumsy jests told around the village grocery stove.

"I wanted to tell you that I read that last story of yours," said Millie, sociably, when I had strolled over to her counter, "and I liked it, all but the heroine. She had an 'adorable throat' and hair that 'waved away from her white brow,' and eyes that 'now were blue and now gray.' Say, why don't you write a story about an ugly girl?"

"My land!" protested I. "It's bad enough trying to make them accept my stories as it is. That last heroine was a raving beauty, but she came back eleven times before the editor of *Blakely's* succumbed to her charms."

Millie's fingers were busy straightening the contents of a tray of combs and imitation jet barrettes. Millie's fingers were not intended for that task. They are slender, tapering fingers, pink-tipped and sensitive.

"I should think," mused she, rubbing a cloudy piece of jet with a bit of soft cloth, "that they'd welcome a homely one with relief. These goddesses are so cloying."

Millie Whitcomb's black hair is touched with soft mists of gray, and she wears lavender shirtwaists and white stocks edged with lavender. There is a Colonial air about her that has nothing to do with celluloid combs and imitation jet barrettes. It breathes of dim old rooms, rich with the tones of mahogany and old brass, and Millie in the midst of it, gray-gowned, a soft white fichu crossed upon her breast.

In our town the clerks are not the pert and gum-chewing young persons that story-writers are wont to describe. The girls at Bascom's are institutions. They know us all by our first names, and our lives are as an open book to them. Kate O'Malley, who has been at Bascom's for so many years that she is rumored to have stock in the company, may be said to govern the fashions of our town. She is wont to say, when we express a fancy for gray as the color of our new spring suit: "Oh, now, Nellie, don't get gray again. You had it year before last, and don't you think it was just the least leetle bit trying? Let me show you that green that came in yesterday. I said the minute I clapped my eyes on it that it was just the color for you, with your brown hair and all."

And we end by deciding on the green.

The girls at Bascom's are not gossips—they are too busy for that—but they may be said to be delightfully well informed. How could they be otherwise when we go to Bascom's for our wedding dresses and party favors and baby flannels? There is news at Bascom's that our daily paper never hears of, and wouldn't dare to print if it did.

So when Millie Whitcomb, of the fancy goods and notions, expressed her hunger for a homely heroine, I did not resent the suggestion. On the contrary, it sent me home in thoughtful mood, for Millie Whitcomb has acquired a knowledge of human nature in the dispensing of her fancy goods and notions. It set me casting about for a really homely heroine.

There never has been a really ugly heroine in fiction. Authors have started bravely out to write of an unlovely woman, but they never have had the courage to allow her to remain plain. On Page 237 she puts on a black lace dress and red roses, and the combination brings out unexpected tawny lights in her hair, and olive tints in her cheeks, and there she is, the same old beautiful heroine. Even in the "Duchess" books one finds the simple Irish girl, on donning a green corduroy gown cut square at the neck, transformed into a wild-rose beauty, at sight of whom a ball-room is hushed into admiring awe. There's the case of Jane Eyre, too. She is constantly described as plain and mouse-like, but there are covert hints as to her gray eyes and slender figure and clear skin, and we have a sneaking notion that she wasn't such a fright after all.

Therefore, when I tell you that I am choosing Pearlie Schultz as my leading lady you are to understand that she is ugly, not only when the story opens, but to the bitter end. In the first place, Pearlie is fat. Not plump, or rounded, or dimpled, or deliciously curved, but FAT. She bulges in all the wrong places, including her chin. (Sister, who has a way of snooping over my desk in my absence, says that I may as well drop this now, because nobody would ever read it, anyway, least of all any sane editor. I protest when I discover that Sis has been over my papers. It bothers me. But she says you have to do these things when you have a genius in the house, and cites the case of Kipling's "Recessional," which was rescued from the depths of his wastebasket by his wife.)

Pearlie Schultz used to sit on the front porch summer evenings and watch the couples stroll by, and weep in her heart. A fat girl with a fat girl's soul is a comedy. But a fat girl with a thin girl's soul is a tragedy. Pearlie, in spite of her two hundred pounds, had the soul of a willow wand.

The walk in front of Pearlie's house was guarded by a row of big trees that cast kindly shadows. The strolling couples used to step gratefully into the embrace of these shadows, and from them into other embraces. Pearlie, sitting on the porch, could see them dimly, although they could not see her. She could not help remarking that these strolling couples were strangely lacking in sprightly conversation. Their remarks were but fragmentary, disjointed affairs, spoken in low tones with a queer, tremulous note in them. When they reached the deepest, blackest, kindliest shadow, which fell just before the end of the row of trees, the strolling couples almost always stopped, and then there came a quick movement, and a little smothered cry from the girl, and then a sound, and then a silence. Pearlie, sitting alone on the porch in the dark, listened to these things and blushed furiously. Pearlie had never strolled into the kindly shadows with a little beating of the heart, and she had never been surprised with a quick arm about her and eager lips pressed warmly against her own.

In the daytime Pearlie worked as public stenographer at the Burke Hotel. She rose at seven in the morning, and rolled for fifteen minutes, and lay on her back and elevated her heels in the air, and stood stiff kneed while she touched the floor with her finger tips one hundred times, and went without her breakfast. At the end of each month she usually found that she weighed three pounds more than she had the month before.

The folks at home never joked with Pearlie about her weight. Even one's family has some respect for a life sorrow. Whenever Pearlie asked that inevitable question of the fat woman: "Am I as fat as she is?" her mother always answered: "You! Well, I should hope not! You're looking real peaked lately, Pearlie. And your blue skirt just ripples in the back, it's getting so big for you."

Of such blessed stuff are mothers made.

But if the gods had denied Pearlie all charms of face or form, they had been decent enough to bestow on her one gift. Pearlie could cook like an angel; no, better than an angel, for no angel could be a really clever cook and wear those flowing kimono-like sleeves. They'd get into the soup. Pearlie could take a piece of rump and some suet and an onion and a cup or so of water, and evolve a pot roast that you could cut with a fork. She could turn out a surprisingly good cake with surprisingly few eggs, all covered with white icing, and bearing cunning little jelly figures on its snowy bosom. She could beat up biscuits that fell apart at the lightest pressure, revealing little pools of golden butter within. Oh, Pearlie could cook!

On week days Pearlie rattled the typewriter keys, but on Sundays she shooed her mother out of the kitchen. Her mother went, protesting faintly: "Now, Pearlie, don't fuss so for dinner. You ought to get your rest on Sunday instead of stewing over a hot stove all morning."

"Hot fiddlesticks, ma," Pearlie would say, cheerily. "It ain't hot, because it's a gas stove. And I'll only get fat if I sit around. You put on your black-and-white and go to church. Call me when you've got as far as your corsets, and I'll puff your hair for you in the back."

In her capacity of public stenographer at the Burke Hotel, it was Pearlie's duty to take letters dictated by traveling men and beginning: "Yours of the 10th at hand. In reply would say . . ." or: "Enclosed please find, etc." As clinching proof of her plainness it may be stated that none of the traveling men, not even Max Baum, who was so fresh that the girl at the cigar counter actually had to squelch him, ever called Pearlie "baby doll," or tried to make a date with her. Not that Pearlie would ever have allowed them to. But she never had had to reprove them. During pauses in dictation she had a way of peering near-sightedly over her glasses at the dapper, well-dressed traveling salesman who was rolling off the items on his sale bill. That is a trick which would make the prettiest kind of a girl look owlish.

On the night that Sam Miller strolled up to talk to her, Pearlie was work-ing late. She had promised to get out a long and intricate bill for Max Baum, who travels for Kuhn and Klingman, so that he might take the nine o'clock evening train. The irrepressible Max had departed with much eclat and clat-ter, and Pearlie was preparing to go home when Sam approached her.

Sam had just come in from the Gayety Theatre across the street, whither he had gone in a vain search for amusement after supper. He had come away in disgust. A soiled soubrette with orange-colored hair and baby socks had swept her practiced eye over the audience, and, attracted by Sam's good-looking blond head in the second row, had selected him as the target of her song. She had run up to the extreme edge of the footlights at the risk of teetering over, and had informed Sam through the medium of song—to the huge delight of the audience, and to Sam's red-faced dis-comfiture—that she liked his smile, and he was just her style, and just as cute as he could be, and just the boy for her. On reaching the chorus she had whipped out a small, round mirror and, assisted by the calcium-light man in the rear, had thrown a wretched little spotlight on Sam's head.

Ordinarily, Sam would not have minded it. But that evening, in the vest pocket just over the place where he supposed his heart to be, reposed his girl's daily letter. They were to be married on Sam's return to New York from his first long trip. In the letter near his heart she had written prettily and seriously about traveling men, and traveling men's wives, and her little code for both. The fragrant, girlish, grave little letter had caused Sam to sour on the efforts of the soiled soubrette.

As soon as possible he had fled up the aisle and across the street to the hotel writing-room. There he had spied Pearlie's good-humored, homely face, and its contrast with the silly, red-and-white countenance of the unlaundered soubrette had attracted his homesick heart.

Pearlie had taken some letters from him earlier in the day. Now, in his hunger for companionship, he strolled up to her desk just as she was putting her typewriter to bed.

"Gee! This is a lonesome town!" said Sam, smiling down at her.

Pearlie glanced up at him, over her glasses. "I guess you must be from New York," she said. "I've heard a real New Yorker can get bored in Paris. In New York the sky is bluer, and the grass is greener, and the girls are prettier, and the steaks are thicker, and the buildings are higher, and the streets are wider, and the air is finer, than the sky, or the grass, or the girls, or the steaks, or the air of any place else in the world. Ain't they?"

"Oh, now," protested Sam, "quit kiddin' me! You'd be lonesome for the little old town, too, if you'd been born and dragged up in it, and hadn't seen it for four months."

"New to the road, aren't you?" asked Pearlie.

Sam blushed a little. " How did you know?"

"Well, you generally can tell. They don't know what to do with themselves evenings, and they look rebellious when they go into the dining-room. The old-timers just look resigned."

"You've picked up a thing or two around here, haven't you? I wonder if the time will ever come when I'll look resigned to a hotel dinner, after four months of 'em. Why, girl, I've got so I just eat the things that are covered up—like baked potatoes in the shell, and soft boiled eggs, and baked apples, and oranges that I can peel, and nuts."

"Why, you poor kid," breathed Pearlie, her pale eyes fixed on him in motherly pity. "You oughtn't to do that. You'll get so thin your girl won't know you."

Sam looked up, quickly. "How in thunderation did you know—?"

Pearlie was pinning on her hat, and she spoke succinctly, her hatpins between her teeth: "You've been here two days now, and I notice you dictate all your letters except the longest one, and you write that one off in a corner of the writing-room all by yourself, with your cigar just glowing like a live coal, and you squint up through the smoke, and grin to yourself."

"Say, would you mind if I walked home with you?" asked Sam.

If Pearlie was surprised, she was woman enough not to show it. She picked up her gloves and handbag, locked her drawer with a click, and smiled her acquiescence. And when Pearlie smiled she was awful.

It was a glorious evening in the early summer, moonless, velvety, and warm. As they strolled homeward, Sam told her all about the Girl, as is the way of traveling men the world over. He told her about the tiny apartment they had taken, and how he would be on the road only a couple of years more, as this was just a try-out that the firm always insisted on. And they stopped under an arc light while Sam showed her the picture in his watch as is also the way of traveling men since time immemorial.

Pearlie made an excellent listener. He was so boyish and so much in love and so pathetically eager to make good with the firm, and so happy to have someone in whom to confide.

"But it's a dog's life, after all," reflected Sam, again after the fashion of all traveling men. "Any fellow on the road earns his salary these days, you bet. I used to think it was all getting up when you felt like it, and sitting in the big front window of the hotel, smoking a cigar and watching the pretty girls go by. I wasn't wise to the packing, and the unpacking, and the rotten train service, and the grouchy customers, and the canceled bills, and the grub."

Pearlie nodded understandingly. "A man told me once that twice a week regularly he dreamed of the way his wife cooked noodle-soup."

"My folks are German," explained Sam. "And my mother—can she cook! Well, I just don't seem able to get her potato pancakes out of my mind. And her roast beef tasted and looked like roast beef, and not like a wet red flannel rag."

At this moment Pearlie was seized with a brilliant idea. "To-morrow's Sunday. You're going to Sunday here, aren't you? Come over and eat your dinner with us. If you have forgotten the taste of real food, I can give you a dinner that'll jog your memory."

"Oh, really," protested Sam. "You're awfully good, but I couldn't think of it. I—"

"You needn't be afraid. I'm not letting you in for anything. I may be homelier than an English suffragette, and I know my lines are all bumps, but there's one thing you can't take away from me, and that's my cooking hand. I can cook, boy, in a way to make your mother's Sunday dinner, with company expected look like Mrs. Newlywed's first attempt at 'riz' biscuits. And I don't mean any disrespect to your mother when I say it. I'm going to have noodle-soup, and fried chicken, and hot biscuits, and creamed beans from our own garden, and strawberry shortcake with real—"

"Hush!" shouted Sam. "If I ain't there, you'll know that I passed away during the night, and you can telephone the clerk to break in my door."

The Grim Reaper spared him, and Sam came, and was introduced to the family, and ate. He put himself in a class with Dr. Johnson, and Ben Brust, and Gargantua, only that his table manners were better. He almost forgot to talk during the soup, and he came back three times for chicken, and by the time the strawberry shortcake was half consumed he was looking at Pearlie with a sort of awe in his eyes.

That night he came over to say good-by before taking his train out for Ishpeming. He and Pearlie strolled down as far as the park and back again.

"I didn't eat any supper," said Sam. "It would have been sacrilege, after that dinner of yours. Honestly, I don't know how to thank you, being so good to a stranger like me. When I come back next trip, I expect to have the Kid with me, and I want her to meet you, by George! She's a winner and a pippin, but she wouldn't know whether a porterhouse was stewed or frappéd. I'll tell her about you, you bet. In the meantime, if there's anything I can do for you, I'm yours to command."

Pearlie turned to him, suddenly. "You see that clump of thick shadows ahead of us, where those big trees stand in front of our house?"

"Sure," replied Sam.

"Well, when we step into that deepest, blackest shadow, right in front of our porch, I want you to reach up, and put your arm around me and kiss me on the mouth, just once. And when you get back to New York you can tell your girl I asked you to."

There broke from him a little involuntary exclamation. It might have been of pity, and it might have been of surprise. It had in it something of both, but nothing of mirth. And as they stepped into the depths of the soft black shadows he took off his smart straw sailor, which was so different from the sailors that the boys in our town wear. And there was in the gesture something of reverence.

Millie Whitcomb didn't like the story of the homely heroine, after all. She says that a steady diet of such literary fare would give her blue indigestion. Also she objects on the ground that no one got married—that is, the heroine didn't. And she says that a heroine who does not get married isn't a heroine at all. She thinks she prefers the pink-cheeked, goddess kind, in the end.

NOBLESSE

Mary E. Wilkins Freeman

Like the female and the slave bodies, the monstrous body exists in societies to be exploited for someone else's purposes.

. . . In Victorian America, the exhibition of freaks exploded into a public ritual that bonded a sundering polity together in the collective act of looking. In a turbulent era of social and material change, the spectacle of the extraordinary body stimulated curiosity, ignited speculation, provoked titillation, furnished novelty, filled coffers, confirmed commonality, and certified national identity. From the Jacksonian to the Progressive Eras, Americans flocked to freak shows.
—Rosemarie Garland Thomson, "Introduction: From Wonder to Error:
A Genealogy of Freak Discourse in Modernity"

There remains one true physical freak in modern culture: the obese person. . . . Being fat is so stigmatized in American culture that fat people are often perceived as having mental, emotional, and even moral impairments.
—Andrea Stulman Dennet, "The Dime Freak Show Reconfigured"

◇

Margaret Lee encountered in her late middle age the rather singular strait of being entirely alone in the world. She was unmarried, and as far as relatives were concerned, she had none except those connected with her by ties not of blood, but by marriage.

Margaret had not married when her flesh had been comparative; later, when it had become superlative, she had no opportunities to marry. Life would have been hard enough for Margaret under any circumstances, but it was especially hard, living, as she did, with her father's stepdaughter and that daughter's husband.

Margaret's stepmother had been a child in spite of her two marriages, and a very silly, although pretty child. The daughter, Camille, was like her, although not so pretty, and the man whom Camille had married was what Margaret had been taught to regard as "common." His business pursuits were irregular and partook of mystery. He always smoked cigarettes and chewed gum. He wore loud shirts and a diamond scarf-pin which had upon him the appearance of stolen goods. The gem had belonged to Margaret's own mother, but when Camille expressed a desire to present it to Jack

26

Desmond, Margaret had yielded with no outward hesitation, but afterward she wept miserably over its loss when alone in her room. The spirit had gone out of Margaret, the little which she had possessed. She had always been a gentle, sensitive creature, and was almost helpless before the wishes of others.

After all, it had been a long time since Margaret had been able to force the ring even upon her little finger, but she had derived a small pleasure from the reflection that she owned it in its faded velvet box, hidden under laces in her top bureau drawer. She did not like to see it blazing forth from the tie of this very ordinary young man who had married Camille. Margaret had a gentle, high-bred contempt for Jack Desmond, but at the same time a vague fear of him. Jack had a measure of unscrupulous business shrewdness, which spared nothing and nobody, and that in spite of the fact that he had not succeeded.

Margaret owned the old Lee place, which had been magnificent, but of late years the expenditures had been reduced and it had deteriorated. The conservatories had been closed. There was only one horse in the stable. Jack had bought him. He was a worn-out trotter with legs carefully bandaged. Jack drove him at reckless speed, not considering those slender, braceleted legs. Jack had a racing-gig, and when in it, with striped coat, cap on one side, cigarette in mouth, lines held taut, skimming along the roads in clouds of dust, he thought himself the man and true sportsman which he was not. Some of the old Lee silver had paid for that waning trotter.

Camille adored Jack, and cared for no associations, no society, for which he was not suited. Before the trotter was bought she told Margaret that the kind of dinners which she was able to give in Fairhill were awfully slow. "If we could afford to have some men out from the city, some nice fellers that Jack knows, it would be worth while," said she, "but we have grown so hard up we can't do a thing to make it worth their while. Those men haven't got any use for a back-number old place like this. We can't take them round in autos, nor give them a chance at cards, for Jack couldn't pay if he lost, and Jack is awful honorable. We can't have the right kind of folks here for any fun. I don't propose to ask the rector and his wife, and old Mr. Harvey, or people like the Leaches."

"The Leaches are a very good old family," said Margaret, feebly.

"I don't care for good old families when they are so slow," retorted Camille. "The Fellers we could have here, if we were rich enough, come from fine families, but they are up-to-date. It's no use hanging on to old silver dishes we never use and that I don't intend to spoil my hands shining. Poor Jack don't have much fun, anyway. If he wants that trotter—he say's it's going dirt cheap—I think it's mean he can't have it, instead of your hanging on to a lot of out-of-style old silver; so there."

Two generations ago there had been French blood in Camille's family.

She put on her clothes beautifully; she had a dark, rather fine-featured, alert little face, which gave a wrong impression, for she was essentially vulgar. Sometimes poor Margaret Lee wished that Camille had been definitely vicious, if only she might be possessed of more of the characteristics of breeding. Camille so irritated Margaret in those somewhat abstruse traits called sensibilities that she felt as if she were living with a sort of spiritual nutmeg-grater. Seldom did Camille speak that she did not jar Margaret, although unconsciously. Camille meant to be kind to the stout woman, whom she pitied as far as she was capable of pitying without understanding. She realized that it must be horrible to be no longer young, and so stout that one was fairly monstrous, but how horrible she could not with her mentality conceive. Jack also meant to be kind. He was not of the brutal—that is, intentionally brutal—type, but he had a shrewd eye to the betterment of himself, and no realization of the torture he inflicted upon those who opposed that betterment.

For a long time matters had been worse than usual financially in the Lee house. The sisters had been left in charge of the sadly dwindled estate, and had depended upon the judgment, or lack of judgment, of Jack. He approved of taking your chances and striking for larger income. The few good old grandfather securities had been sold, and wild ones from the very jungle of commerce had been substituted. Jack, like most of his type, while shrewd, was as credulous as a child. He lied himself, and expected all men to tell him the truth. Camille at his bidding mortgaged the old place, and Margaret dared not oppose. Taxes were not paid; interest was not paid; credit was exhausted. Then the house was put up at public auction, and brought little more than sufficient to pay the creditors. Jack took the balance and staked it in a few games of chance, and of course lost. The weary trotter stumbled one day and had to be shot. Jack became desperate. He frightened Camille. He was suddenly morose. He bade Camille pack, and Margaret also, and they obeyed. Camille stowed away her crumpled finery in the bulging old trunks, and Margaret folded daintily her few remnants of past treasures. She had an old silk gown or two, which resisted with their rich honesty the inroads of time, and a few pieces of old lace, which Camille understood no better than she understood their owner.

Then Margaret and the Desmonds went to the city and lived in a horrible, tawdry little flat in a tawdry locality. Jack roared with bitter mirth when he saw poor Margaret forced to enter her tiny room sidewise; Camille laughed also, although she chided Jack gently. "Mean of you to make fun of poor Margaret, Jacky dear," she said.

For a few weeks Margaret's life in that flat was horrible; then it became still worse. Margaret nearly filled with her weary, ridiculous bulk her little room, and she remained there most of the time, although it was sunny and noisy, its one window giving on a courtyard strung with clothes-lines and teeming with boisterous life. Camille and Jack went trolley-riding, and made shift to entertain a little, merry but questionable people, who gave them passes to vaudeville and entertained them in their turn until the small hours. Unquestionably these people suggested to Jack Desmond the scheme which spelled tragedy to Margaret.

She always remembered one little dark man with keen eyes who had seen her disappearing through her door of a Sunday night when all these gay, bedraggled birds were at liberty and the fun ran high. "Great Scott!" the man had said, and Margaret had heard him demand of Jack that she be recalled. She obeyed, and the man was introduced, also the other members of the party. Margaret Lee stood in the midst of this throng and heard their repressed titters of mirth at her appearance. Everybody there was in good humor with the exception of Jack, who was still nursing his bad luck, and the little dark man, whom Jack owed. The eyes of Jack and the little dark man made Margaret cold with a terror of something, and she knew not what. Before that terror the shame and mortification of her exhibition to that merry company was of no import.

She stood among them, silent, immense, clad in her dark purple silk gown spread over a great hoopskirt. A real lace collar lay softly over her enormous, billowing shoulders; real lace ruffles lay over her great, shapeless hands. Her face, the delicacy of whose features was veiled with flesh, flushed and paled. Not even flesh could subdue the sad brilliancy of her dark-blue eyes, fixed inward upon her own sad state, unregardful of the company. She made an indefinite murmur of response to the salutations given her, and then retreated. She heard the roar of laughter after she had squeezed through the door of her room. Then she heard eager conversation, of which she did not catch the real import, but which terrified her with chance expressions. She was quite sure that she was the subject of that eager discussion. She was quite sure that it boded her no good.

In a few days she knew the worst; and the worst was beyond her utmost imaginings. This was before the days of moving-picture shows; it was the day of humiliating spectacles of deformities, when inventions of amusements for the people had not progressed. It was the day of exhibitions of sad freaks of nature, calculated to provoke tears rather than laughter in the healthy-minded, and poor Margaret Lee was a chosen victim. Camille informed her in a few words of her fate. Camille was sorry for her, although not in the least understanding why she was sorry. She realized dimly that Margaret would be distressed, but she was unable from her narrow point of view to comprehend fully the whole tragedy.

"Jack has gone broke," stated Camille. "He owes Bill Stark a pile, and he can't pay a cent of it; and Jack's sense of honor about a poker debt is about the biggest thing in his character. Jack has got to pay. And Bill has a little circus, going to travel all summer, and he's offered big money for you. Jack can pay Bill what he owes him, and we'll have enough to live on, and have lots of fun going around. You hadn't ought to make a fuss about it."

Margaret, pale as death, stared at the girl, pertly slim, and common and pretty, who stared back laughingly, although still with the glimmer of uncomprehending pity in her black eyes.

"What does—he—want—me—for?" gasped Margaret.

"For a show, because you are so big," replied Camille. "You will make us all rich, Margaret. Ain't it nice?"

Then Camille screamed, the shrill raucous scream of the women of her type, for Margaret had fallen back in a dead faint, her immense bulk inert in her chair. Jack came running in alarm. Margaret had suddenly gained value in his shrewd eyes. He was as pale as she.

Finally Margaret raised her head, opened her miserable eyes, and regained her consciousness of herself and what lay before her. There was no course open but submission. She knew that from the first. All three faced destitution; she was the one financial asset, she and her poor flesh. She had to face it, and with what dignity she could muster.

Margaret had great piety. She kept constantly before her mental vision the fact in which she believed, that the world which she found so hard, and which put her to unspeakable torture, was not all.

A week elapsed before the wretched little show of which she was to be a member went on the road, and night after night she prayed. She besieged her God for strength. She never prayed for respite. Her realization of the situation and her lofty resolution prevented that. The awful, ridiculous combat was before her; there was no evasion; she prayed only for the strength which leads to victory.

However, when the time came, it was all worse than she had imagined. How could a woman gently born and bred conceive of the horrible ignominy of such a life? She was dragged hither and yon, to this and that little town. She traveled through sweltering heat on jolting trains; she slept in tents; she lived—she, Margaret Lee—on terms of equality with the common and the vulgar. Daily her absurd unwieldiness was exhibited to crowds screaming with laughter. Even her faith wavered. It seemed to her that there was nothing for evermore beyond those staring, jeering faces of silly mirth and delight at the sight of her, seated in two chairs, clad in a pink spangled dress, her vast shoulders bare and sparkling with a tawdry necklace, her great, bare arms covered with brass bracelets, her hands incased in short, white kid gloves, over the fingers of which she wore a number of rings—stage properties.

Margaret became a horror to herself. At times it seemed to her that she was in the way of fairly losing her own identity. It mattered little that Camille and Jack were very kind to her, that they showed her the nice things which her terrible earnings had enabled them to have. She sat in her two chairs—the two chairs proved a most successful advertisement—with her two kid-cushiony hands clenched in her pink spangled lap, and she suffered the agony of soul, which made her inner self stern and terrible, behind that great pink mask of face. And nobody realized until one sultry day when the show opened at a village in a pocket of green hills—indeed, its name was Greenhill—and Sydney Lord went to see it.

Margaret, who had schooled herself to look upon her audience as if they were not, suddenly comprehended among them another soul who understood her own. She met the eyes of the man, and a wonderful comfort, as of a cool breeze blowing over the face of clear water, came to her. She knew that the man understood. She knew that she had his fullest sympathy. She saw also a comrade in the toils of comic tragedy, for Sydney Lord was in the same case. He was a mountain of flesh. As a matter of fact, had he not been known in Greenhill and respected as a man of character as well as of body, and of an old family, he would have rivaled Margaret. Beside him sat an elderly woman, sweet-faced, slightly bent as to her slender shoulders, as if with a chronic attitude of submission. She was Sydney's widowed sister, Ellen Waters. She lived with her brother and kept his house, and had no will other than his.

Sydney Lord and his sister remained when the rest of the audience had drifted out, after the privileged hand-shakes with the queen of the show. Every time a coarse, rustic hand reached familiarly after Margaret's, Sydney shrank.

He motioned his sister to remain seated when he approached the stage. Jack Desmond, who had been exploiting Margaret, gazed at him with admiring curiosity. Sydney waved him away with a commanding gesture. "I wish to speak to her a moment. Pray leave the tent," he said, and Jack obeyed. People always obeyed Sydney Lord.

Sydney stood before Margaret, and he saw the clear crystal, which was herself, within all the flesh, clad in tawdry raiment, and she knew that he saw it.

"Good God!" said Sydney, "you are a lady!"

He continued to gaze at her, and his eyes, large and brown, became blurred; at the same time his mouth tightened.

"How came you to be in such a place as this?" demanded Sydney. He spoke almost as if he were angry with her.

Margaret explained briefly.

"It is an outrage," declared Sydney. He said it, however, rather absently. He was reflecting. "Where do you live?" he asked.

"Here."

"You mean—?"

"They make up a bed for me here, after the people have gone."

"And I suppose you had—before this—a comfortable house."

"The house which my grandfather Lee owned, the old Lee mansion-house, before we went to the city. It was a very fine old Colonial house," explained Margaret, in her finely modulated voice.

"And you had a good room?"

"The southeast chamber had always been mine. It was very large, and the furniture was old Spanish mahogany."

"And now—" said Sydney.

"Yes," said Margaret. She looked at him, and her serious blue eyes seemed to see past him. "It will not last," she said.

"What do you mean?"

"I try to learn a lesson. I am a child in the school of God. My lesson is the one that always ends in peace."

"Good God!" said Sydney.

He motioned to his sister, and Ellen approached in a frightened fashion. Her brother could do no wrong, but this was the unusual, and alarmed her.

"This lady—" began Sydney.

"Miss Lee," said Margaret. "I was never married. I am Miss Margaret Lee."

"This," said Sydney, "is my sister Ellen, Mrs. Waters. Ellen, I wish you to meet Miss Lee."

Ellen took into her own Margaret's hand, and said feebly that it was a beautiful day and she hoped Miss Lee found Greenhill a pleasant place to— visit. Sydney moved slowly out of the tent and found Jack Desmond. He was standing near with Camille, who looked her best in a pale-blue summer silk and a black hat trimmed with roses. Jack and Camille never really knew how the great man had managed, but presently Margaret had gone away with him and his sister.

Jack and Camille looked at each other.

"Oh, Jack, ought you to have let her go?" said Camille.

"What made you let her go?" asked Jack.

"I—don't know. I couldn't say anything. That man has a tremendous way with him. Goodness!"

"He is all right here in the place, anyhow," said Jack. "They look up to him. He is a big-bug here. Comes of a family like Margaret's, though he hasn't got much money. Some chaps were braggin' that they had a bigger show than her right here, and I found out."

"Suppose," said Camille, "Margaret does not come back?"

"He cold not keep her without bein' arrested," declared Jack, but he looked uneasy. He had, however, looked uneasy for some time. The fact was, Margaret had been very gradually losing weight. Moreover, she was not well. That very night, after the show was over, Bill Stark, the little dark man, had a talk with the Desmonds about it.

"Truth is, before long, if you don't look out, you'll have to pad her," said Bill; "and giants don't amount to a row of pins after that begins."

Camille looked worried and sulky. "She ain't very well, anyhow," said she. "I ain't going to kill Margaret."

"It's a good thing she's got a chance to have a night's rest in a house," said Bill Stark.

"The fat man has asked her to stay with him and his sister while the show is here," said Jack.

"The sister invited her," said Camille, with a little stiffness. She was common, but she had lived with Lees, and her mother had married a Lee. She knew what was due Margaret, and also due herself.

"The truth is," said Camille, "this is an awful sort of life for a woman like Margaret. She and her folks were never used to anything like it."

"Why didn't you make your beauty husband hustle and take care of her and you, then," demanded Bill, who admired Camille, and disliked her because she had no eyes for him.

"My husband has been unfortunate. He has done the best he could," responded Camille. "Come, Jack; no use talking about it any longer. Guess Margaret will pick up. Come along. I'm tired out."

That night Margaret Lee slept in a sweet chamber with muslin curtains at the windows, in a massive old mahogany bed, much like hers which had been sacrificed at an auction sale. The bed-linen was linen, and smelled of lavender. Margaret was too happy to sleep. She lay in the cool, fragrant sheets and was happy, and convinced of the presence of the God to whom she had prayed. All night Sydney Lord sat down-stairs in his book-walled sanctum and studied over the situation. It was a crucial one. The great psychological moment of Sydney Lord's life for knight-errantry had arrived. He studied the thing from every point of view. There was no romance about it. These were hard, sordid, tragic, ludicrous facts with which he had to deal. He knew to a nicety the agonies which Margaret suffered. He knew, because of his own capacity for sufferings of like stress. "And she is a woman and a lady," he said, aloud.

If Sydney had been rich enough, the matter would have been simple. He could have paid Jack and Camille enough to quiet them, and Margaret could have lived with him and his sister and their two old servants. But he was not rich; he was even poor. The price to be paid for Margaret's liberty was a bitter one, but it was that or nothing. Sydney faced it. He looked about the room. To him the walls lined with the gleams of old books were lovely. There was an oil portrait of his mother over the mantel-shelf. The weather was warm now, and there was no need for a hearth fire, but how exquisitely home-like and dear that room could be when the snow drove outside and there was the leap of flame on the hearth! Sydney was a scholar and a gentleman. He had led a gentle and sequestered life. Here in his native village there were none to gibe and sneer. The contrast of the traveling show would be as great for him as it had been for Margaret, but he was of the male of the species and she the female. Chivalry, racial, harking back to the beginning of nobility in the human, to its earliest dawn, fired Sydney. The pale daylight invaded the study. Sydney, as truly as any knight of old, had girded himself, and with no hope, no thought of reward, for the battle in the eternal service of the strong for the weak, which makes the true worth of the strong.

There was only one way. Sydney Lord took it. His sister was spared the knowledge of the truth for a long while. When she knew, she did not lament; since Sydney had taken the course, it must be right. As for Margaret, now knowing the truth, she yielded. She was really on the verge of illness. Her spirit was of too fine a strain to enable her body to endure long. When she was told that she was to remain with Sydney's sister while Sydney went away on business, she made no objection. A wonderful sense of relief, as of wings of healing being spread under her despair, was upon her. Camille came to bid her good-by.

"I hope you have a nice visit in this lovely house," said Camille, and kissed her. Camille was astute, and to be trusted. She did not betray Sydney's confidence. Sydney used a disguise—a dark wig over his partially bald head and a little make-up—and he traveled about with the show and sat on three chairs and shook hands with the gaping crowd, and was curiously happy. It was discomfort; it was ignominy; it was maddening to support by the exhibition of his physical deformity a perfectly worthless young couple like Jack and Camille Desmond, but it was all superbly ennobling for the man himself.

Always as he sat on his three chairs, immense, grotesque—the more grotesque for his splendid dignity of bearing—there was in his soul of a gallant gentleman the consciousness of that other, whom he was shielding from a similar ordeal. Compassion and generosity so great that they comprehended love itself and excelled its highest type, irradiated the whole being of the fat man exposed to the gaze of his inferiors. Chivalry, which rendered him almost god-like, strengthened him for his task. Sydney thought always of Margaret as distinct from her physical self, a sort of crystalline, angelic soul, with no encumbrance of earth. He achieved a purely spiritual conception of her. And Margaret, living again her gentle lady life, was likewise ennobled by a gratitude which transformed her. Always a clear and beautiful soul, she gave out new lights of character like a jewel in the sun. And she also thought of Sydney as distinct from his physical self. The consciousness of the two human beings, one of the other, was a consciousness as of two wonderful lines of good and beauty, moving for ever parallel, separate, and inseparable in an eternal harmony of spirit.

EVEN AS YOU AND I

Fannie Hurst

A more subtle mechanism is involved in cases where the victim instead of pretending to agree with his [sic] "betters" actually does agree with them, and sees his own group through their eyes. This process may underlie assimilationist strivings and be the factor that leads the individual to lose himself totally in the dominant group as soon as his level of possessions, customs, and speech makes him indistinguishable from the majority. But more mysterious are the cases where the individual is hopelessly barred from assimilation and yet mentally identifies himself with the practices, outlook, and prejudices of the dominant group. He accepts his state.

—Gordon Allport, "Traits Due to Victimization"

◇

There is an intensity about September noonday on Coney Island, aided and abetted by tin roofs, metallic facades, gilt domes, looking-glass fronts, jeweled spires, screaming peanut- and frankfurter-stands, which has not its peculiar kind of equal this side of opalescent Tangiers. Here the sea air can become a sort of hot camphor-ice to the cheek, the sea itself a percolator, boiling up against a glass surface. Beneath the tin roofs of Ocean Avenue the indoor heat takes on the kind of intense density that is cotton in the mouth and ringing in the ears.

At one o'clock the jibberwock exteriors of Ocean Avenue begin fantastic signs of life. The House of Folly breaks out, over its entire façade, into a chickenpox of red and green, blue and purple, yellow, violet, and gold electric bulbs. The Ocean Waves concession begins its side-splitting undulations. Maha Mahadra, India's foremost soothsayer (down in police, divorce, and night courts as Mamie Jones, May Costello, and Mabel Brown, respectively), loops back her spangled portiere. The Baby Incubator slides open its ticket-windows. Five carousals begin to whang. A row of hula-hula girls in paper necklaces appears outside of "Hawaii," gelatinously naughty and insinuating of hip. There begins a razzling of the razzle-dazzle. Shooting-galleries begin to snipe into the glittering noon, and the smell of hot spiced sausages and stale malt to lay on the air.

Before the Palace of Freaks, a barker slanted up his megaphone, baying to the sun.

35

"Y-e-a-o-u! Y-e-a-o-u! The greatest show on the Island! Ten cents to see the greatest freak congress in the world. Shapiro's freaks are gathered from every corner of the universe. Enter and shake hands with the Baron de Ross, the children's delight, the world's smallest human being; age, forty-two years, eight months; height, twenty-eight inches; weight, fourteen and one-half pounds, certified scales. Enter and see the original and only authentic Siamese Twins! The Ossified Man! You are cordially invited to stick pins into this mystery of the whole medical world. Jastrow, the world's most famous strong man and glass-eater, will perform his world-startling feats. Show about to begin! Our glass-eater eats glass, not rock candy—any one doubting same can sample it first. We have on view within, and all included in your ten-cents admission, the famous Teenie, absolutely the heaviest woman in captivity. We guarantee Teenie to tip the certified scales at five hundred and fifty-five, a weight unsurpassed by any of the heavy-weights in the history of show business. Come in and fox-trot with Teenie, the world wonder. Come in and fox-trot with her. Show begins immediately. Y-e-a-o-u! Y-e-a-o-u!"

Within the Palace of Freaks, her platform elevated and railed in against the unduly curious, Miss Luella Hoag, all that she was so raucously purported to be, sat back in her chair, as much in the attitude of relaxing as her proportions would permit.

There is no way in which I can hope to salve your offended estheticisms with any of Miss Hoag's better points. What matters it that her skin was not without the rich quality of cream too thick to pour, when her arms fairly dimpled and billowed of this creaminess, and above her rather small ankles her made-to-order red-satin shoes bulged over of it, the low-cut bosom of her red and sequin dress was a terrific expanse of it, her hands small cushions of it, her throat quivery, and her walk a waddle with it. All but her face; it was as if the suet-like inundation of the flesh had not dared here. The chin was only slightly doubled; the cheeks just a shade too plump. Neither was the eye heavy of lid or sunk down behind a ridge of cheek. Between her eyes and upper lip, Miss Hoag looked her just-turned twenty; beyond them, she was antediluvian, deluged, smothered beneath the creamy billows and billows of self

And yet, sunk there like a flower-seed planted too deeply to push its way up to bloom, the twenty-year old heart of Miss Hoag beat beneath its carbonaceous layer upon layer, even skipped a beat at spring's palpitating sweetness, dared to dream of love, weep of desire, ache of loneliness and loveliness.

Isolated thus by the flesh, the spirit, too, had been caught in nature's sebaceous trick upon Miss Hoag. Life had passed her by slimly. But Miss Hoag's redundancy was not all literal. A sixth and saving sense of humor lay like a coating of tallow protecting the surface of her. For nature's vagary, she was pensioned on life's pay-roll at eighteen dollars a week.

"Easy money, friends," Miss Hoag would *ad lib.* to the line-up outside her railing; "how would some of you like to sit back and draw your wages just for the color of your hair or the size of your shoes? You there, that sailor boy down there, how'd you like to have a fox-trot with Teenie? Something to tell the Jackies about. Come on, Jack Tar, I'm light on my feet, but I won't guarantee what I'll be on yours. Step up and have a round."

Usually the crowd would turn sheepish and dissolve at this Terpsichorean threat. In fact, it was Miss Hoag's method of accomplishing just that.

In the August high noon of the Coney Island Freak Palace, which is the time and scene of my daring to introduce to you the only under-thirty-years, and over-one-hundred-and-thirty-pounds, heroine in the history of fiction, the megaphone's catch of the day's first dribble of humanity and inhumanity had not yet begun its staring, gaping invasion.

A curtain of heat that was almost tangible hung from the glass roof, the Ossified Man, sworn by clause of contract impervious alike to heat and cold, urged his reclining wheel-chair an imperceptible inch toward the neighboring sway of Miss Hoag's palm-leaf. She widened its arch, subtly.

"Ain't it a fright?" she said.

"Sacred Mother of the Sacred Child!" said the Ossified Man, in a *patois* of very south Italy.

Then Miss Hoag turned to the right, a rail partitioning her from the highly popular spectacle of the Baron de Ross, christened, married, and to be buried by his nomenclature in disuse, Edwin Ross Mac Gregor.

"Hot, honey?"

The Baron, in a toy rocker that easily contained him, turned upon Miss Hoag a face so anachronistic that the senses reeled back. An old face, as if carved out of a paleolithic cherry-stone; the ears furrowed in; the eyes as if they had seen, without marveling, the light of creation; even the hands, braceleted in what might have been portiere-rings, leanly prehensile. When the Baron spoke, his voice was not unlike the middle C of an old harpsichord whose wires had long since rusted and died. He was frock-coated like a clergyman or a park statue of a patriot.

Of face, a Chaldean sire; of dress, a miniature apotheosis of the tailor's art; of form, a paleolithic child.

"Blow me to an ice-cream cone? Gowann, Teenie, have a heart!"

Miss Hoag billowed into silent laughter. "Little devil! That's six you've sponged off me this week, you little whipper-snapper."

The Baron screwed up into the tightest of grimaces.

"Nice Teenie——nice old Teenie!"

She tossed him a coin from the small saucerful of them on the table beside her. He caught it with the simian agility of his tiny hands. "Nice Teenie! Nice old Teenie!"

A first group had strolled up, indolent and insolent at the spectacle of them.

"Photographs! Photographs! Take the folks back home a signed photograph of Teenie—only ten cents, one dime. Give the kiddies a treat—signed photograph of little Teenie!"

She would solicit thus, canorous of phrase, a fan of her cardboard likenesses held out, invitational.

Occasionally there were sales, the coins rattling down into the china saucer beside her; oftener a mere bombardment of insolence and indolence, occasionally a question.

This day from a motorman, loitering in uniform between runs, "Say, Skinnay, whatcha weigh?"

Whatever of living tissue may have shrunk and quivered beneath the surface of Miss Hoag was further insulated by a certain professional pride—that of the champion middle weight for his cauliflower ear. Of the beauty for the tiny mole where her neck is whitest, the *ballerina* for her double joints.

"Wanna come up and dance with me and find out?"

"Oh Lord!"—— receding from the crowd and its trail of laughter. "Oh Lord! Excuse me. Good night!"

A CHILD: Missus, is all of you just one lady?

"Bless your heart, little pettie, they gimme a good measure, didn't they? Here's a chocolate drop for the little pettie."

"Come away! Don't take nothing from her!"

"I wouldn't hurt your little girl, lady. I wouldn't harm a pretty hair of her head; I love the kiddies."

"Good-bye, Missus."

"Good-bye, little pettie."

A MAN: Say, was you born in captivity—-in this line of work, I mean?

"Law, no, friend! I never seen the light of the show business up to eight year ago. There wasn't a member of my family, all dead and put away now, weighed more'n one-fifty. They say it of my mother, she was married at ninety pounds and died at a hundred and six."

"You don't say so."

"I was born and raised on a farm out in Ohio. Bet not far from your part of the country, from the looks of you, friend. Buckeye?"

"Not a bad guess at that—-Indiana's mine."

"Law! to my way of thinking, there's no part of the Union got anything on the Middle States. Knock me around all you want, I always say, but let me buried in the Buckeye State. Photographs? Signed photographs at ten cents each. Take one home to the wife, friend, out in Indiana. Come, friends, what's a dime? Ten cents!"

The crowd, treacle-slow, and swinging its children shoulder-high, would shuffle on, pause next at the falsetto exhortations of the Baron, then on to the collapsibilities of the Boneless Wonder, the flexuosities of the Snake-charmer, the goose-fleshing, the terrible crunching of Jastrow, the

Granite Jaw. A commotion, this last, not unlike the steam-roller leveling of a rock road.

Miss Hoag retired then back to her chair, readjusting the photographs to their table display, wielding her fan largely.

"Lord!" she said, across the right railing, "Wouldn't this weather fry you!"

The Baron wilted to a mock swoon, his little legs stiffening at a hypotenuse.

"Ice-cream cone!" he cried. "Ice-cream cone, or I faint!"

"Poor Jastrow! Just listen to him! Honest, that grinding goes right through me. He hadn't ought to be showing today, after the way they had to have the doctor in on him last night. He hadn't ought to be eating that nasty glass."

"Ain't it awful, Mabel!"

"Yes, it's awful, Mabel A fellow snagging up his insides like Jastrow. I never knew a glass-eating artist in my life that lived to old age. I was show-ing once with a pair of glass-eating sisters, the Twins Delamar, as fine a pair of girls as ever———"

"Sure, the Delamars—— I know 'em."

"Remember the specialty they carried, stepping on a piece of plate glass and feeding each other with the grounds—-"

"Sure."

"Well, I sat up for three weeks running, with one of them girls—-the red-haired one, till she died off of sorosis of the liver—-"

"Sure enough—-Lizzie Delamar!"

"Lida, the other one, is still carrying the act on street-fair time, but it won't surprise me to hear of her next. That's what'll happen to Granite Jaw one of these days, too, if he—-"

"Pretty soft on the Granite Jaw, ain't cha? M-m-n! Yum—yum! Pretty soft!"

When the Baron mouthed he became in expression Punchinello with his finger alongside his nose, his face tightening and knotting into cunning. "Pretty soft on the Granite Jaw! Yum—yum—yum!"

"Little devil! Little devil! I'll catch you and spank you to death."

"Yum! Yum!

"It's better to have loved a short man
Than never to have loved atall."

"Little peewee, you! Jastrow ain't short. Them's thick, strong-necked kind never look their height. That boy is five feet two is he's an inch. Them stocky ones is the build that make the strong kind. Looka him lift up that cannon-ball with just his left hand. B-r-r-r! Listen how it shakes the place when he lets is fall. Looka! Honest, it makes me sick! It's a wonder he don't kill himself.

"Better to have loved a short man
   Than never to have loved atall."

The day, sun-dash riddled, stare-dash riddled, sawdusty, and white with glare, slouched into the clanging, banging, electric-pianoed, electrifying Babylonia of a Coney Island Saturday night. The erupting lava of a pent-up work-a-week, odiferous of strong foods and wilted clothing, poured hotly down that boulevard of the bourgeoise, Ocean Avenue. The slow, thick circulation of six days of pants-pressing and boiler-making, of cigarette rolling and typewriting, of machine-operating and truck-driving, of third-floor-backs, congestion and indigestion, of depression and suppression, demanding the spurious kind of excitation that can whip the blood to foam, The terrific gyration of looping the loop. The comet-tail dash plunge of shooting the shoots; the rocketing skyward, and the delicious madness at the pit of the stomach on the downward swoop. The bead on the apple juice, the dash of mustard to the frankfurter, the feather tickler in the eye, the barker to the ear, and the thick festival-flavored sawdust to the throat. By eleven o'clock the Freak Palace was a gelatinous congestion of the quickened of heart, of blood, of tongue, and of purse. The crowd stared, gaped, squirmed through itself, sweated. By twelve o'clock from her benchlike throne that had become a straitjacket to the back, a heaviness had set in that seemed to thicken Miss Hoag's eyelids, the flush receding before doughiness.

A weary mountain of the cruelly enhancing red silk and melting red sequin paste, the billowy arms inundated with the thumb-deep dimples lax out along the chair-sides, as preponderous and preposterous a heroine as ever fell the lot of scribe, she was nature's huge joke—a practical joke, too, at eighteen dollars a week, bank-books form three trust companies, and a china pig about ready to burst.

"Cheer up, Ossi! It might be worse," she said across the left rail, but her lips twitching involuntarily of tiredness.

"Sacred Mother of the Sacred Child!" said the Ossified Man, in Italian.

The sword-swallower, at the megaphone instance of the barker, waggled suddenly into motion, and, flouncing back her bushy knee-skirts, threw back her head and swallowed an eighteen-inch carpenter's saw to the hilt. The crowd flowed up and around her.

Miss Hoag felt on the undershelf of her table for a glass of water, draining it. "Thank God," she said, "another day done!" and began getting together her photographs into a neat packet, tilting the contents of the saucer into a small biscuit-tin and snapping it around with a rubber band.

The Baron de Ross was counting, too, his small hands eager at the task. "This Island is getting as hard-boiled as an egg," he said.

"It is that," said Miss Hoag, making a pencil insert into a small memo-randum-book.

"You!" cried the Baron, the screw lines out again. "You money-bag tied in the middle! I know a tattooed girl worked with you once on the St. Louis World's Fair pike says you slept on a pillow stuffed with greenbacks."

"You're crazy with the heat," said Miss Hoag. "What I've got out of this business, I've sweated for."

Then the Baron de Ross executed a pirouette of tiny self. "Worth your weight in gold! Worth your weight in gold!"

"If you don't behave yourself, you little peewee, I'll leave you to plow home through the sand alone. If it wasn't for me playing nurse-girl to you, you'd have to be hiring a keeper. You'd better behave."

"Worth your weight in gold! Blow us to an ice-cream cone. Eh, Ossi?"

The crowd has sifted out; all but one of the center aisle grill-arc lights flickered out, leaving the Freak Palace to a sputtering kind of gloom. The Snake-charmer, of a thousand irridescencies, wound the last of her devitalized cobras down into its painted chest. The Siamese Twins untwisted out of their embrace and went each his way. The Princess Albino wove her cotton hair into a plait, finishing it with a rapidly wound bit of thread. An attendant trundled the Ossified Man through a rear door. Jastrow the Granite Jaw flopped on his derby, slightly askew, and strolled over toward that same door, hands in pocket. He was thewed like an ox. Short and as squattily packed down as a Buddha, the great sinews of his strength bulged in his short neck and in the backs of the calves of his legs, even rippled beneath his coat. It was as if a compress had reduced him from a great height down to his tightest compactness, concentrating the strength of him. Even in repose, the undershot jaw was plunged forward, the jowls bonily defined.

"Worth your weight in gold! Blow us to an ice-cream cone. Eh, Jastrow? She's worth her weight in gold."

Passing within reach of where the Baron de Ross danced to his ditty of reiteration, Jastrow the Granite Jaw reached up and in through the rail, capturing one of the jiggling ankles, elevating the figure of the Baron de Ross to a high-flung torch.

"Lay off that noise," said Jastrow the Granite Jaw, threatening to dangle him head downward. "Lay off, or I'll drown you like a kitten!"

With an agility that could have swung him from bough to bough, the Baron de Ross somersaulted astride the rear of Jastrow the Granite Jaw's great neck, pounding the little futile fists against the bulwark of head.

"Leggo of me! Leggo!"

"G-r-r-r-r! I'll step on you and squash you like a caterpillar."

"Don't hurt him, Mr. Jastrow! Don't let him fall off backwards. He is so little. Teenie'll catch you if you fall, honey. Tennie's here in back of you."

With another double twist, the Baron de Ross somersaulted backward off the should of his captor, landing upright in the outstretched skirts of Miss Hoag.

"Yah, yah!" he cried, dancing in the net of skirt and waggling his hands from his ears. "Yah, yah!"

The Granite Jaw smoothed down the outraged rear of his head, eyes rolling and smile terrible.

"Wow!" he said, making a false feint toward him. The Baron, shrill with hysteria, plunged into a fold of Miss Hoag's skirt.

"Don't hurt him, Jastrow. He's so awful little! Don't play rough."

THE BARON (*projecting his face around a fold of skirt*): Worth her weight in go-ould——go-ould!

"He's always guying me for my saving ways, Jastrow. I tell him I ain't got no little twenty-eight-inch wife out in San Francisco sending me pin-money. Neither am I the prize little grafter of the world. I tell him he's the littlest man and the biggest grafter in the show. Come out of there, you little devil! He thinks because I got a few hundred dollars laid by I'm a bigger freak than the one I get paid for being."

Jastrow the Granite Jaw flung the crook of his walking-stick against his hip, leaning into it, the flanges of his nostrils widening a bit, as if scenting.

"You old mountain-top," he said, screwing at the up-curving mustache, "who'd have thought you had that pretty a penny saved?"

"I don't look to see myself live and die in the show business, Mr. Jastrow."

"Now you've said something, Big Tent."

"There's a farm out near Xenia, Ohio, where I lay up in the winter that I'm going to own for myself one of these days. I've seen too many in this business die right in exhibition, and the show have to chip in to buy 'em, for me not to save up against a rainy day."

"Lay it on, Big Tent. I like your philosophy."

"That's me every time, Mr. Jastrow. I'm going to die in a little story-and-a-half frame house of my own with a cute little pointy roof, a potato-patch right up to my back steps, and my own white Leghorns crossin' my own country road to get to the other side. Why, I know a Fat in this business, Aggie Lamont—"

"Sure, me and the Baroness played Mexico City Carnival with Aggie Lamont. Some heavy!"

"Well, that girl, in her day, was one of the biggest tips to the scale this business ever seen. What happens? All of a sudden, just like that – pneumonia!—down to three hundred sixty-five pounds and not a penny saved. I chipped in what I could to keep her going, but she just down and died one night. Job gone. No weight. In the exhibit business, just like other line, you got to have a long head. A Fat's got to look ahead for a thin day. Strong for a weak day. That's why I wish, Mr. Jastrow, you'd cut out that glass-eating feature of yours."

"How much you got, Airy-Fairy? Lemme double your money for you!"

"She's worth her weight in gold."

"Lemme double it!"

"Like fun I will. A spendthrift like you!"

"Which way you going?"

"We always go home by the beach. Shapiro made it a rule that the Bigs and the Littles can't ever show themselves on Ocean Avenue."

"Come on, you little flea; I'll ride you up the beach on my shoulder."

"Oh, Mr. Jastrow, you—you going to walk home with me and—Baron?"

"Come on is what I said."

He mounted the Baron de Ross to his bulge of shoulder with veriest toss, Miss Hoagg, in a multifold cape that was a merciful shroud to the bulk of her, descending from the platform. The place had emptied itself of its fantastic congress of nature's pranks, only the grotesque print of it remaining. The painted snake-chests closed. The array of gustatory swords, each in flannelet slip-cover. The wild man's cage, empty. The tiny velocipede of the Baron de Ross, upside down against rust. A hall of wonder here. A cave of distorted fancy. The Land of the Cow Jumped Over the Moon and the Dish Ran away with the Spoon.

Outside, a moon, something bridal in its whiteness, beat down upon a kicked-up stretch of beach, the banana-skins, the pop-corn boxes, the gambados of erstwhile revelers violently printed into its sands. A platinum-colored sea undulated in.

The leaping, bounding outline of Luna Park winked out even as they emerged, the whole violent contortion fading back into silver mist. There was a new breeze, spicily cool.

Miss Hoag breathed out. "Ain't this something grand?"

"Giddy-ap!" cried the Baron, slappity-slappity at the great boulder of the Granite Jaw's head. "Giddy-ap!"

They plowed forward, a group out of phantasmagoria—as motley a threesome as ever strode this side of the land of Anesthesia.

"How do you like it at Mrs. Bostum's boarding-house, Mr. Jastrow? I never stop anywheres else on the Island. Most of the Shapiro concession always stops there."

"Good as the next," said Mr. Jastrow kicking onward.

"I was sorry to hear you was ailing so last night, Mr. Jastrow, and I was sorry there was nothing you would let me do for you. They always call me 'The Doc' around exhibits. I say—but you just ought to heard yourself yell me out of the room when I come in to offer myself—"

"They had me crazy with pain."

"You wasn't so crazy with pain when the albino girl come down with the bottle of fire-water, was he, Baron? We seen him throwing goo-goos at albino, didn't we, Baron?"

THE BARON (*impish in the moonlight*): He fell for a cotton-dash top.

"He didn't yell the albino and her bottle out, did he, Baron?"

"It's this darn business," said Mr. Jastrow, creating a storm of sand-spray with each stride. "I'm punctured up like a tire."

"I been saying to the Baron, Mr. Jastrow, if you'd only cut out the glass-eating feature. You got as fine a appearance and as fine a strong act by itself as you could want. A short fellow like you with all your muscle-power is a novelty in himself. Honest, Mr. Jastrow, it—it's a sin to see a fine set-up fellow like you killing yourself this way. You ought to cut out the granite-jaw feature."

"Yeh—and cut down my act to half-dash pay. I'd be full of them tricks—wouldn't I? Show me another jaw act measures up to mine. Show me the strong-arm number that ever pulled down the coin a jaw act did. I'd be a sweet boob, wouldn't I, to cut my pocket-book in two? I need money, Airy-Fairy. My God! How I got the capacity for needing money!"

"What's money to health, Mr. Jastrow? It ain't human or freak nature to digest glass. Honest, every time I hear you cruching I get the chills!"

Then Mr. Jastrow shot forward his lower jaw with a milling motion:
"Gr-r-r-r-r!"

"She's sweet on you, Jastrow, like all the rest of 'em.

"Better to have loved a short man
Than never to have loved atall."

"Baron—I—I'll spank!"

"Worth her weight in gold!"

"Where you got all that money soaked, Big Tent?"

"Aw, Mr. Jastrow, the Baron's only tormenting me."

"She sleeps on a pillow stuffed with greenbacks."

"Sure I got a few dollars saved, and I ain't ashamed of it. I've had steady work in this business eight years, now, ever since the circus came to my town out in Ohio and made me the offer, but that's no sign I can be in it eight years longer. Sure I got a few dollars saved."

"Well, whatta you know—a big tent like you?"

"Ain't a big tent like me human, Mr. Jastrow" Ain't I—ain't I just like any other—girl—twenty years old—ain't I just like— other—girls—underneath all this?"

"Sure, sure!" said Mr. Jastrow. "How much you to the good, little one?"

"I've about eleven hundred dollars with my bank-books and pig."

"'Leven hundred! Well, whatta a you know about that? Say, Big Tent, better lemme double your money for you!"

"Aw, you go on, Mr. Jastrow! Ain't you the torment, too?"

"Say, gal, next time I get the misery you can hold my hand as long as you're little heart desires. 'Leven hundred to the good! Goodnight! Get down off my shoulder, you little flea, you. I got to turn in here and take a drink on the strength of that. 'Leven hundred to the good! Good night!"

"Oh, Mr. Jastrow, in your state! In your state alcohol is poison. Mr. Jastrow—please—you mustn't!"

"Blow me, too, Jas! Aw, say—have a heart; blow me to a bracer, too!"

"No, no, Mr. Jastrow, don't take the Baron. The little fellow can't stand alcohol. His Baroness don't want it. Anyways, it's against the rules—please—"

"You stay and take the lady home—flea. See the lady home like a gentleman. 'Leven hundred to the good! I'd see a lady as far as the devil on that. Good night!"

At Mrs. Bostrum's boarding-house, one of a row of the stair-faced packing-cases of the summer city, bathing suits drying and kicking over veranda rails, a late quiet had fallen, only one window showing yellowy in the peak of its top story. A white-net screen door was unhooked from without by inserting a hand through a slit in the fabric. An uncarpeted pocket of hall lay deep in absolute blackness. Miss Hoag fumbled for the switch, finally leaving the Baron to the meager comfort of his first-floor back.

"Y'all right, honey? Can you reach what you want?"

The Baron clambered to a chair and up to her. His face had unknotted, the turmoil of little lines scattering.

"Aw!" he said. "Good old tub, Teenie! Good old Big Tent!"

A layer of tears sprang across Miss Hoag's glance and, suddenly gaining rush, ran down over her lashes. She dashed at them.

"I'm human, Baron. Maybe you don't know it, but I'm human."

"Now what did I do, Tennie?"

"It—it ain't you, Baron; it—it ain't nobody. It—it's—only I just wonder sometimes what God had in mind, anyways—making our kind. Where do we belong—"

"Aw, you're a great Heavy, Teenie—and it's the Bigs and the Littles got the cinch in this business. Looka the poor Siamese. How'd you like to be hitched up thataway all day. Looka Ossie. How'd you like to let 'em stick pins in you all for their ten cents worth. Looka poor Jas. Why, a girl's a fool to waste any hearache gettin' stuck on him. That old boy's going to wake up out of one of them spells dead someday. How'd you like to chew glass because it's big money and then drink it up so fast you'd got to borrow money off the albino girl for the doctor's prescription—"

The tears came now, riveleting down Miss Hoag's cheeks, bouncing off to the cape.

"Oh God!" she said, her hand closing over the Baron's, pressing it. "With us freaks, even if we win, we lose. Take me. What's the good of ten million dollars to me—twenty millions? Last night when I went in to offer him help—him in the same business and that ought to be used to me—right in the middle of being crazy with pain, what did he yell every time he looked at me, 'Take her away! Take her away!'"

"Aw now, Teenie, Jas had the D.T.'s last night; he—"

"'Take her away!' he kept yelling. 'Take her away!' One of my own kind getting the horrors just to look at me!"

"You're sweet on the Granite Jaw; you are, Teenie; that's what's eating you—you're sweet on the Granite Jaw—"

Suddenly Miss Hoag turned, slamming the door afterward so that the silence re-echoed sharply.

"What if I am?" she said, standing out in the hall pocket of absolute blackness, her hand cupped against her mouth and the blinding tears staggering. "What if I am? What if I am?"

Within her own room, a second-floor-back, augmented slightly by an immaculate layout of pink celluloid toilet articles and a white water-pitcher of three pink carnations, Miss Hoag snapped on her light where it dangled above the celluloid toilet articles. A summer-bug was bumbling against the ceiling; it dashed itself between Miss Hoag and her mirror as she stood there breathing from the climb and looking back at herself with salt bitten eyes, mouth twitching. Finally, after an inanimate period of unseeing stare, she unhooked the long cape, brushing it, and, ever dainty of self, folding it across a chair-back. A voluminous garment, fold and fold upon itself, but sheer and crisp dimity, even streaming a length of pink ribbon, lay across the bed-edge. Miss Hoag took it up, her hand already slowly and tiredly at the business of unfettering herself of the monstrous red silk.

Came a sudden avalanche of knocking and a rattling of door-knob, the voice of Mrs. Bostrum, landlady, high with panic.

"Teenie! Jastrow's dyin' in his room! He's yellin' for you! For God's sakes—quick—down in his room!"

In the instant that followed, across the sudden black that blocked Miss Hoag's vision, there swam a million stars.

"Teenie! For God's sakes—quick! He's yellin' for you—"

"Coming, Mrs. Bostrum—coming—coming—coming!"

In a dawn that came up as pink as the palm of a babe, but flowed rather futilely against the tired speckled eye of incandescent bulb dangling above the Granite Jaw's rumpled, tumbled bed of pain, a gray-looking group stood in whispered conference beside a slit of window that overlooked a narrow clapboard slit of street.

THE DOCTOR: Even with recovery, he will be on his back at least six months.

MISS HOAG: Oh, my God! Doctor!

THE DOCTOR: Has the man means?

THE BARON: No a penny. He only came to the concession two months ago from a row with the Flying-Fish Troupe. He's in debt already to half the exhibit.

THE LANDLADY: He's too weeks in arrears. Not that I'm pestering the poor devil now, but Gawd knows I—need—

THE DOCTOR: Any relatives or friends to consult about the operation?

MISS HOAG (*turning and stooping*): 'Ain't you got no relations or friends, Jastrow? What was it you hollered about the aerial-wonder act? Are they friends of your? 'Ain't you got no relatives, no long—no friends, maybe, that you could stay with a while? Sid? Who's he? 'Ain't you, Jastrow, got no relations?

The figure under the sheet, pain-huddled, limb-twisted, turned toward the wall, palm slapping out against it.

"Hell!" said Jastrow, the Granite Jaw.

THE DOCTOR (*drawing down his shirt-sleeves*): I'll have an ambulance around in twenty minutes.

MISS HOAG: Wherefore, Doctor?

THE DOCTOR: Brooklyn Public Institute, for the present.

THE LANDLADY (*apron up over her head*): Poor fellow! Poor handsome fellow!"

MISS HOAG: No, Doctor. No! No! No!

THE DOCTOR (*rather tiredly*): Sorry, Madame, but there is no alternative.

MISS HOAG: No, no! I'll pay, Doctor. How much? How much?

THE BARON: Yeh. I'll throw in a tenner myself. Don't throw the poor devil to charity. We'll collect from the troup. We raised forty dollars for a nigger wild man once when—

THE DOCTOR: Come now; all this is not a drop in the bucket. This man needs an operation and then constant attention. If he pulls through, it is a question of months. What he actually needs then is country air, fresh milk, eggs, professional nursing, and plenty of it!

MISS HOAG: That's me, Doc! That's me! I'm going to fix just that for him. I got the means. I can show you three bank-books. I got the means and a place out in Ohio I can rent 'til I buy it some day. A farm! Fresh milk! Leghorns! I'll take him out there, Doc. Eighty miles from where I was born. I was thinking of laying up a while, anyways. I got the means. I'll pull him through, Doctor. I'll pull him through!

THE BARON: Good God! Teenie—you crazy—

FROM THE BED: Worth her weight in gold. Worth her weight in gold.

In the cup of a spring dusk that was filled to overflowing with an ineffable sweetness and the rich, loamy odors of turned earth; with rising sap and low mists; with blackening tree-tops and the chittering of birds—the first lamp-light of all the broad and fertile landscape moved across the window of a story-and-a-half white house which might have been either itself or its own outlying barn. A roof, sheer of slant, dipped down over the window, giving the façade the expression of a coolie under peaked hat.

"Great Scott! Move that lamp off the sill! You want to gimme the blind staggers?"

"I didn't know it was in your eyes, honey. There—that better?"

Silence.

A parlor hastily improvised into a bedroom came out softly in the glow. A room of matting and marble-topped bottle-littered walnut table, of white iron hospital-cot and curly horsehair divan, a dappled-marble mantelpiece of conch-shell, medicated gauze, bisque figurines, and hot-water kettle; in the sheerest of dimity, still dainty of ribbon, the figure of Miss Hoag, hugely, omnipotently omnipresent.

"That better, Jas?"

Silence.

"Better? That's good! Now for the boy's supper. Beautiful white egg laid by beautiful white hen and all beat up fluffy with sugar to make boy well, eh?"

Emaciated to boniness, the great frame gutting and straining rather terribly to break through the restraint of too tight flesh, Mr. Jastrow rose to his elbow, jaw-lines sullen.

"Cut out that baby talk and get me a swig, Teenie. Get me a drink before I get ugly."

"Oh, Jastrow honey, don't begin that. Please, Jastrow, don't begin that. You been so good all day, honey—"

"Get me a swig," he repeated through set teeth. "You and a boob country quack of a doctor ain't going to own my soul. I'll bust up the place again. I ain't all dead yet. Get me a swig—quick, too."

"Jas, there ain't none."

"There is!"

"That's just for me to whip up five drops at a time with your medicine. That's medicine, Jas; it ain't to be to be took like drink. You know what the doc said last time. He ain't responsible if you disobey. I ain't—neither. Please, Jas!"

"I know a thing or two about the deal I'm getting around here. No quack boob is going to own my soul."

"Ain't it enough the way you nearly died last time, Jas? Honest, didn't that teach you a lesson? Be good, Jas. Don't scare poor old Teenie all alone here with you. Looka out there through the door. Ain't it something grand? Honest, Jas, I just never get tired looking. See them low little hills out there. I always say they look like chiffon this time of evening. Don't they? Just looka the whole fields out there, so still—like—like a old horse standing up dozing. Smell! Listen to the little birds! Ain't we happy out here, me and my boy that's getting well so fine?"

Then Jastrow the Granite Jaw began to whimper, half-moans engendered by weakness. "Put me out of my misery, shoot!"

"Jas—Jas—ain't that just an awful way for you to talk? Ain't that just terrible to say to your poor old Big Tent?"

She smoothed out his pillow and drew out his cot on ready casters, closer toward the open door.

"See, Jas—honest, can you ever get enough of how beautiful it is? When I was a kid on my pap's farm out there, eighty miles beyond the ridge, instead of playing with the kids that used to torment me because I was a heavy, I just used to lay out evenings like this on a hay-rack or something and look and look and look. There's something about this soft kind of scenery that a person that's born in it never gets tired of. Why, I've exhibited out in California, right under the nose of the highest kind of mountains; but gimme the little scenery every time."

"I'm a lump—that's what I am. Nine months of laying. I'm a lump—on a woman, too."

"Why, Jas, Teenie's proud to have you on—on her. Ain't we got plans for each other after—you get well? Why, half the time I'm just in heaven over that. That's why, honey, it only you won't let yourself get setbacks! That's all the doctor says is between you and getting well. That's all that keeps you down, Jas, you scaring me and making me go against the doctor's order. Last week your eating that steak—that drink you stole—ain't you ashamed to have got out of bed that way and broke the lock? You—you mustn't ever again, Jas, make me go against the doctor."

"I gets crazy. Crazy with laying."

"Just think, Jas; here I've drew out my last six hundred, ready to make first payment down on the place and us already to begin to farm it. Ain't that worth holding yourself in for? It wouldn't be right, Jas; it would be something terrible if we had to break into that six hundred for medicine and doctors. I don't know what to make of you, honey, all those months so quiet and behaved on your back, and, now that you're getting well, the—the old liquor thirst setting in. We never will get our start that way, Jas. We got plans, if you don't hinder your poor Teenie. The doctor told me, honey—honest, he did—one of them spells—from liquor could—could take you off just like that. Even getting well the way you are!"

"I'm a lump; that's what I am."

"You ain't, Jas; you're just everything in the world."

"Sponging off a woman!"

"'sponging'! With our own little farm and us farming it to pay it off! I like that!"

"Gimme a swig, Teenie. For God's sake, gimme a swig!"

"Jas—Jas, if you get to cutting up again, I'm going to get me a man-nurse out here—honest I am!"

"A swig, Teenie."

"Please, Jas—it's only for bad spells—five drops mixed up in your medicine. That's six dollars a bottle and only for bad spells."

"Stingy gut!"

"Looka down there, honey – there's old man Wyncoop's cow broke tether again. What you bet he's out looking for her. See her winding up the road."

"Stingy gut!"

"You know I ain't stingy. If the doctor didn't forbid, I'd buy you ten bottles, I would, if it cost twenty a bottle. I'm trying to do what the doctor says is best, Jas."

"'Best'! I know what's best. A few dollars in my pocket for me to boss over and buy me the things I need is what's best. I'm a man born to having money I his pocket. I'm none of your mollycoddles."

"Sure you ain't! Haven't you got over ninety dollars under you pillow this minute? 'Ain't the boy got all the spending-money he wants and nowheres to spend it? Ain't that a good one, Jas? All the spending-money and nowheres to spend it. Next thing the boy knows he's going to be working the farm and sticky with money. Ain't it wonderful, Jas, never so showing for us again? Oh God! ain't that just wonderful?"

He reached up then to stroke her hand, a short pincushion of a hand, white enough, but amazingly inundated with dimples.

"Nice old Big Tent!"

"That's the way, honey! Honest, when you get one of your nice spells, you're poor old Teenie would do just anything for you."

"I get crazy with pain. It makes me ugly."

"I know, Jas—I know—anyway, you fix it, honey. I 'ain't got a kick coming—a tub like me to have you."

She loomed behind his cot, carefully out of his range of vision, her own gaze out across the drowsing countryside. A veil of haze was beginning to thicken, whole schools of crickets whirring into it.

"If—if not for one thing, Jas, you know—you know what—? I think if a person was any happier than me, she—she'd die."

"Let's play I'm Rockefeller laying on his country estate, Teenie. Come on; let's kid ourselves along. Gimme the six hundred, Teenie—"

"Why don't you ask me, Jas, except for what I'd be the happiest girl? Well, it's this. If only I could wear a cloak to when I got in it you couldn't see me! If only I never had to walk in front of you so—so you got to look at me!"

"You been a good gal to me, Big Tent. I never even look twice at you— that's how used a fellow can get to anything. I'm going to square it up with you, too."

"You mean it's me will square it with you, Jas—you see if I don't. Why, there'll be nothing too much for me to do to make up for the happiness we're going to have, Jas. I'm going to make this the kinda little home you read about in the magazines. Tear out all this rented junk furniture, paint it up white after we got the six hundred paid down and the money beginning to come in. I'm even going to fix up the little trap-door room in the attic, so that if the Baron or any of the old exhibit crowd happens to be showing in Xenia or around, they can visit us. Just think, Jas—a spare room for the old crowd. Honest, it's funny, but there's not one thing that scares me about all these months on the place alone here, Jas, now that we bought the gun, except the nightmares sometimes that we—we're back exhibiting. That's why I want to keep open house for them that ain't as lucky as us. Honest, Jas—I—I just can't think it's real, not, anyways, till we've paid down sex hundred and—the fellow you keep joking about that wears his collar wrong side 'fore comes out from Xenia to read the ceremony. Oh, Jas, I—I'll make it square with you. You'll never have a sorry day for it!"

"You're all right, Big Tent," said the Granite Jaw, lying back suddenly, lips twitching.

"Ain't you feeling well, honey? Let me fix you an egg?"

"A little swig, Teenie—a little one, is all I ask."

"No, no—please, Jastrow; don't begin—just as I had you forgetting."

"It does me good, I tell you. I know my constitution better than a quack country boob does. I am a freak, I am—a prize concession that has to be treated special. Since that last swig, I tell you, I been a different man. I need the strength. I got to have a little in my system. I'm a freak, I tell you. Everybody knows that there's nothing like a swig for strength."

"Not for you! It's poison, Jas, so much poison! Don't you remember what they said to you after the operation? All your life you got to watch out—just the little prescribed for you is all your system has got to have. Wouldn't I give it to you otherwise—wouldn't I?"

"Swig, Teenie! Honest to God, just a swig!"

"No, no, Jas! No, no, no!"

Suddenly Jastrow the Granite Jaw drew down his lips to a snarl, his hands clutching into the coverlet and drawing it up off his feet.

"Gimme!" he said. "I've done it before and I'll do it now—smash up the place! Gimme! You're getting me crazy! This time you got me crazy. Gimme—you hear—gimme!"

"Jas—for God's sakes—no—no!"

"Gimme! By God! You hear—gimme!"

There was a wrenching movement of his body, a fumbling beneath the pillow, and Mr. Jastrow suddenly held forth in crouched attitude of cunning, something cold, something glittering, something steel.

"Now," he said, head jutting forward and through shut teeth—"now gimme, or by God—"

"Jas—Jas—for God's sake, have you gone crazy? Where'd you get that gun? Is that where I heard you sneaking this morning—over to my trunk for my watch-dog? Gimme that gun—Jas! You—you're crazy—Jas!"

"You gimme, was what I said, and gimme quick! You see this thing pointing? Well, gimme quick."

"Jas—"

"Don't *Jas* me. I'm ugly this time, and when I'm ugly, *I'm ugly!*"

"All right! All right! Only, for God's sakes, Jas, don't get out of bed, don't get crazy enough to shoot that thing. I'll get it. Wait, Jastrow; it's all right, you're all right. I'll get it. See, Teenie's going. Wait—wait—Teenie's going—"

She edged out, and she edged in, hysteria audible in her breathing.

"Jas, honey, won't you please—"

"Gimme, was what I said—gimme and quick!"

Her arm under his head, the glass tilted high against his teeth, he drank deeply, gratefully, breathing out finally and lying back against his pillow, his right hand uncurling of its clutch.

She lifted the short-snouted, wide-barreled, and steely object off the bed-edge gingerly, tremblingly.

"More like it," he said, running his tongue around his mouth; "more like it."

"Jas—Jas, what have you done?"

"Great stuff! Great stuff!" he kept repeating.

"If—if you wasn't so sick, honey—I'd don't know what I'd do after such a terrible thing like this—you acting like this—so terrible—God! I—I'm all trembling."

"Great stuff!" he said, and reaching out and eyes still closed, patting her. "Great stuff, nice old Big Tent!"

"Try to sleep now, Jas. You musta had a spell of craziness! This is awful! Try to sleep. If only you don't get a spell— Sleep—please!"

"You wait! Guy with a collar on wrong side wrong—he's the one; he's the one!"

"Yes—yes, honey. Try to sleep!"

"I wanna dream I'm Rockefeller. If there's one thing I want to dream it's Rockefeller."

"Not now—not now—"

"Lemme go to sleep like a king."

"Yes, honey."

"Like a king," I said.

She slid her hand finally into one of the voluminous folds of her dress, withdrawing and placing a rubber-bound roll into his hands.

"There, honey. Go to sleep now—like a king."

He fingered it, finally sitting up to count, leaning forward to the ring of lamplight.

"Six hundred bucks! Six hundred! Wow—oh, wow! If Sid could only see me now!"

"He can, honey—he can. Go to sleep. 'Sh-h-h-h!'"

"Slide 'em under—slide 'em under—Rockefeller."

She lifted his head, placing the small wad beneath. He turned over, cupping his hand in his cheek, breathing outward deeply, very deeply.

"Jas!"

"Huh?"

"Ain't you all right? You're breathing so hard. Quit breathing so hard. It scares me. Quit making those funny noises. Honey—for God's sake—quit!"

Jastrow the Granite Jaw did quit, so suddenly, so completely, his face turned outward toward the purpling meadows, and his mouth slightly open that a mirror held finally and frantically against it did not so much as cloud.

At nine o'clock there drew up outside the coolie-faced house one of those small tin motor-cars which are tiny mile-scavengers to the country road. With a thridding of engine and play of lamps which turned green landscape, gray, it drew up short a rattling at the screen door following almost immediately.

"Doctor, that you? Oh my God! Doctor, it's too late! It's all over, Doctor—Doctor—it's all over!"

Trembling in a frenzy of haste, Miss Hoag drew back the door, the room behind her flickering with shadows from an uneven wick.

"You're the Fat, ain't you? The one that's keeping him?"

"What—what—"

"So you're the meal-ticket! Say, leave it to Will. Leave it to that boy not to get lost in this world. Ain't it like him to the T to pick a good-natured Fat?"

There entered into Miss Hoag's front room Miss Sidonia Sabrina, of the Flying-Fish Troupe, World's Aeronaut Trapeze Wonder, gloved and ringleted, beaded of eyelask and pink of ear-lobe, the teeth somewhat crookedly but pearlily white because the lips were so red, the parasol long and impudently parrot-handled, gilt-mesh bag clanking against a cluster of sister baubles.

"If it ain't Will to the T! Pickin' hisself a Fat to sponge on. Can you beat it? Mm! Was you the Fat in the Coney concession?"

"Who— Whata you want?"

"We was playin' the Zadalia County Fair. I heard he was on his back. The Little in our show, Baroness de Ross, has a husband played Coney with youse. Where is he? Tell him his little Sid is here. Was his Sid fool enough to beat it all the way over here in a flivver for eight bucks the round trip? She was! Where is he?"

"He— Who— You—"

"You're one of them good-natured simps, ain't you? So was I, dearie. It don't pay! I always said of Will he could bleed a sour pickle. Where is he? Tell him his little Sid is here with thirty minutes before she meets up with the show on the ten-forty, when it shoots through Xenia. Tell him she was fool enough to come because he's flat on his back."

"I— That's him—Jastrow—there— Oh my God—that's him laying there,

Miss! Who are you? Sid— I thought— I never knew— Who are you? I thought it was Doc. He went off in a flash. I was standing right here— I— Oh God!"

There seemed to come suddenly over the sibilant Miss Sidonia Sabrina a quieting down, a lessening of twinkle and shimmer and swish. She moved slowly toward the huddle on the cot, parasol leading, and her hands crossed atop the parrot.

"My God!" she said. "Will dead! Will dead! I musta had a hunch. God! I musta! All of a sudden I makes up my mind. I jumps ahead of the show. God! I musta had one of my hunches. That lookin glass I broke in Dayton. I—I—musta!"

"It come so sudden, Miss. It's a wonder I didn't die, too, right on the spot. I was standing here and—"

Suddenly Miss Sabrina fumbled in the gilt-mesh bag for her kerchief, her face lifting to cry.

"He spun me dirt, Will did. If ever a girl was spun dirt, that girl was me, but just the same—it's my husband laying there—it's my husband, no matter what dirt he spun me. Oh God—Oh—Oh—"

At half after ten to a powdering of eye-sockets, a touching up with lipstick, a readjustment of three-tiered hat, Miss Sidonia Sabrina took leave. There were still streaks showing through her retouched cheeks.

"I left you the collar—and—cuff box with his initials on, dearie, for a remembrance. I give it to him the first Christmas after we was married, before he got to developing rough. I been through his things now entire. I got 'em all with me. If there's such a thing as recordin angel, you'll go down on the book. Will was a bad lot, but he's done with it now, dearie. I never seen the roughness crop up in a man so sudden the way it did in Will. You can imagine, dearie, when the men in the troupe horsewhipped him one night for the way he lit in on me one night in drink. That was the night he quit. Oh Gawd! Maybe I don't look it, dearie, but I been through the mill in my day. But that's all over now, him layin there—my husband. Will was a good Strong in his day—nobody can't ever take that away from him. I'm leavin you the funeral money out of what he had under his pillow. It's a godsend to me, my husband laying up that few hundred when things ain't so good with me. You was a good influence, dearie. I never knew him to save a cent. I'd never have thought it. Not a cent from him all these months. My legs for the air-work ain't what they used to be. Inflammatory rheumatism, y'know. I've got a mind to buy me a farm, too, dearie. Settle down. Say, I got to hand it to you, dearie—you're one fine Fat. Baby Ella herself had nothing on you, and I've worked as fine Fats as there is in the business. You're sure one fine Fat, and if there's such a thing as a recordin angel—I got to catch that train, dearie—the chauff's honkin'—no grandmother stories goes with my concession. God, to think of Will laying on a cool six hundred! Here's twenty-five for the funeral. If it's more, lemme know. Sidonia Sabrina, care Flying-Fish Troupe, State Fair, Butler County, Ohio. Good-bye, dearie, and God bless you!"

Long after the thridding of engine had died down, and the purple quiet flowed over the path of twin lamplights, Miss Hoag stood in her half-open screen door, gazing after. There were no tears in her eyes; indeed, on the contrary, the echo of the chug-chugging which still lay on the air had taken on this rhythm:

Better to have loved a short man
   Than never to have loved atall.

Better to have loved a short man
   Than never to have loved atall.

FAT

Grace Sartwell Mason

In many cultures and historical periods women have been proud to be large—being fat was a sign of fertility, of prosperity, of the ability to survive. . . . Fat activists suggest that making women afraid to be fat is a form of social control. Fear of fat keeps women preoccupied, robs us of our pride and energy, keeps us from *taking up space.*
—The Boston Women's Health Book Collective, *Our Bodies, Ourselves*

◇

The limousine as it waited for the traffic signal was like a glittering cage of glass. The scarlet and gold monogram on the door stood for Payton Michael Tierney. Within was Mrs. Tierney, the lower of her two chins resting snugly upon the back of what had once been a mink, a lively lad slipping in and out of icy brooks. Dozens of his brothers fended the wintry blast from the rest of Mrs. Tierney.

When Mrs. Tierney moved her knees a lap robe of civet cat came alive. Each little animal bore a furry lyre on its back. With the twitching of Mrs. Tierney's knee the glass cage became full of leaping black and white bodies; it hummed with syncopated music. From Mrs. Tierney's hat floated the airy and languorous tail of an exotic bird. And the mink, the civet cats, the exotic bird, were more alive than Mrs. Tierney as she sat there, drowsily waiting for the limousine to start.

It was mid-afternoon. Had she looked ahead of her down the Avenue she would have seen scarfs of blue-gray chiffon, fold on airy fold, floating about the knees of white cliff-buildings. She would have seen the orchid in the vase behind the chauffeur's head, dying for want of air and water. But she did not look. She had no love of fantasy nor of flowers.

High aloft in the traffic tower an eyelid came down over a ruby eye; a green one shone out. As gently as if Mrs. Tierney were dynamite the chauffeur started the car. It moved down the Avenue. The tail of the exotic bird shivered and floated against the glass. Mrs. Tierney slapped a powder puff against her chins and sighed:

"Always just one thing after another. No sooner catch a wink of sleep than the traffic starts up again. And then I'm there. And I have to get out and do somethin'." She yawned. "Some day I'm goin' to tell Sandy to drive

56

round the Park a couple o' hours and I'm just going to sleep right through."

Sleep, a pleasant thought. But it had its unpleasant association too for it reminded her of the p'fessor. The professor at the School of Health and Beauty had said that was the trouble with her—she slept too much. Then she recalled—she always ruminated by association—that some one had said, or had she read it in a magazine or a newspaper or something?—that if you wanted to get thin you must sleep cold.

Ugh! Her face drooped. Its curves, as meaningless as marshmallows, reversed themselves. Where at the thought of sleep they had curled upward they now curved down. But after an instant of dissatisfied musing Mrs. Tierney rebelled. Her mouth buttoned itself defiantly.

"It's too much!" She liked to talk aloud in the limousine and in the bathtub with the water running. And as she spent a great deal of time in her bath and alone in the limousine, talking aloud to herself had become a habit. "It's too much. Take last night. The eiderdown slipped offa me and I was mis-'able. I was simply mis'able. I have to sleep warm. I'll do most anything they expect me to do but sleep cold. Haven't I cut down on my sleep? Well then, what sleep I do have I'll have warm, thank you."

Soothed, she looked through the clear window at the pedestrians. It was a raw day, unpleasantly slushy underfoot. While Mrs. Tierney felt sorry for the walkers slopping along and being spattered now and then by limousines, she was at the same time cheered by them. They made her feel snug and warm and set apart.

The limousine slid through the traffic. Vague wisps of discontented thought drifted like dun-colored clouds across the featureless landscape of Mrs. Tierney's mind. "Mayonnaise—some of these tea shops make it so it isn't fattening, I've heard—I must find out. The p'fessor says no more chicken Maryland—just as I've got Frieda so she can do it my way—can you beat it? There's a good hat—wonder if Mad'moiselle would make me one—but no—that girl's got one of those thin faces—young, too—well, I guess I'm not old—not old—forty-six isn't really old—Payt's forty-eight—but a man—you don't think about a man's age—it isn't fair—a man never does a thing to keep his figure—eats and eats—but if a woman gets the least little bit plump—the things he says! Bulgy—he called me bulgy—"

She stared fixedly at the silver-mounted clock and vanity case in front of her. Nothing moved in the sky of her mind save the one word—bulgy. And from it resentment, like a thin bitter rain, dripped down upon her spirits.

She thought about Payt, her husband, with a vague venom. Just why he had of late taken to being sarcastic about her figure she could not understand. For years he had been comfortably indifferent. An unreasonable man, Payt had become. He had always been a hard man like a rock. But a rock was a good thing to cling to. Safe. Only a man ought not to be rude to his wife. He ought not to tell her she bulged. Not with a certain kind of smile.

The limousine came to a stop. A blood-red eye looked watchfully down upon its roof. Mrs. Tierney turned her gaze toward the window. Then this vague glance sharpened, fixed itself, pointing like the nose of a setter dog. For the limousine had halted exactly opposite the window of Henri's, a world-famous sweet shop.

Cruelly close was this window. On crystal plates French bonbons were heaped. In little gilt baskets tied with sea-green ribbons were candied fruits like frosted jewels. With a rich brown sheen upon them chocolates sat snug in their boxes, plump with a delicious melting plumpness. Their brown coats concealed creams and nuts and fruits. Beyond the window as Mrs. Tierney well knew were other delights. Bouillon with cream, rich salads, frosted chocolates, *marrons glacés*, frozen puddings.

These things were to Mrs. Tierney what poetry or jewels or green seas are to others.

Formerly Henri's had been her club, her garden of fulfillment. One could sit contentedly even though alone, in Henri's, watching the fashions, listening to other women's conversation and lunching—ah, but lunching, reverently, upon sweetbreads in cream, asparagus in butter. Or having tea and muffins, topped off with maple mousse. Time passed like a pleasant dream at Henri's.

But that had been before Mr. Tierney, with the unpleasant smile upon his face, said she bulged. She had given up Henri's.

It was peculiarly unfortunate that to-day of all days Sandy had halted the limousine directly in front of that window. For yesterday the p'fessor had put her upon diet number two, a cruel diet, only one turn of the screw from starvation. "My stummick is simply clapping together!" she whimpered.

This was no exaggeration. Where before there had been for years a complacently comatose organ, now there was a fierce animal, an animal trapped and gnawing. A tireless animal that never failed day and night to remind her of its fury. Of late, moreover, it had become wily. It was forever whispering to her suggestions that were rank treason to the p'fessor.

"Might get me just a little hot chocolate—leave off the baked potato for dinner—"

Sweets. Mrs. Tierney pressed her nose close to the limousine window. Her mouth watered so that she had to lick the corners of it. It twittered a little, as a cat's when it watches a bird on the lawn. The gnawing inside her was terrible. It was real. She could taste the thick smooth taste of the chocolate, the soft crunch of nuts in cream. A moisture came into her eyes. Her hand went out to the door handle.

But at that instant in the strip of mirror over his head she met the cool eye of the chauffer. The young wretch! As lightly as a caress he started the car.

Well, she had not meant to go into Henri's anyway. But it was hard. Her chin quivered and she felt to the full how pitiful this quivering was. It wasn't as if she couldn't afford Henri's. For years now her bead bag had been stuffed with bank notes all the time. And at home she had the best cook she had ever had. It was hard to starve, to deny herself, to do those hateful exercises—

She fetched a tremulous breath. Well, she was doing it for Payt—if that was any consolation. She was a good wife taking note of her husband's whims. Working herself practically to the bone to please him. Practically to the bone.

The car turned east, Sandy saluting the policeman. All was the same as usual. The same dim gray men in the club window, the same entrance next door to the beauty parlor where she had been wont to loll for hours in a perfumed steam—only the p'fessor had stopped all that now. And the same lovely marble museum at the end of the block, at which she had never looked twice. Everything without was quite the same as usual.

But within the limousine something extremely unusual had occurred. It must be that a thought had slipped in. A thought too much like a sharp slim sword for that upholstered interior. It hung directly in front of Mrs. Tierney's eyes where she could not but see it. It silenced the eternal monologue upon her lips. It swept the sky of her mind clear of vague clouds. It even struck the little civet cats, and the tail of the exotic bird.

"If Payt was dead," glinted the thought, "you could eat every day at Henri's. You would never need to go again to the p'fessor. You could sleep and sleep and sleep."

So unaccustomed was Mrs. Tierney to any thought whatsoever, much less a thought so starkly naked, that she sat transfixed, staring at the silver-topped bottles in the vanity case. She sat in perfect stillness in a vacuum where there was nothing, where no air stirred, no cloud drifted across the sky. Where there was nothing save a thought like an ironic sword.

Then the car bumped slightly over a manhole. At once blessed movement saved Mrs. Tierney. The furry lyres of the civet cats twanged under her twitching knee, the feathers of the exotic bird swirled as she jerked back her head.

"I cert'n'y don't know what's the matter with me to-day. It must be my stummick. You have funny thoughts when your stummick is empty like mine is this minute—I've been a good wife—I've cert'n'y been a good wife to Payt Tierney. Why, I lo—yes, I do love him like a wife ought to. See what I'm going through with for him. Starving myself—exer—"

The word broke in two of its own accord. A faint horror stiffened the curves of her face. For it was there again, the presence, indecently unclothed. Almost as if it had a voice it spoke: "Love? He's a husband. A husband's a rock to cling to. But love? You forgot how, years ago."

Mrs. Tierney's hand jerked toward the speaking tube. "Sandy! Sandy, stop at that drug store on the corner, and get me a glass of bi-carb."

When she stepped out of the car at the gymnasium she felt better, almost as well as if she had never encountered a thought. She told the chauffeur he need not wait for her, she would walk home.

Within the door of the School of Health and Beauty the sound of machines, pounding, grinding, rubbing, thumping, met her, and the smell of talcum and steam. She liked the drowsy smell but she hated the sound. And there was the p'fessor turning away from the window with a sardonic glance. "Ah, Mrs. Tierney, I see you rode again to-day."

She shook a finger archly. Now, P'fessor, don't you scold me. If you could know how weak I am. Honest, that diet number two is—"

"Aw, Mrs. Tierney, that's what you always say. Snap into your togs now and I'll give you your work myself to-day."

Dejectedly she climbed the stairs to the dressing-rooms. She had hoped for the milder direction of one of the girl attendants but this was not her lucky day.

A little later in a long white robe she stood as in a vise between wooden rollers that went clickety-click, clickety-click. Their fingers inhumanly massaged her redundancy. She looked about at the other women. When she observed one who was plumper than herself she smiled benevolently. But when a slim girl passed she curled her lip. The sight of one as slim as a wand endeavoring to get slimmer affronted her like an insult. She stared with hostility at the ridiculous creature. What was the world coming to?

There was one patron of the gymnasium because of whom she felt a particular grievance. She was coming down the stairs now, tall and excessively slender in black satin knickers and a peach-colored sweater. As Mrs. Tierney stood in the massaging machine this young woman—she was golden-haired and rather pretty—lay down on the gymnasium mat and touched her toes over her head. She made a perfect hoop of herself. Insufferably lithe and thin she was. Mrs. Tierney could not bear to look at her.

"What's *she* here for?" she whispered to an attendant crossly. "She's too thin now."

"Oh, she's here to put it on!"

Mrs. Tierney sighed. A world in which there were persons trying to put it on while she labored so cruelly to take it off offended her beyond speech.

She changed to an unsympathetic rubber garment, to woolen bloomers and a great woolly sweater. She trundled without enthusiasm into the gymnasium. Ah, the bliss of lying down on the mat, relaxed, sprawling—Oh dear, the p'fessor!

"Now, let's put some snap into it to-day, Mrs. Tierney. Left leg and right arm. Up—up—faster—higher—higher—up—down—"

The p'fessor prowled on catlike feet, jeering in a scornful bark. "Treat 'em rough and they'll come back for more," was his motto and on this simple platform he had become famous. A very hard young man with a beautiful waist. He made Mrs. Tierney feel quite desperate. She wondered if her heart would stand it.

Before many minutes everything had become a blur except the p'fessor's bark: "Now circle the right leg—*one*—two—three. Aw, way back, Mrs. Tierney—w-a-a-y up! *One*—two—three— What? Not dying so soon? Again. *Again*, I said. You heard me the first time. *One*—two—three—"

Would he never let her rest? She dared not suggest such a thing, being in terror of his biting tongue. But she knew that one more kick at that nasty sodden ball would kill her. It was cruel. But she'd take it out on Payt—he could just get her a silver fox for this—ouch!

"Fifteen—sixteen—oh, put a little punch in that kick, Mrs. Tierney. Eighteen—ha! Gettin' mad, are we, now? Great stuff! Who's this we have with us, now—Red Grange himself, eh? Twenty-two—twenty-three—oh, yes you will—twenty-five—"

One last feeble kick with legs as heavy as lead. "Rest."

She lay gasping, aching. If Mr. Tierney could just once see what she was going through for him—but he wouldn't appreciate it. Men didn't. She felt a sudden distrust of everything she had ever heard or read or imagined about beauty culture. Was it worth it? And why? She gazed gloomily up at the ceiling. Then the voice of the p'fessor:

"Up! Now, the good ol' medicine ball. Oh, yes you can too. What do you think this is, Mrs. Tierney—an invalid's rest cure? Now. Snap to it. Over your head—under—over—under—"

Panting and resentful she chased the most slippery ball in the world about the largest room ever built, while weeks dragged past. "Now the horse, Mrs. Tierney. Give her a good sharp gallop, Maudie. Then the bicycle."

Hope and the power of resistance died within Mrs. Tierney. But the electric horse though it jiggled unpleasantly gave her a chance to get her breath and the p'fessor, having gone on his way, one could converse with the lady being ironed out in the nearest machine.

"This your first course?"

"Oh, no. My fifth. You have to keep it up, you know."

"Oh, dear, I suppose so. Does that machine take it off your hips? It don't make a dent in mine."

"What diet you on? Oh, mercy! That diet is simply poison for me. Ever try that new health bread at Petersen's?"

Then the bicycle, mile after mile encased in a bright hot inferno with only her perspiring face sticking out. One eye on the clock.

But at last the part she enjoyed—the electric cabinet bath. She stepped willingly into the mirror-lined box, the white radiance of the electric bulbs streamed over her, stinging her flesh, soothing her aching muscles. She slumped on a stool, the cabinet was closed about her throat, only her head protruded. The icy bandage wrapped about her temples was delicious, the cold water held to her lips was nectar. Her hands that had grown bleached and puffy in years of idleness relaxed upon her plump thighs. Her diamond rings sputtered tiny blue flames in the white glare—"I always say no one can steal my diamonds when they're on me—"

The room was darkened. At right and left of her were other heads resting bodiless upon the tops of other boxes. They talked about what they could and could not eat and whether they perspired easily or with difficulty.

"My cook," said the head on Mrs. Tierney's left, "makes an Indian pudding with a creamed maple sugar sauce that simply melts in the mouth. You know, one of those steamed Indian—"

"Don't!" groaned Mrs. Tierney faintly.

Then unexpectedly to herself she laughed aloud. For Indian pudding had reminded her of corn meal, and corn meal had taken her back eighteen years to the year Payt sold his interest in the Lucky Augusta mine and with the money became a Napoleon in Wall Street.

Corn meal and canned tomatoes, that was what they had got down to long before Payt put through the deal. The coffee, the dried fruits, the molasses had given out but Payt just shut that mouth of his and hung on, dickering. And she was wild for something sweet. Twenty miles from town they were and their last penny gone. One day she had scraped the little molasses firkin to the white, she had boiled up the cup of splinters and strained off the sirup. She had licked it out of a spoon with rapture.

And now stirring with her soft heavy body silvered by the rows of lamps and reflected in the strips of mirrors she tasted again the thin sweetness of molasses flavored with barrel staves. She felt again the pangs of hunger she had suffered during those long-ago days.

"To-day," she thought, "I could buy out Henri's and I can't eat a chocolate cream! Life is funny."

"What did you say?" inquired the head on her left.

"I was saying I always did have a great sweet tooth."

"Me too. But let me so much as sniff at a box of candy and up goes my weight. I've heard there's a new kind of chocolate that's not fattening—"

"It's no good. It's got no taste to it, no taste a-tall." Mrs. Tierney spoke with melancholy firmness.

"Oh, well, that's always the way." And silence brooded over the darkened room.

The thin blond girl, inconsiderately sipping a glass of rich milk, passed through on her way to the dressing rooms. Mrs. Tierney had her shower. And a little later she lay prone, wrapped in a blanket. The electric vibrator had been played over her spine. Like a furious bee it had buzzed up and down, filling her with apprehension and drowsiness.

It was dark in this corner where she rested. If she pulled the blankets higher over her head they would forget she was there and she could get a wink of forbidden sleep. She burrowed deeper and lay still with a pleased sense of defiance.

She may have slept for a moment but suddenly she was wide awake. She had not perceptibly stirred under the blankets but she had stiffened. Cautiously her hand crept up to lift a fold of the blanket away from her ear. For she had heard a number called on the telephone not ten feet from the couch where she rested, a familiar number. Some one was calling Payt on his private wire. A woman's voice.

In the obscurity of her corner Mrs. Tierney stealthily uncovered one eye. At a table with the telephone in front of her, under a frank ceiling light, sat the thin blond girl. She was dressed now for the street, sleekly perfect. She murmured into the telephone that she would be a little late for tea.

"But, Payton," she drawled, "get our usual table, will you, and order for me, there's a dear? Oh, anything—a creamed chicken *paté* and a good rich sweet, I suppose. They say I must tuck in more calories. Disgusting, isn't it? But what do you think? This will please you: I've gained two pounds! Yes, really. And all for you, my dear."

In the darkened corner the heap of blankets after a while heaved as Mrs. Tierney struggled out of them. Dazedly she fumbled at her clothes. With the circular motion of a cat washing its face she blindly patted a powder puff over her chin and nose. She felt her way downstairs. "Good night, Maudie. Good night, P'fessor."

"Good night, Mrs. Tierney!"

At the curb she looked for Sandy before she remembered that she was to walk home. Could you beat that? Just when she needed the limousine it was not there. Well, she would walk. And probably she would be run over by a truck or something. And as Payt leaned over her shattered body in the hospital she would murmur, "Payt, I forgive you. I know all about you and that hussy, but I forgive—no! I won't forgive him, either. Not even in a hospital I wouldn't forgive him—"

Mrs. Tierney's elbows went out, her heels clicked. She would just make him suffer. She would do something—something— But in the meantime, since she had to walk, she would go by way of the Avenue where there would be windows to take her mind off her wrongs.

A ball of fur on inadequate feet she trundled up an Avenue into which all of civilization had poured its finest flowers. In the twilight gold streamed out of windows and poured itself across the steel-black pavements. Spires and enchanted castles rose ahead of her against a streak of clear primrose in the sapphire of the sky. In the canyon of the castles two currents of life flowed like swift rivers, one north and one south. At her elbow were jade and orchids, ivory and silks from the ends of the earth.

But in the narrow echoing caverns of Mrs. Tierney's mind there was nothing but a phrase, a few words:

"Creamed chicken *paté* and a good rich sweet—"

The phrase made a rhythm to which her empty stomach danced, gnawing at the bars of its cage. She felt for herself an enormous pity. Three motorcycles like screaming meteors made way for an ambassador and a great general. But Mrs. Tierney's back was turned. She had reached Henri's window. She stood in front of it motionless, regarding the bonbons, the candied fruits, the chocolates that sat so richly in their boxes.

"Creamed chicken *paté* and a good rich sweet—"

She was scarcely aware of the worlds for she was saying to herself that she would be iron; she would fight; she would get slim and buy herself some new clothes; and she'd show Payt and that scrawny girl that she was not to be trifled with.

But it was hard to fight on an empty stomach. "I'm cer'nly going to need my strength."

With a defiant duck she went in at the door of Henri's. And the sweet-sour-perfumed air, so familiar, so long abstained from, greeted her eager nostrils. "Just a cup of bouillon, Lily, and no whipped cream." Bouillon without cream was not fattening, even the p'fessor admitted that.

Sternly she sipped the clear drink. She wrinkled her nose a trifle. It was good but it lacked body. "Uh—Lily! Just a little bit of whipped cream. Thanks. Put it down there. I'll just take a spoonful—"

Ah, better, but still not suave enough. Another spoonful of cream, absently. She sipped rapidly. There! The bouillon was finished except for a tiny pool in the bottom of the cup. She drained it. Unsatisfied she reflected on the smallness of the portions served these days. She looked about her. Women lingering over substantial teas; buttered muffins, anchovy sandwiches, trays of pastries jeweled with bits of ruby and emerald jelly.

Sitting in front of her empty cup Mrs. Tierney suffered a swift loneliness. She felt bereaved of something that had nothing to do with Payt. Existence seemed to have no point to it. With a sudden despair she ate the last spoonful of whipped cream.

She pushed the dish away from her. Now she had to think what she was going to do about Payt and his shameless conduct. Something firm, effective. Renounce him? "Payt, I am through. I've been a good self-denying wife to you but now I—am—*through*."

And what would Payt say? She knew too well. He was a hard man, Payt Tierney was, with an eye that could bore unpleasantly. Well then—maybe she had better put it more diplomatically: "Payt, you've just got to give up that—"

Oh, dear, if only her stomach would stop that gnawing. Maybe considering the trying circumstances she owed it to herself—

"Lily, bring me a cup of hot chocolate."

As Lily hastened with the tall steaming cup Mrs. Tierney's nose met it lovingly halfway. Um—m—delicious! She consumed it in large sips. Slowly it soothed her, revived a faith in her pattern of life. Each tiny bit that made up that pattern began to tick into accustomed place. An hour ago a rude hand had jogged them out of alignment, confusing her; but now they began to make a clear familiar design.

A necessary part of that design by which she lived was Henri's, warm, bright, full of the latest fashions and of talk and delicious smells. And at a table in Henri's, herself, alone, to be sure, but yet not alone. For there were other women to be appraised; there were the waitresses whose names she knew, whom she tipped with a gesture; there was the menu to be studied, more provocative each day. There was her bead bag stuffed with bank notes, ready to buy for her any delicacy she fancied—

A sudden thought chilled this dreamy mood. Suppose Payt, when she had issued her ultimatum, did not take it so well—you couldn't tell about Payt, ever—suppose the flow of bank notes were dried up by Payt's anger? Suppose the bead bag grew limp and empty, deprived of its sole source of supply?

A table at Henri's was no place for an empty purse. With the bead bag empty there would be no ministering friendly Lily, no boxes of chocolates taken in the limousine, no rich luncheons, no delicious teas—nothing. Nothing.

Nothing is a dreadful word. It takes steel and the airy stuff of dreams to bear that word. And Mrs. Tierney was made of neither. With one hand she clutched at the bead bag and with the other she beckoned as if in panic fright. "Lily! Bring me—"

When Lily had ministered and gone away again Mrs. Tierney wielded the fork and spoon of a person who has much to make up. A person who has been out in the cold and is grateful for warmth. Rapidly she vanquished that dreadful word nothing. Rapidly she put in the place of it good rich sustaining food.

And stone by stone the puny wall she had begun to build between herself and disintegration crumbled. Never again would she be quickened by disturbing thought, nor whipped to salutary struggle. The prison of her flesh received her. And there fell away from her, defeated, all the little annoyances of the afternoon. Nothing was left of them save one tear, the last she was ever to shed. It rolled down her cheek and missing the creamed chicken *paté*, gave an agreeable saltiness to the banana-marrons-pecan mousse.

THIS WAS MEANT TO BE

Alberta Hughes Wahl

Round is female. Round females are the visual symbols of strength, of love, of life-giving. When you start getting in touch with the fact that being round and being big is very female, then you begin to understand why the men have asked us to go away. They want us to be little, to be smaller than they are. We have tremendous sexual energy, we have sensuous soft round soft bodies that just have to be touched. Fat women typically become involved with thin people. This is because we have learned to hate other fat people. But what is it that draws these thin people to our beds? It is that they know what we are beginning to find out: there's nothing quite like making love to a warm round body. Somewhere in the mind of the human race is the memory of who we are and what we represent. The cultures that produced thousands of images of fat women knew this about us, that we represent the ultimate female, full, round, big, strong, soft, warm woman. The moon is round, the earth is round, cycles are round, and so are we.

—Kelly, "The Goddess is Fat"

◇

As Jeffrey came into the drawing-room Mrs. Carstair looked over her daughter's head and smiled at him, a secret understanding smile. This was the beginning of the conspiracy they had planned.

"You remember my daughter, don't you?" she said, putting her hand caressingly on Alison's soft bright hair. The subdued pleasant chatter of the Carstairs' party rose and fell against their conversation.

"Of course I remember Alison," Jeffrey said, coming over. "The question is, does she remember me?" His forced heartiness made him uncomfortable.

Alison Carstair gave him her hand and a stiff little smile. "Oh yes, Mr. Hartshorne. You helped my brother and me with our Christmas tree one year, remember?"

"That's right! So I did." Now that he had been reminded of it, Jeffrey wondered how he could have forgotten anything so pleasant. Six or seven years ago he had come here to a cocktail party on the afternoon before Christmas and, wandering into the library in search of his current girl, had found, instead, Alison and her younger brother, Roger, trimming their tree.

They were having a very fine time, not feeling at all sorry for themselves because their famous and gregarious parents were not helping with the tree. At the moment Jeffrey had walked in, they were confronted with a problem. The tree was so tall the silvery spire for the top couldn't be slipped on.

"I'll tell you what," Jeffrey said. "If you have some cardboard and poster paints I'll paint you an angel. You can fasten her on from the back."

They had agreed that would be very nice indeed. Not ever family had their top-of-the-tree ornament painted by someone the Times art critic had called "the most promising of the younger landscape artists."

Everyone, including Jeffrey, agreed that it was a first-rate angel—a blue-eyed golden-haired angel with the rear view of her curls and the folds and pleats of her gown drawn and painted more carefully, if anything, than the front. "Just *because* it won't show," Jeffrey had said. Roger had snorted at the idea of any work that didn't show, but Alison had nodded her head in under-standing assent.

Now, still holding her hand and enveloped for an instant in a pleasant nostalgia for all Christmases past, Jeffrey exclaimed, "Do you know, I see already exactly how I'm going to paint you. I *am* going to, you know."

Mrs. Carstair said sharply, "Jeffrey!" And her look said, *this isn't the right way to go about it at all.*

But Jeffrey paid her no attention because he was sure now that he could put across this tender little scheme of Olive Carstair. "She's eighteen and she's so diffident," Olive had told him, her beautiful face troubled. "She's still in the awkward age and she has no confidence in herself as a woman. I feel like a betrayer talking about her this way, but she's so miserable at dances and with boys. I've thought up a plan. She's not at all pretty," she went on, "but she's such a darling, Jeffrey. She only needs something, someone, to discover what she really is and then she will bloom. And you're just the one to do it, darling. She thinks you're the most marvelous painter alive, and if she thought *you* thought her worth painting—"

Jeffrey remembered the next part with amusement. (Olive, for all her beauty and fame, was as good a businesswoman as he had ever met.) "I'll give you a check as soon as it's done, of course, and I should think after a year perhaps—I could tell her Bill and I liked the portrait so well we had insisted on your selling it to us."

It was precisely the sort of homemade plot an actress would cook up and Jeffrey had told Olive so, but he had agreed to play his part. Olive had bought his pictures when no one else had thought them worth buying, she had given him tea and sandwiches when tea was not merely a pleasant social habit but a very welcome addition to his daily intake of calories. Moreover she had introduced him and talked about him to people who could and eventually did buy his pictures. And she had done all this not through any romantic interest—she was fifteen years his senior and most happily mar-ried—but because she liked him and wanted to help. Jeffrey was happy to have a chance to repay part of his debt to Olive, but he was a painter, not an actor, and he had been afraid of muffing his lines.

Having looked at Alison with a painter's eye, he was no longer worried. Her mother had been right in saying she wasn't pretty. She was short and still in the chubby stage. He suspected she was always going to have to worry about plumpness. And her button of a nose was never going to change into a Grecian feature. But her skin was good, her plainly cut light brown hair heavy and shining, and her eyes really very fine—widely spaced, with thick lashes much darker than her hair. Pansy eyes, he thought, his mind already reaching for the colors to blend to get that deep-piled velvety texture.

"Apricot velvet," he was thinking out loud. "One of those Renoirish hats with plums and a muff. And we'll play The Dance of the Little Swans while I'm painting because that's what you remind me of."

Alison looked at her mother uncertainly. Having gone through the stage himself not too many years ago, Jeffrey was near enough in years to recognize the ever-present never-solved dilemma of the not-quite-grown-up who thirsts for excitement, adventure and romance, yet hesitates to reach for them for fear of being made a fool.

Mrs. Carstair was delighted. An experienced and gifted actress, she could tell at once when someone playing with her "got his teeth into a part."

"But Jeffrey," she protested. "When, may I ask, have you taken to portrait painting?"

"I haven't, really. But I like to do about one a year, to please myself and see if I'm any good at it. Will you, Allison? I warn you; it's drudgery."

He was afraid she was going to cry. "May I? May I, Mother?"

Jeffrey, who had just thought of something he was sure Olive had forgotten too, groaned with sincere regret. "But the time! Good Lord, Easter's two days gone. Won't you have to be going back to school?"

"Not for a month," Alison said. "Not for a whole month. Because so many girls have had the flu. We're going to make up for it by going two weeks longer in June. Mr. Hartshorne, is a month long enough?"

"Just about," said Jeffrey, looking at Olive with respect. "You see, Olive, this was meant to be."

"I see that *you* mean it to be," said Mrs. Carstair, laughing such a delightful proper maternal laugh that she deserved to be spanked. "Are you sure, Alison, you want to give up so much of your holiday? Don't bother to answer. I see you've made up your mind. And I don't blame you. You ought to be terribly flattered; Jeffrey never volunteered to paint *my* portrait."

"You should have asked Providence prettily and well ahead of time for pansy eyes," he said with friendly malice.

Alison looked quickly at her mother, then at Jeffrey. He knew exactly what she was thinking. Was it possible that he, Mr. Hartshorne, an artist, found any feature of hers prettier than her beautiful mother's? This being just what he wanted her to think, Jeffrey smiled down at Alison warmly. For all he was such a worldly young man, Jeffrey had a tenderness for those who could be so easily hurt.

Olive rewarded him with the deep-throated chuckle that was her trademark. "Alison gets her eyes from her father, but I'll bet you never noticed them on him! Now, there is old Mrs. Irwin. I must go be nice to her. Jeffrey, you and Alison work out the times for her sittings between you."

Jeffrey gave Alison no time to retreat into self-consciousness. He looked at his watch. "It's not quite five. What do you say we skip the rest of this party, Alison, and go see Madam Celestine about a costume for you?"

Her eyes widened. "Madame Celestine! But she's awfully expensive and she takes weeks to make anything. She's doing Mother's third-act dress and Mother's having fits over how long it's taking."

Jeffrey laughed. "Oh well, your mother's one of her customers."

"But what—" Alison stopped and blushed.

Jeffrey knew at once why. He was aware that he had the reputation—not entirely deserved—of being loved by many women. And he was uncertain of just what to say. Olive, in handing over Alison to him, had taken for granted that he would not take advantage of her youth and inexperience. And she had been right in taking it for granted. On the other hand he and Alison were going to have to make conversation for a good many hours these next few weeks and she looked intelligent. Hanged if he was going to start off by pretending she was still a child.

He said gently, "You needn't have stopped. I haven't had and I'm not having an affair with Madame Celestine. I'm one of her favorites for a very human reason. Because once she was able to do me a great kindness."

Alison's eyes showed a quick understanding but with a tact hardly to be expected at eighteen, she did not ask what the favor had been. He told her.

"Madame got me through a tough go of pneumonia when I was a kid just getting started, and without a cent to pay for doctors or hospital care. Ever since then," he concluded with affectionate irony, "she can't do enough for me."

"It is nice of you to let her do it," Alison said. "Sometimes it's awfully hard just to let people do for you."

How nice and how wise she is, he thought. Olive wasn't wrong in calling her a darling.

Madame Celestine was brown-skinned, middle-aged, ugly and enormously elegant in a black wool dress. She embraced Jeffrey affectionately and demanded in a torrent of French that snapped and crackled like her black eyes, how he was, what he had been doing, and why he had not been to see her for so long. Then, placing one thin brown hand over the other and holding them in front of her waistline in a sculptured Renaissance attitude, she listened and nodded while Jeffrey explained and sketched. "The heavy velvet, not the sof'. But of course I understand. Not salmon, *non*. Aprico', the color weeth brown in it somewhere."

Having removed Alison temporarily to a fitting room so that her measurements could be taken, she brought her back to Jeffrey, announcing with approval that Mademoiselle had a "truly French figure."

Madame cried out in pain when Jeffrey told her he wanted the dress in three days. "One week. Jus' one week," she implored.

"Good strong basting'll do, so long as the line is right. She's not going to walk in it."

Madame capitulated with a look of such submissive devotion that Jeffrey was afraid to look at Alison for fear one or the other would laugh aloud.

He turned Madame around by the shoulders, declaring, "I can never understand how you get your wings to fold so nicely under a dress like this."

Madame's face sparkled with pleasure. She said, with an apologetic look at Alison for such foolishness, "Ah, that! It is because they are so very small!"

Outside the spring dusk held the cool light fragrance of expensive toilet water. Alison drew a deep breath. "Spring's never as nice anywhere else as it is in New York, do you think so? Probably because there's so little, and you never know when to expect it, that when it comes it's—"

"Like so much velvet," finished Jeffrey, delighted that she too loved what was to him the most beautiful and exciting city. "Would you like to walk back to Sutton Place?"

"Oh yes! That is—if you haven't another engagement," she finished politely.

"Nothing that can't wait," Jeffrey chuckled mentally over what Miss Leila Harmer would say if she heard herself so described. But it was true, tonight. When they weren't going to the theater Leila like to dine late.

After a moment Alison said, "You and Madame talk as though I ought to be glad I have a French figure."

"Well, aren't you? The French have been doing pretty well with it for a long time."

"I know, but it's not the style. Nowadays if you haven't nice long legs you might as well not have anything."

"Fashions can be changed," observed Jeffrey sententiously.

"I know. By people like Mother, or Katherine Cornell, or somebody. But not me. I haven't one speck of glamour."

"Glamour is a vastly overrated quality. Don't try to change too much, Alison. You're practically perfect, just as you are."

She didn't answer and thinking he might, somehow, have said the wrong thing, he looked down. She was smiling to herself, a comforted tucked-in smile that made him smile with relief and satisfaction. He put his hand down to hers and drew her arm up inside of his elbow.

Toward the end of the evening Leila said suddenly, "For heaven's sake, Jeffrey, stop smiling into your champagne like a cat in a sardine factory. What on earth are you looking so smug about?"

Jeffrey removed the smile. But he went on thinking about something that had happened earlier in the evening. In one of the intervals during which Leila had left him to repair a face in no need of repairs, Albert Geer had come upon Jeffrey in the bar.

Albert was a fat little man whose gossip column was the most widely read in New York. His writing had been rated by a fellow wit as the poison-ring, rather than the poison-pen variety—its style being as exquisitely wrought, its content as deadly.

Hauling his bouncing-ball body with difficulty up to the high bar stool, Albert had said, "And how is Winslow Homer these days?"

In that instant a great idea took shape in Jeffrey's mind. He twirled his glass and said absently, "Very nicely, thank you, Albert. I'm just starting my annual busman's holiday and I'm looking forward to it immensely."

"Busman's holiday?"

"Didn't I ever tell you? Why, once a year or so, I do a portrait to please myself. I pick my own subject and I don't get paid for it. It's swell."

Albert's eyes flickered beadily like those of a toad eyeing a fly just within reach. "Who's the subject? Leila?"

"No. Olive Carstair's daughter, Alison."

"I don't believe I know her," said Albert almost humbly. "Pretty?"

Jeffrey managed a supercilious smile. "She's very paintable. A remarkable combination of femininity and character."

Albert's curiosity was greater than his pride. "What's she do?"

"Goes to college. She's only eighteen."

"I suppose she'll be going on the stage?"

"Good Lord, I shouldn't think so. She's a very scholarly person."

"Well, it's nice to have seen you, Jeffrey. Sorry you wouldn't have that drink with me." Albert slipped down from his stool, ready to move on down the bar like a trapper inspecting his line of traps.

Jeffrey, perfectly aware that he hadn't been offered a drink, said cheerfully, "Thanks just the same, Albert. Sorry I didn't have anything exciting for you."

Remembering how nicely he had managed all this, Jeffrey had good reason to be smug. But he was sure to be in Leila's black book after she had read Albert's column. So, gazing appreciatively at Leila's white and gold perfection, he said soothingly, "I'm afraid I was painting away in my mind. It goes so much better when I haven't a brush in my hand."

Alison rang Jeffrey's doorbell so promptly the next morning he suspected she had walked around the block until time to climb the three flights of the brownstone house to his studio. Helping her off with her coat he wondered gloomily that he had ever thought her paintable. She was wearing a very short blue flannel pleated skirt and a pale pink sloppy Joe sweater. But when she turned to him, saying apologetically, "Mother said I wasn't to dress up," he felt again a rush of protective affection.

He said, "It's just as well you didn't. This morning I'm just going to figure out how to pose you and what sort of background I want. Would you like to see my place first?"

There was nothing much to see—the entrance hall, one great sparsely furnished room with a skylight, a bathroom and a kitchenette. Having shown her around, Jeffrey said, "Look, will you have a cup of coffee with me before we start?"

"Yes, please," said Alison smiling.

She didn't hear him when he came back from the kitchenette with the tray. She had found his good-luck piece, a snowstorm paperweight that had originally been his grandmother's. Having just shaken it, she was watching the miniature storm with absorbed delight.

This was the way he would paint her, Jeffrey instantly decided, her face, free of the social immaturity that stiffened and masked it, foreshadowing the woman she would become.

He set down the tray. "Alison, before you come next time will you have your mother's hairdresser cut your hair in thick Victorian bangs?"

She flushed with humiliation. "My forehead's too high, isn't it?"

"It isn't too high at all," said Jeffrey crossly. "Try to get out of the habit of running yourself down, will you? It's just that your dress and hat are going to be Victorian so your hair ought to look that way too. Here, have your coffee!"

A month later it was she who was scolding him. It was Alison's last sitting and since it was in the afternoon, Jeffrey had splurged on pastry and nuts and French chocolates for their tea, spending far too much, in Alison's opinion. Jeffrey listened to her with mock humility and an amused appreciation of the reversal in their roles.

He could hardly believe now how she had looked, that first visit to his studio. In the delectable face beneath the Sarah Bernhardt bangs it was already difficult to find a trace of the awkward schoolgirl. When he looked at the graceful swelling curves of that "truly French" figure, buttoned snugly into its apricot velvet, he found it hard to believe in the existence of a sloppy Joe sweater and skirt.

"And besides I oughtn't to eat pastry," she was saying. "I've gone on a diet."

"Don't you dare," protested Jeffrey.

"What difference would it make? The picture's finished."

"You'll lose all your beaux," Jeffrey warned her.

"Then I'll get new ones who like nice skinny girls," said Alison cheerfully.

She was being contrary with the delightful perversity of a woman, conscious of, and with confidence in, her charm.

And you were the one who said you couldn't change a fashion!"

"I haven't," said Alison simply. "You did."

She was so truly herself. She hadn't disintegrated under the freakish spotlight of publicity; instead, it was as her mother had predicted. Alison's personality had flowered in the warmth of Jeffrey's apparent admiration; but it was no hothouse blossom that stood forth, thus revealed.

"Just the same it isn't I they take out to Hamburger Heaven and Rockefeller Center and the Sutton Cinema," he reminded her.

Alison grinned. "Boys are sheep. But some of them," she added thoughtfully, "are nice sheep."

"Is the one you're going tea-dancing with today one of the nice ones?"

"Who? Fred? Goodness no, he's a wolf!" And she laughed delightedly at Jeffrey's expression.

"Now look here, Alison, don't go running—Oh hand, there's someone at the door!"

It was, incredibly, Leila Harmer. Jeffrey was so surprised he stood staring, forgetting his manners. To be sure, Leila had long since forgiven him for Albert Geer's squib about Alison's portrait and all the publicity it had aroused. Jeffrey had taken Leila to the theater only two nights ago and it had never been Leila's policy to go after a man. She didn't have to.

"Aren't you going to ask me in? I've been having tea with Marian Donald downstairs and when she reminded me you were in the same house I couldn't resist ringing your bell."

"I wouldn't have forgiven you if you hadn't," said Jeffrey, flattered, even though she was here only by accident. "This is a wonderful surprise, Leila. Come in."

Watching her move into the entrance hall ahead of him, he realized that he was always forgetting how very beautiful she was. It was really too bad she hadn't happened by when he was alone.

He said, "Go right in. Alison Carstair is here; I've just finished her picture."

Leila lifted one hand in graceful protest. "Oh, I don't want to interrupt."

"You're not," said Jeffrey brusquely. He called, "Alison, we have a visitor. You've heard me speak of Miss Harmer."

Alison had risen. She stood waiting for them with an expression Jeffrey had not seen before on her face, a mature look of watchful caution.

Leila went forward, hands outstretched. "Hello, Alison. You probably don't remember me. Last time I saw you, you were the darlingest chubby little schoolgirl. But I would have known you anywhere. She hasn't changed much, has she, Jeffrey?"

"Enough," said Jeffrey. "The line between being chubby and being nicely rounded seems to be about as easy to cross as the one between genius and insanity. But what I can't figure out is how all the wolves in town know when somebody has crossed it."

Leila smiled knowingly at Alison. "I imagine most of them can read. And the papers have been as helpful as if you had a press agent."

Jeffrey, aware that Alison had not said a word, suddenly realized that Leila was up to something. What was the matter with her? Alison was only a kid and no competition for one of the town's leading belles. All his pleasure in her visit evaporated and he looked at his watch, wishing she'd go. It was almost five and time for Alison to be leaving for her date but he wasn't going to let her go for the last time with Leila still here.

Leila had not missed his covert glance at his watch. She said with the affectionate possessiveness he had rather liked until now. "I'm keeping you from your work, I'm afraid, darling, but I'm not going without seeing the famous picture. May I, Alison?"

"Yes, of course," said Alison quietly. "It's right there beside you."

Jeffrey turned the picture toward the light. Standing beside Leila he tried to see his work objectively. He had not wanted to do the typical period piece, full of prettiness and sentiment. All his creative ability and technical skill had been directed toward one aim—that of interpreting character in terms of color and form. The pansies pinned to the muff, the bright colors of the tiny figure immured within the glass of the paperweight and the glowing apricot tones of Alison's dress were all subordinated to that grave face, where, for a brief time, a child and a woman were together and at peace.

It was a face that was a touchstone for those who looked at it and he noticed how swiftly Leila turned her eyes away. She was prettily enthusiastic. "It is charming, simply charming. You know you *are* clever, darling."

Jeffrey saw Alison flush at the inference. Leila went on, "You won't have to worry about having this picture left on your hands, will you? I'm sure Olive will insist on buying it when she sees how good it is."

That's ruined everything, thought Jeffrey. Leila hadn't forgiven him for choosing Alison as his subject. She had thought and thought about his reasons until she had hit upon the truth. And she had come here today purposely to make sure Alison knew the truth too. Well, she wasn't going to get away with it; he wasn't going to have her hurt Alison. He could have used Olive's check very nicely, but, since there was no other way—

He said, "I have no intention of letting this one out of my hands. I'm much too fond of it. With Alison's permission I'm going to hang her picture right where she can see all my visitors and decide which ones are proper company for me."

That was unkind and Jeffrey would not have blamed Leila for being violently angry. But when she turned, with a smile like a scimitar on her lips, he saw he had forced her to a woman's last resort. She was never going to speak to him again if she could help it and he was surprised to discover he didn't care.

"I must run. Good-by, Alison. I suppose you are anxious to get back to your school. It must be an excellent one. I can see they feed you properly and that's always a good sign, isn't it?"

After she had gone, Jeffrey said, "Whew!" and Alison said reproachfully, "You were awfully mean to her, Jeffrey."

"She's a nasty piece," said Jeffrey happily, "and she deserved it. Now I know what they mean by beauty being only skin-deep. And she's spoiled your last afternoon. You'd better go change, Alison, or you'll be late for your wolf."

She came back in a few minutes, tying the bow at the neck of her new spring suit. She had let down her hair in back and tied an angelic band of cornflowers behind her bangs. "Do I look all right?"

"Your nose is shiny or is that another new fashion?"

"Oh golly. Well, I'll wait till I get there."

"Wait a minute," said Jeffrey. "I haven't put my name to this masterpiece."

Alison watched him brush in his name with firm simple strokes. "It is beautiful, isn't it? Not me—the picture."

"I only painted what I saw."

"But no one else saw me like that until you did. And your seeing it has made everything different."

"And happier?"

"Oh much! Because when you like people it's nice not feeling all thumbs with them. But frightened and excited, sort of. As if something had ended and something else was just beginning."

"That's a pretty good description of the beginning of growing up," said Jeffrey. "Good luck to you, Alison, all the way."

"I think you must be just about the nicest person in the whole world," she said impetuously. She looked up at him, her face alight with gratitude and Jeffrey, without thinking, bent down and kissed her.

It was a light gentle kiss; he thought if he had met Alison for the first time in the dark and kissed her he would have known she was eighteen. But the kiss had been an end and a beginning for him too.

Why, he *loved* Alison! He looked at her incredulously and found it to be so. She was everything he had waited for, without knowing until now why he had waited. There was no mystery, when he came to think of it, about why she was. In one month he had come to know her better than anyone else in the world. And, knowing her, he loved her the way you ought to love the one you want to spend the rest of your life with—loved her stubbornness as well as her honesty, her plumpness as well as her pansy-blue eyes.

It's the silliest thing I ever heard of, he thought and looked down at her again to see her expression. A month ago she would have been crimson with embarrassment; today she was interested, pleased and expectant.

He said lightly, "Only one to a customer. That's for being such a good subject. Now good-by, kitten. Beat it!"

He couldn't tell her. Not because he was twenty-seven and she was eighteen but because she must have time and opportunity to make her choice as he had made his. He knew he'd made his once for all because he remembered something forgotten until now—that he came from a long line of one-woman men. Nevertheless it would be a good idea not to let her get too far away.

She was almost at the door. He said, "Write to me once in a while, Alison, will you?"

She turned. "You want me to? Honestly?"

He wanted to say more than yes, but in fairness he couldn't tie even the lightest thread of obligation around her finger. He said, "I'd rather have you write to me than anyone else I know."

Although she didn't quite believe him, she was terribly pleased. "Then I will," she cried. "And you write to me too. I'll write you once a week," she promised earnestly, "but you don't have to answer that often."

She started to open the door. "Thank you for the kiss, Jeffrey," she said over her shoulder. "It was the best of all."

The door closed behind her. Jeffrey couldn't move. How much had his kiss meant to her? How much would she remember?

He went to the front window, opened it and stuck his head out. There she was, running as hard as she could toward the other corner and a wolf named Fred. And toward all the other wolves and all the corners of the world. He waited until she had turned the corner before he pulled his head in and closed the window.

He walked over to the writing table and rummaged in the drawer for paper. He picked up his pen. Reaching behind him with his foot, he hooked up a chair, sat down and started to write.

"Dear Alison," he began.

Good-bye, Old Laura

Lucile Vaughan Payne

There is nothing funny about being fat in America. Every fat child learns this early in life. We are jeered, reviled, spat upon, physically and mentally pushed around, and joked about to our faces almost incessantly. Where is the humor in a life like that?

No, there's nothing funny about fat. Fat people learn that they must laugh first, and they think that people will then be laughing with them, not at them. Unfortunately that's only partly true. When fat people assume their traditional clown role, people are laughing with them and at them. Being fat and funny does give you a modicum of control over a situation—you make the jokes so you decide when people laugh. But the point is that people will tolerate fat people only when they are clowns. Fat people quickly find that that is the only route to even the outskirts of slim society, and we grow used to having our few minutes as the life of the party via our masochistic humor, and then fading away when the dancing starts.
—Lynn Mabel-Lois, "Position Paper: Humor"

A shrewd teacher had once looked thoughtfully at Laura Stanley and remarked to a colleague, "She's an island unto herself." The other teacher had laughed and said, "Laura? She's practically a whole continent." But the two teachers had not been talking about the same thing.

Laura Stanley was seventeen years old and she weighed two hundred pounds.

She had short dark hair, a face so round and full that its bone structure was invisible, and remarkable eyes. Nobody ever noticed them. Everybody was too busy listening to her contagious laughter, or looking forward to one of her parties, or enjoying one of Laura's jokes, to notice her eyes. They were gray, beautiful, and full of very cool, very guarded intelligence.

She was quite easily the most popular girl in school.

Usually her crowd met at the drugstore, when classes were out, for a postmortem to the day's events. Today Laura was late, arriving after the others had already gathered. They could see her through the plate glass windows as she moved toward the entrance.

"Good old Laura," said Pete Skinner. "Like a fish in an aquarium. She kind of floats."

"Like a whale, you mean," said Wanda Myers.

"Aw, c'mon," said Jim Roberts, but he laughed with the others. Under the table he reached for Sue Price's hand, and they both forgot all about Laura.

At a table in the rear of the store another girl glanced up. "There's your girlfriend, Tubby," she said.

"Aww—" said Tubby. "Listen, Grace," he said, his voice cracking, high with embarrassment, "there was something I wanted to ask you today—"

"Well, she is your girl, isn't she?"

"Laura? Heck, no! I mean, well, we go around in the crowd, you know, but she's not my girl or anything like that."

"Oh." Grace regarded Tubby with small bright eyes. He was the son of the leading attorney in town, a member of *the* crowd, Laura's crowd, the one that by tacit consent "ran the school" and set the pattern for everybody else. Grace McGuire's ruling passion for two years had been to become part of that crowd; she was an intelligent girl in an academic, rather brightly insistent way, but she had a kind of finicking, overnice manner that had earned her the title of "the Deeb," which in the crowd's language was short for "deadly bore." At this moment Grace knew that Tubby Dickinson was on the verge of asking her for a date. Tubby wasn't much of a catch, but dating him might mean acceptance into the crowd, or at least its fringes. She patted her hair and simpered. "What was it," she asked, "you were going to ask me?"

Outside the drugstore Laura reached absently for the door, just as another hand pulled it open. In the moment's imbalance her armload of books slipped and fell to the sidewalk. "Whoa!" she said, laughing, looking down at the books. "Oh, hello," she added to the surprised, familiar face of the boy who had opened the door.

"You didn't even *try* to catch them," he said. He didn't say it accusingly; he sounded thoughtful. Behind his horn-rimmed glasses his narrow dark eyes were keen and friendly.

"Of course not," said Laura. "I don't believe in throwing my weight around. You live next door to me, don't you?"

He picked up her books and handed them to her. "Yes. Just got moved in last week."

"I know all about you," said Laura. "You're a pre-med at the University, your name is George Grant, and your home town is in Ohio. Thanks for picking up the books. I'm Laura Stanley."

"Aha," said George. "So you're that FBI agent I've been trying to shake." He leaned toward her and spoke *sotto voce* from the corner of his mouth. "Who squealed?"

"I got spies all over," said Laura. She grinned and added, "Mostly Special Agent Slade—your landlady. Your room is practically in our back yard, you know, and the boys who live there usually spend half their time on our patio. I've been meaning to ask you over." Her manner was completely without coquetry. "Any time you're lonesome or bored, just jump out the window and make yourself at home."

No wonder she's so popular, thought George Grant. He had already noticed the activity on the patio. Other students were constantly dropping in, lounging in the bright-striped chairs, eating and drinking and listening to the record player. Left alone, Laura was usually reading. Once he had glanced toward the Stanley house and had seen her sitting in the living room, simply sitting, in an attitude of such stillness and concentration that he had glanced quickly away, feeling that he had intruded on her privacy.

"Thanks," he said. "I will. Can I get you something to drink?"

"No thanks. Friends waiting." She moved on.

"Hello, you all," said Laura to the two couples sitting in the booth. Couples, she thought, and something moved softly in her mind, like a door that opened slightly, then closed.

"Hi," said Sue Price languidly, and the others echoed her greetiung. Nobody stirred to make room.

"Scoot over, Pete," said Jim Roberts. He was a tow-headed, handsome boy with the big square hands and tall slouch of a basketball player. "If you can scoot far enough," he added.

Laura laughed and sat down heavily, squeezing her bulk into the space beside Pete, but for a fraction of a moment she kept her lids lowered over her muted eyes. If I hadn't been late, I could have steered them to a table, she thought; they know how I hate booths.

They know. Again the door in Laura's mind was pushed open, and understanding came like a sliver of light in a dark room. She saw Sue and Wanda exchange long, pained looks. They had not mentioned anything to her today about meeting at the drugstore. Two girls plus two boys made a date; five made a crowd.

They don't want me, she thought. It was not the first time she had faced this thought—for under the placid, smiling, exterior Laura was a core of ruthless honesty, a hard and brilliant self-knowledge embedded like a diamond in fat. She knew what the others did not know, that her charm and hospitality had kept the crowd together and kept her own place in it secure for a long time, and that her time was running out. They wanted to pair off, to enter private worlds that would not and could not include her. Always before she had been able to make them forget that she was actually excess and unwieldy baggage in a boy-meets-girl society. She had made them want her. Now they were older, less pliable. I have graduated, she thought cynically, from diversion to intrusion.

"Hot-fudge sundae," she said to the waitress. "With plenty of whipped cream," she added. She had been trying to cut down on rich food, but had given the order out of some inner compulsion, an instinct to show the enemy that she was not afraid.

"Eeek," said Sue, "and poor little me drinking tomato juice!"

"Why, I wouldn't want to order a thing like that," Laura said. "I might get fat."

They laughed, and she felt safe again. "I have to watch my figure, you know," she said, deliberately spooning up on whipped cream. She felt obscurely shamed, but she could not help herself. "After all, I have a lot at stake."

Their laughter braced her somewhat, but the obscure sense of shame still persisted.

"Hey," said Pete Skinner, "dig Tubby, back at the goon table."

"With the Deeb, imagine," said Wanda.

"Man," said Pete, "he really looks like he's grounded."

Laura raised her eyes and saw Tubby talking earnestly, with flushed face. Was it possible that he was trying to date the Deeb? Not only possible, but probable. Laura knew that he had tried before to date more popular girls, without success. They laughed him off. He was considered more or less Laura's property. Although he was fat and rather dull and so painfully embarrassed by his fatness that everybody else was embarrassed by it too, he was at least a boy. He and Laura could give the appearance of a couple when the occasion demanded it. In a crowd she could endure Tubby; alone with him, she could hardly disguise her boredom. So why should I care, she thought, if he dates the Deeb?

She knew why she would care. All the charm and intelligence and hospitality in the world wouldn't get her out of this one. A silly, pretentious girl like Grace McGuire was preferable as a date to fat Laura Stanley.

They were watching her. "My," she said, in a rich parody of sentiment, "ain't that the sweetest."

"Man, he's really scraping bottom," said Pete.

"Good old Tubby," said Laura. She spooned up ice cream and thick chocolate, coolly despising the small fat hand that held the spoon, the dimpled white wrist. She gave her friends a face of pure smiling pleasure. He's fat, she thought, fat as I am, but because he's a boy he can find a girl who will go out with him, even though it's only the Deeb. While I . . . She checked a secret surge of self-pity. Self-pity was the luxury of fools. But imagine yourself, she thought, looking into Jim Roberts' eyes the way Tubby is looking into the Deeb's. Oh, funny. Very, very funny.

She put down her spoon very carefully.

"We were just talking about the sock hop next week," said Sue Price.

"Oh," said Laura. She turned her curious, muted eyes on the two couples. "Yes, that ought to be fun." The crowd always went together to the sock hops; at least it had been that way last year.

"Jim finally broke down and asked me," said Sue, laughing up at the fair-haired boy. "And Pete's taking Wanda." Her question was casual but pointed: "Are you going, Laura?"

So it was a "couple thing," after all, not a "crowd thing," and Laura was being told right away how it was. All three of the girls knew this instantly.

Laura met Sue's glance and read it clearly: *I want Jim Roberts to myself, at the dance, and before it, and after it.*

Laura wondered briefly if Sue had ever suspected how she, Laura, felt about Jim Roberts. No, she thought, I've been too careful; they would all have made my life miserable if they had known. And his. Under the big, unassuming boy's grin she could see a deep kindness, a genuine friendliness for her as a person. Laura would have cut her throat before embarrassing him with the knowledge that the school fat girl dreamed of him constantly, lived only for those moments she could be near him—even like this, at the table of a drugstore booth, with another girl at his side. He was the only real reason that she had kept the crowd so close together, why she had so many parties. When the others came, he came.

But now the chips were down, at least for the sock hop; it was couples or nothing—and nothing meant no party afterward at home, with Jim near for another hour. *Are you going, Laura?*

She reached for the right touch of broad humor. "Well, now, I guess I could take myself. That's practically the same as two."

They laughed, as always. "Oh, Tubby'll take you," said Wanda. "Hey, Tubby!" she called. "C'm'ere!"

Tubby shambled over toward the booth. Laura laughed, a lazy, untroubled sound, thinking, as she listened to her own laughter, how skillful she had grown in its use. She could do nothing now but play out the scene. "They're ganging up on us, Tubby," she said gaily. "How would you like to take me to the sock hop next week?"

"Gee, Laura," Tubby gasped. His color grew high; his voice squeaked. "I'm sorry—I can't. I mean, well, I've already got a date."

"Tubb-eeee!" shrilled Sue and Wanda. "Why, you rat, you!"

"With the Deeb?" Jim Roberts asked. "Gee whiz!" He shook his head wonderingly.

At the table in the rear, out of earshot, the Deeb preened and smiled. "The goons have got him," Pete muttered.

"Oh, shut up, Pete," said Laura sharply. "I'm glad, Tubby. I think that's swell. Don't let these guys get you down. Listen, I was just thinking of having a party the weekend school's over. Why don't you bring your girl?"

"Well, gee, Laura. Okay. Fine. I'll ask her."

Laura felt a sudden weakness, a trembling under her skin, as though layer after layer of fat, held momentarily in chill suspension, had turned to jelly. The worst was over. The idea of a party had rescued everybody from embarrassment.

"Goody!" cried Sue. "Jim, I'm inviting you to take me, right now."

"Caught!" said Jim.

Laura felt the onrush of an emotion rare to her: anger. "What makes you think you're invited?" she asked sharply.

"Gosh," said Sue, "aren't we?"

Laura stood up. "Sure," she said, holding out her laugh like an offering. "The whole crowd."

"She always has swell parties," Wanda said thoughtfully, watching Laura go slowly out of the drugstore.

A small frown creased Jim Roberts' brow. "Laura's a good kid," he remarked to nobody in particular.

"Who's that guy at the fountain, the one with the horn-rimmed glasses?" Sue whispered to her friend.

"I don't know," said Wanda, craning. "But I'll take it."

"I think he's been watching us," Sue murmured. "I caught his eye two or three times in the mirror." She rolled her eyes. "You can be the bridesmaid, dear."

"What are you two clacking about?" demanded Pete.

At the fountain George Grant picked up his check and left.

FROM "PROBLEMS IN OBESITY:
A CASE STUDY" *page 3*

Assurances were obtained from the family physician, Dr. Edward Norquist, that Miss Stanley's overweight was not due to glandular imbalance. He stated that she could and should reduce and that he had on several occasions prescribed a diet. She was, at her last medical checkup, approximately seventy pounds overweight.

Dr. Norquist believed that the case had special difficulties because Miss Stanley liked being fat. She had achieved a unique popularity, actually a following among the high-school students. Because of her father's high income as owner of a department store, her life was unusually comfortable.

He discounted the "neglected-child" or "lack of love" theory. Mr. Stanley was deeply concerned about the welfare of his daughter, and apparently their relationship was a happy one. The young woman's tendency toward overweight was observed before the death of the mother, who was a woman of unusual beauty, charm, and talent.

On the Stanley patio June sun lay warmly on the red-tiled floor and dappled with chairs where Laura and George Grant sat, a Scrabble board on the table between them. George swallowed a last mouthful of strawberry shortcake and groaned contentedly. "Laura," he said happily, "you are undoubtedly the best cook in the world."

"I know it," said Laura placidly. "I can play *Chopsticks*, too. And I'm awfully good at Scrabble."

She was, he reflected, extraordinarily good at Scrabble. She seemed to need only one glance at the board with those wise, muted eyes to see every possibility of play. Out of six games in the last two weeks, she had won all but two. Her vocabulary was impressive, but it was her instantaneous mental connections, her ability to see wholly and clearly the potential of the board in relation to any jumble of letters she held, that made her such a formidable Scrabble player. And that's not vocabulary, he thought; that's intelligence.

He had not imagined, a week earlier, when the fat girl had first invited him with that air of lazy good nature which he found himself liking and faintly despising at the same time, that he would find her remotely interesting. It was his Olympian judgment, as a third-year university honor student, that all high-school girls were lisping infants with minds bounded on one side by freshman English and on the other by the Beatles. Laura at first dumbfounded, then delighted him. His status as a college man did not seem to impress her in the least. The truth is, he thought one night just before he went to sleep, that she accepts me as an equal. The thought tickled him so that he laughed aloud.

He sensed that he was getting acquainted with a Laura that the high-school crowd didn't know existed. With them she masked her intelligence in slang and fat-girl humor; her mind, like a strong, bright bird, hid its plumage in its nest of fat. She never lets them see it, he thought shrewdly; it would set her even more apart.

Whatever emotional life Laura had, it was bound up with her high-school crowd. George was half-exasperated by the complete absence of any romantic overtones in his own relationship with her. Not that he wanted them. He had been determined to avoid them at all costs. But it was a little unflattering to realize that as far as his masculine charms were concerned he didn't even exist for Laura. It was a long time before he realized Laura had simply set aside this area of human relations as the province of others. She was too honest to interpret their growing friendship as anything except what it was—mutually interesting companionship. Most high-school girls, he knew, would have capitalized on it. It would be easy to tell her friends at school, "I'm dating a college man." Laura would be contemptuous of such pretense.

"It's your play," she reminded him now.

He cursed his luck. He saw only one possible play on the board. He held an "f"; the only opening on the board he could use was in front of the word "at." He could make "fat," with a triple score on the "f."

"Guess I'll have to pass this one."

"Let's see our letters," said Laura abruptly.

"Not on your life, nosey."

"You've got an 'f.'"

"So?"

"Use it, stupid. It's a triple-letter score."

"Mmmm. I'm saving it for better things."

A flush spread up Laura's throat. She knows very well why I wouldn't do it, he thought, half-angrily. Why did she put me on the spot? Wordlessly, Laura spelled out "obese."

"So you see," she said ironically, "you might as well have spelled 'fat' and made it count."

He sensed that they were on perilous ground. "You're so good to me," he said lightly.

"Of the two words," said Laura invincibly, "I think I prefer 'fat' to 'obese.'"

"I'll try to bear that in mind."

"Please do. If you're obese, you're just a mound of something—thick, somehow immovable, stupid. 'Fat's' a nicer word. At least it's got some laughs in it." George looked at her silently, and she went on, her gray eyes on the line of evergreens beyond the patio. "People are afraid of words. Dad's friends, for example. 'Poor Laura,'" she mimicked expertly, "'she's a little overweight, of course—' Why don't they say she's fat as a sow, which would be truer?"

"Very funny. Am I supposed to laugh now?"

"You're afraid of words," she said mockingly. She leaned back in her chair and closed her eyes. "I'm fat. I knew it before you did, so you don't need to keep it from me. I'm fat, and I wish you'd kindly refrain from being so all-fired delicate about it."

"Somebody," said George, "ought to knock your teeth out."

"Oh?"

He took a deep breath. "So you're fat. Why beat yourself on the head with it? What goes with this joke compulsion? I've never seen you pass up an opportunity to crack wise about yourself or laugh at yourself. Why?"

Laura's eyes flickered. "I'm fat, so I'm funny, so I laugh. All very simple. When you can't do anything about a situation, laugh. Nutshell philosophy for today."

"Nutshell baloney."

"You wouldn't know," said Laura. The look she gave him was so direct and profoundly wounded that he was shocked and moved by it. But the look left her eyes as quickly as it came. "Skip it," she said amiably. She was again the lazy, good-natured friend.

He continued insistently. "What do you mean you can't do anything about it?"

"Look pal, I said skip it."

"Now who's afraid of words?"

Her eyes challenged him. "All right. I know because I've tried. Call it laziness, or lack of will power, or the cat died and I'm eating to forget. I can't stick to a diet, period. And anyway, who cares? Things are all right with me the way they are."

He thought of the day he had first seen her in the drugstore. "Are they, Laura?" he asked soberly.

During her fifteenth year Miss Stanley had made a final, strenuous attempt to reduce under the supervision of her Aunt Edith, her father's sister. Her aunt offered to stay at the Stanley home for as long as it took to get an acceptable routine established and to see some progress made. She was a brisk, efficient woman, active in charitable organizations and club work.

In two weeks Miss Stanley lost ten pounds, but she became morose, sullen, and painfully self-conscious. Her aunt held frequent club and committee meetings at the Stanley home. The girl was aware that all the women were aware of the aunt's campaign and that she was a frequent subject of discussion and conjecture.

Entertainment at the aunt's various club meetings was usually furnished by daughters of members. Attempting to overcome Miss Stanley's growing self-consciousness, Aunt Edith asked her to sing for one of the meetings. Miss Stanley refused and was enraged by her aunt's offer of special refreshments if she would consent, which she considered an insult to her intelligence. She pointed out that she did not pretend to be a good singer and that she had no intention of exposing herself further to the group's criticism, however sympathetic. Her aunt persisted. "You're a lovely girl," she said, "and you sing beautifully."

But at that point the aunt had completely lost the battle. Miss Stanley answered, quite calmly, "I am not a lovely girl, and I can't sing for sour apples." She then proceeded to help herself to a tremendous serving of dessert, announcing to her aunt that she was through. Her aunt departed the next day. Miss Stanley resumed her outwardly placid life and her ten pounds very quickly.

George lounged indolently on the patio while Laura rustled back and forth to the house, bringing out some wax candles, napkins, and stacks of records for the player. "What goes?" he asked.

"Party tonight," said Laura briefly. She settled temporarily in the chair beside him and added grouchily, "I got myself into it last month, and it's too late to get out now."

"Why try to get out of it? I thought you liked parties."

With me on a diet? Oh, it's going to be peachy, just peachy. I should never have let you talk me into it."

"Me? I never said a word about having a party. I haven't even been invited."

"I mean the diet, not the party. The whole thing is plain stupid."

He refrained from pointing out that she herself had done most of the talking; he had simply listened and offered to help, and before she had known it, Laura had committed herself. He had to admit it had played havoc with his peaceful hours on the patio; after two days of dieting Laura was acting like a bear with a sore head. "You've just got the third day jumps," he said lightly. "Relax. Who's coming to the party?"

"Oh, the usual." She added rather ungraciously, "You can come if you want to."

"No thanks. Uncle's too old. But," he added, grinning, "I do appreciate the wonderful sincerity of your invitation."

Laura laughed in spite of herself. "Sorry. I meant it, really. Come on over. Music, food, and beautiful girls. Or at least one beautiful girl. But that's her opinion, not mine."

"It's your spirit of loving-kindness when you diet that I like," said George. "Is the beautiful-she-thinks girl the one I've heard over here a couple of times? The one that neighs?"

Laura shot him a look of malicious pleasure. "That would be Wanda. The one I meant is Sue Price. She doesn't neigh, she glubbers."

"Oh. What's a glubber?"

"It's the mating cry of a tarantula—I'm being mean. Sue's really a very sweet girl. She has hair like sunshine, a twenty-four-inch waistline, and a mind like a wet biscuit."

George grinned. "Sounds like my dish. Give me a thumbnail sketch of the rest of your dearest friends."

Laura shrugged. "You've probably seen most of them over here. Or heard them. Draw your own conclusions."

"I've drawn them."

"Well, what are they?"

"Never mind. Who's the tall blond boy? The one I saw in the drugstore the day I ran into you?"

Laura paused. She said shortly, "Jim Roberts."

"Aha," said George.

"Oh, don't be silly."

"All I said was 'aha.'"

"That was too much." Laura's voice was unfriendly.

"Sorry." He began leafing through his neglected textbook, whistling tunelessly. "Toss me that pencil, will you? I bet you can't define a tibia."

"No," said Laura sulkily.

"Ignorant girl. It's something you play in a band."

Laura snorted.

"Next question: define a clavicle." He peered at her over his glasses professorially.

It was a game Laura could never resist. "A clavicle is a decayed spot in a tooth," she said.

"No," said George, "you're thinking of a calamity. A clavicle is a seventeenth-century musical instrument. Now give me the definition of 'sacro-iliac.'"

"It's the Greek book that came out about the same time as the sacro-Odyssey."

"Right!" shouted George. "What is 'inflammation'?"

"It's what you ask for when you can't find a telephone number. Just for the record, George—about that 'aha' business—Jim Roberts is just a nice boy in the senior class. I don't think of him any other way." She added painfully, "Under the circumstances, it would be pretty silly."

She was talking seriously about the problems of a fat Laura now, he realized. Not joking, but talking. The joke approach was out; he had made that perfectly clear already—he wanted nothing to do with it. When he had told her that she made herself the butt of her own humor simply as a defense and that it was silly and self-destructive, she had said quietly, "I know it," and she never played the buffoon with him again. He listened and said nothing.

"Maybe I did like him—of course I did, I guess it's silly to be coy about it—nobody knew it, but I liked him a lot. But that's all over. He's no different from all the others, so why kid myself? They're all alike."

"How do you mean?"

"They're cannibals. Junior-grade cannibals, every one of them." She looked straight at George now and said with a cool sincerity that was more devastating than anger: "I hate them all."

Laura knew what her Aunt Edith would have said if she had heard that remark. Reproof, a brisk dismissal of any truth in it, a lecture on loyalty to friends. Or her father—shocked and sorry, shaking his head helplessly. She wondered what George would say, not caring very much, but in effect testing him against the sharp, ragged edges of her hidden anger. She was hungry, wild with irritation at the world and everybody in it, ready to quarrel at the merest hint of reproof or disagreement. If he gives me that calm, reasonable line about "just being hungry," I'll murder him, she thought. All right, let's have it, smart boy. I've just told you that I hate every one of my best friends. What do you do with that one?

George yawned and stretched. "Of course you do," he said.

FROM "PROBLEMS IN OBESITY:
A CASE STUDY" *page 28*

Miss Stanley had an unusual ability to laugh; that is to say, not only did she laugh frequently, but the quality of her laughter was extraordinarily attractive. It was rich, warm, and contagious. She used laughter as an expert musician uses a fine instrument, providing any nuance or inflection that the situation demanded. She had actually, though subconsciously, trained herself in its use. She confessed that she had bridged many painful moments with her laughter. When others enjoyed a joke at her expense, she seemed to enjoy it even more than they. She used her gift of laughter to disarm her enemies and charm her friends. Regardless of her hidden feelings of humiliation and resentment, her laughter seemed spontaneous and delightful. It was her chief weapon of defense. Unfortunately, it was also a great liability. It was too convincing. It challenged her friends to more and more humor at her expense. None of them would have believed that she was capable of being hurt or insulted.

She knew the party wouldn't be easy, and it wasn't. She watched with smoldering resentment as the piles of sandwiches disappeared, as empty glasses returned for refills, as lips smacked over creamy cheese dip, salted nuts, fat black olives. At least they don't notice that I'm not eating, she thought contemptuously; they're too busy filling their own faces. "Food!" they had screamed happily. "Count on Laura to have good food, and puh-lenty of it!"

The record player was going full blast on the patio. Even Tubby was dancing, and the Deeb was in transports, full of high, nervous chatter and an annoying pathetic eagerness to seem perfectly at ease. Sue Price looked beautiful in a swirl-skirted new dress of white wool, and was perfectly aware of the effect she was having on Jim Roberts. The candles made patches of yellow light under the stars The night was just right for dancing outdoors.

Laura's father seemed pleased with the party. He liked to see her have a good time. "Where's George this evening?" he asked.

"Studying," said Laura.

"I guess this crowd's a little young for him, at that," said Sam Stanley.

"Have a Coke," said Laura.

"See," said Tubby to the Deeb, "I told you that Laura always has swell parties."

"She looks sort of worried or something," said Grace.

"Who, Laura?" Tubby laughed, his voice ending on a squeak. "Gosh, she never worries."

"Oh!" cried Wanda. "A rumba!"

"Hey, get Laura!" shouted Pete. "Make her do a rumba for us."

"We want Laura, we want Laura—" They were beginning to chant it from the patio.

"Come on, Laura," said Wanda, tugging at her arm. "Give us a solo. Command performance."

Anger shot through Laura. What do they think I am, a performing seal? They think I'll stand up there and lumber around, give them a good laugh. Oh, yes, Laura's always good for a laugh. "Sorry," she said crisply and emphatically, "I'm sitting this one out."

She reached her chair and sat down, trembling with anger. Or was it merely hunger? Somebody near her in the semi-darkness was crunching potato chips. She could feel it; her own nerve ends might have been splitting between those teeth. On the table near her chair were bottles of soft drinks and a platter of food. It would be so easy to fill a glass and a plate and eat, eat, *eat*. . . . She glanced toward the rectangle of George Grant's window and set her jaw.

Around her the music and laughter eddied. Oh she knew how to give a good party, all right, all right. "Mom thinks I'm studying at Janice's," murmured a girl's voice behind her. "Wouldn't she have a fit if she knew I had a date?"

So now they're using my house as a hideaway, thought Laura. She sat quite still in her chair and let the anger build up inside herself, feeling it in her throat like a hot drink, alive with the power of it. . . .

"Golly, I'm thirsty!" Sue Price laughed, let the dazzle of her blond hair brush Jim Roberts' shoulder. "Jim, you are the most *marvelous* dancer—I need a Coke—hey, Fatsy dear, how about a Coke?"

Fatsy dear . . . She did not remember standing; she was simply carried to her feet on a wave of pure rage. "A Coke? Why, yes, of course, a Coke . . ." Carefully, almost calmly, she filled a paper cup, turned, and threw the drink straight at the pretty, astonished face.

"Why you . . . you . . . *fat* . . . *slob!*" Sue was gasping, dashing liquid from her eyes and patting wildly at her stained dress. She lunged for Laura, but Jim Roberts held her back firmly.

"All right," he said. "Take it easy, Sue."

Sue was sobbing with rage. "Who does she think she is, throwing that stuff all over me . . . look at my dress . . . ruined . . . let *go* of me . . ."

The noise of the party had subsided to a scared murmur. The record player ground on. Laura reached for it, ripping the needle across the disc. "All right, go home," she said in the startled silence. "All of you. The free lunch is over. *Get out.*"

They began to leave, awkwardly, silently. Nobody seemed to know exactly what happened. "Gee," they muttered, "What happened to Laura!"

Sue Price was nearly hysterical. "A new dress! What did I do, I'd like to know? What did I *do*? When my mother sees this . . ."

"You shouldn't have called her a fat slob, though," said Jim Roberts.

It was the talk of the crowd all summer.

FROM "PROBLEMS IN OBESITY:
A CASE STUDY" *page 37*

Miss Stanley's relations with her mother may provide a clue to her tendency toward obesity even as a very young child. Her mother was a woman of great charm but was extremely temperamental. Miss Stanley recalled that she had once disobeyed her mother by playing with an extremely valuable china figurine and had broken it. The child was terrified by the prospect of the punishment she thought she would receive, but when she confessed her crime, her mother had simply laughed and kissed her. However, at another time her mother had been enraged when the child had disarranged a centerpiece before a dinner party. Miss Stanley was never sure what her mother's reaction would be to a given situation.

Mrs. Stanley was an ambitious and talented amateur actress. She spent considerable time away from home and left her child in the care of a maid. She always brought the child a present in the form of some kind of sweet after she had been out. Miss Stanley remembers that she always got the sweet, regardless of her mother's mood, which was sometimes overwhelmingly affectionate and sometimes sharp and irritable. The child never knew what to expect. But she knew what to expect from the candy. It was always sweet.

She was agonizingly, terrifyingly hungry. She could not sleep. Laura switched on the light and sat up in bed, aware of intense stillness. It was very late. She glanced up at the mirror and felt a spreading horror at the image of herself—the bland, round face, the dimpled arms, the tentlike nightgown. She pressed her hands against her sides; her flesh felt flabby and weak.

What's the use? She asked herself despairingly. She had lost twelve pounds and it hardly showed; there was only a faint easing of her clothes, and this sense of flabbiness and anguish. She had too far to go; it was hopeless. . . .

Her friends were lost. Now when she met them on the street she passed unsmiling. It was all stupid, stupid . . . friends discarded, an easy, pleasant way of life thrown away, even the comfort of decent food denied. At lunch she ate, grimly and silently, her boiled egg, her cottage cheese and carrot sticks and lettuce. This rabbit fare, and pride, were all she had to keep her going now.

It was not enough. Why should she go on with it? Why this torture of the flesh, this idiot martyrdom to nothing? She had lost everything but weight; the twelve pounds were meaningless. George had said it would get easier; it did not get easier. And what did he care, really; what business was it of his? Furiously Laura threw on a robe and started for the kitchen. I'm going to eat, she thought. And suddenly she was jubilant, free, walking on air. Food! A hamburger . . . with all the trimmings; a thick malt. She almost ran to the kitchen.

Under the broiler the hamburger sent out a heavenly fragrance. She dumped ice cream and a bottle of coffee cream into the blender, tossed in lavish spoonfuls of malt. Oh, she groaned inwardly, food, food, at last!

She nearly laughed aloud with pleasure. Dieting! I've had it, boys and girls. I am through. Let 'em eat cake, said the queen. Give that lady sixty-four silver platters full of Stanley's Special Hamburgers.

Suddenly, there was George.

He was tapping on the window. She opened the door. He looked about, half-awake. "Come in, Frowzy," said Laura happily, "and smell the smells."

"I saw your light," he said. "Figured something like this might be going on."

"How right you were. I don't care," she said, seeing his unsmiling look. "I can't stand it any longer . . . Oh, smell that!" She closed her eyes and inhaled deeply. "Oh, George, I feel like a freed slave! Here, I'll fix one for you, too." She extracted her own hamburger and went to the refrigerator to get another. The whirr of the blender stopped suddenly. She turned, and under her appalled eyes the creamy malt mixture went down the sink. The garbage disposal ground viciously.

"No!" Laura cried. "No, stop that!" But her hamburger was gone. Nothing remained but the smell.

Her fury and frustration were beyond speech. Her face turned bright red. In one wild movement she lunged toward him and slapped his face.

In the shocked silence that followed, he stood looking at her. "Go get dressed," he said evenly.

"You must be crazy." Her voice shook.

"Hurry up, get dressed."

"Why?"

"We're going for a walk."

"Oh," she cried suddenly, "why don't you leave me alone?"

"Go on, Laura," he said with great gentleness. "The exercise will tire you, and you'll forget about being hungry."

"I . . ." Her voice broke. "I don't see. . . ." She turned blindly and started for her room. George's face was drawn and tired. He had classes the next morning, early. He had probably been on his way to bed when he saw her light. Yet he wanted to take her walking at midnight. At the door she said in a muffled voice, her back still turned to him, "Why worry about me?"

"When I start something," he said, "I like to finish it."

She turned dumbly and went to her room.

FROM "PROBLEMS IN OBESITY:
A CASE STUDY" *page 40*

The striking similarity of the problems of obesity and of alcoholism must be observed. The alcoholic attempts to drown his submerged or subconscious self in alcohol; a compulsive eater buries this self under layers of fat. In each case, the food or drink consumed tends to erase an immediate problem but increases the problem as a whole. The compulsive eater has deep feelings of inferiority because of overweight, feelings that the pleasure of food can temporarily overcome. Thus the victim of obesity is caught in a vicious circle.

Furthermore, an abnormally obese person is mentally as well as physically less comfortable in the first stages of dieting. The accumulated fat seems to act as insulation against defeat and humiliation. As fat begins to disappear, but before any obvious improvement in appearance can be noted, the dieter may become oversensitive and emotional, with a prevailing sense of hopelessness.

Her coat was voluminous now. With the first frost of October Laura felt the cold through the loose coat, through her wrinkled blouse and the baggy skirt pinned at the waistline. I ought to get some new clothes, she thought. She walked lightly, easily, noting with a kind of scientific curiosity how her legs pumped her up the front steps at home, firmly, without that disgusting quiver and flap of loose flesh that she had once despised and ignored. Her father had urged her to get a whole new outfit, anything she wanted; if she didn't want to get it at their own store, she could buy it elsewhere. Laura remembered the years of special-order dresses, the outsizes, all the smothered longing for the bright, narrow-waisted dresses that other girls wore. But she refused now to look at new clothes. She would buy new clothes when the time came. The time was not yet.

Maybe what I really want, she thought, her lips twisting ironically as she began preparations for dinner, is to knock them dead with one of those Cinderella transformations. Size 20 in a Mother Hubbard today, size 14 in a sequined sheath tomorrow. With Hollywood scouts standing by to offer contracts and all the other girls livid with envy. She smiled to herself, genuinely amused by the childish fantasy and by the germ of truth in it. But her reluctance to get new clothes or to pay any more attention than strictly necessary to her looks went deeper than that. She knew that the other girls talked about it behind her back—"Sure, she's lost a lot of weight, but look how sloppy she is. Why doesn't she fix herself up?"

The eyes turned on her at school were curious, sometimes friendly. But Laura went silently from class to class, stiff-arming questions or comment by her manner. Only Jim Roberts had come close to breaking through the wall she put between herself and the others.

"I'm sorry about what happened at that party, Laura," he said, uneasily shifting books from one hand to the other.

She was conscious of her straggling hair, her sagging skirt and flapping blouse. "Oh, that's all right, Jim. Forget it."

She had reached a dead spot, and she knew it. She ate what she was supposed to eat, mechanically, no longer thinking about it or feeling hungry. She exercised, she studied, she slept deeply and dreamlessly. She felt dull, unwanted and unwanting. Sometimes she thought of George Grant with a kind of wonder; why did he help her? Deliberately she let him see her at her worst—with her hair stringing, without makeup, flapping about in the kitchen in old bedroom slippers and baggy jeans.

His manner was unchanging: friendly, firm, unshakable and unshockable. "I like that boy," her father said. And he added, twinkling, "He seems to like you, too, young lady."

Laura looked at her father almost with pity. He could never possibly understand her relationship to George Grant; it would be pointless to explain. George was about as romantic as a page of beginning algebra; he was a college boy, practically another generation; and he knew far too much about her. Of course he liked her. But he didn't "like" her in the way her father meant. You didn't "like" a girl you had seen at her worst, a quivering mountain of flesh who had exposed all her weaknesses, slapped your face, ruthlessly turned the lights on in every dark corner of her mind.

She told George about Jim Roberts' apology. "Have you apologized yet?" he asked.

"Me? Of course not."

"You will," he said smugly.

"Be darned if I will."

"Sure," he said. He pinched her cheek. "Firming up," he said in a pleased way. He picked up her arm and shook it. "Another month and you'll be rid of every bit of that flab. Practically gone now."

Suddenly Laura laughed with the old rich humor. "You . . . you *scientist*, you! Oh, I could brain you! 'Firming up!'" she mimicked. "Oh, George!" She could feel mirth swiftly coming, laughter moving down on her like a spring avalanche. "What I love," she gasped, "is that . . . rich . . . poetic . . ." She leaned helplessly against the sink. ". . . exalted . . . you make me feel," she screamed gently, "like something . . . hanging feet up . . . at the county fair!"

"Haw!" said George. Her laughter was like music hitting his ribs; it was buoyant, free, luxurious, a splendid contagion. "Haw!" and he was off, guffawing. Their laughter rocketed through the house, bringing in Laura's father to look at them in astonishment. Laura lifted a hand weakly to point at him, closed her eyes and quietly caved in with mirth.

That laugh, thought George. You can't listen to it without catching it. It was the first time Laura had laughed in weeks, and this was a hundred times more delectable than her old laugh; this was real. When they were sober enough to talk again, Laura remained sitting on the floor, her baggy jeans billowing. She pulled a lank string of hair across her face and held it under her nose like a mustache, her gray eyes still brimming with laughter. "I ought to get this cut."

"Get the scissors," he said.

"Oh no," said Laura hastily, scrambling to her feet, "no, thanks. I'll get my hair cut when I'm good and ready."

"Well, when is that, for Pete's sake?"

"When I can wear a size 14 dress," said Laura airily.

"It's a deal," said George. "Let's go."

"Go? Go where?"

"To get a size 14 dress, Jughead."

"Don't treat me like a moron."

"Oh, come off your high horse. I know how to pick clothes. Even my sister admits it. Every time I go home she tries to get me to go shopping with her. She says I have really ex*qui*site taste. She mispronounces it, but she says it."

"Nobody's talking about your ex*qui*site taste. When am I supposed to wear this size 14—about ten years from now?"

"Christmas," answered George promptly. "No reason at all why you can't be a size 14 by Christmas. Come on."

"Holy cats," said Laura simply. "No. Not with you, Mastermind. Not yet. Thanks just the same."

"When?" he asked inexorably.

"When I take care of a couple things," said Laura. She knew suddenly why she had waited, and what she had to do.

> FROM "PROBLEMS IN OBESITY:
> A CASE STUDY" *page 41*
> In certain cases it may be advisable for the reducing patient to cut himself off from his usual friends and activities, thus gaining the opportunity to see himself as a person apart from the group and independent of it. The personality of the patient must be the deciding factor.

School was dismissed early the day before the long Christmas holidays began. Students were already pouring out of the building; Laura looked quickly along the corridor, afraid she had missed Sue Price. But the slender blond girl was still there, standing near the stairway talking to Jim. Laura made her way toward them. They were completely engrossed in each other; Laura saw Jim's big hand reach out and tug gently at a strand of the girl's shining hair. It was a tender and strangely touching gesture. They turned and saw her only when she spoke.

"May I speak to you, Sue? And Jim."

Jim dropped his hand self-consciously. Sue's eyes were suddenly unfriendly and suspicious. Her look went up and down Laura, taking in the pinned skirt, the enormous, baggy sweater. Laura stood quietly, waiting. "What do you want?" Sue asked stiffly.

"I want to apologize for what happened at the party last summer," said Laura. "I'm sorry about it, and I wish I could have apologized sooner, but I couldn't."

Sue's eyes filled with tears. She bit her lip and stared at Laura.

"I want to tell you I'm sorry, too, Jim," Laura said quietly. "Merry Christmas to you both. I guess that's all."

She turned to go, but Sue's hand was on her arm. "I'm sorry, too," she whispered. "Oh, Laura . . . I've missed you!"

"So've I," said Jim gruffly.

Her own eyes smarted with tears. She had forgotten how nice they were, how really kind under the silly, superficial chatter of the past. And yet she could not truly say, as Sue had said, "I've missed you," and mean quite the same thing. She had fought her battle without them, and although she had thought of them at first with pain and anger, it had been a long time since she had really thought of them at all. "Good-bye," she said, touching their hands lightly, her smile a sudden illumination.

I had to do it in my old clothes, she thought.

She left the school and went straight to the dress department of her father's store. The clerk failed to recognize her. "What'll it be?" she asked laconically.

I look like a ragpicker, thought Laura, amused. She doesn't want to waste her time on me. "I want a bright-colored dress," she said firmly. "Really bright, size 14, wool, with a full skirt, and I don't care what it costs."

"We have one," said the clerk with renewed interest.

It was burnished gold, and it hung like a banner among the collection of drab, limp garments which she wore. She never even tried it on. She flapped about the house in her baggy jeans like a scarecrow, waiting for Christmas and miracles. George was on vacation, too. He couldn't go home for the holidays because of some work which he had to finish for one of his classes. The professor had given him an extension of time. When he wasn't studying, he was abstracted and moody. He paced the floor and glared at her. "Why in the name of all that's holy don't you fix up your face and get some clothes?"

"Mind your own business," said Laura. "It isn't Christmas yet."

"Do it now," he wheedled.

She looked at him curiously. Was he really that sick of looking at her in her present state? "You don't have to look at me, you know," she pointed out.

"Oh, all right," he said glumly.

Maybe he's homesick, she thought contritely. Maybe he was thinking about his pretty sister at home and how she looked, or maybe he was just tired and needed cheering up. He had been working hard on his term paper. I could do it, she thought. He might even see that I'm a girl. . . . Unaccountably she blushed.

The next day she had her hair cut, hurrying home to look long and privately in her mirror. Oh, no, she thought, that can't be me. Her hair lay in a soft dark bang across her brow, curled neatly against her ears. *Why, I'm sort of pretty,* she thought amazed. I'm not myself at all, I'm a different person. She took off all her clothes and turned around before the mirror. Of the old mountain of fat only a faint roundness remained, like the ghost of another Laura; the flesh had melted away from the good bones of her face, and under the wide arched brows her eyes were vivid, startling. She could not get used to her new head; she cuffed her ears and peered disbelievingly at her profile. Her battered jeans and her father's old shirt lay on the floor where they were dropped.

"Good-bye, old Laura," she said, stepping over them. She took the new dress from the closet and laid it carefully on the bed. This was a day of miracles. It would fit. Very carefully, she began to dress.

FROM "PROBLEMS IN OBESITY:
A CASE STUDY" *page 43*
Obviously, it is good practice to give the patient on a reducing diet some definite goal to work toward, such as a new dress or a new suit which is purchased in advance, in the size desired, for use on a specific date. This commits the patient more completely to the diet program, is a concrete symbol of reward, and provides a needed stimulus by its presence. Care should be taken to keep the goal within the range of possibility, so that the dieter is not faced with such difficulties that the program is given up in despair. A study of size and weight charts, an analysis of bone structure, and an adequate medical history provide ample information for the physician in setting a goal.

"Something's eating you," said George. "You've changed."

Laura gave him a brief look and then glanced away with mounting color. They were sitting in her living room, rather stiffly facing each other in the fireside chairs. Laura looked down at her feet, still incredible in those delicate high heels, at the soft blue folds of her brushed wool skirt ("Buy out the store!" her father had shouted happily after seeing her in the gold dress; "Shoot the works!"), at her immaculate red-tipped nails, at the feet opposite her own on the hearth rug, George's feet, in carefully shined shoes, somewhat worn . . . and none of it seemed quite right or very real. There was something unfamiliar about those shoes, as though she hadn't seen them a hundred times propped up on a kitchen chair. She had a silly desire to touch them. Her hands were cold.

"We used to sit in the kitchen."

"Or the patio," he said. He was smiling at her now. "What's the trouble, Laura?"

"Have you got some new shoes?" she asked stupidly?

"These? Nope."

She raised her eyes and felt her heart thump heavily like a logy bird. "Let's go out in the kitchen." She longed suddenly, passionately for her old baggy jeans and shirt. It was because she was so dressed up that she felt so queer.

"I like it here," said George. "I practically lived in that kitchen all semester, and now I'm on vacation. Entertain me. Make like a hostess."

He had been feeling good for two days, ever since he had turned in the work for one of his courses. This should have been the best time of all, thought Laura, but nothing is right somehow. The old easiness was gone.

It was ridiculous. Ever since she had put on the new dress, things had been different. Her hands got cold for no reason at all, she was afraid to look George in the eye, she wanted to hide when she saw him coming and wanted to weep when she didn't see him coming.

"It's getting dark," she said. "I'll turn on the tree lights." She stood by the lighted tree for a moment, staring out at the icebound December dusk. It would be Christmas in two days. "You ought to have a tree," she said.

"Oh, I'll share yours," said George comfortably. "Then I can sit around and look at you."

She didn't know how to answer. She tried to smile, and it didn't come off. She came back to the fireplace and stood looking at him with tears in her eyes. "George," she said, "I don't know how to be a girl."

"You wait," he said reassuringly. "It'll all come naturally."

If he would only touch me, she thought. Just take my hand or touch my hair. . . . She thought of Jim Roberts standing in the corridor with Sue Price, tugging gently at that lock of hair. Her breath stopped short with shock. Oh, no, she thought. Not George. I can't be . . . he couldn't . . . she turned dazed eyes on his face. He was looking at her queerly.

In that moment she nearly said it. The habit of utter frankness with him was so strong that the words almost got away: *Why, George, I love you.* The room seemed to fade and recede around them; it was a moment explosive with meaning. Laura clapped her hand over her mouth to keep back the words.

Yes, she thought with a kind of brilliant delight, it all comes naturally. She tumbled into the chair opposite him, her eyes slanting toward him with a mischief older than history.

She had always learned quickly.

FROM "PROBLEMS IN OBESITY:
A CASE STUDY" *page 45*
In the course of her diet Miss Stanley dropped from 200 pounds to 125. Indications are that her weight will be stabilized at about 125. Frequent physical checkups have established that the functioning of all vital organs has been improved and in no way impaired. Blood pressure is now normal. All strain has been taken off the heart. Daily exercise and out-of-doors walking have resulted in good muscle tone. Blemishes of the facial skin have disappeared. Indeed, Miss Stanley's only remaining problem is one of readjustment to the social group to which she belongs. Her natural qualities of leadership should make this step very easy.

Laura still thought George should have a tree. The day before Christmas she bought one for him. She stopped long enough at home to pick up some extra ornaments and a bag of artificial snow, and then ran next door. The landlady answered her knock.

"He ain't in, Laura," said Mrs. Slade. "I think he went shoppin'. My you look nice. You sure did thin down, didn't you?"

Laura laughed. "I sure did. Look, do you suppose I could set up this little tree in his room while he's gone and surprise him with it?"

"Sure," said Mrs. Slade. "Let me get the key." She walked down the hall with Laura and opened the door of Room 6. "I wouldn't do this for anybody else," she said, "but, my land! That boy practically lives over to your place, and I've known you forever, almost. So you go right on in and fix it up pretty."

"The desk was the best place, she decided, near the window. She peeped out through the shutters at her own backyard; the patio was covered with snow now. Her mouth curved gently. What was life like before he came, anyway? How was it possible? Her eyes dreamed over the patio. *That's where it all started. What an accident love is.*

She stirred, finally, and bent to the little tree. Her eyes fell on a slip of paper clipped to a manila folder. She saw the big *A*+ first and felt a stir of pride—naturally George's work would be superior. She read the professor's notation above the grade: "Excellent and unusual piece of work. Worth waiting for." So this was the paper George had needed an extension of time for. She wondered idly what it was about and flipped open the manila cover to glance at the title. Her eyes froze on the words: PROBLEMS IN OBESITY: A CASE STUDY. George Oliver Grant.

In that instant she knew.

She read it all. Everything was there, everything. He had split her wide open as he would a rabbit and held up each part for examination and discussion. It had all been planned, from the very first moment. He had been looking for an experiment in medical psychology; one look at her and he had whetted his knife. He had wanted to see her in her new clothes before Christmas, crown his efforts with a size 14. She was not a girl to him; she was a case study worth an *A*+. All these months he had watched her life like a bug under a microscope.

The manuscript was still in her hands when she heard George at the door. He came in whistling, his arms full of packages. He said, "Hey!" his voice pleased and surprised. Then he saw the folder.

The room grew completely still. The little evergreen lying on the desk gave the air a faint fragrance. Laura laid the manuscript down and walked toward the door, very steadily. She did not look at him.

"Laura?" he said questioningly. "Look, Laura . . ."

She walked on, not looking back, letting herself out the front door and walking heedlessly in her high heels through the drifted snow on the lawn and up the path. The wind cut through her coat and whipped her legs, but she felt nothing. He caught up with her as she reached the patio and blocked her way.

"You shouldn't have read that, Laura. Not yet."

She looked past him, her eyes on a distant snowy roof. "Were you saving it for me . . . for Christmas?"

He gripped her arm. "Don't be like that, Laura. Please."

"I thought you were my friend," she said. "That's funny, isn't it?" Her voice broke. "That's very funny."

"I was your friend. I *am* your friend." He needed a shave. He looked suddenly haggard, a little wild. "If we're not friends, then nothing makes any sense. You think I spent all those months with you for just a lousy term paper?"

"Yes," said Laura. "That's what I think." She moved to go, but his hand was on her arm, hard and angry.

"That's not so," he said. "And you know it. But what if it was so? Wasn't it worth it? Look at yourself now. Look at yourself. You're a beautiful girl, and the world is your oyster. Am I supposed to be ashamed of that? You can have anything you ever wanted. That old crowd of yours . . . one snap of your fingers, and they'll come running . . ."

"That old crowd . . ." Her smile was as wintry as the weather. Didn't he know that she could never fit into the old crowd now, even if she wanted to? More than the shape of her figure had changed in the past months: the whole shape of her mind had changed. "Do you really think that means anything to me now?"

He let go of her arm and stared. "It doesn't, does it?" he said in a changed voice. His eyes were dark, surprised. "Of course it doesn't. I thought I could give it all back to you, that I had to. But . . . you've left it all behind."

She turned again to go. "Laura?" he said. "Don't leave *me* behind."

She stopped, stunned by something in his voice she had never heard before, and searched his face. He looked strange, a little shy. "You're cold," he said, as though he had just discovered the weather. He pulled her scarf closer to her neck. "I love you," he said. "Don't you know that?" He buttoned her coat and turned up the collar. "When I went up to my room and saw you I had this great feeling, just seeing you there. And then when you left . . ." He traced her hairline with his finger and brushed the snow from her shoulders and picked up her hand. He studied it very carefully, as if he had never seen a hand before. "Don't ever walk away from me like that again," he said. "Don't *ever*." Laura said in a shaken voice, "I never could, again. But hold me. Hold me anyway."

When they finally turned to walk toward the warmth of the house, their feet were numb with cold, but neither of them noticed, and the snow, coming down steadily now, fell on their shoulders like spring flowers.

THE FOOD FARM
Kit Reed

At different times throughout history, the fat figure was looked upon as the ideal, desirable figure. For example, at the turn of the century, Lillian Russell—at a weight of over 200 pounds—was a reigning sex symbol. Today, the American cultural aesthetic of beauty ranges from the thin supermodel whose figure's proportions are unrepresentative of the naturally occurring shape of the human female, to an emaciated, sunken-eyed look termed "heroin chic."

Historically, men have gained credibility from their accumulated wealth and power, and at different times throughout history, fatness was seen as an indicator of wealth and abundance, and thus viewed as desirable. . . .

Based on anecdotal evidence, five to ten percent of the population has a sexual preference for a fat partner. Since fat partners are not considered attractive or desirable by modern American society, there is a high degree of stigmatization associated with such a preference. Due to this societal, peer, and parental pressure, individuals with such a preference see the preference itself as abnormal or shameful. As a result, most individuals who prefer fat partners suffer from self-doubt and often public ridicule. Many decide to stay "in the closet" about their preference because of this opposition. This denial of one's preference may lead to a disruption in personal growth and inadequate development of social and interpersonal skills. It may also lead to unhappy relationships with average-size partners chosen simply to conform to society's norms or to please parents, employers, or friends. As a result of this social stigma, relationships between fat people and their admirers are often unnecessarily difficult, and many people who could form happy, successful relationships never have the opportunity to meet.

—The National Association to Advance Fat Acceptance

◇

So here I am, warden-in-charge, fattening them up for our leader, Tommy Fango; here I am laying on the banana pudding and the milkshakes and the cream-and-brandy cocktails, going about like a technician, gauging their effect on haunch and thigh when all the time it is I who love him, I who could have pleased him eternally if only life had broken differently. But I am scrawny now, I am swept like a leaf around corners, battered by the slightest wind. My elbows rattle against my ribs and I have to spend half the day in bed so a gram or two of what I eat will stay with me, for if I do not, the fats and creams will vanish, burned up in my own insatiable furnace, and what little flesh I have will melt away.

Cruel as it may sound, I know where to place the blame.

It was vanity, all vanity, and I hate them most for that. It was not my vanity, for I have always been a simple soul; I reconciled myself early to reinforced chairs and loose garments, to the spattering of remarks. Instead of heeding them I plugged in, and I would have been happy to let it go at that, going through life with my radio in my bodice, for while I never drew cries of admiration, no one ever blanched and turned away.

But they were vain and in their vanity my frail father, my pale, scrawny mother saw me not as an entity but a reflection of themselves. I flush with anger to remember the excuses they made for me. "She takes after May's side of the family," my father would say, denying any responsibility. "It's only baby fat," my mother would say, jabbing her elbow into my soft flank. "Nelly is big for her age." Then she would jerk furiously, pulling my voluminous smock down to cover my knees. That was when they still consented to be seen with me. In that period they would stuff me with pies and roasts before we went anywhere, filling me up so I would not gorge myself in public. Even so I had to take thirds, fourths, fifths, and so I was a humiliation to them.

In time I was too much for them and they stopped taking me out; they made no more attempts to explain. Instead they tried to think of ways to make me look better; the doctors tried the fool's poor battery of pills; they tried to make me join a club. For a while my mother and I did exercises; we would sit on the floor, she in a black leotard, I in my smock. Then she would do the brisk one-two, one-two and I would make a few passes at my toes. But I had to listen, I had to plug in, and after I was plugged in naturally I had to find something to eat; Tommy might sing and I always ate when Tommy sang, and so I would leave her there on the floor, still going one-two, one-two. For a while after that they tried locking up the food. Then they began to cut into my meals.

That was the cruelest time. They would refuse me bread, they would plead and cry, plying me with lettuce and telling me it was all for my own good. My own good. Couldn't they hear my vitals crying out? I fought, I screamed, and when that failed I suffered in silent obedience until finally hunger drove me into the streets. I would lie in bed, made brave by the Monets and Barry Arkin and the Philadons coming in over the radio, and Tommy (there was never enough; I heard him a hundred times a day and it was never enough; how bitter that seems now!). I would hear them and then when my parents were asleep I would unplug and go out into the neighborhood. The first few nights I begged, throwing myself on the mercy of passers-by and then plunging into the bakery, bringing home everything I didn't eat right there in the shop. I got money quickly enough; I didn't even have to ask. Perhaps it was my bulk, perhaps it was my desperate subverbal cry of hunger; I found I had only to approach and the money was mine. As soon as they saw me, people would whirl and bolt, hurling a purse or wallet into my path as if to slow me in my pursuit; they would be gone before I could even express my thanks. Once I was shot at. Once a stone lodged itself into my flesh.

At home my parents continued with their tears and pleas. They persisted with their skim milk and their chops, ignorant of the life I lived by night. In the daytime I was complaisant, dozing between snacks, feeding on the sounds which played in my ear, coming from the radio concealed in my dress. Then, when night fell, I unplugged; it gave a certain edge to things, knowing I would not plug in again until I was ready to eat. Some nights I had to go into the streets, finding money where I could. Then I would lay in a new supply of cakes and rolls and baloney from the delicatessen and several cans of ready-made frosting and perhaps a fletch of bacon or some ham; I would toss in a basket of oranges to ward off scurvy and a carton of candy bars for quick energy. Once I had enough I would go back to my room, concealing food here and there, rearranging my nest of pillows and comforters. I would open the first pie or the first-half gallon of ice cream and then, as I began, I would plug in.

You had to plug in; everybody that mattered was plugged in. It was our bond, our solace and our power, and it wasn't a matter of being distracted, or occupying time. The sound was what mattered, that and the fact that fat or thin, asleep or awake, you were important when you plugged in, and you knew that through fire and flood and adversity, through contumely and hard times there was this single bond, this common heritage; strong or weak, eternally gifted or wretched and ill-loved, we were all plugged in.

Tommy, beautiful Tommy Fango, the others paled to nothing next to him. Everybody heard him in those days; they played him two or three times an hour but you never knew when it would be so you were plugged in and listening hard every living moment; you ate, you slept, you drew breath for the moment when they would put on one of Tommy's records, you waited for his voice to fill the room. Cold cuts and cupcakes and game hens came and went during that period in my life, but one thing was constant; I always had a cream pie thawing and when they played the first bars of "When a Widow" and Tommy's voice first flexed and uncurled, I was ready, I would eat the cream pie during Tommy's midnight show. The whole world waited in those days; we waited through endless sunlight, through nights of drumbeats and monotony, we all waited for Tommy Fango's records, and we waited for that whole unbroken hour of Tommy, his midnight show. He came on live at midnight in those days; he sang, broadcasting from the Hotel Riverside, and that was beautiful, but more important, he talked, and while he was talking he made everything all right. Nobody was lonely when Tommy talked; he brought us all together on that midnight show, he talked and made us powerful, he talked and finally he sang. You have to imagine what it was like, me in the night, Tommy, the pie. In a while I would go to a place where I had to live on Tommy and only Tommy, to a time when hearing Tommy would bring back the pie, all the poor lost pies. . . .

Tommy's records, his show, the pie . . . that was perhaps the happiest period of my life. I would sit and listen and I would eat and eat and eat. So great was my bliss that it became torture to put away the food at daybreak; it grew harder and harder for me to hid the cartons and the cans and the bottles, all the residue of my happiness. Perhaps a bit of bacon fell into the register; perhaps an egg rolled under the bed and began to smell. All right, perhaps I did become careless, continuing my revels into the morning, or I may have been thoughtless enough to leave a jelly roll unfinished on the rug. I became aware that they were watching, lurking just outside my door, plotting as I ate. In time they broke in on me, weeping and pleading, lamenting over every ice cream carton and crumb of pie; then they threatened. Finally they restored the food they had taken from me in the daytime, thinking to curtail my eating at night. Folly. By that time I needed it all, I shut myself in with it and would not listen. I ignored their cries of hurt pride, their outpourings of wounded vanity, their puny little threats. Even if I had listened, I could not have forestalled what happened next.

I was so happy that last day. There was a Smithfield ham, mine, and I remember a jar of cherry preserves, mine, and I remember bacon, pale and white on Italian bread. I remember sounds downstairs and before I could take warning, an assault, a company of uniformed attendants, the sting of a hypodermic gun. Then the ten of them closed in and grappled me into a sling, or net, and heaving and straining, they bore me down the stairs. I'll never forgive you, I cried, as they bundled me into the ambulance. I'll never forgive you, I bellowed as my mother in a last betrayal took away my radio, and I cried out one last time, as my father removed a hambone from my breast: I'll never forgive you, And I never have.

It is painful to describe what happened next. I remember three days of horror and agony, of being too weak, finally, to cry out or claw the walls. Then at last I was quiet and they moved me into a sunny, pastel, chintz-bedizened room. I remember that there were flowers on the dresser and someone watching me.

"What are you in for?" she said.

I could barely speak for weakness. "Despair."

"Hell with that," she said, chewing. "You're in for food."

"What are you eating?" I tried to raise my head.

"Chewing. Inside of the mouth. It helps."

"I'm going to die."

"Everybody thinks that at first. I did." She tilted her head in an attitude of grace. "You know, this is a very exclusive school."

Her name was Ramona and as I wept silently, she filled me in. This was a last resort for the few who could afford to send their children here. They prettied it up with a schedule of therapy, exercise, massage; we would wear dainty pink smocks and talk of art and theater; from time to time we would attend classes in elocution and hygiene. Our parents would say with pride that we were away at Faircrest, an elegant finishing school; we knew better—it was a prison and we were being starved.

"It's a world I never made," said Ramona, and I knew that her parents were to blame, even as mine were. Her mother liked to take the children into hotels and casinos, wearing her thin daughters like a garland of jewels. Her father followed the sun on his private yacht, with the pennants flying and his children on the fantail, lithe and tanned. He would pat his flat, tanned belly and look at Ramona in disgust. When it was no longer possible to hide her, he gave in to blind pride. One night they came in a launch and took her away. She had been here six months now, and had lost almost a hundred pounds. She must have been monumental in her prime; she was still huge.

"We live from day to day," she said. "But you don't know the worst."

"My radio," I said in a spasm of fear. "They took away my radio."

"There is a reason," she said. "They call it therapy."

I was mumbling in my throat, in a minute I would scream.

"Wait." With ceremony, she pushed aside a picture and touched a tiny switch and then, like sweet balm for my panic, Tommy's voice flowed into the room.

When I was quiet she said, "You only hear him once a day."

"No."

"But you can hear him any time you want to. You hear him when you need him most."

But we were missing the first few bars and so we shut up and listened, and after "When a Widow" was over we sat quietly for a moment, her resigned, me weeping, and then Ramona threw another switch and the Sound filtered into the room, and it was almost like being plugged in.

"Try not to think about it."

"I'll die."

"If you think about it you *will* die. You have to learn to use it instead. In a minute they will come with lunch," Ramona said and as The Screamers sang sweet background, she went on in a monotone: "A chop. One lousy chop with a piece of lettuce and maybe some gluten bread. I pretend it's a leg of lamb, that works if you eat very, very slowly and think about Tommy the whole time; then if you look at your picture of Tommy you can turn the lettuce into anything you want, Caesar salad or a whole smorgasbord, and if you say his name over and over you can pretend a whole bombe or torte if you want to and . . ."

"I'm going to pretend a ham and kidney pie and a watermelon filled with chopped fruits and Tommy and I are in the Rainbow Room and we're going to finish up with Fudge Royale . . ." I almost drowned in my own saliva; in the background I could almost hear Tommy and I could hear Ramona saying,

"Capon, Tommy would like capon, canard a l'orange, Napoleons, tomorrow we will save Tommy for lunch and listen while we eat . . ." and I thought about that, I thought about listening and imagining whole cream pies and I went on, ". . . lemon pie, rice pudding, a whole Edam cheese . . . I think I'm going to live."

The matron came in the next morning at breakfast, and stood as she would every day, tapping red fingernails on one svelte hip, looking on in revulsion as we fell on the glass of orange juice and the hard-boiled egg. I was too weak to control myself; I heard a shrill sniveling expression and realized only from her expression that it was my own voice: "Please, just some bread, a stick of butter, anything, I could lick the dishes if you'd let me, only please don't leave me like this, please . . ." I can still see her sneer as she turned her back.

I felt Ramona's loyal hand on my shoulder. "There's always toothpaste but don't use too much at once or they'll come and take it away from you."

I was too weak to rise and so she brought it and we shared the tube and talked about all the banquets we had ever known, and when we got tired of that we talked about Tommy, and when that failed, Ramona went to the switch and we heard "When a Widow," and tomorrow we would put off "When a Widow" until bedtime because then we would have something to look forward to all day. Then lunch came and we both wept.

It was not just hunger: after a while the stomach begins to devour itself and the few grams you toss it at mealtimes assuage it so that in time the appetite itself begins to fail. After hunger comes depression. I lay there, still too weak to get about, and in my misery I realized that they could bring me roast pork and watermelon and Boston cream pie without ceasing; they could gratify all my dreams and I would only weep helplessly, because I no longer had the strength to eat. Even then, when I thought I had reached rock bottom, I had not comprehended the worst. I noticed it first in Ramona. Watching her at the mirror, I said, in fear:

"You're thinner."

She turned with tears in her eyes. "Nelly, I'm not the only one."

I looked around at my own arms and saw that she was right: there was one less fold of flesh above the elbow; there was one less wrinkle at the wrist. I turned my face to the wall and all Ramona's talk of food did not comfort me. In desperation she turned on Tommy's voice, but as he sang I lay back and contemplated the melting of my own flesh.

"If we stole a radio we could hear him again," Ramona said, trying to soothe me. "We could hear him when he sings tonight."

Tommy came to Faircrest on a visit two days later, for reasons that I could not then understand. All the other girls lumbered into the assembly hall to see him, thousands of pounds of agitated flesh. It was that morning that I discovered I could walk again, and I was on my feet, struggling into the pink tent in a fury to get to see Tommy, when the matron intercepted me.

"Not you, Nelly."

"I have to get to Tommy. I have to hear him sing."

"Next time, maybe." With a look of naked cruelty she added, "You're a disgrace. You're still too gross."

I lunged, but it was too late; she had already shot the bolt. And so I sat in the midst of my diminishing body, suffering while every other girl in the place listened to him sing. I knew then that I had to act; I would regain myself somehow, I would find food and regain my flesh and then I would go to Tommy. I would use force if I had to, but I would hear him sing. I raged through the room all that morning, hearing the shrieks of five hundred girls, the thunder of their feet, but even when I pressed myself against the wall I could not hear Tommy's voice.

Yet Ramona, when she came back to the room, said the most interesting thing. It was some time before she could speak at all, but in her generosity she played "When a Widow" while she regained herself, and then she spoke:

"He came for something, Nelly. He came for something he didn't find."

"Tell about what he was wearing. Tell what his throat did when he sang."

"He looked at all the *before* pictures, Nelly. The matron was trying to make him look at the *afters* but he kept looking at the *befores* and shaking his head and then he found one and put it in his pocket and if he hadn't found it, he wasn't going to sing."

I could feel my spine stiffen. "Ramona, you've got to help me. I must go to him."

That night we staged a daring break. We clubbed the attendant when he brought dinner, and once we had him under the bed we ate all the chops and gluten bread on his cart and then we went down the corridor, lifting bolts, and when we were a hundred strong we locked the matron in her office and raided the dining hall, howling and eating everything we could find. I ate that night, how I ate, but even as I ate I was aware of a fatal lightness in my bones, a failure in capacity, and so they found me in the frozen food locker, weeping over a chain of link sausage, inconsolable because I understood that they had spoiled it for me, they with their chops and their gluten bread; I could never eat as I once had, I would never be myself again.

In my fury I went after the matron with a ham hock, and when I had them all at bay I took a loin of pork for sustenance and I broke out of that place. I had to get to Tommy before I got any thinner; I had to try. Outside the gate I stopped a car and hit the driver with the loin pork and then I drove to the Hotel Riverside, where Tommy always stayed. I made my way up the fire stairs on little cat feet and when the valet went to his suite with one of his velveteen suits I followed, quick as a tigress, and the next moment I was inside. When all was quiet I tiptoed to his door and stepped inside.

He was magnificent. He stood at the window, gaunt and beautiful; his blond hair fell to his waist and his shoulders shriveled under a heartbreaking double-breasted pea-green velvet suit. He did not see me at first; I drank in his image and then, delicately, cleared my throat. In the second that he turned and saw me, everything seemed possible.

"It's you." His voice throbbed.

"I had to come."

Our eyes fused and in that moment I believed that we two could meet, burning as a single, lambent flame, but in the next second his face had crumpled in disappointment; he brought a picture from his pocket, a fingered, cracked photograph, and he looked from it to me and back at the photograph, saying, "My darling, you've fallen off."

"Maybe it's not too late," I cried, but we both knew I would fail.

And fail I did, even though I ate for days, for five desperate, heroic weeks; I threw pies into the breach, fresh hams and whole sides of beef, but those sad days at the food farm, the starvation and the drugs have so upset my chemistry that it cannot be restored; no matter what I eat I fall off and continue to fall off; my body is a halfway house for foods I can no longer assimilate. Tommy watches, and because he knows he almost had me, huge and round and beautiful, Tommy mourns. He eats less and less now. He eats like a bird and lately has refused to sing; strangely, his records have begun to disappear.

And so a whole nation waits.

"I almost had her," he says, when they beg him to resume his midnight shows; he will not sing, he won't talk, but his hands describe the mountain of woman he has longed for all his life.

And so I have lost Tommy, and he has lost me, but I am doing my best to make it up to him. I own Faircrest now, and in the place where Ramona and I once suffered I use my skills on the girls Tommy wants me to cultivate. I can put twenty pounds on a girl in a couple of weeks and I don't mean bloat, I mean solid fat. Ramona and I feed them up and once a week we weigh and I poke the upper arm with a special stick and I will not be satisfied until the stick goes in and does not rebound because all resiliency is gone. Each week I bring out my best and Tommy shakes his head in misery because the best is not yet good enough, none of them are what I once was. But one day the time and the girl will be right—would that it were me—the time and the girl will be right and Tommy will sing again. In the meantime, the whole world waits; in the meantime, in a private wing well away from the others, I keep my special cases; the matron, who grows fatter as I watch her. And Mom. And Dad.

JELLY ROLLS
Jyl Lynn Felman

The negative reactions and anxieties aroused by obesity cannot be adequately explained by the argument that obesity is unhealthy. Many other things we do to ourselves are unhealthy, yet they do not incite the same kind of shame, hostility, and disapproval. Furthermore, many people have strong reactions to weight even when a person is not fat enough for health to be affected.

Clearly, obesity has become mythologized in our culture into something much more than a physical condition or a potential health hazard. Being overweight is now imbued with powerful symbolic and psychological meanings that deeply affect the person's identity in the world. In other words, the state of being fat is felt to express something basic about a person's character and personality.
— Marcia Millman, *Such a Pretty Face: Being Fat in America*

"Is this where the bus for Durham comes in?"

Edith Jeanne Drinkwater needed an answer to the exact same question, so she turned half a circle around. When she saw that she was facing a fat woman, Edith wanted to immediately complete the circle. But she couldn't do that because the fat woman had got hold of one of her eyes and wasn't letting go until Edith answered her question.

Edith had a thing about eye contact; it was just plain impolite to ignore someone else's eyes when they were aimed at you. So she looked, expecting to see a single big eye in the middle of a huge face. Much to her surprise the woman had two eyes just like she did. And the woman's eyes were the exact same color as her very own.

Unbelievable, Edith said to herself, not because she thought she had the only pair of green hazel eyes in the world; it was just that—Edith was laughing to herself—who would have thought that *fat* women had green eyes?

Before she knew what she was doing, thirty-five-year-old Edith found herself agreeing with the woman that Gate Three was their gate. Edith had never agreed with a fat woman in her entire life. She did not know what to do. She worried that the woman would assume friendship—think that the two of them could share a seat on the bus. Edith knew what she was going to have to do and she didn't like it one bit. She was going to have to force herself to take up an entire row of seats. In order to accomplish that—

because the size of her own body was so small—she now planned to spread her packages out over both seats instead of putting them on the rack above her as she usually did.

For the next fifteen minutes—to make her own position perfectly clear—Edith planned to ignore the fat woman. They had absolutely nothing in common; it was sheer coincidence that had the two of them riding the same bus to the same place this Sunday night. Edith's ears filled up. She knew that fat people always sounded like they were addressing the entire world with a single breath; they did not have small voices. The woman was trying to appear as though she were not addressing anyone in particular. When a young boy finally announced the bus's arrival time, "6:15," Edith leaned over to make sure she had heard right. After all, it was her bus too.

Quickly she stomped her sturdy Thom McAns on the floor of the Greyhound station. She had to keep her body firmly in place. Edith wondered if this woman understood the difference between herself and the rest of the human race. Edith knew the difference; she had always known the difference, ever since she was a little girl, and her mother had pointed all the way down the street at a blue bonnet. "That, E.J., is a fat woman; we don't mess with them. So don't let me catch you bringing one of them home for a glass of whole white milk and one of my homemade walnut-pecan butterscotch brownies. Friends like that you don't need—they're contagious." Edith had never forgotten her mother's wisdom. In fact last week she'd decided to point out that same blue bonnet to her daughter, next time they walked down the street together.

Edith felt green hazel eyes hanging onto her feet. She knew better than to think that anyone would stare like that at a single pair of Thom McAns, no matter how small the feet were that wore them. Edith was scared. For the first time since she'd entered the bus station, she wasn't precisely clear about what was going on around her. That wasn't like her; she wasn't herself today. She wasn't sure about anything and after a few more minutes of feeling fat green eyes move up and down her entire body, Edith's fear turned into panic. The fat woman was seeing something she shouldn't be seeing. Holding her packages close to her small breasts, Edith begged her feet to move her body forward. It had to be time to leave. Once she got on the bus, she knew she'd feel more like herself.

As she started for the gate, Edith felt an entire army coming after her. There must be some mistake; everybody had begun to follow Edith. This had never happened to her. She was no leader. She knew her place, and that had always been toward the end of every line. She was not one to push her way forward. Thin people never had to push and shove. Thin people were always sandwiched in between the larger people so that nothing would happen to them. That was the way Edith had always seen life work.

She found herself glancing around for the fat woman, who she saw, much to her dismay, was bringing up the end of the army. Because Edith had decided to wait and board last, what Edith had most feared *might* happen, already *had* happened. Everyone going to Durham, New Hampshire, had assumed the two women were travelling together, and that they knew when to board the bus. Edith sincerely hoped the woman would take over the lead; then the confusion would clear up once and for all.

Somewhere in the background their bus was called and the fat woman took over the lead at the same time. Edith had stopped moving. When the announcement was over, the woman's ticket was in the driver's hand. Edith smiled at her feet, feeling almost like her old self again. The fat woman had taken over the responsibility for leading the people home. That was the way all life should be. In case there was any danger, it would happen to the fat woman first. Besides, there was always a draft at the beginning of the line. Edith knew that fat people didn't get cold like the rest of them. She had only seen their kind dressed in thin coats with hardly any buttons. That was definitely the only lucky part about being a fat person; you didn't feel the cold. Edith was cold now, and although that meant she might be sick in bed tomorrow, it also meant she wasn't fat.

She had been standing in one place for so long that everyone had passed her up. She was the last passenger to board the bus. Edith gave the driver her ticket without looking him in the face. She was keeping her green-hazel eyes to herself and she was putting one foot directly in front of the other. She wasn't going to look for a seat until she was smack at the front of the aisle. No single individual was going to get this very cold but thin woman to lift her eyes until she was ready. When her feet were in place Edith was amazed. The confusion was still not over.

The problem was that the fat woman had seated herself directly behind the driver, while all the real passengers had seated themselves behind the entire first row. How could they do this to her: leave her up front with that woman? What if her daughter had been travelling with her? How could she have explained to such a young child why they had to sit in the fat section? Edith lifted her eyes slowly; before she took her seat she was going to have her say. She made her eyes go from seat to seat until they'd been up and down the whole aisle; she wanted the people to know that Edith Jeanne Drinkwater knew exactly what had happened; they had deserted her, one of their own. Only the fat woman met her gaze, waiting for Edith to take the row of seats across the aisle from her own row. Edith stared into the eyes of her people. *Thank you, each and every one of you for making my dream come true. All day I was praying for the first seat on this bus. That way, as soon as we turn down Main Street, my daughter will see—even before I get off the bus—that her mother has come home. You are all good people and I thank you.*

Edith had made her eyes carry all the way to the back of the bus. Satisfied that she had excluded the fat woman from her gaze and that she had redeemed herself, she sat down, calmly waiting for the bus to begin its journey. Her own mother would have been proud of her. Edith had seen the heat of the fire coming straight for her, but she'd turned it ice-cold without ever getting burned. For the first time since this whole mess had started, she'd almost forgotten the fat woman existed. With a little more concentration, she was sure she could finish her off for good.

She'd just close her eyes and see if she could imagine the woman's seat giving way. Then the fat woman would be left out in the road. In order to keep moving, the back wheels of the bus would have to roll right over her.

Edith thought she could do it. She'd been in strong control of her imagination ever since she was a child. But when Edith closed her eyes, nothing happened. She blinked fast and closed them again tighter, in case there had been a mistake. This time she concentrated more. But behind her eyes was no fat woman falling through the floor of the bus. There was nothing but the black of the night behind those green hazel eyes.

Edith knew from past experience that some things took more work than others. She would try harder. After all, they were *her* eyes; if she couldn't get them to see what she wanted to see, nobody else could. She closed her eyes again, but had to open them immediately. Clearly there had been some confusion. She would close her eyes one more time to make sure that what she thought she was seeing, she wasn't seeing at all. There was no mistaking what was going on behind Edith's eyes. Food. Lots of food. It was the fat woman up to no good, and Edith wasn't going to stand for it. Just because they both had green-hazel eyes did not mean they had to see the world the same. Never before had she lost her own clear sight and never before had she closed her eyes and seen only food.

The bus was not due in Durham for over an hour. That was long enough to regain her own sight. Edith remembered there had been a single occasion in her youth when her eyesight had been impaired. She had not listened to her mother, who had told her never to look straight into the sun or she might go blind for life. Edith hadn't gone blind for life though, she'd only lost sight for a few seconds. For those few seconds, she had felt separated from the entire human race. That had been the most horrible feeling she had ever hoped to feel. Even as a child she could not stand being separated from her people. Although that seemed to be happening again, only this time right in front of her eyes.

Edith could feel her body resting; she was tired from all the confusion. Her eyes closed. The food came back into view but Edith didn't even try to make it go away. At the same time her small body spread out small across the entire seat. She was careful not to interfere with her packages. It felt good to be going to sleep. She was one of them after all; Edith had seen lots of her people sleeping on buses, spread out in all directions. Everything was going to be fine.

In the middle of her dreams, Edith woke to find herself staring at the fat woman's stomach. The woman had slumped over and spread out in all directions just like Edith had done. The woman had no right to copy Edith's body position. The fat woman was even taking up both seats. Edith could see absolutely no reason why they had to sit in identical positions. She moved her body immediately, careful not to squash her husband's sweet rolls.

Edith tried to bring her legs together before the bus driver looked into his rear view mirror and noticed the unladylike position she'd gotten herself into. But nothing happened. She couldn't get her eyes to remove themselves from the fat woman's stomach. Never before had she lost so much control of her faculties. She was clearly not herself today. She would have to try again to move her legs, because as long as Edith had known her husband he had refused to eat his sweet rolls if they were the least bit flat. Any minute her right thigh was going to flatten those jelly rolls out for good.

Just as she tried lifting her legs, Edith's eyes started talking inside her head. She wondered what exactly was inside the fat woman's stomach. Maybe, if she stared hard enough, she could see in through all that thick flesh. Her eyes imagined thick piles of white powdered sugar where she supposed the top of the woman's stomach began. She stared harder; Edith laughed to herself. The white powder was turning into a giant jelly roll.

She got hold of herself fast. She did not like the idea of the fat woman and her husband eating the same food even if it was only for breakfast. That meant her husband's stomach could one day look like the fat woman's stomach. Edith knew she could never serve a fat man dinner at her table. She was going to act faster than she had ever acted in her entire life. Edith's hand reached to secure from under her thigh the bag which held her husband's jelly rolls.

That was when Edith noticed the fat woman's mouth opening and closing while she slept. It appeared the woman was eating the air. When her mouth closed, anyone could see she was chewing and swallowing. Edith knew eating when she saw it, and the fat woman was eating in her sleep. Edith felt her left hand open her husband's jelly roll bag. She knew what she had to do to keep her husband from turning into a fat woman. Her hand sank fast and deep into the white powdered sugar. She crumpled some powder between her fingers while she watched the fat woman eating the very air on the bus. The next time the fat woman's mouth opened, Edith's mouth opened right along with hers. Slowly at first, just to get the feeling of chewing on a moving bus. It felt good; Edith got her jaw moving in the same round motion as the fat woman's jaw.

She hummed to herself, softly so she wouldn't wake the woman. She was beginning to feel weightless, which was not hard for someone of Edith's small size. Her hand caught hold of one of the big jelly rolls. All she had to do to save her man was bring that roll up to her mouth while her lips were parted. If she got it up there while her lips were closed, Edith didn't know what would happen. She might push the roll back into the bag fast and stop all this rescue work immediately. She pictured her kitchen table which was only big enough for three small people. She saw her husband sitting down to his breakfast and getting up too big to ever sit down again. Quickly she stuffed the entire sweet roll into her mouth.

Powdered sugar was everywhere. Edith couldn't see clearly because some of the white stuff was floating right in front of her eyes. She waved her arms, hoping her vision would clear. When she could see again, she saw the fat woman staring straight at her husband's bag of red jelly rolls. Edith said NO! out loud. Faster than she had done before, she stuffed another jelly roll into her mouth. The woman just kept staring as if Edith hadn't said a word. Edith tried to chew faster. Eating on the bus wasn't so bad after all; it helped pass the time.

She knew there were exactly twelve rolls left. She'd bought fourteen—a week's supply. They had all been for her husband, who ate two a day with black coffee. After a week the jelly dried up and her husband said the white powder started cracking. He wouldn't have to worry about that this week. Edith ate two more sweet rolls in time with the turning bus wheels. The fat woman was still staring at Edith's bag as if she understood what Edith was doing. But she couldn't possibly understand. Edith assured herself that she was only eating to save her husband. She was certainly not eating because she was hungry.

She swallowed hard; she had almost choked on the sixth jelly roll. She had stopped paying full attention to what she was doing. She had begun to think hard about the fat woman. She hoped that the woman did not assume they suffered from the same illness. Edith was positive that she had nothing in common with that woman. Their kind ate to save themselves, but Edith was eating to save her family. There was a huge difference. She had only four rolls left; she was going to miss all that white powder floating down in front of her. She had almost forgotten where she was; she'd actually begun to float like when the dentist filled her up with gas. Edith knew she was not quite in control of her faculties, but that didn't matter anymore. She felt good. She had no idea red sweet jelly rolls made you feel so lightheaded.

Her whole body was jumping. Instead of feeling heavy and full, she had those female twitches between her legs. Her thighs pushed into each other; she felt her whole body puffing up like a fresh hot roll coming straight from the oven to the table. Just as Edith pictured the baker filling the roll with all that sweet red jelly, she gave out a bigger groan than she'd ever remembered giving out while lying right next to her very own man. Her thighs were calming down. She almost hated to let go of all that sweetness between her legs. But she'd finished the last jelly roll; there was no more white powder blocking her vision. Quickly, Edith commanded her legs to relax. She looked down at her feet just to make sure her Thom McAns were still there. Then she pulled her dress down as far over her knees as it would go.

The fat woman's head was nodding to the same beat as Edith's head. Edith looked at where the woman's thighs ought to be; she panicked. She couldn't make out two thighs in all that slumped-over body. But she wasn't exactly looking for thighs; she was more looking for why their heads were nodding together at the exact same time. The fat woman seemed to be feeling real good. As if she felt what Edith had just been feeling when she finished off the last jelly roll to save her family. Then Edith did it; she couldn't stop herself. She locked her own green-hazel eyes straight onto the fat woman. Then her vision cleared, clearer than it had been all day. The fat woman had got what she wanted. She was nodding her head slowly, pushing something from her head directly into Edith Jeanne Drinkwater's.

Edith had no choice but to accept what the woman was giving her; she had locked their eyes together. Besides she had been waiting her whole life for a single moment of truth. She'd always known she was capable of visions sent by the Lord, only Edith never expected to receive from a fat woman riding on a moving bus. Here they were, taking up the whole front row including the aisle; it was unavoidable. That was the way her mother said the Lord always worked—He was unavoidable when you most wanted to be avoided. Edith decided to act with courage. If this was her moment, she was going to receive and be hallowed. Only it was too bad she had come to peace through the fat woman's eyes. Edith decided to prepare herself. She quit thinking altogether and opened her eyes as wide as she possibly could.

She shook her head, shaking out what the Lord was sending in. She was seeing herself staring out at her from the fat woman's eyes. Only it wasn't exactly Edith. It was, as far as she could tell, Edith—a wee bit deformed. She was still five feet one-and-a-half inches tall and her arms were still short and slender, but her stomach had been pulled way out of shape. In the eyes of that woman Edith was fat, so fat that her stomach took up both of the woman's eyes. Edith was horrified; she had never seen such a big stomach before. She was not at all clear that this was what the Lord Jesus had wanted her to see when she gave her eyes to the fat woman.

Her stomach grumbled; the picture was making her ill. She thought for a moment that if she could just open the moving bus window, she could throw up all fourteen jelly rolls into the street and let the bus roll right over them, killing the red jelly out flat. Then she could forget everything. But Edith knew that was impossible. She'd swallowed hard every single bite of those sweet red rolls; she'd taken them in as if in preparation for her single moment of truth.

Edith was still staring at herself in the fat woman's eyes when she noticed her neck had disappeared into her stomach. All of a sudden she saw one head after another rise up out of the stomach and take over. There must be some mistake. The heads had begun to look like her mother's and her mother's sister's heads. It was horrible; the fat woman was gulping down all the women Edith had ever known. Finally, Edith's own head came back. She smiled out at herself, only the smile seemed far away. She forced her eyes to focus. The smile was hiding under a thick veil and Edith was wearing a blue bonnet. She was becoming that woman. They all were were becoming one giant fat woman. Edith began to think that inside every thin woman was a fat woman waiting to get out.

Edith took her eyes back. What if all the other passengers had seen what just happened to her? She sucked her stomach in; nobody was going to call Edith Jeanne Drinkwater fat. Nobody on this bus was going to know what Edith knew. It was okay for Edith to know that all of them—all the women on the bus—were one and the same. But she wasn't going to be the one shouting out the new gospel, even if the vision had come her way first. She reminded herself that she'd never been one for leadership; she had no ability there. She could follow through, without losing a single step. Edith made a decision to walk off the bus as if nothing had happened. As if nothing concerning the order of things had changed. She was going to hold her stomach in for the rest of her life, just to make sure no one guessed the truth. Oh, she'd come around once the others did. But not until then; she was going to keep it all to herself just as her mother had done with her. She would not point out that blue bonnet to her daughter after all. Edith was going to keep silent and keep her stomach in.

When the bus finally stopped moving, it stopped where it always did. She was glad for that. At least some things never changed. The bus stopped, even with the flagpole which was right across the street from Young's Coffee Shop. The fat woman stood up at the same time Edith did. In fact, they almost bumped into each other stepping into the aisle. Edith couldn't wave to her daughter who she knew was standing right in front of the flagpole. She was too busy trying to avoid connecting with the fat woman. But she saw she needn't worry. The woman was holding back, letting Edith go first. That was the polite thing to do, she told herself. Those people had to learn to wait their turn. Edith choked on the end of that thought.

When the driver opened the doors of the bus, Edith felt like her own stomach was opening up. The doors opened straight down the middle. She could breathe again. Her left Thom McAn led her into the aisle. There still seemed to be some confusion as to who was going out first. She thought it had all been decided. So it had. Just as Edith's left foot took the lead, the woman opened her mouth, "You go first, honey. I'm in no hurry. Besides, it doesn't matter anyway." Edith wanted to stop in the middle of the aisle, turn around and head straight back to her seat. But she'd already put both feet on the ground and the fat woman was right behind her, putting down her own two feet on the very same ground.

HE WAS A MAN!
(BUT HE DID HIMSELF WRONG)

J. California Cooper

I realize now that I tolerate a level of disrespect from people about being fat that I would never, ever permit about being Black or female. It is a tolerance born of shame, an undercurrent so pervasive that I have trouble even typing the word *fat*. . . . I can still be persuaded, when I'm not in my right mind, that thin people are happier, prettier, more focused, more balanced. At those moments I can still be persuaded that thin people have richer lives, that they're better people than I am. But that is the wounded me. And I am learning, at last, to love and care for her as best I can.

—Rosemary Bray, "Heavy Burden"

I have always been the kind of person who wonders about people and things and I have some neighbors who have kept me pretty busy with plenty to wonder about! It's not real important how or where Smitty and Della met, the main thing is they were married nine years when I got to know them. At first, because of the way the world looks at things, they seemed an unlikely, funny couple. He was short, 5 feet or so, 125 pounds, while Della was 5'7" or so, and 207 pounds. You pictured them making love and in your mind it was really funny, but you shouldn't do that picturing stuff because making love, real love, is never funny! Remember the heart has its own way of picking a partner and never asks for measurements.

Anyway, Smitty was a feisty, loudmouthed, bragging, aggressive little man. Always trying to out-talk or out-do some taller man. But Della loved him even beyond the love-is-blind thing. Anything Smitty did was alright with Della.

I mean even the way she cooked his meals; he had so many things he disliked and his food had to be just right. I mean JUST RIGHT! He was the kind of man who even liked gravy on his lamb chops! Very few vegetables, hardly any fruit and all that! All of which made Della gain more weight because of course she had to taste it to be sure it was just right. She could make homemade bread that would make you kill yourself. She did everything, Della did. Wash, cook, clean, garden, shop, chauffeur, watch football games, listen to him lie, pet, massage, and make love too. Maybe more, you know. I don't know everything.

I know he was proud of Della, he was always bragging down there at the pool hall and at work about her, but he never told her, thinking just staying with her was enough. Well, after nine years, maybe he was right. Their marriage musta been strong because they got over some real big hurdles which made me wonder at the way it all turned out.

Like, one time I ran over to their house. They had a nice little house, sitting all by itself on a neat little lot, that they rented. Anyway, I went over there and he was standing on a box directing her how to tie a rope over a beam so he could hang her. SHOUTING "I am the man! You gon have to do what I say! I ain't taking NO shit!" Della just crying, trying to tie that rope like he telling her. Well, I talked them out of it that time. I think he was glad because he didn't know no other way to back down and give her her life back. I told her later "You are a fool! Big as you is, you gonna let that littler man kill you? Help him kill you?!" That's when I found out it wasn't the first time. Anyway she just said, "I don't think he was really gonna do it!" and smiling, went on about cooking him something special. I just really want you to know she thought he was special, that he had power, black and otherwise! Whatever he said she believed him. I mean . . . that man had him a woman!

Now there's always a little hell waiting round paradise and Della's hell was that every once in awhile, Smitty hit her, abused her. It hurt and it didn't hurt! But it seemed to do so much for him, being so small and all, hitting a woman so large, she never tried to hit him back. He would tell everyone down at the pool hall and work (again) that "I know I am boss!" He pranced as he told them, his chest stuck out in pride, he had a lot of that! He had whipped his woman, all 207 pounds of her! . . . all those pounds that loved him.

Their bed had to be braced up by bricks underneath so the mattress wouldn't tilt when Della got in bed and bring him crashing over to her side, reminding him of his size. One night when they were sleeping, someone broke into the house. Don't know what they came for cause Della and Smitty didn't have nothing much special. Just one of these crazy people that don't have sense enough to be honest and ain't got sense enough to know how to be dishonest and rob somebody with something! Anyway, Della heard the noise and woke Smitty up. He lay there a moment then said "Let's go see what's going on." He hollered from the bed, "Who's there! Who's in this house?"

They got up and went into the hall and there was this dope addict or something looking raggedy and holding a gun. Smitty ran past him, going to get his gun, I guess, and Della got scared and tried to follow him past the robber, who was then squashed against the wall with Della screaming at him to let her go! She must have hit him or something, he was really trying to get out of that tight spot with all that mouth wide open screaming in his ears, and probably hoping somebody would come in and save him from his victims, but their house stood all alone and the café-bar across the street made so much noise, nobody could hear them. The gun went off around that time and Della thought Smitty had saved her when Smitty came rushing around a corner hollering Della's name, guess he thought she had been shot, and the robber slid down the wall at her feet, dead.

Smitty hadn't been able to find his gun. They grabbed each other and looked at the dead man; he had shot himself with Smitty's gun . . . accidentally. Della said, "We gotta call the police!" Smitty said back, "Wait a minute! Let's talk about this!" So they did. Smitty continued. "Now listen. . . if we call them cops we gon have a lot of trouble! That's my gun! And I ain't got no license for it! And I can't prove I didn't pull that trigger and put that gun in his hand! All them cops look at TV and ain't no tellin what they gon decide happened here!" Della's eyes grew even wider. "Well, what else can we do? We can't throw him outside in the street!" Smitty shot back, "Oh yes we can! That's just what we got to do."

He ran to look out the window with Della following him, her large white flannel gown billowing around her. No one was in sight and the music blasting from the café. It was settled in Smitty's mind . . . the dead man was going outside. Della started crying til Smitty slapped her into just whimpering and sniffling. She went to get her robe and a cap and Smitty went to get an old blanket out of his car. She noticed the blood that had flowed from the man's wound and went to get a bandaid, Smitty came back and snatched it and stuck it in the man's shirt pocket. In fact, they did all the wrong things you see on TV. They rolled the man up and when the café closed and all was dark they carried the corpse over to the empty lot and left it! Went home, cleaned up, wiped off the gun, put it back in the drawer and went to bed with Smitty explaining, "I didn't kill him, you didn't kill him, so we ain't got nothing to do with it! He broke in our house, took our gun (everything was suddenly 'our') and shot his own self! We didn't know him before, we don't know him now! So go to sleep and forget the whole thing!". . . So they did. See, what I mean, something that's big like death, they stepped over that like it was a broom!

Anyway, the police found the body the next day, took it somewhere and did something and since the man was black the case was closed, even with all those clues, stamped "killed by person or persons unknown . . . CLOSED!" and that was that. Smitty and Della picked up their life and went on as usual. He felt real smart cause he had handled it real smart so he began to add, when they had arguments, "You ain't got no sense! If it wasn't for me, a man in this house, ain't no telling what would happen to you!" Della smiled at all that, she was used to it and she loved her Smitty!

Then this thing happened that made me wonder at them because they had been through such big things and this seemed little to me, you might say.

It was a day that Della had not been feeling well; maybe lost a baby or something almost as important; she was always talking bout having a baby and Smitty was always trying to make one. Also, her special cake for Smitty had burned while she was trying to untangle something in the washing machine wringer and when she put the cake on the sink, she burnt her hand and in flinging her arm out she hit the filled dish drainer rack. It fell to the floor and dishes and glass flew everywhere! She was barefoot and cut her foot tipping across the floor. She burst into loud, dreadful tears and ran into the hall past the sign that read, "God Bless This Home" through the pink door she had painted because pink made her feel like a woman going into a romantic bedroom. She flung herself across the bed onto the spread she had crocheted painstakingly to laugh and love on. She cried herself to sleep.

When Smitty came home, he did his lion's roar at the door and receiving no answer he went through the house and found Della asleep and . . . he got mad! He started stomping around and shouting at her about the dirt (there was no dirt). The filthy kitchen (just broken dishes, that's all). No dinner (well, there was none, but my lord!) The messed up favorite cake (as if it was on purpose) and anything else his little mind could come up with! He never did ask her what was wrong. He kept shouting, "A man this and a man that."

Della swung her legs around and sat on the edge of the bed and tried to smile and explain. She was still trying to smile and explain when Smitty came rushing up and slapped her twice! One way and then back the other! Her arm must have shot out instinctively in reaction and she caught him solid and he flew all way cross the room, through the door and hit the wall in the hall and blacked out! Now, that alone was bad enough but Della went and picked him up and placed him in bed! That Della was strong! So when he woke up, an hour or so later, he looked around him and . . . cried. Now he really was a man, ain't no question, but he cried . . . him! . . . Smitty!

Della came rushing into the room at the sound of the crying and when she saw him she started crying too. "What's wrong? Are you hurt daddy? What's the matter, baby?" But he pushed her away, snot and spit flying, then he snarled at her from his pain . . . an ego can be a dangerous, painful thing. "Get away from me! Get away! I hate you, you big, fat, ugly bear! You a ape! A gorilla! You ain't no woman!"

"But, Smitty," she began to whine and try to ease him but he wouldn't have any of that! He got up trying to move without showing his pain and got the little raggedy suitcase (they didn't never go anywhere so they didn't need no new ones) and began to throw things in it. Della's eyes were big and red and swollen, she kept trying to grab his shirts and underwear from him, but he done stopped crying now and was really talking mean to her, calling her all kinds of names, sloppy fat bitches and things like that! It was untrue and it hurt her. You could almost see her drawing up, shrinking, every time a word struck her. Seemed like the words were razor blades cutting her to ribbons. This was her Smitty talking to her!

As Smitty got to the door he turned, "I can't never live with you no more!

You always gonna think you bettern me! That's what you want . . . to be the man! Well, I ain't staying nowhere I can't be the man! You get yourself and your stuff together and get out of my house as soon as you get you some money! I'm takin all we got now cause I done made it all white you sat chere on your ass! You the man now, you can get you some more!" Della reached for him, "Please daddy, baby, please daddy, don't go! Don't leave me! I'm SORRY (she screamed that). I didn't mean to hit you! Please don't go. I'm begging you! Daddy, I'm begging you!" She grabbed his arm and such a hate in his face went down to his arm and he struck her so hard she just let go and stood there with her arms hanging and her tears pouring, down. He left, leaving the door open so she could watch him leaving, wobbling away dragging that suitcase, taking the car. She finally shut the door and went to bed, for two weeks.

I tended her and checked on her but she wouldn't eat nothing or talk and usually she's a big talker. But time takes care of everything and time took care of her. Pretty soon she got up and got on out to find work. She was still grieving, but with every bad there's some good and she was losing weight like thunder. Smitty got him a room somewhere and was busy telling everybody everywhere that he done left Della. "Wasn't gonna keep no woman who wants to be the man in his family, Della didn't know how to treat no man but she would before he sat foot in that house again." He meant it too . . . he said! But every day when he come out of that door at work, lunch and quitting time, he seem to be looking for somebody. Pretty soon, he would go to the windows and peer out all through the day, but nobody was there . . . least not Della. He let everybody know where he lived, but she didn't go there either!

I caught her one day, just a cussing to herself, crying. I said, "What's the matter with you Della?" "Nothing," she answered, "Just repeating all the names Smitty called me so I don't forget and go running out there after him." Well, that was Della's formula and it seemed to work. She didn't go! As she kept crying and grieving she grew thinner and her clothes began to hang on her. She looked terrible, but didn't care. I tried to make her eat but she wouldn't.

There was a church social coming up and I talked two days to get her to go and even helped her to buy some new things to wear that fit her. I can tell you honestly that Della at 135 pounds was a whole new better Della than she was at 207 pounds! She was good looking! And with that big, sweet, innocent, sad smile, she was pretty and the men let her know it! She danced every dance once I got her started, and laughed and laughed and laughed with happiness! Smitty wasn't there, he was probably at the pool hall bragging bout his hold on her. I ain't gonna say a lot about it, but there was a nice man there named Charles . . . and he took to Della like wet takes to water! Soon, they was going out together, being seen a lot. Smitty heard about it. He wanted to come around and save his ego at the same time so he began to come around the house and tell her she had to move out, he needed a place. I know he wanted her to say, "Come on home then," but she didn't. Instead she said, "Give me a month to see what I'm gonna do and how, then I be gone." He didn't really want that house, he wanted Della, but his pride and ego kept him from tellin her. I don't really know what would have happened if he had told her, but anyway, Charles told her to move in with him, he was buying his own house. She just said she would think about it.

One day Smitty came by to check on his "house" and Charlie was there. Smitty said, blustering, "Well, I'm here now and you better go! This is a husband talking to his wife and you oughta leave!"

Charlie answered softly, "Well, Smitty, I didn't come to see you at your invitation . . . I came to see Della at her invitation, so you can't tell me to go . . . only Della can do that!" Smitty said, taken aback, "This is my house! I say what goes on here! And this is my wife!" Della said softly, "This the landlord's house and I been paying the rent Smitty, so it's not your house." She looked neat and clean and pretty and you could smell the food cooking! Smitty repeated, stubborn, "I want to talk to my WIFE!" Charlie said, just as stubborn, "When she tells me to go, I will!" Della said, "I invited him to supper Smitty, I can't tell my company to go!" Smitty said, "I'm your man, invite me to supper!" Della said back "No . . . you said you wasn't my man, that I was the man. Charlie don't think I'm a man."

Smitty, quick to think wrong, "Why don't he think you a man? What you been doin with him?" He balled his fist up! Charlie put in "I hope to marry Della some day."

Smitty said, "She already married! To me!" They both looked surprised when Della said, "I ain't made up my mind about anything!" She looked thoughtful for a minute then continued, "Charlie will eat supper, then he will go, then you can come back and talk." Smitty was outdone! "Come back?" he asked. Della was up to it. "If you want to!"

So Smitty left, but before he was out the door completely Charlie said, standing in the doorway like it was his, "Smitty, I am interested in Della and she is my friend, so if I leave it ain't so you can do whatever you want to her. Don't hurt her, don't touch her, because I will know about it!" Smitty left mumbling to hisself that wasn't nobody gonna do nothing to him!

Now, all the time I been knowing Della, she always said how Smitty didn't remember no birthday presents or Valentines day or nothing, she always gave him things, but when Smitty came back he was dressed up and had a bag of candy I his right hand and some flowers in his left hand. But he came in fussing, "Ain't you gon offer me no dinner or cake or nothin? Are you just gonna give some to that Charles that don't want nothing but to go to bed with you? Then he gon be gone, just like he done all them other women I done heard of!" Della jumped up and went to get some cake and don't you think Smitty didn't take heart from that! "Sure," she said, "I got plenty cake. You want some coffee?" Smitty leaned back, smiling, "Yes, I would like some coffee, too!"

As he ate the cake, Della was quiet but he talked a lot about how well he was doing. "And I been thinking bout takin a trip, like a vacation!" Della sighed, he went on talking, "Maybe putting some money in this house to make it look a little better!" Della looked around the room and nodded. He smiled and went on "Might even go-head and try to get one of my own!" Della's eyes opened wide and she said "It must be nice to own your own house!" That encouraged him, his chest came out and he decided to play his ace card and hit Della with something that would wake her up and make her realize she didn't want to lose him!

"Della," he said, serious-like in a new deep voice, as he wiped the last cake crumb from the saucer with his finger, "Della, we gon have to do something . . . now . . . or I'm going to get a divorce!" The room was real quiet while Della stared at Smitty, her man for so long.

"You done found somebody else you love, Smitty?"

He laughed. "No, I don't want none of these women that keep running after me! They worry me to death!" He flecked off a speck from his pants as he waited for her to cry out "I don't want no divorce Smitty!" But she didn't. She just sat there staring down at the floor and pretty soon tears came slowly down her cheeks. Smitty saw this and felt his point was won. He stood up and stuck his chest out saying, "Well Della, we can't go on like this . . . I'm a man!" Della looked up and the tears stopped and dried. "I need a woman! and if it's gonna be you then say so, if it ain't, then I better get on bout my business and . . . (he leaned toward her) get my divorce!" He waited a moment for her to say the words that would give him his old good life back, but there was only silence, Della looking at the floor again. He straightened up and looked around the home toward the bedroom where he really wanted to go and lay his big pride down. He tried to think of a way to stretch his visit out, but had played his ace too soon, so he cleared his throat and gave himself the next invitation. "I'll be by in a few days to get your answers and I'm gonna come with my bags, Della!" It was said almost like a question.

Della started crying and he went to put his arms around her and rub on her back. "Della, you know I'm your man, now act like you got some sense girl and cut out all this dating and stuff! You my wife and you lucky and he lucky I didn't kick ass this day!" She stepped back from his arms. He continued, "Go wash your face and go to bed, no more company tonight! I'll be back in a few days, Friday, with my bags and get your life back together again cause you acting like a fool!" (Sometimes I wonder about people.) She let him kiss her and then led him to the door and he left feeling good about being a man about the whole thing.

Della didn't sleep much that night and got up saying she "might as well get this over with" and went down town and got a lawyer and filed for a divorce, which takes 30 days in this town, then came home and moved most of her stuff in my house. When Friday came she went over and sat on a chair right in front of the door and waited for Smitty. He came grinning in with his suitcase without knocking and she handed him the papers saying, "This what you want Smitty, if you want it, it must be right! But I like married life so I'm gonna be marrying up with Charles when this is final. I done moved so here is your house . . . now, I'll be going!" He cussed her again but didn't try to hit her and he told her "I don't want this house, ain't nothin' in it!" She left first, then he did and the next day she moved all her stuff back in it!

She was true to her word. When the divorce was final, the marriage plans was made. I wondered about all that so I ask her, "Don't you think you rushin into one marriage after another?" She always takes her time to answer, "No. . . ." she said, "I really done learned a lot. I have learned in these few months when I been workin on a job and workin this stuff out with Smitty. I know bout cookin and not havin to cook. I know about a peaceful house when you alone in it . . . havin your own money or waiting for somebody to bring you some . . . and sleepin alone, or with a husband! My life ain't never gonna be like it was before . . . ever again! But . . . I like havin a husband, I want a man of my own!" So the marriage plans went on.

I was just sitting at home sewing and wondering about people when about two days before the little wedding, Della came running and screaming over to my house, tears streaming down, she was what you call hyster . . . rical! She couldn't say a word, just screaming "Smitty," so I followed her over to her house. Smitty was hanging from that same rafter he was always going to hang Della from, looked like he had kicked the chair over. Me, I believe it was an accident and that chair fell over. I think he was either trying to fix it so Della would catch him in time to stop him and realize she loved him, or he was fixin it for her and the chair fell over! Anyway, he was hanging there dead. I took her home and called Charles and he took care of everything, like a man. She didn't have to do anything except sign some papers for the insurance. She wanted to put the wedding off but Charles wouldn't have none of that!! And all those rangements made too!!

They got married and she moved into her new home. It's been a year or so now and they seem happy and peaceful and Della is gaining her weight back, up to 200 pounds and just as happy as she can be. Sometimes when she gets to thinking bout Smitty, she says "I still blieve if I had been there, he wouldn't have done that. He would have used me instead and we'd all be alive today!" I tell her, "Better for that fool to accidentally kill hisself like a fool than for you to be a fool and let him kill you!" Sometimes I wonder bout Della!!

THE FEEDER
Maria Bruno

I really have a thing about society deciding what we should look like. . . . If your husband feels like that [negative about your weight], get rid of him, get him out of your face. Your job is to start believing that God didn't make no mistakes.
—Roxanne Brown, "Full-Figured Women Fight Back"

Men who genuinely love women fantasize about being smothered in sofa-sized breasts and pillowed in marshmallow thighs. Pert is okay but pneumatic is heaven. Not for them the bite-size morsel. They revel in handfuls, fistfuls, and armfuls of lusty lady. Of course, millions of men don't really like women very much. They only tolerate us emaciated, depilated, and deodorized. Men who count your calories and stand over you with a stopwatch while you do sit-ups invariably claim to be doing it for your own good. Baloney! They're simply closet woman-haters—flesh-fearing, fat-baiting misogynists. They don't lust for me. The repugnance is mutual.
—Vanessa Feltz, "Who Says Fat Isn't Sexy?"

That summer day Alma Winters came to lunch, I noticed she had lost weight. She had lost the fullness of her breasts, the pinkish flesh of her cheeks, and could have been a small boy sitting there, instead of a grown woman playing with the food on her plate. Her once fiercely platinum hair was a faded brown, cropped close to her head with rigid sprouts standing upright at her crown and temples. Her gray eyes seemed much larger than I ever remembered, glass marbles fixed in a dull yellowed skin. Alma did not look at me as she arranged the meal into forced geometric designs on her plate. There was a sense of primordial ritual as she played with the food, separating it into squares and triangles with the tines of her fork, then pushing the food together into a larger rectangle. It was only after several minutes of this ceremonial rite that she took a bite. She showed no measure of enjoyment in her food, which could have been tasteless stones, the way she labored to swallow. Periodically she would lay down her fork, reach for her water goblet, and take measured mechanical sips, her lips never leaving the rim of the glass.

I felt like a cow next to her. My breasts were round and full from nursing my daughter Jenny, and David had joked just that morning that my arms and legs were getting to look like baby sea whales. I felt misshapen, a flesh balloon, sweat trickling down my inner thighs, making my print shift stick to my skin. I smelled of cooking grease and soured milk. I was uncomfortable in the late summer heat. Alma was cool and composed.

Jenny, who was seated in her highchair, squirmed momentarily and threw a large pastry noodle on the floor. She whined and I knew she wanted my breast. I lifted her out of the highchair, wiped the tomato sauce away from her face with a napkin, and opened the top button of my dress. Jenny maneuvered herself into a comfortable position, letting her smooth cheek disappear into the soft white breast, her lips blowing little fish kisses until she reached the nipple. Alma did not look up. She rearranged the food on her plate.

"It's too bad David can't be home for lunch," I said, shifting Jenny deeper into my arm for more leverage. "He would have loved to have seen you."

"Oh really?" she asked, taking a small even bite of the noodle.

"But then, I'm kind of glad we had this time to talk alone."

Alma neatly wiped her mouth with the cloth napkin, appearing to be finished, even though a great deal of food was left on her plate. I noticed fine strands of brown hair growing above her lip, alien shadows to this formerly very feminine creature.

"So," I paused, "When did you begin losing all this weight?"

"Oh, it's all come about gradually," she answered.

The breast milk from my untended breast seeped through the fabric of my dress, I was embarrassed, and shifted Jenny, who at nine months seemed too big and cumbersome to nurse. She eagerly reached for the swollen nipple of my other breast, while I wiped myself with a cloth diaper that I carried on my shoulder.

"I've been losing weight for a while now," Alma continued, placing her silverware on her plate and pushing the plate forward. "Everytime I look in the mirror, I see fat. It seems my stomach is an inevitable fate." She pinched a thin line of skin where her stomach should have been through the fabric of her tailored blouse. "You know, I don't even have my periods any more. I love it."

"Alma, I'm worried about you."

"Don't be."

"How does Cal feel about this?"

"Oh Calvin. He's been a bit of a brute. But let's not talk about me, please."

And so I launched into a self-conscious monologue about my life, my life with baby, my life with David. The night feedings, the diapers, the baby edging herself around the coffee table like a plump duck, giggling and cooing one moment, engaged in a tirade the next. I talked at considerable length about my body, all round and sagging, laced with white ribbons of stretch marks, and how the heat made me feel like a swollen pear, all thick and ripe and miserable. I talked about David and the business, how he liked his shirts ironed, that he liked his phone messages written neatly in ink, and how he wrote me a little note every morning before he left for work. "Sylvia, stick to your diet." And then I talked of the baby again, the La Leche League, the parenting group meetings, how zinc oxide is better for diaper rash than anything commercial on the market, how I intended to nurse Jenny until she was two years old even though my mother-in-law thought the whole idea disgusting. And it struck me as I spoke that I had no idea what language I spoke before this Baby Talk. What could I have possibly thought or said before there was a David or a Jenny? My head was filled with every movement that Jenny made, every monosyllable that she uttered, every new and startling skill she mastered. And when I did not speak of Jenny, it was David and his business, David and his needs, his desires for the family. I vaguely remember a young woman, with long black hair and black eyes, a literature major at a small university, who romped in a woolen turtleneck and faded blue jeans, carried a Greek woven bag she had bought in Europe, laced leather sandals up her calves, who met friends in dark campus taverns, political rallies, and in the dormitory rooms late at night. I vaguely remember her speaking, but the language and tools of speech are alien to me now, and the faces and names of her cohorts are impossible to remember. And this woman adopted a new language, and spoke to a woman who politely listened, but who did not share the language either.

Alma once had told me she had graduated from Stephens College in Missouri when Stephens was a finishing school devoted solely to preparing each young woman for a life with a successful man. Alma had jokingly mentioned once there was a mini-course in "the art of pouring tea" and she laughed, "the art of wearing gloves." She had been waiting for Calvin when he came along, she said. She was attracted to his angular frame and Nordic coloring, and she was bored with Stephens and her courses, and she fell for him so passionately that she forgot who she was and why she had ever gone to college in the first place. She quit Stephens her junior year and married Cal in a large ceremony somewhere out East.

I managed to finish college, but I fell hard for David, much like Alma did for Cal. David told me he didn't usually like literature majors because he found them flighty and unpredictable, but he thought he could handle me and mold me into the perfect wife. I remember telling him, this abrasive young man I had only known for two weeks, that you can only mold gelatin and cheese, neither of which I remotely resembled. He roared at that one, and later he told me he had decided that night he wanted to marry me. Something about the anger in my eyes intrigued him.

As I rambled on, Alma sat composed, smooth like carved marble, smiling a thin line of a smile, her hands, a small child's hand, folded neatly in her lap, Jenny was asleep at my breast.

After Alma had left, and I had put Jenny in her crib, I remembered back to the time when I had first met Alma. It was the night she and her husband Cal had thrown a celebration party honoring his new partnership with my husband, David. She was much rounder then, her face a soft pink, her blonde hair like a child's doll, and she was open, receptive, not the frigid mannequin that measured every move, every bite of food. She laughed appreciatively at everything her husband said that night, as if his words were golden, or god inspired, and she sat with her tea, her lacquered nails tapping delicately on the porcelain cup, smiling, giggling, winking at the other guests. I remembered the earrings and the fine golden chains that dangled from her neck and fell into the crevice of her then fuller breasts. She dressed flamboyantly, in odd-glittered colors, and men crowded around her. These same men often congratulated Cal on how lucky he was to find such a fine hostess and a good wife, and the other wives in the room envied her, myself included, because she was many things we were not. I hadn't had Jenny yet, and I sat at the dinner table, my pregnant belly resting in folds, straining in a slanted position, my puffed legs sprawled beneath me. David kept laying his hand on my stomach saying things like "That better be my cake baking in this oven," and he patted my stretched flesh, as if I wasn't even there, merely a receptacle for some precious cargo. Alma laughed heartily at David's humor, along with the other men at the table who spat and choked and roared, and I sat back, grinning, pretending I enjoyed all this attention. I remembered at one point the baby gave a strong kick and David raised his hand with an almost religious gesticulation and shouted, "Goddamn, it's going to be a first-string linebacker, sure as hell." I remember sipping my mineral water, amidst the laughing, and wondered what exactly a first-string linebacker did.

Alma sought me out later in the evening. "I'm so glad our husbands are going to be partners. We're going to be fast friends, I can tell. I want to hear all about your baby." And before I had a chance to respond, she had flittered away, off to Cal's side, crawling into the folds of his arms, and he steadied her, positioned her, and her form became fluid as she melted into a cool liquid in his grasp.

Several months had passed after that summer lunch with Alma, and I did not think much about her. I was engrossed with Jenny and the house, and my diet, which was David's pet obsession as well as mine. David had devised a curious regimen he had found in an old Air Force manual. He had written down my instructions neatly on a legal pad, detailing the precise amount of sit-ups, leg lifts, arm twirls that I was to do each day. By each category, there was a box to be checked each time the prescribed exercises were completed. Every morning, next to his "Daily Notes for Sylvia" ("Don't touch that Jamoca Almond Fudge ice cream, Syl, I'll check the level when I get home"), he left the annoying Air Force regimen, with a newly sharpened pencil laid next to it. I often greeted the note with a half-eaten banana or toasted bagel dangling from my mouth, and in an act of silent defiance, I checked the little squares perfunctorily as I dipped my finger into the Jamoca Almond Fudge.

I decided to have Alma over for lunch again in November. She arrived promptly, dressed in a roomy t-shirt that swallowed her boyish frame. Her hair was shorter, swept back above her ears, and she had lost more weight. She seemed to be in even more control, her posture rigid, almost military, her hands tight and folded in her lap, the purplish veins transparent, like frozen rivers in her flesh. I stared at her face, the skin still yellowed, but now deep grey circles swelled around the eyes, and her smile, much tighter, stretched like a violet string across her face. I had fixed something rich and pasty, I wanted to fatten her up, but she no longer bothered to lift the food to her mouth. She neatly separated it and let it converge again with each mechanical movement of her fork.

"Alma," I began, "Is it possible that you could have lost more weight? You really didn't need to." I saw in her form the frozen pictures of war and famine that lay like a sheet of cellophane over my consciousness.

"When I look into the mirror all I see is fat. It's funny, but I find I can live quite nicely on some meat broth and a sliver of fruit."

"But that's not enough, Alma. You need more."

"No, you're wrong," she shook her head. "I need nothing. I'm in complete control now."

"What do you mean you're in control?"

"My body is my own."

"Has Cal said anything about this to you?"

She laughed, and said nothing for a moment, then straightened herself in the chair. "Oh he forces me to eat. He pinches the food between his fingers and forces it into my mouth. I swallow it all right, but I throw it up later." She laughed again. "You think I'm crazy, don't you?"

"No, I don't think that," I answered. "But you and Cal were always so close."

"Oh really? Is that what you thought?" I heard the faint stirrings of Jenny in the upstairs bedroom. She's probably hungry, I thought, and my breasts ached. "I think that's the baby, Sylvia," Alma said, and stood to leave.

"Alma, please stay. You just got here. Have dessert. I made it special."

"Sylvia, please don't worry about me."

"How can I help you?"

"You can't."

I noticed the bruise as she was putting on her overcoat. It lay under her arm, large, circular, the deep purple of a summer plum.

"Alma!" She jerked, I must have startled her. "What happened to you?" I heard Jenny wailing in the upstairs bedroom. My attention shifted in the direction of the bedroom door, then back to Alma, who was quickly buttoning up her overcoat.

"Oh, that. A gift from Calvin. He had a bad day at work."

She lifted the woolen hood over her head, opened the door, and walked rigidly into the brutal wind. I felt a chill as the wind crept into the open weave of my sweater. I folded my arms across my chest and hid my hands under each arm. I closed the door behind her and stood for a moment ignoring the persistent cries of my child.

"She's the joke of the office," David said that night at dinner. "Mort Kreiners calls her 'Alma from Auschwitz.'"

"That's so sick." I said. "I can't believe you can even repeat that."

"Alma used to be some broad," he continued. "Cal was considered lucky going home to that every night. Mort says you couldn't pay him to lay her now."

"Mort Kreiners is an asshole."

"Mort Kreiners sold three houses last week."

"How can you defend him?"

"Like I said, he sold three houses last week."

"Anyway, I tried to get her to eat. I made Lasagne. She just played with it. Wouldn't take a bite."

"I figure if you can't get her to eat, no one can," he smirked, patting the meat of my thighs. "You're always feeding everyone, including yourself." He reached for his coffee, and swirled the black brew with his spoon. He smiled. "Did you do your leg lifts today?"

"I didn't have time." He let that one slip in, I thought, he's a real professional, him and his little calculated doses of disapproval. I had covered my advancing weight that winter with oversized sweaters and pants, and had been careful to keep my arms covered and my legs hidden under large towels after a shower, and then safely lost under a lounging gown. Even though Jenny had several teeth and was increasingly mobile, I was still nursing her and my breasts were still huge and swollen and laced with purple veins. That's it I thought. No more nursing, Jenny, you're going cold turkey tomorrow. No more feeding off of Momma.

"I think Cal has been hitting Alma and I'm worried," I said, looking for some type of reaction in David's face. I folded my hands across my breasts hoping to minimize my misshapen body.

"He says he has to get tough with her to make her eat. It's none of your business, Syl. Now drop it." He got up from the table and turned, "Cal is my friend, my partner, and we get along fine. Just drop all of this."

I took David's advice, letting it go, hoping Alma could resolve what was troubling her on her own, after all, she herself said I couldn't help her. Months later in the spring, when I had all but forgotten about Alma, and David ceased to even mention her in conversation, I became absorbed with

Jenny and her expanding vocabulary. I wrote down every new word she acquired and the day she uttered it into a little journal I had been keeping since her birth. Her newest phrase was "I want, I want," and she followed me around the house playfully reiterating her new sentence. David had left a note for me one morning in the spring, and instead of his usual "Stick to your diet, Syl!" there was a set of terse instructions: "Get a hold of Alma Winters. Invite her and Cal to dinner tonight. I'll explain later."

Alma was distant on the phone, and responded in short, brittle sentences: "Yes. That will be fine. We can make it. Thank you. Good-bye." Her voice was a bizarre parody of one of those computer toys that respond verbally to a child's persistent finger punches. I heard a grey undercurrent of pain, not the whinings of a hungry child that I was so used to responding to, but the low, hollow moans of the wounded. Her voice made me think of that morning when I lay in bed, startled by the imperiled quakings of a small bird trapped in our roof that the workman had finished repairing the day before. It was a sparrow or a Brewers blackbird, which often nests in the soffits and gutters of the neighborhood homes. I stared at the sloped ceiling, directed my attention to where the bird had been entombed between the rafters. The scratchings became more frantic as I envisioned the bird flapping its fragile wings in the darkness, in blind panic, buffeted only by the freshly laid insulation. I threw off my covers and stood on the mattress.

"What are you doing Sylvia?" David had asked, turning in a half sleep. I lifted my fingertips and grazed the ceiling.

"There's a bird trapped in the ceiling. Can't you hear him?"

"He'll die soon. Let it go."

"Can't we get it out?"

"Now, how are we going to get it out, Syl? We just paid eight hundred dollars to have the roof fixed, and you want to save some damn bird?"

"I can't stand listening to it die."

"Then go downstairs and fix me some coffee."

"How can you stand it, David?"

"It's easy," he had answered, sitting up in bed. He turned on the radio.

The dinner party was Cal's idea. He had hoped that if Alma was around familiar faces, she might eat. He admitted to David she was losing more weight, that he had found her vomiting several more times in the bathroom and that he had to get physical with her. He had to watch her constantly now, following her to the bathroom and having to force-feed her in the mornings before he went to work and at night when he got home. He thought it was time to involve a doctor, but Alma had refused.

The dinner surprisingly went well. Alma mad a visible effort to eat, not toying with the food, but actually scooping large amounts of food onto her fork and shoving them into her mouth. David and Cal made a deliberate attempt to not watch Alma, and were engaged in a raucous retelling of some more office antics of Mort Kreiners. He had, so they said, deliberately spilled coffee on Miss Kendall's bosom, in hopes of getting to wipe it away with his pocket handkerchief. Miss Kendal, the secretary, was noticeably upset when old Mort dropped his handkerchief down her cleavage and proceeded to retrieve it. David recounted that "Her jugs were just a-jiggling" at the sight of Kreiners' hand, and she poured another cup of coffee on his three-piece-pin-stripe. I often wondered how a man I could be married to could defend a man who had such an open contempt for women. It seemed to me that David and Cal, and all men for that matter, had a fierce camaraderie, impenetrable, a shared, personal knowledge, fraternity, partnership, that excluded women. It is a code, an unspoken devotion. I felt jealous of Cal and David and Mort, much like I felt in high school when I saw the male athletes on a football or basketball squad hug each other on the field, while I enviously sat in the stands, surrounded by the other girls, yearning for that type of camaraderie. The girls would cheer and wave at the men hoping for some form of recognition or male attention. But we were all separate entities, failing to acknowledge each other, only interested in extrapolating a small fragment of this male fraternity.

Alma asked for seconds of the dessert after finishing two helpings of the main course, and Cal smiled appreciatively at me. David nodded. She smiled and took large chunks of the cheesecake onto her fork and dropped them into her mouth. I reached for a piece of the cheesecake for myself, hoping that David was so lost in his reverie with Cal that he would not notice, but, as if on cue, he tapped my elbow with the prongs of his fork and whispered so Cal and Alma could almost certainly hear, "Not tonight, Darling, you've had enough as it is." So I continued to minister the meal, monitoring everyone's plate, standing, then sitting, treating each portion of food as a personal gift to the taker.

After coffee, Alma excused herself and left the table. Calvin gave me a sour, pleading look, so I offered to walk her up to the bathroom using the excuse that I wanted to check on Jenny. David winked at me, letting me know I had done the right thing.

I stood by the bathroom door. I heard the low gutteral sounds, the heavings, the moans, and then the sudden flash of the toilet. I wondered if I should knock, and then the door opened. Alma stood in the doorway, not surprised to see me at all, her dull hair matted and wet, fresh yellow balls of sweat beading her forehead and the pronounced hair above her lip. "Please don't tell Cal, Sylvia." I felt as if we shared a small closet, suffocating in the dark, acrid smell of vomit, and I felt the sad, sick walls of enclosure. She lifted her sweater and showed me several side strips of surgical tape wrapped around her emaciated body. "He did this," she announced, and headed down the stairs, her form distinctly masculine in nature. Her body was propelled by some ethereal energy, giving her strength, and as she disappeared down the stairway, I knew I would say nothing.

Alma called three weeks later, her voice was different, not the clipped military sentences, but a series of unpunctuated fragments. She asked to see me. It was urgent. I remembered a doctor's appointment I had made that day for Jenny's inoculations, and the promise to pick up David's pinstripe at the cleaners and my luncheon meeting with David's mother. "Yes, Alma. Please come. I'll be waiting here for you."

I suddenly felt the same fear I did the night I stood in the imaginary closet, the stale air that hung low around me, the feeling of hopeless enclosure. Jenny had tripped over a line of toys in front of her and held out her arms for solace, a green plastic frog lodged in one hand, the other tugging at the fabric of my shirt, pleading to nurse. I walked into the kitchen and poured her a cup of juice, she tagging behind me, at first resisting the cup, still tugging at the cloth of my shirt. "No, Jen, you use a cup now. Momma has no more milk."

Ten minutes later Alma stood in the doorway in a pair of denims and a bloodied white shirt. There was a large untended bruise, split and bleeding on her forehead. I ushered her in, her frail body quaking, her hands, like strings of bones, convulsing. She bit into her shaking hand, making small indentations in the skin, trying by the self-induced pain, to steady herself. She composed herself, transfixed by the tiny dots that filled with blood and steamed the hollows of her skin. "Let me take care of that cut, Alma. Please." I sat her in the living room and then ran for some disinfectant and some bandages. When I returned, Jenny was yelling, "Hurt, Momma, hurt!" Shaking I spilled the bright orange Mercurochrome over the wound. Jenny pummeled my legs, disturbed at my behavior, tugged demandingly at my slacks, and then sat curiously to watch the bright spectacle, the Mercurochrome spreading like ink on white paper, creating a Rorschach on Alma's face. I took some tissue out of my pocket and gently wiped away the excess, placed some soft gauze over the wound, finishing with two strips of adhesive tape.

"I thought I was strong enough to kill him," she began. "I worked at being strong . . . in control . . . I thought I could do it this time, this time . . . I waited so long for just the right time . . . I thought I had the power . . . I had the power . . ."

"Alma, what are you saying?" I grabbed her fists that were wound tight like hoarded string.

"I thought he couldn't touch me anymore . . . I thought my body was my own . . . I felt strong . . . did everything, everything right . . ."

"Alma . . ."

"But oh oh that bastard that bastard he walks in on me in the bathroom I had to vomit that toast he made me eat that morning and he walked in that bastard and he grabbed me and he still can beat me he still can hurt me and it still hurts still hurts and I thought I had the power to make him stop. I yelled I was going to leave him and he said 'You skinny bitch, I'll kill you yet.'"

"Alma, please, calm down, slow down."

Her trembling ceased and I wrapped my arms around her. Jenny, surprised by the sudden silence, edged into our circle, and with a surge of compassion that young children often intuitively display, reached for both of us. We sat there a very long time, arms entwined, heads together, listening to the ancient rhythm of our blood. And in this human huddle, we shared a secret knowledge, a silent, undying bond, a communion that only females can share.

Later in the day, David walked into the kitchen and found Alma, quiet and contemplative, sitting at the kitchen table warming her hands around a cup of tea. Jenny was in her highchair fingerpainting with a Jell-O salad, tossing bits of strawberry gelatin onto the linoleum floor. David grabbed me by the arm and led me outside to the living room.

"Get her out of here, Sylvia," he said.

"She's hurt, David. She needs help."

"Cal said she got hysterical this morning, trying to puke her breakfast into the toilet. He says he's having her committed."

"He's the one that should be committed. He's an animal."

"Can't you see she's fucking nuts?" he yelled, and then more quietly. "Listen honey. She's his wife. This is his business. You're my wife, and I want you to get her out of here."

"I can't."

"He's my friend, Sylvia. He's my partner. This is his mess. I'm calling him." He picked up the phone and began to dial.

"David, please, don't."

"Do what I say Sylvia. Get your daughter, clean up that fucking mess she's made in there, and then start dinner. I'm not coming home to this kind of thing, I mean it!"

I walked into the kitchen, went over to Jenny, and lifted her from the highchair and wiped her hands and face with a dishrag. I looked at the bowl of Jell-O on the floor and the little strawberry hills that peppered the tiles. I looked up at Alma, whose flushed and bruised face registered nothing. She sipped her tea. "Come on, Alma. We're going." She looked up. "Come on, I'm getting you out of here. David is calling Cal. He'll be here soon." She didn't move. I felt as if my chest was exploding. My anger was so rich, so deep, surging like volcanic lava, a grit that burned my throat, enflamed my voice. God, I thought. It's not only Alma that had to get out of there.

As we drove off, all three of us in the front seat, huddled together again, as soldiers do in combat trenches, I looked through the rear view mirror to see David in the driveway, yelling, I suppose, my name. As we pulled farther and farther away, I saw our roof, still neatly repaired, and I thought of that lost sparrow, entombed in the darkness, shrouded with its broken wings.

BLOOMINGDALE'S

Perri Klass

Young children inhabit their bodies, round or angular, with a happy lack of self-consciousness that is part of what we call innocence. Look at a 3- or 4-year-old, supremely comfortable in her own skin. Watch how a 5-year-old takes up space, exulting in the joy of motion. But then something happens, particularly to girls. An 8-year-old girl recently confided to me that she avoids swimming because she doesn't want people to look at her in a bathing suit. Maybe someone in her class made a cruel remark; maybe the insanely thin bodies in magazines and music videos got to her. And for one hot, angry moment, I wanted to storm the barricades, incinerate the Barbie dolls, do anything that would keep this child happy and comfortable. And I was deeply grateful for her mother's good sense as she piped in, "You're beautiful, and anyone who says anything different is talking nonsense." It may not be enough to counter all those negative messages, but it's a start, right at home, where it matters most of all.

—Perri Klass, "What Really Shapes a Girl's Self-Image"

The Paramus branch of Bloomingdale's is holding three afternoon lectures for local home economics classes. Each afternoon will cover one important subject for teenage girls: fashion, makeup, and diet and exercise. Since all the girls will have to miss school those afternoons, they must get their parents to sign permission slips.

The home economics teacher says to the home economics class: "And I hope you will remember that you are representing our school and dress accordingly. No jeans, please."

"Are other pants okay?" a girl asks.

"I think we'll say double knit is fine, but corduroy is out," the teacher says, and the girls nod.

There is one girl in the room who looks different. Some are fatter, some have worse acne, but she is the only one who does not seem to have made an effort. Her name is Maggie. She is one of very few girls to wear no makeup, her jeans are baggy, her man's teeshirt is an ugly brown, and her hair looks a little dirty. The other fat girls wear clothes that the magazines say will distract attention from their waists, and they take special trouble with their hair. Just by looking, you could not tell that Maggie is the only overweight girl who isn't on a perpetual diet, but that's true too. She is sitting next to her best friend, who has also made little obvious effort, but manages to look quite all right in her jeans and shirt. Maggie's best friend is thin and her skin is clear. She sits hunched over, covertly doing French under the desk.

[It is so hard to give any dignity to high school. And I am afraid to tell you the truth. Because the truth would be I was the fattest, the ugliest, the one on whom a thousand full skirts, interesting necklines, and layers of Cover Girl makeup would have been useless. And my best friend was one of those people who cannot make a graceless move, and her blond hair swung around her face perfectly, and even her handwriting was beautiful . . . but the truth would make my story less convincing; you might write it off as the leftover self-hatred and jealousy of an unhappy teenager, so I will tone it down to where you will begin to believe me.]

The home economics room is full of sewing machines. They sit around the sides of the room and wait for the girls to sew. There is a bulletin board with a poster on it, released by the Simplicity Pattern Company, which shows six very pretty teenage girls in dresses made from Simplicity patterns. The writing on the bottom of the poster says these are the winners of Simplicity's "Sew It and Model It Contest" and copies of the poster, along with rules for next year's contest, are available from Simplicity for seventy-five cents.

There is another bulletin board with charts of the four basic food groups on it. That is for the advanced home economics class, in which girls learn about planning a family's meals. It is coordinated with the senior health class, in which girls learn about the other kind of family planning.

Maggie shifts down in her chair so her feet sprawl out. Her best friend, who is artistic, draws a very clever caricature of the teacher and shows it to Maggie, who grins. The bell rings and they all go off to gym.

Once, a year ago, Maggie dressed up for school. She wore jeans that the lady in Bamberger's said were just her size, and a flowered shirt with pearly buttons. The clothes felt very tight. She borrowed some of her mother's face powder and held her hair back with two matching barrettes. She was not comfortable that day, but she held a picture of her prettiness in her mind and moved with care and deliberate grace. Gym period came, and she faced the full-length mirror in the locker room, and she bulged out of the clothes and her face looked greasy. It has been so long since then that probably no one can remember her in anything but the baggy clothes she is wearing now. Home economics is required, and so is gym.

[In fact, everything we took was required that year, even music, where the teacher, who wore fake stick-on sideburns, had a special program called "Jukebox Jury," in which we rated the top ten songs every week, then discussed their musical qualities, and later had to identify lyrics on a test. So you see, I don't need to exaggerate.]

Maggie comes to school the day of the first trip to Bloomingdale's in a skirt and teeshirt, and all the girls get on the school bus. Maggie sits with her best friend, and everybody sings for a while, starting with "Found a Peanut" and going on to a football song. Maggie knows all the words (that was their first music lesson) and she lets herself sing softly until she catches her best friend's eye and feels obliged to giggle. She looks out her window at Paramus, New Jersey, shopping center capital of the world. All over Paramus there are enormous shopping malls. Some are enclosed in super-buildings, with trees along the indoor promenades between the stores. Waterfalls tumble off the roofs of department stores onto Styrofoam rocks in lily ponds (the lilies are plastic, as are the frogs crouching on them), and one mall has a bunch of automated plastic cows (life-size) grazing on the Astroturf.

The Bloomingdale's mall is one of the classier ones. Maggie and most of her classmates are more familiar with some of the cheaper stores at the more plebeian malls. The bus parks, the girls climb out and follow the teacher into Bloomingdale's. As they move toward the escalator, they finger the scarves, stroke the tweed blazers, and a few of the daring try a spritz from one of the sample perfume bottles.

Maggie is at the back of the group; she sees the first girls rising into the quiet heights of Bloomingdale's on the escalator. She has always been slightly afraid of escalators, but she gets on and off without hesitation. The girls are led around the handbag tables and into a small auditorium. It is almost full of other home economics classes; there are just enough seats left. They all sit down. The faces are young and pretty, colored with creams and powders, the bodies are dressed in pastels, the necks are circled by thin gold chains dangling crosses, stars, charms, and hearts onto shirts or into necklines.

[And yet they couldn't all have been pretty, could they? I could watch them in the hall at school and see individual flaws. Some of them were beautiful, some were pretty and some fit in only by virtue of careful attention to detail. But all together, they blended into a pretty group, a group of pretty girls.]

It takes five minutes to quiet the girls down. A woman walks onto the stage and welcomes them all. She is handsome, wearing a dark red suit, and she handles herself easily. She comments on what a nice-looking group they are and how pleased Bloomingdale's is to welcome them. The first topic, she announces, will be fashion. Several Bloomingdale's people come on the stage and talk: the lady from the College Boutique, the man from Teen Sportswear, finally the lady from Lingerie. The girls giggle. "Now," she says, "there is nothing funny about underwear. After all, we're all girls together here." They giggle again.

The Bloomingdale's people pick six pretty girls out of the audience, ask them to come up on the stage, and analyze their clothes. They tell one to put on a blue sweater ("See how it pulls your whole look together?") and another to put on a plastic belt painted to look as if it were made of linked chewing-gum wrappers ("See how the right accessories highlight your outfit!"), and soon they are all festooned with Bloomingdale's merchandise.

"I bet everyone goes down and buys those things right after the lecture," Maggie whispers to her best friend.

"There'll be thirty people wearing that belt in school tomorrow," whispers her best friend, and they giggle.

The next week they pick six girls and have them take off all their own makeup with cold cream. Then a very effeminate man ("faggy," the girls whisper) with a tie printed to look like gum wrappers applies makeup to them while he explains what he is doing: "brings out" "conceals" "shadows" "plays up" "shapes" "highlights" "brightens" "plucks" and "covers." The six decorated girls then walk around the room so everyone can get a good look, while the man answers questions.

"What can I do about my freckles?"

"My brows never come out even."

"What liner goes well with green eye shadow?"

"Is it better to have your lipstick match your blush exactly?"

Maggie whispers to her best friend, "I dare you to ask how to cover serious birth defects." Maggie thinks makeup looks silly and has never been really tempted to use it, so she is able to laugh. Still, she sometimes imagines she is Cybill Shepherd posing for Cover Girl makeup ads. These are the kinds of fantasies she tries not to have, and she is ashamed of herself for having them. She feels that to daydream about being Cybill Shepherd is just the sort of silly irony she should avoid.

[In case you wonder, I can also still recognize Susie Blakely, and Lauren Hutton, and every other model who ever glowed on the cover of *Mademoiselle* in her autumn-russet cheek gloss and peach-coral lip paint, hair by Sassoon.]

The makeup man produces a little blue plastic thing; it looks like a tiny propeller. When he presses a switch it spins like a fan and he explains that it is a battery-operated eyeliner dryer. Maggie laughs aloud and everyone looks at her.

The third week is diet and exercise. The girls are told to eat fruit instead of candy and to get fresh air during their menstrual periods (giggles). It is suggested that they make a habit of chewing each mouthful of food thirty-two times ("Your jaws will get tired and you won't take so many mouthfuls!"), and that they spend twenty minutes a day doing some simple exercises. To demonstrate the exercises the Bloomingdale's people pick six overweight girls. Maggie sees the woman coming toward her and tries to look both hostile and invisible. The woman picks her, leads her to the stage, where she stands with the other overweight girls, all embarrassed and fidgeting.

"Lie down on your backs," the woman says. "Now lift your legs off the floor." Maggie does not lift her legs. She lies on her back in the soft Bloomingdale's carpet. The woman says, "Now, we're not trying." She picks up Maggie's ankles, rather gingerly.

Maggie screams. The lady drops her ankles. All the other girls jump up. Maggie lies there. The lady touches her shoulder and Maggie screams again and kicks the carpet. Maggie's teacher hurries up to the stage, and Maggie is on her feet with bits of lint in her hair. She is so angry that her head burns. She is so angry she wants to spit. She spits at her home economics teacher, who shrieks.

Maggie is standing alone on the stage and crying, and everyone stares at her, and if there is understanding in the eyes of the other five fat girls she does not see it. Maggie wraps her arms around herself and shudders, wishing she were invisible, weightless. She has a sudden tearstained picture of herself flying above Bloomingdale's, holding on to a battery-operated blue plastic propeller.

THE DREAM DIET

Susan Dyer

1. Diets don't work.
2. Dieting is hazardous to your health.
3. Dieting reduces self-esteem.
4. Diets reinforce body hatred.
5. Diets cause food/weight obsession.
6. Diets are a leading cause of eating disorders.
7. Dieting perpetuates fatphobia.
8. Dieting supports an oppressive multi-billion dollar industry.
9. Dieting is social control of women.
10. Dieting kills.

—Largesse, the Network for Size Esteem

My jolly fat grandmother, who made the best apple tarts I ever ate, had a sampler hanging over her well-used stove that read:

THE AMBITIONS OF WOMEN

TO GROW UP
TO FILL OUT
TO SLIM DOWN
TO HOLD IT IN
TO HELL WITH IT

I'm still aiming for the third ambition, though there are times when it seems to be a losing battle. I've been dieting off and on since I was a teenager, when I would have given my eyeteeth to be able to walk down the beach in a bikini.

I gave up on the bikini idea a long time ago, but I'd still like to look nice in an ordinary swimsuit. I get depressed just thinking about it, and usually end up raiding the refrigerator to console myself.

But I keep trying. Last year I got together with some other women to form a diet club. Three of my best friends joined too. Madge and I have shared our dieting woes since high school. She weighs even more than I do, so just being with her is some consolation. She's also the nicest, most generous person I know, and doesn't deserve to be fat.

Harriet, on the other hand, is slim enough to make the rest of us jealous, but she thinks of herself as fat, and is just as desperate to reduce as we are. She's pretty strict about dieting. Being a math teacher, she keeps track of our weights and tells us how we're doing. We've made her president of the club.

Then there's crazy Arabella. Her favorite outfit has pink and purple stripes going the wrong direction, if that tells you anything. The diets she comes up with are never boring, though they're sometimes inedible. She also has a great sense of humor, which helps a lot when you're dieting.

My husband refers to us as the "fork and spoon girls," but we call ourselves the Diet-of-the-Month Club. Because none of us were able to stick to any diet for more than thirty days at a time, we decided to have a member present a new one every month. We can vote to keep any diet that we really like, but so far we haven't. Harriet tells us how much weight the average member has lost at the end of the month. That way, we don't embarrass any one person in particular.

I think I had better confess right now that I was the one to blame for last December. I'd come up with a brand-new diet imported from Japan consisting of seaweed and raw fish, both very healthy and slimming. But with all the turkey and cranberry sauce, eggnog, Christmas cookies and fruitcake around, none of us were able to stay on the plan. In fact, everyone gained weight and ended up mad at me. Harriet reported that the average weight gain was eleven and a half pounds, though Madge gained quite a bit more, and she herself quite a bit less.

I didn't dare take December again, so I traded with Madge for April. I could see by mid-March, though, that April was going to be a tough assignment too, because ever since January—with our New Year's resolutions and the extra eleven and a half pounds behind us (so to speak)—we'd all been desperately trying to lose weight in time for the swimsuit season. We had nearly starved ourselves doing it, but when the club met on the last Wednesday in March, together we had managed to lose an average of ten pounds each. Now it was up to me to keep us on our steady course.

Unfortunately, three months of deprivation had left us all pretty crabby. Arabella, who happened to have been divorced that year, had gone through three boyfriends in three months. The oldest daughter of Sarah, a new member, had run away from home to live with a friend until her mother had finished her dieting. None of our husbands were speaking to us, and even gentle Madge had nearly been thrown out of a supermarket for fighting with the fruit man over the price of bananas.

"Now, who has the April diet?" Harriet inquired once she'd called the meeting to order. There was a general groan as I raised my hand; no one had forgotten my December fiasco. "All right, Penny," said Harriet, "but it better be good."

"No grapefruit!" grumbled Arabella.

"Nothing exotic, either!" pleaded Madge.

"And it has got to be cheat-proof," snapped Sarah.

"Furthermore," added Harriet, who has to get her oar in, "it has to cheer us up!"

There were mutterings of agreement and then everyone turned to glare at me. "Well?" said Harriet. "Can you come up with a simple, delicious diet by next week?"

"I'll try," I croaked, ready to burst into tears.

By Friday I'd found a new fat-melting diet and called Harriet to tell her. She said scornfully that fat only melted in a frying pan; I'd have to do better than that.

I worked on the problem all weekend and came up with a very sensible plan: no junk food, no seconds, no fats, no alcohol. How could we go wrong? I ran into Arabella at the store on Monday and told her about it. "It's got no pizzazz," she objected, "and besides, it isn't cheat-proof!"

Tuesday evening, in desperation, I went to the public library and devoured shelf after shelf of diet books—not literally, of course, though in my half-starved condition, I won't say I wasn't tempted. The trouble was, we'd already tried all of the big-name ones. I had to come up with something different.

They were just announcing that the library would close in fifteen minutes, when, down on my knees scanning the bottom shelf, I noticed a small pamphlet crammed in behind some larger books. I dislodged it and smoothed it out on the floor.

"The Anti-Craving Diet," it said, "by Dr. Oswald Rasswilder." The publication date was 1932, and though the paper was old and brittle, the pamphlet looked as if it had never been checked out. I opened it gingerly and began to read. It was the answer to all our prayers. . . .

At the meeting on Wednesday, even before I got to my seat, I heard bickering and hissing and nasty remarks all around me. Captain Hook's crew was a tea-party by comparison.

Harriet seemed especially out of sorts. "Well, I suppose I'll have to open the meeting," she snarled, as if she'd been asked to carry out a dead rat. "Penny will present the April diet, heaven help us." That was all the introduction I got.

Nevertheless, I stood up clutching my trusty pamphlet and started in. "Fellow dieters," I quavered as I began. "Tonight I want to propose an entirely new approach to dieting. It's called the Anti-Craving Diet by Dr. Oswald Rasswilder." I held up the precious pamphlet for all to see.

"What do we have to do?" growled Sarah.

"We better not have to eat grapefruit," roared Arabella.

I wiped my sweaty palms on my skirt. People were muttering and watching me with narrowed eyes. I felt like a plump gazelle that has accidentally stumbled into a pack of hungry hyenas.

"Well," I said, "the idea is to eat exactly what you want, however much of it you want, whenever you want it."

There was a stunned silence in the room. Finally Harriet spoke. "It'll never work."

"Wait a minute," I said. "You have to hear the theory."

"Yes, let's hear the theory," said Madge, who was always fair-minded about things. "How can we possibly lose weight on a diet like that?"

"Dr. Rasswilder says," I began, "that obesity is caused by unnatural cravings for food; these cravings are really just natural cravings that have been denied for too long. They get out of hand and become compulsions."

"You're talking my language, baby," said Arabella.

I nodded my appreciation for her support, but I had to go on with my speech before I forgot it. "Dr. Rasswilder's theory is that the problem of obesity can never be overcome until the problem of the unnatural cravings is addressed and resolved. Therefore, the first step in his diet is to defuse the cravings by gratifying them."

"For example, he says"—I opened my pamphlet to a well-worn page, because I knew unless I read it they wouldn't believe me— "'If your particular craving is chocolate cake à la mode, you should make two chocolate cakes, one to eat and one to keep in reserve, and you should keep an extra gallon of ice cream on hand at all times.'"

"Oh, dear God!" cried Madge.

"I think I'm going to swoon," Arabella declared.

"It'll never work," said Harriet.

I ignored these interruptions, flipped to another page and continued. "Dr. Rasswilder warns that 'a lifetime of unsatisfied cravings may take time to appease, but eventually a new sense of confidence will evolve—the confidence that what you want will be available whenever you want it—and your unnatural cravings will diminish until they become a perfect guide to sensible, healthy eating.'"

I looked around triumphantly. The entire Diet-of-the-Month Club was hanging desperately on my every word. Some of them were actually drooling.

"The most important thing," I concluded, "is not to rush the project, or to try to skip over the early gorging phase, because the whole success of the diet depends upon gratifying the appetite."

"What kind of doctor is this Rasswilder?" Harriet demanded. Is he a medical doctor or a psychologist?"

"Neither," I said. Harriet raised a well-tweezed eyebrow and looked archly around the room. I knew if she didn't approve of the diet she could bully the others into voting it down, but I had one more ace up my sleeve. "As a matter of fact, Dr. Rasswilder was a distinguished professor of mathematics at the University of Vienna."

"Mathematics!" Harriet gasped.

I opened the pamphlet to Appendix B and held it up for all to see. "Dr. Rasswilder says you can calculate mathematically exactly how long the diet will take with these formulas." There was a whole page of impressive equations, chock-full of functions and variables. "All you have to do is fill in the amount gained or lost, the number of days since the start of the Anti-Craving Diet and a few other things."

Harriet was impressed. "Well, in that case," she said, "it's worth a try." I bowed graciously and took my seat to the applause of the entire club.

Ordinarily, we sit around for quite a while on Wednesday nights, complaining about our troubles, confessing our lapses and debating whether vertical stripes or basic black make better camouflage. But tonight the meeting adjourned early. We couldn't wait to get started on the April diet.

Arabella, Madge, Harriet and I didn't even wait to get home. We went out to our favorite restaurant to celebrate. Madge ordered a banana split, Arabella took a huge plate of spaghetti and meatballs, and I settled on a double cheeseburger with french fries and a malted milk shake.

Harriet said she'd just have a cup of black coffee, but we reminded her that the diet said to gratify every craving, and finally she decided she'd have a tiny dish of maple walnut ice cream. It was a start, anyway.

By the end of the first week everyone had gained about seven pounds, except Harriet, who only gained four—we suspected she may have been cheating. Some of the members were worried, but I counseled patience and read inspiring passages from Dr. Rasswilder. After that everyone cheered up and went off to the second week with renewed determination and enthusiasm.

By the end of the next week, only Harriet was still wearing a size twelve. The routine weigh-in brought groans of despair from everyone. Members were losing their nerve left and right, and a small contingent thought perhaps we ought to go back to a more conventional diet.

"But Dr. Rasswilder said this would happen," I assured everyone. "If we just keep at it, pretty soon we'll start *losing* weight." But even I wasn't quite as confident as I sounded.

On the good side, our tempers had improved dramatically. Our husbands were talking to us again, Sarah's daughter had moved back home, and Arabella had *two* boyfriends.

By the third week, the testimonials were pouring in. Madge reported that her husband was so impressed with Dr. Rasswilder's diet that he'd gone on it too. "And I've never been able to get Rodney to go on a diet before!" she marveled.

Then another member stood up and said, "I woke up the other night at three A.M. craving Moo Goo Gai Pan, and my husband went right to an all-night Chinese take-out to get me some. I haven't had so much fun since I was pregnant!"

Harriet looked pretty skeptical as she recorded our weights in her book. "I just don't see how this can be working," she said.

"But it's all right here in the pamphlet," I reminded her.

"Let me see that." She browsed through the complicated equations in Appendix B. "May I borrow this till next Wednesday?" she asked. "I think I'll work out these equations and give a report at the next meeting."

"Oh great," I replied. But in spite of my bravado, I felt anxious. What if Harriet discovered that the diet wasn't working?

By the time the Wednesday of reckoning finally came, we had all gained about twenty pounds. We took our seats and prepared to hear Harriet's report.

Harriet stood before us opening her burgundy attaché case and taking out several pages of yellow, legal-size paper covered with numbers and mathematical symbols. She smiled so that we could see every one of her front teeth. "Do you want to hear the good news or the bad news first?" she asked.

"The good news!" everyone cried.

Harriet cleared her throat. "The diet is going to work," she announced.

A round of applause went up in the meeting room. Arabella pulled a kazoo out of her purse and started zooing away. Two or three of the women got up and danced a hora. Order was finally restored with difficulty.

"And now for the bad news," she continued. Boos and catcalls were heard. Harriet waited till we were absolutely silent. "It won't work in time for summer."

There was a murmur of disappointment. Then Madge stood up bravely and said, "But it isn't the short term we're in for, Harriet, it's the long term. If we're going to lose weight in the long term, it's worth it. I've never been so happy on a diet in my life."

I could have hugged her. Madge sat down, and Sarah got up.

"I agree with Madge. I haven't fought with my daughter for a whole week. And the diet is going just as it's supposed to. I say we vote to continue the April diet for the rest of the year."

Everyone in the room seconded the motion except Harriet. We'd almost forgotten she was there. The fact that she was still smiling gave me a queasy feeling in the pit of my stomach. "Uh, Harriet," I said. "Just *how* long term are we talking?"

Harriet adjusted her glasses and referred to her yellow sheets. "According to my calculations," she said, the diet is following a parabolic curve." She looked over her glasses at the rest of us to see if anyone cared to challenge that assertion. No one did. "I have calculated definitively that on this diet the curve will peak in ten years at an average weight of three hundred pounds per person."

It was so quiet in the room that you could have heard a button pop.

"After that," Harriet said smugly, "there will be a gradual but steady decrease to our respective ideal weights, which we will reach, on the average, at age seventy-two."

There was a huge groan.

Then a miserable silence.

Then Arabella started to laugh. Someone else giggled and a few other women joined in. Pretty soon we were all laughing till the tears rolled down our cheeks. Some of us may have been crying too, but it didn't seem to matter.

When we finally sobered up, Harriet was assigned the May diet. "It won't be as much fun as the April diet," she said, "but at least we might lose some weight."

"It was too good to be true," said Arabella, shaking her head.

Madge stood up. "I have an idea," she said, "Let's do the Anti-Craving Diet again—in December!"

Thus it was unanimously approved that we'd adopt the April diet every December, as a kind of Christmas present to ourselves.

"Well, it was fun while it lasted," Harriet admitted as we walked to our cars afterward. "But we don't want to turn into a bunch of jolly fat ladies, do we?"

"No, of course we wouldn't want that," I agreed. But in my mind I saw my jolly fat grandmother, and I thought, "There are worse things we could be."

A MAMMOTH UNDERTAKING

Roz Warren

To feel the body heavy, when it is in fact light on the balance, shows a worse state of health, than to feel it weighty when it is really so. On the other hand, to feel it light when it is heavy on the balance, shows an excellent state of health.
—Catherine Beecher, *Never Too Thin: Why Women Are At War With Their Bodies*

◇

My best friend and roommate Eliza Haley woke up one morning with the sudden conviction that she had to become very fat, as soon as possible.

She immediately got out of bed and went to look at her naked body in the full length mirror in her bathroom. Eliza was average weight for her height. She worked out. She ran. She has always worked hard on her appearance and had been satisfied with the results. Now, she looked unfinished to herself, an uninspiring collection of skin and bones.

Standing there on the bathroom scale under the fluorescent light, she realized that she resembled a neat, sparse, sturdy piece of modern furniture, like a Scandinavian coffee table. She suddenly yearned to be a comfy chair—plush, overstuffed and yielding.

She got off the scale, pulled on her bathrobe, and marched down to the kitchen. Instead of her usual breakfast of black coffee and yogurt, she made herself a batch of whole what pancakes, doused them in maple syrup and butter, and polished off every last bite. She was on her way.

Within a week, she had gained five pounds. They formed a neat little bulge at her belly and sat tentatively on her hips. "Progress is being made!" she said to me happily, scrambling some eggs for us one morning.

"You're nuts," I said.

"No I'm not," she said. "I simply want to be a fat person. The fatter the better."

"What for?"

"Because I want to be all that I can be."

"You're nuts."

"I'll make you eat those words," she vowed.

She steadily put on weight. However, watching television one evening, she had a sudden insight—she wasn't putting on the proper kind of weight. In order to gain, she had been eating too much of her favorite foods. But that wasn't enough. Being a Real Fat Person didn't mean merely ingesting excess of salad and whole wheat bread. It meant cutting loose entirely—washing down a double helping of macaroni and cheese with a gallon of chocolate milk, and following it up with a plate of Twinkies.

For lunch the next day, she proudly served me a huge sandwich made of a mass of pre-packaged luncheon meat slices and American cheese singles between two slices of Wonder Bread, oozing with glops of Miracle Whip.

"It took me hours to unwrap all the plastic," she said, "but you're worth it."

"You're crazy," I said, contemplating the preposterous sandwich.

"Trust me. I'm into something very significant here."

"Yeah—it's called high blood pressure."

Concerned, I got Eliza a subscription to Weight Watchers Magazine. I was a bit nervous as she pulled the first issue from the mailbox and examined it. Although we were close, she had always been rather thin-skinned and could be touchy about such a critical gesture. However, she merely smiled. Later, I crossed my fingers as Eliza disappeared into her bedroom with the magazine and a fresh bag of corn chips.

She emerged several hours later, still smiling. "I love it!" she cried.

"You do?"

"It's inspired me! For instance, there's an article about a woman who used to sneak downstairs every morning at three while her family was asleep and prepare cake mixes Then she'd eat the entire thing, right out of the mixing bowl! Why on earth didn't I think of that?"

The next night, Eliza dreamed that she took part in an elaborate awards ceremony in which Captain Crunch, Ronald McDonald and the Pillsbury Dough Boy presented her with a beautiful patchwork quilt. The quilt was made up of millions of American kitchens at midnight. In the center of each kitchen stood a sleepy fat person, putting together and then devouring cake mix.

"We present you with this coveted award, Eliza Haley," the Pillsbury Dough Boy said in his distinctive, high-pitched, giggling voice, "for your heroic effort to become larger than life." Happily, Eliza took the quilt, wrapped it around herself, and strode proudly from the platform to thunderous applause.

Then she awoke, to find herself standing on the scale in her bathroom, her electric blanket draped about her shoulders. Peering into the mirror, she let the blanket drop. To her profound joy, her outline, which only weeks before had been hard and lean, was now fuzzy and indistinct. She had acquired a pale luminous softness, like the women in Renoir's paintings. Her physique had traveled back in time—she had mysteriously evolved into a glowing, voluptuous, nineteenth century beauty.

"Renoir would have adored me!" she exalted.

"But Renoir is dead," I said when she told me of this vision the next day. "Cindy Sherman would probably cross the street to avoid having to look at you. And not only is all this weight unstylish, but it's also unhealthy!"

"You can't be sure," she said. "For centuries, doctors thought that being *large* was healthy. The current emphasis on being thin could turn out to be completely misguided. Why, in a few years health food stores could be selling blocks of cholesterol instead of tofu! I wouldn't be surprised if doctors discovered that the key to a long life is a positive outlook combined with an additional fifty pounds. I personally have never felt better."

This was undeniably true. At 160 pounds, Eliza seemed happier than I'd ever seen her.

At 175 pounds, all of Eliza's hard edges vanished completely. As if to compensate, she developed a sharp wit. Everyone enjoyed her company and adored her wonderful new sense of humor.

One of them, Ralph, soon confessed his love for her.

"I always wanted you," he said to her as they lay in bed the first night they made love. "But you seemed so cold—so hard and unapproachable. Now I feel completely comfortable and relaxed with you."

Eliza merely smiled and patted her ample belly in the darkness. "I'm up for a midnight snack, darling," she said tenderly. "Want to split a pot roast?"

"Okay," I said to her after he left the next morning. "He's adorable. But I still maintain that you're throwing yourself away."

"On the contrary," she said. "I'm finally finding myself. All my life, I've worked and slaved and struggled to be thin. What if that was completely wrong? You know how they say that inside every fat person, there's a thin person longing to be released?"

I nodded.

"What if inside certain thin people there's really a fat person being slowly crushed to death?"

"Eliza," I said, stunned. "Are you telling me that you've really been a fat person all along?"

"That's what I have to find out," she said. "And the only way is to take this as far as it can go."

"But how far is that?"

"My goal," she said, "is to reach that point where life is reduced to three fundamentals—procuring food, preparing food, and devouring food."

"And everything else," I said, "will be—you'll forgive the expression—icing on the cake?"

"Exactly."

"And what then?"

"Who knows?" she said with a mysterious smile, reaching for another handful of bon bons.

Almost a year after she had begun her great project, Eliza Haley woke up in the middle of the night. She heaved herself out of bed, moved majestically to the bathroom scale, and climbed aboard. The needle danced crazily back and forth, in a desperate attempt to adjust Eliza's increased poundage. Then, with an anguished Clunk! the scale broke.

"Jackpot!" breathed Eliza to her reflection. The fat lady in the mirror grinned back happily.

Giggling, she tore off the voluminous flannel nightgown she wore, raced out into the night.

"Hallelujah!" she cried. "I'm fat at last!"

The noise she made woke up her neighbors. We all went to our windows and looked out, then watched, mesmerized by the unique sight of all three hundred pounds of naked Eliza Haley joyfully jitterbugging across her back lawn in the moonlight.

It should have been awkward, or ugly. She should have been grotesque. But it wasn't in the least bit ugly. Instead, it was one of the most touching, enchanting and beautiful sights we'd ever seen.

We had each feared in our heart that we were ugly in some way. Seeing Eliza, we lost all fear. All we wanted to do was to join her, to laugh and dance with relief and happiness.

But as we moved to do so, Eliza stopped dancing and spread her arms wide. A great rush of wind came and caught her and she began to rise, like a succulent cookie in an oven, or an old fashioned zeppelin loosened from its moorings. As we watched, dumbfounded, she rose quickly into the night sky and disappeared forever.

And everybody who rushed out of their homes and into their backyards that night swears that her disappearance from sight coincided exactly with the appearance in the sky of a brand new cluster of stars, which the astronomers named Zorga Molar Constellation, but which Eliza's neighbors always refer to knowingly as The Fat Lady.

And those of us who slip downstairs at night to finish off the roast chicken, or settle down on a Sunday afternoon with a good book and a box of chocolates, know that she watched over our meager efforts to duplicate her art, tenderly, eternally smiling and supportive, and, at long last, satiated.

FAT LENA
Wanda Coleman

In some ways, as an African-American woman, I have a smidgen of leeway amongst my own—not a lot, but African cultures appreciate large, full-bodied women. Living in America, we're also influenced by what the dominant culture promotes as its ideals.

Other facets of racism also color the picture. As a Black woman who is often around European-Americans, I feel a particular urgency not to be the disdained, laughed-at, fat Black woman so ridiculed in white American consciousness. There's that level where white Americans project what they don't want to see in themselves as belonging to the realm of Black people. Whites are thus allowed to feel smug and superior as they discount us.

I don't want to fulfill that role. My stance here parallels why I never ate watermelon as a kid: It was expected that I would just love watermelon and grow up to be Aunt Jemima, fat and cooking happily for whites. I bridled fiercely against satisfying a stereotype no one will admit to holding.

White women are kept in line by racist devices as well—their beauty measured by how much they don't look like people of color. We are said to wear the characteristics, like weight on a woman's body, that are deemed unacceptable by white American beauty standards.

—Donna Allegra, "Fat Dancer"

◇

She riding in the car next to her husband he be rubber-neckin' at all the pretty womens age no object and Fat Lena feel herself gettin' fatter by the minute wonderin' why he don't reserve his lust for her cuz they married anyway and she like to fuck as much as he do even if she new at it and not nearly as experienced but he want a virgin and that what he got Fat Lena never had a boy break her cherry till he come along she had a few hold her hand and squeeze up all around her and two or three try a kiss and one day Fat Lena go to the liquor store for her Mama this young man just come up on her and feel her titty where it ought to be but there's just barely enough to grab hold to and he tear the button off her jumper and ran away when she scream in a fear totally new to her not knowing why she was supposed to be afraid of that skinny little ugly brown boy so that was when Mama began to explain sex sort of and Fat Lena married at last and moved out and all day she lay up and watch television and eat junk and wait for her husband to come home

151

and maybe they go somewhere and do something but lately she not so happy as she was cuz he started eyeballing other womens and not even hiding it from her he whistles and carries on like she's not there or is just another man and it hurts her feelings real bad but Fat Lena she don't know how to tell him and one day he pull up at a stop light and while he lookin' off in another direction an old man steps off the curb and the old man catch sight of Lena and he grin a big grin at her and lick his tongue out at her as he passes in front of the car and Lena grinned back at him and suddenly she feel good and warm deep inside like God done told her there's hope for her yet.

On Ward G

Judy Freespirit

[Because I was still so anemic] I spent my birthday last week in the emergency [room] checking my Hb [blood count]. It was 9 [still low]; I left depressed as usual. There was a death, people were crying. I asked the reception clerk about the matter. He said it was a heart attack. It is nothing, he said, just a very, very, very fat man. So to him it is normal for a fat man to die of a heart attack. So I said "how very, very, very fat was he?" He looked at me shyly and said "just like you." I felt sorry for the poor dead man and his family. They were crying so much, old and young men and women. It was not just a fat man to them but a loved soul and kind heart.

—Fatima Parker, "Shedding Light on Fat Discrimination"

I asked the ER nurses why if being fat caused "all health problems," then the hospital must be full of fat people, so why didn't they have more accommodating resources for us. It makes no sense that they would not have an extra-large gown in the ER or on a floor of the hospital or even readily accessible.

You come into the ER because you are sick or injured, so you have to wait for them to find a wheelchair big enough for you to sit in so you can even get inside. A lot of the doctors' offices now have wheelchairs available and they are all skinny seats. I just don't understand if the majority of America is fat and fat causes health problems then why isn't the health care industry more accommodating?

—Cheryl Olsen, cheryl@midmo.net

"How old does someone have to be," one of our models asked one day, "before she dies of old age instead of being too fat?"

—Debbie Notkin, *Women En Large: Images of Fat Nudes*

The clock on the wall over the nurses' station says 5:05. I forgot to bring my watch when I left home at 1:30 A.M. to drive myself once again into Emergency at Kaiser Hospital. My asthma is especially bad this time, and again it's happening when I have my bloods. I wonder what the connection is.

There was a patient in the waiting room smoking a cigarette when I arrived. She was holding it down below the eye level of the receptionist and sort of cupping it in her hand. I could smell it the instant I opened the door. Someone was also wearing very heavy perfume, the receptionist, I think. I stood in the open doorway, gasping for air as I got up the nerve to speak to the woman with the cigarette.

"I'm having an asthma attack," I wheezed at her, "and I need you to put that out."

She put it out but not before grumbling some obscenities under her breath. She looked pissed as hell. Then, when the nurse took me ahead of her, she was really steamed.

"How come you're taking her first?" she complained, "I could be dying of pneumonia out here."

The nurse just told her it was because I couldn't breathe. That's all I heard anyway. I didn't blame her for being pissed, but I sure was glad they took me right away, cause I was real sick this time.

The young doctor on duty was the same one who had seen me last night and he remembered me. This time he looked sort of scared. Not the nurse though. She was totally cool. She just kept working real fast, zipping those needles into my arm and saying "stick" just before she jabbed me. That juice they shoot me full of is a speed freak's dream. But me, I don't like that high, nervous feeling it gives me. It reminds me of all those years I was on diet pills as a kid. I used to feel like climbing the walls. I never learned to like it the way some people do.

The nurse stuck me a bunch of times and gave me a treatment on the breath therapy machine. They took my blood pressure which was really high. That usually happens when I'm having an asthma attack. They don't volunteer the information about how high it is, but I always ask. They have to tell you now, it's the law.

The medicine was making me shake a lot. My teeth were rattling in my head, but the wheezing just stuck with me. I knew it would. I could tell the doctor knew too, but they have this procedure they have to go through, so we tried all the things first that we both knew weren't going to work. Then the doctor told me I'd probably need to be on IVs and stay the night on Ward G.

That's the name they use here at Kaiser for the holding ward. It's a kind of Never Never Land between Emergency and one of the regular wards. They keep you on G hoping you'll get better in 8 or 12 hours and that will save them the trouble and paperwork of admitting you to the hospital. I'm an old hand at Ward G.

The best things about being on G Ward are they give you a real bed which is a lot more comfortable than a gurney, you get a table across the bed so you can write and the nurses don't smoke on duty like they do in Emergency.

It's about 6 A.M. now. There's a voice coming over the loud speaker saying, "Code Blue, room 620." She has said it three times now, real calm and gentle-like. "Code Blue, room 620," she says, like nobody's gonna know that someone in room 620 is probably dying. Now she's doing it again! What's wrong? Isn't anybody responding? God, I hate how helpless I am in the hospital, how dependent. She's saying it again! *Please will someone go to 620 already? I can't stand the pressure.* OK, she finally stopped. I hope they got there in time. I'm afraid tonight, more afraid than usual, of dying.

I was saying before what's good about G Ward. The best thing is having a bathroom right near the bed, just a few yards away. In Emergency if you get put in one of the rooms where they put the sickest people, the bathroom is a city block away. And since they put me in this stupid night shirt, or whatever you call it, that closes in the back and only goes half way around my fat body, my whole back is exposed. I have to walk through the hallway dragging this IV pole and my backside is sticking out for everyone to see. The halls are filled with patients and their friends and family and various staff people. It's really too much.

Now for the bad. The worst part for me is that G is where the staff refrigerator, microwave and coffee machine are. Doctors, nurses, aides, maintenance men and security guards are coming in every few minutes, getting food and coffee and yackin' up a storm. Real early this morning there was this big box of Colonel Sanders Kentucky Fried Chicken in the refrigerator, and each staff person came in, took some out and put it in the microwave. The smell of greasy chicken was all over the ward. They kept taking out potato salad and cole slaw and apples and juice and milk. I'm in the bed right across from the refrigerator and I'm starving. I want to ask for something to eat, but I know it's for the staff. They don't feed the patients during the night. If I were a thin woman I'd have asked for some anyway, but I didn't want to provide them with a funny story about the fat lady who wanted their food.

I've been up for 48 hours now and it's been over 12 since I last had anything to eat. In a few hours they'll bring me breakfast. I can guess from experience what it will be: an asthmatic's nightmare! A cheese omelet, Wonder Bread with butter, a glass of milk, and some apple juice. Everything that makes me wheeze more. I'll eat it anyway, whatever it is. They don't know a thing about nutrition and diet for allergies. I wonder what they teach dieticians in all those years of schooling.

For a while there last night I got real scared. I don't know why except that it was unusually hard for me to breathe and suddenly it occurred to me that I might die tonight. I flashed on this scene form the movie *Resurrection* where this woman dies in a car accident and she goes to this place that's like a tunnel with bright light at the end. All her dead relatives and neighbors are there, welcoming her. Well, I began to feel like I might be seeing my Bubbie tonight, and I started to cry. I suddenly missed her so much. I never really let myself feel how much I missed her till now. I could see her in my mind like she was when I was a kid. She died when I was 11 or 12 years old. She was very short, maybe 4 feet 10 inches, fat and wrinkled. She had the finest, most pure white hair I've ever seen; a bobby pin wouldn't stay in it for 2 seconds. And she had soft brown eyes. Even though she didn't speak much English and I didn't speak much Yiddish, we managed to communicate somehow.

I was crying and thinking about seeing my Bubbie and then I said, "No! I'm not ready to go yet. I still have more stories to write and more women to know and love. It's too soon. I'm only 47 and I just started living 10 years ago when I came out as a lesbian. It's too soon. I won't go."

Then I looked at the door to the hallway in the wall next to the refrigerator and saw this thick white tape spelling out the word "No!" It was about eight inches high and I looked at that word "No!" and I said to myself, "I'll just keep looking at it to remind me that I can't die today. For one thing, nobody knows I'm here."

I realized how alone I am when the woman in the next bed came in a few hours after I was admitted. Her daughter was with her, and it made me think about how I don't have anyone here with me, no family. I have friends, and even a lover or two, but nobody I feel like I want to ask to drive me to the emergency or check in to see how I'm doing. It's easier this way. If I call someone they get all upset and then I have to take care of them and it takes more energy than just coming in by myself. So anyway I can't die tonight because nobody would know. I'd just disappear. Of course eventually somebody would see I wasn't at a meeting or didn't make a lunch date and they'd ask each other, "Have you seen Malka lately?" Sooner or later somebody would call the hospital and they'd be told I'd died days ago. Since the hospital has no information about "next of kin" they had just given me a pauper's funeral. You can't leave a smelly old body lying round indefinitely, you know. Anyway, I'm going to live this time, so it doesn't matter. Next time I'd better make some arrangements.

I almost blew it with the male nurse when I first came in. I mean it's as important for the patient to have the right bedside manner as it is for the staff. Even more important since we're talking about survival here. I've developed a system over the past few years. The theory goes like this: The best of nurses is overworked and the worst just couldn't care less. The more you can do for yourself the better; that way when you do need to ask for something, they're more likely to be willing to do it for you. So I straighten my own sheets, push the red button on the IV machine when it starts beeping, get myself water, things like that. The other thing is that you have to be polite, but not too polite, or they'll ignore you. The most effective method I've found is to be assertive and appreciative at the same time. For example, when I first came to G Ward tonight I realized I'd need some sanitary napkins. Now if I had been mealy-mouthed about it I'd have gotten them eventually, but the nurse might have been hostile and seen me as a simpering weakling, and done as little as possible after that to make me comfortable. So in a strong voice, level but not pushy, I said, "I'll need some sanitary napkins and some ice water and that should do it." He brought them to me right away and I smiled slightly, not too friendly but acknowledging the effort. Then he hooked up the IV bag to the machine. Now that's where I made my first mistake. Instead of keeping my mouth shut, I said, "I'll just unplug and take this in with me when I need to go to the bathroom." "No," he said, "you have to call me each time, and if you have to go too often we'll have to give you a bedpan. The doctor put you on bed rest."

"Well," I thought, "we'll see about that, Honey. I'm not using any goddamned bed pan as long as I'm conscious." So, I'd just quietly slip out of bed and slip back into bed when I was done and plug back in. I think by the third time he must have realized what was happening. He just ignored it.

It's after 9 o'clock now. Around 7 A.M. I could hear the night nurse filling in the next shift, but I couldn't see who she was. When I finally did see her I knew I had my work cut out for me. It was Sharmina, tough as nails and slow as a snail. Not only that, but I was so hungry by this time I could have eaten the bedclothes, and Sharmina has this thing about taking her good old time about feeding patients, especially about feeding me.

The first time I was on Ward G, about a year ago, I made the mistake of telling Sharmina at 7 a.m. that I was hungry. I ate around 10 a.m. that time. Now I know she's fat phobic and I have to charm her to get anything at all. So when she came to check my IV around 8 o'clock I smiled and said, "They could use three more of you on this shift. They sure do give you a lot of work to do." She smiled and then I said, "I love your ring." She liked that. I got my breakfast about 8:30.

Manipulation sometimes doesn't hurt anybody and it can help me survive. I wish I didn't have to do it. I'm not sorry I did though, even if I was right about the breakfast. It was worse than I had expected—French toast made with two thin slices of Wonder Bread, two soggy bacon strips and a carton of milk. There were two orange slices too, which had been heated with the French toast in the microwave. I ate them anyway. I was tempted to pour some of the honey-cinnamon syrup on the styrofoam dish and see how that would taste, but I squelched that idea. I can't afford to die of styrofoam poisoning when I'm in the middle of writing a story. I left the milk and the dish and ate everything else. I'm still starved. Maybe later I can get someone to come over and bring me some real food.

It's now 9:30 and the doctor who came in at 9:15 said I'm not sounding very good. I could have told him that. They can only keep me on G Ward till noon and then evaluate whether they should admit me or send me home. Either option scares me.

I'm feeling really uptight now, scared, pissed, wheezy and panicky. About half an hour ago I phoned my boss to say I'm in the hospital and I don't know if they are going to let me out or not. She sounded tight-lipped, not happy at all. "So what does that mean?" she wanted to know. I said, "Well, I'll know around 12:00 or 1:00 if they're letting me out or admitting me and I'll call you then." She just said, "OK, let me know when you know." Then she hung up.

I spent the next 5 minutes doing a scenario in my head, a confrontation where I go to work and she says to me, "Now look, I want to be fair, but I have a business to run here and you're missing too much time. I know you haven't used all of your sick leave, but you're out when I need you, and it's really a problem." So I say, "OK Carla, what exactly is it you want me to do?" and she says, "I just can't have this. I need to be able to depend on you. I want you to be here when you're supposed to be here."

"You're saying you don't want me to be sick and miss work, right?"

"Well, yes, I guess so."

"OK Carla, I won't be sick any more."

"Now wait a minute," she says, "How can you promise you won't be sick?"

"It's just as reasonable for me to promise," I say, "as it is for you to ask me to." I leave her on that. She's very guilt ridden and liberal as hell. She also has a lot of power over my life. She pays me a good hourly salary and gives me holidays and sick leave, but she won't pay into unemployment or disability so I'm at her mercy. If I lose my job or become physically unable to work, I'm out of luck. So I'll come in to work as much as I can, unless I'm really dying. Meantime I think I ought to look for a job where they're not so nice but where I can get unemployment and disability benefits. I feel really sad. I hope the fantasy doesn't have to be played out all the way. I like working for Carla.

Around noon Sharmina comes over to my bed with a big syringe of medicine and she starts to inject it into the IV tubing. I say, "Wait a minute, what's that?" She says, "It's just some more Solumedral." "What do you mean 'some more'? What is it? Is it steroids?" "Yes," she says, "you've been getting it all night and it's time to put in some more." Now I'm pissed. I say, "Nobody told me they were putting steroids in the IVs. I specifically asked in E.R. to be told if they were going to give me steroids." "Look honey," Sharmina snaps, "I can't control what they do or don't do in E.R. I'm just giving you what the doctor ordered." I want to cry. Damn them, those arrogant, fucking-bastard-prick doctors.

I decided to let myself cry. I was just getting into it, allowing the tears to splash onto the blankets when this doctor I hadn't seen before comes by to make his rounds. It's been hours since I've seen a doctor, and just when I'm trying to have a good cry, he shows up and says, "Why the tears?" "I'm really angry," I tell him. "I just found out they're giving me steroids. They promised they'd tell me before they did that. I wanted to check with my own doctor first. I've been on steroids for 5 months now and I've been cutting down, trying to get off them. Now they've upped my dose and I'm really mad that I wasn't informed like I was promised."

"Well," he says, puffing himself up to his full height, "if you've been on them for 5 months that's all the more reason to increase them if you're having an attack."

I'm not convinced. "I'm angry about not being told," I say. "What's at issue here is informed consent. I feel totally out of control of what's happening to me."

"Now, now," he says, "we're giving you the best treatment we know how." Then he leaves as suddenly as he arrived.

I'm chewing on that last piece of drama when Maude, the nurse who's now assisting Sharmina, arrives and sees me writing in my journal. Are you keeping a diary?" she asks. That's when I make my second mistake of the day. "No," I say, "I'm writing a short story. I figure something ought to come out of this experience." The minute it's out of my mouth I know it's a mistake. I don't know how it will come down, but I know I'm going to have to pay for that one. Maude doesn't disappoint me. Next thing I know she's coming over almost seductively, placing a thermometer in my mouth and saying, "I hope you're putting good things about the nurses in your story."

"Of course I am," I answer quickly. "The nurses are the best thing going around here." The next thing I know she's telling me how she's trying to lose 15 pounds. I mean I'm sitting here in bed, all 300 plus pounds of me, and this 5'-9" woman who weighs maybe 150 or 160 at most is telling me that she's on a diet. Now I don't want to hear about it, but I'm not in such a favorable position here. I don't want to make things worse, so I just say, "Why are you dieting? You look fine to me." "Oh," she says, "I need to lose 15 pounds. I lost 50 pounds not so long ago. I got down to a size 3 and I felt sooooooooooo good. But then there was all this food around. You know I hardly eat anything at home, but here at the hospital they give us free donuts every morning, and I just keep eating. I gained back 15 pounds so I have to lose it." All the time she's talking she's acting real coy and charming in a way she wasn't doing before. I say to myself, "Hey now, what's going on here?" Then suddenly it comes to me. She's auditioning! I mean she wants me to write about her in my story. She keeps coming back and talking to me every few minutes. At lunch she gives me an extra roast beef sandwich when I say I'm really hungry. Now this is unheard of behavior from my past experience. So she wants to be in my story? OK, so she's in my story.

It's 2 P.M. now and I want this story to end, but it keeps going on and on. I'm getting very exhausted and I feel worse than I did when I came in last night. I'm breathing better, but I'm feeling sicker somehow. My hands and legs ache especially badly, but really I'm in pain all over. I think it's from the medicine they're giving me. Another doctor came by around 12:30 and said that the other doctor had told him I was upset. He listened to my complaints and said I certainly had reason to be upset. I should have been told what medicine was being given to me. He thought I'd be going home soon and he wanted to get a white blood count to see if I had an infection. He looked into my eyes and at my tongue and listened for a long time to my heart. Then he asked if I felt nauseous and I told him I didn't. He seemed very concerned. I'm sure he's the staff P.R. person, the one they send in when they're afraid of a lawsuit. He's got that smooth "I understand just what you mean" kind of manner specially suited for disarming and defusing.

It's 2:45 now and the P.R. doctor just gave me the word that I can leave. I'm relieved. I think one more hour of this and I'd be screaming and tearing the place apart. My head is aching. Earlier this afternoon I heard a nurse from another floor saying they had just sprayed for ants on her ward and all the patients are complaining of headaches. On top of that, the cleaning woman has just left after mopping the floor around me with some foul smelling disinfectant. Chemicals of any kind make my asthma worse. So now my head aches and I'm starting to feel dizzy and wheeze more than I had before she came.

It's 4 P.M. and I'm home now. As I was leaving, I gave Sharmina a hug and told her, "Hey, let's get together socially sometimes. I don't want to have to keep meeting like this." She just laughed. She's really not so bad. Kind of cute, in fact. I hope I never have to see her again.

SKANKS

Rennie Sparks

Contemporary girls are in trouble because we are experiencing a mismatch between biology and culture. At this moment in our history, young women develop physically earlier than ever before, but they do so within a society that does not protect or nurture them in ways that were once a hallmark of American life. Instead of supporting our early-maturing girls, or offering them some special relief or protection from the unrelenting self-scrutiny that the marketplace and modern media both thrive on, contemporary culture exacerbates normal adolescent self-consciousness and encourages precocious sexuality. Too often popular culture and peer groups, rather than parents or other responsible adults, call the cadence in contemporary teenage life. Contemporary girls seem to have more autonomy, but their freedom is laced with peril. Despite sophisticated packaging, many remain emotionally immature, and that makes it all the more difficult to withstand the sexually brutal and commercially rapacious society in which they grow up.

—Joan Jacobs Brumberg, *The Body Project:*
An Intimate History of American Girls

There is a hidden culture of girls' aggression in which bullying is epidemic, distinctive, and destructive. . . . Our culture refuses girls access to open conflict, and it forces their aggression into nonphysical, indirect, and covert forms. Girls use backbiting, exclusion, rumors, name-calling, and manipulation to inflict psychological pain on targeted victims. . . . girls frequently attack within tightly knit networks of friends, making aggression harder to identify and intensifying this damage to the victims. . . . girls fight with body language and relationships. . . . In this world, friendship is a weapon, and the sting of a shout pales in comparison to a day of someone's silence. There is no gesture more devastating than the back turning away.

—Rachel Simmons, *Odd Girl Out: The Hidden Culture of Aggression in Girls*

Dawn and me eat scrambled eggs and tomato juice for dinner because we're on a diet. Dawn knows how to throw up so she eats toast and butter too. But, my fingers go so far down my throat and still nothing comes up. I'm a fat cow.

Dawn and me are best friends. I sleep over her house now ever since my stepfather called me a skank for eating all his cocktail onions. I'm waiting for my mom to call and beg me to come back home, but it's been almost two weeks and I'm wondering if maybe their phone is broken.

Sometimes my mom spaces on time. She drinks a lot of green Hi-C mixed with vodka. I've seen her sit down with a drink in the morning just as Oprah's coming on and then it's like the next thing she knows, Hard Copy's coming on and my step-dad's walking in the door screaming, "I can't smell no fucking dinner."

But, I'm over Dawn's house now. We share her single bed with the quilted pink covers. We stay up late smoking cigarettes, talking about love with the ashtray balanced between us on the sheets. Dawn loves guys who give long, wet kisses. I love swollen red circles that last for weeks on my neck so that everyone knows I've been going at it. Dawn and me both agree though mostly we just want to fall in love. That's why we hang out at the mall.

Dawn's mom is divorced and Dawn gets to call her Lorraine instead of mom. We smoke Lorraine's Marlboro Lights at the kitchen table with a green ashtray in the shape of a frog. Lorraine is in the shower with her loofah pad and her pineapple-smelling shampoo, getting ready to go out with an optometrist she met at work. Lorraine works behind the counter at the U-Haul on Motor Parkway and she gets to wear this tight, orange dress that says, "U-Haul" on it. She meets a lot of men because of that dress. Not to mention the fact that any guy who gets divorced ends up at U-Haul sooner or later with a sad look on his face.

Lorraine comes out of the shower and models her new underwear for us. The underwear is red lace with a fishnet heart cut out in the center so you can see Lorraine's hair down there and it's sort of dirty blonde even though Lorraine's hair on top is jet black. There's a long purple scar up Lorraine's stomach from where they pulled Dawn out, but Lorraine's stomach is flat and tight like a boy's. She must know how to throw up too.

"Ta da!" Lorraine says.

"You look fox, Lorraine," Dawn says.

"Yeah," I say. "Definitely."

The optometrist pulls up in a dark, blue Chrysler with duct tape over one tail light. Lorraine runs out of the kitchen, shoving in her earrings, smoothing down a yellow satin dress she bought at Shoes 'N Things. She is blushing and pursing her lips and breathing fast as she lets the optometrist inside. He looks afraid, confused—unprepared to be stepping into a woman's house.

"Dawn," Lorraine says in her giggle voice that is saved for men only. "I'll be home late or not at all."

Dawn rolls her eyes.

"Watch it now, young lady." Lorraine says.

"Okay," Dawn mumbles. "Whatever."

"Okay, Lorraine," the optometrist says, nervously. "Is seafood okay?"

Lorraine just giggles and takes his arm. They head out to the car and drive away and I want to cry thinking of this skanking old guy with his hands all over Lorraine's perfect, tight body and his bony lips pressed against her sparkling, purple mouth. Then I remember that with Lorraine gone, Dawn and me are on our own.

We sit down at the kitchen table, light cigarettes and drink half a glass each of Lorraine's pink zinfandel wine because more than that she notices.

"Man," Dawn says. "I can't wait to get a place of my own. All I'm gonna have in the fridge is pink zinfandel and powdered donuts."

Dawn loves powdered donuts because they are the easiest thing in the world to throw up. Tonight we're off to the Mall to hunt for babes. Dawn says if she falls in love at the Mall she'll go out to the Pit.

"And leave me hanging by the fountain!" I scream.

"No," she says, plugging in her crimping iron. "There'll be a babe for you too. We'll find two babes and fall in love and make them take us to the Pit."

Dawn's in love with the actors Chris O'Donnell and Leonardo DeCaprio and she talks about them like she knows them. "Chris likes chocolate," she will tell me, "But, Leonardo likes white chocolate. Isn't that weird?"

We stare at their pictures taped over her bed. Dawn says she'd wear crotchless panties to go to bed with Leonardo. I say crotchless, edible panties. Dawn says crotchless, edible panties with cherry flavor and we fall off the bed laughing until Dawn's older brother, Carl, screams "Shut up" from the next room. Carl goes to college and reads books about building bridges. He knows nothing about music or movies or anything so we don't even bother talking to him.

Dawn's going to be a stewardess when she graduates high school or work at the U-Haul with Lorraine. I'm going to go to Wilfred Beauty Academy to learn how to do acrylic nails. When I get out of Wilfred, no one will call me a fat cow, they'll call me a nail stylist. The only thing is, I'm going to have to live at home for it to work. If I have to pay rent on an apartment, I will never save enough money for tuition.

I lay on Dawn's bed and swear to god I'll never touch my step-dad's cocktail onions again if my mother will just call. My step-dad is better than my real dad anyway and I shouldn't have pissed him off. My real dad broke my mom's jaw against the bathroom sink. My step-dad just slaps her without a fist and it doesn't look like it hurts much.

I have a new make up stick in dark, dusty pink. I put it on above my eyes like I saw in Beauty Digest. Dawn puts it along her cheekbones and outlines her lips in burnt sienna. She rubs musk behind her ears, filling the room with the smell of a jungle.

We lie flat on Dawn's bed to zip our jeans. When I stand up, there's a roll over the waist band so I borrow a loose sweater from Dawn. Dawn is straight and thin and wears padded bras that make tiny puff breasts under her shirts. Oh, how I wish I could throw up.

We each swallow four of Lorraine's Dexitrims and two of her No-Doz's and then fluff our hair out so we look like wild animals. We only take one each of Lorraine's Xanax because those she counts.

Dawn calls the cab and we wrap maxi pads in tin foil and put them in our purses. Since I've been sleeping over, we get our periods at the same time. With the tin foil around the pads we can open our purses in public and not have some skank scream, "Hey, look who's on the rag!"

The cab lets us off at Sears. We go in through the luggage department, past the gardening center and into the bathroom. Dawn doesn't like the way her hair turned out so she wets it in the sink and kneels under the hand dryer, one knee on the tile floor, to do it over.

I look at myself in the mirror. My hair and nails are perfect, but my cheeks are full and red, not hollow and sharp like Dawn's. Tomorrow, I will eat nothing but baby pickles.

We walk out to the benches around the fountain and spot Carol and Gail. Even from two stores down I can see that Carol has lost weight and I'm instantly jealous. She was always a pudge like me, but then she had to go to the clinic for an abortion and she threw up for two days after the anesthetic. It makes me wonder why no one sells anesthetic to fat people for a diet. I guess it's against the law, but still it isn't fair.

Two weeks before Carol had to go to the clinic she said, "Janine, walk with me to the deli." So, I walked with her to the deli and got a ham sandwich with only a little mayo and even pulled the crusts off. Carol got change for the phone.

She called the clinic and said she got raped and wanted the morning-after pill. This wasn't true. Carol had told me the moment down in the Pit when Scottie Milano finally got off her and she had to squat and search for a full minute before she found the rubber wedged up inside her.

It didn't matter anyway because the clinic said she had to tell the police first if she was really raped so Carol hung up the phone and fell against a gallon jar of pig's feet, crying her eyes out. But, when I tried to put my arm around her and pat her back with my fingers, she said, "You smell like ham, Janine," and pushed me away. I don't care. Dawn's my best friend anyway.

Dawn and me and Carol and Gail are sitting in front of the fountain waiting for babes. Gail is beautiful and goes out with Joey Cosomo who wears bleached-out jeans with holes in the ass and has wild, rock-star hair, but tonight Joey Cosomo is at some monster truck show in Garden City so Gail says she's a free agent.

I never told anyone, but I have a secret about Joey Cosomo. Once I walked by The Shear Shack and saw Joey sitting under a dryer with perm rods in his hair. It made me want him even more seeing the plastic sheet over him, the white towel around his neck and blue and yellow perm rods covering his head like a helmet. Any guy who thinks he ought to try and look good even if he's a babe already, has got to be sort of sweet. I wouldn't cheat on him just because he went to a monster truck show without me. But, I am not beautiful like Gail and the rules are different.

Tonight, Gail has done her eyes in blue liner. Her hair is a soft, golden blonde and curls up at her shoulders. She's long and thin in pink cords and a black sweater that shows a beige bra under her arm when she lifts a hand to flip her hair. It's hard to believe we are both girls. I have never come close to looking anything like her.

"What's up," Gail says, throwing her cigarette into the fountain. There's the hiss as flame hits water."

"Nothing," Dawn says.

"How you feeling," I ask Carol, but she just gives me a look.

"I'm staying at Gail's." She says finally.

"Janine's staying at my house," Dawn says.

"Yeah, my stepfather's a skank," I say quickly, feeling a moment's pride being the center of attention.

"They're all skanks," Gail says. "My stepfather stole a bra from my dresser. He says he wants it for a tool rag. Right . . ."

Out of nowhere, Dawn's elbow sinks into my side.

"Babes!" she whispers, and there they are. Two guys turning the corner from Montgomery Ward's, heading up towards the Sunglasses Hut. We lean back with our toes stretched out in high heels. I can feel the water from the fountain spraying across my back, but I don't move. The waist of my jeans is like an iron band. I can hardly breathe.

Dawn stands. "Janine, let's go."

"But, Dawn," I squeal. "We just sat down."

"Janine," she snarls back at me. "Look at that babe in the red leather. He's checking me out!"

"Can't we just sit awhile?" I whisper.

"Janine," Dawn asks, "Do you want to be a fat cow all your life? The blonde one isn't bad. He's got long hair. Let's go."

We go after the babes. They strut around the corner of Camera Corral with long pink combs sticking out of the back pockets of their jeans. Dawn's right. I have to do something with my life.

We follow them down the north corridor of the Mall. I watch the babe in the red leather. His thin hips jut back and forth in tight black denims. I feel myself slow and heavy at Dawn's side.

They go into Orange Julius and Dawn clicks fast on high heels behind them. The two bomber jackets buy chili dogs, but the red leather buys fries. He turns as he squirts ketchup and he has these unbelievable, sea-green eyes. I feel a bird flapping its wings in my stomach and I could almost collapse with the feel of it, but I force myself to look at the blonde one like Dawn wants even though he's ugly.

"What's up?" The babe in red leather says, staring down at the dirty floor. He smiles and I see his teeth are white and clean like a mouthwash commercial. He has dyed black hair with brown roots.

"Nothing," Dawn says, moving in. I try to give the blonde one a look, but he's worse close up. His hair is long, but hangs flat against the sides of his face and his body is round and square like Barney Rubble. I feel myself bursting against my jeans and I can see from his face that I am just as unappealing to him as he is to me. I manage a weak smile.

They slide into a booth with their food, throwing fries at each other across the table. Dawn and me order cheese fries and sit at the next booth up from them. We suck cheese off the fries then put the fries back on the paper plate. I suck only five fries. Dawn sucks down practically the whole plate. She can. She's already thrown up twice today. Finally, the babe finishes his food and looks across the torn vinyl seats at Dawn.

"Hey," the babe says.

"Hey," Dawn says.

"What's up?" he says.

"Nothing," she says.

"You wanna hang out?"

"Sure," she says. "I'm Dawn. This is Janine."

"Hey," the babe says, looking my way for the briefest moment. He's a definite babe—tall and thin with hollow cheeks and a square chin.

"Listen," Dawn says, leaning in towards him. She gives a perfect look— all eyes and lips. "Janine was checking out your friend here," she whispers, "I think she's in love with him or something."

I push my face down into my fat arms, paralyzed.

"This is Stevie," the babe says. "He's cool." Stevie makes a burping sound at the back of his throat and sends me a crooked smile.

"Cool," Dawn whispers, clicking her nails on the tabletop. She stands, brushing against the babe as she pulls out of the booth. There's the slow sizzle of fabric against fabric and the intake of breath as the two of them stand motionless against each other a moment.

"We'll meet you by the Macy's exit," Dawn says and then she struts fast out of Orange Julius, heading back towards the Sears' bathroom. I follow, running in baby steps on my high heels, trying to keep up.

In the bathroom, I open my eyes as wide as possible, feeling tears welling at the edge of my mascara. "I can't believe you, Dawn," I say. My voice is heavy and scratched. "Telling that guy I was hot for his skank friend."

"He's all right," Dawn says, putting on lip gloss with a fingertip. "He has long hair. What's with you?" She stares at me hard.

"I don't wanna hang out with him is all." I whine.

I press my fingers against the corners of my eyes and they come away black with mascara. There's a noise at the back of my throat that wants to come out, but I know Dawn will be mad if I let it.

My stomach feels huge. The thought of that skanky, Barney Rubble waiting out there makes me want to puke though he's no worse than some of the others I've had to put up with as Dawn's best friend. It's no coincidence that every babe Dawn meets has a skanky-looking friend along with him. That's what people see when they look at Dawn and me. Beautiful people like to have a skank friend to hang around with. It makes them look even more beautiful.

"Oh man," Dawn says. "Are you my best friend or what?"

"You know I am!" My voice cracks in half. Carefully, I wipe away the black tears running down my cheek with a twist of Kleenex. "I just don't want to be with that guy. He's a skank and you know it."

A lady comes into the bathroom carrying a shopping bag. She goes in a stall. Dawn turns the hand dryer on so we can talk privately.

"Look," Dawn whispers. "If you're really my best friend, you'll do this for me because I'll tell you one thing for sure: only my best friend can sleep over my house tonight."

I stand there, weeping. It takes forever to get my breath.

"Janine," Dawn says finally. "Fix your face and let's go."

I get out my compact and brush powder across my cheekbones then re-do my mascara and eyeliner. I work quickly, knowing Dawn will leave me behind if I don't hurry.

"Look," Dawn says, leaning in to me finally, her voice softer now. "You don't have to do anything. I just don't want to be alone with this guy the first time is all. We'll stick together, I promise, and later when we get home we'll eat eggs or something, okay? We'll totally pig out."

I nod my head. My face is glowing again in the mirror. I open my eyes wide, testing my mascara. A toilet flushes and the woman with the shopping bag comes out, smoothing down her skirt. She washes up, staring at herself in the mirror. She slides her lips together, evening out her lipstick. She's old, at least forty. I want to fall over and die thinking about how many horrible years I will have to worry about make-up and hair before I get old enough that no one cares.

We leave the bathroom and head to Macy's. There they are, waiting by the exit. The babe sees us and pulls a wig crooked on a mannequin to show off. I smile. My skin is tight with powder, but underneath it I can feel my face swollen from crying.

"Hey, what's up," the babe says.

"Yeah, what's up," Stevie says. His eyes are a dull, mud brown.

"Hi," I say, bending my lips up into something like a smile. Dawn is giggling with her hand over her mouth.

We head out to the parking lot. It's dark out. Headlights reflect off the passing cars as we walk out to the strip of grass that separates the highway from the Macy's parking lot. Thick green bushes are planted in a row that lead out to the "Entrance" and "Exit" signs separating the traffic in and out of Macy's. Dawn and me lean against "Enter." Stevie and the babe stand across from us. The babe has a pint of Southern Comfort. He passes it around and we all swig.

"So," the babe says, finally. "What's up?"

"I'm cold," Dawn says.

"Here," the babe says. He takes off his red leather and wraps it around her, leaving his arm on his shoulder. Suddenly, they're going at it. She falls against "Enter" with a bang and I move quickly away as he presses into her with his hips and chest, grunting and tangling his fingers into her shining, black hair.

I look at Stevie and past him at the cars streaming by on the highway. He makes a noise in his throat and spits on the grass.

"What's up?" He says.

"Nothing." I say, looking down.

He puts his arm around me. The babe has a hand up Dawn's shirt, kneading her breast. I catch a glimpse of her pink bra under his hand. Stevie's arm curls around my shoulder slowly. The babe breaks away from Dawn a moment and says, "Time to move this party down to the pit?"

Dawn looks at me. "Come on, Janine." I shake my head. She puckers her lips. We go behind the "Exit" sign. She's sweaty, her makeup rising up like a film over her face.

"Janine, you want a place to sleep tonight?" Dawn asks. Her voice is thick, breathless. It's dark enough out that I just let my mascara run. I know Dawn can see, but she just flips her hair and steps back, talking loud so the guys can hear.

"Janine," she says. "You think you can do better?"

I look at her. Even with the wind from the cars and the sweat on her face, she's still something I will never be. From the tiny points of her shoulders to the long swoop of her legs rising up from her pink leather, high heel sandals. I give in.

We cross the highway and take the path down to the woods we call the pit. It's just dug up land from where they took dirt to make cement for the mall a million years ago. Thin pine trees planted along the highway have grown tall to block out the street lights and below, thorny bushes divide the pit into narrow paths where people go to fool around or do drugs or hide from the cops.

Stevie has a hand on my ass. He whispers in my ear, "You got a nice body, okay?"

The babe and Dawn have disappeared into the woods. I call her name, but she won't answer. Up the hill a truck shifts gears, a horn blares, some guy screams, "Dildo!"

Stevie says, "Sssssh. Relax."

We walk further into the pit, passing the dark outlines of couples rolling slowly in the dirt. We find a clearing with an overturned shopping cart and Stevie sits. I go to sit next to him, but he grabs my head tight over my ears so everything sounds like an ocean and behind the roar, I hear him whispering, "I love you, yeah, I really love you, okay . . ." pushing me down to my knees, pushing my face into his zipper and then there's the smell of his penis gagging me through his jeans.

I've been in this position before, lots of times, because of Dawn and because of other girls who were once my best friend and because a few beers convinced me that maybe a guy really liked me. I know I'm supposed to go numb, just open my mouth and let it happen then wait for Dawn to call me to go home. But, this time I can't seem to. This time there is no pretending that I'm doing it for Dawn or for myself or for any reason at all because I can see that Dawn is getting tired of me. Even if I play this right with Stevie, my days are numbered as Dawn's best friend.

I open my eyes. After a moment, the gold thread along the zipper of Stevie's jeans appears. Tears are running into my mouth. My make-up is shot. I try, I try so hard to keep my face pressed against Stevie's zipper but I can't and when his hand comes down and unzips his jeans, I pull away and stand up.

"You're a skank," I hear myself say.

"Hey," he says. "Come on. Help me out here. You can't leave me like this."

I call Dawn's name. No answer. I turn and head back up toward the road.

"Hey," Stevie yells after me. "You on the rag or something?"

"I'm leaving, Dawn," I yell one last time. I know if I walk back to the mall, I'll be doing something awful. I know as soon as I step out of these woods, I won't have a best friend anymore.

"Aaah, get lost fat girl," Stevie yells from behind me. "It's your loss anyways!"

I start to run. I run up out of the woods, and across the highway and through the lines of parked cars and into Macy's. I run through lingerie and pantyhose and piles of scarves. I run to the center of the mall and then stop with a burning cramp squeezing my side, feeling my fat stomach covered in sweat under Dawn's borrowed sweater. I stand there, panting, my face aching with dried tears. No one seems to notice me.

The benches by the fountains are empty and something tells me, if I've lost Dawn, I've lost Gail and Carol too. I've lost all the girls that sit at Dawn's lunch table at school. I am all alone and I have nowhere to sleep tonight.

I go into Little Anthony's Pizzeria and buy three slices with pepperoni with the last of my money. I eat as fast as I can with warm grease dripping down my neck.

Inside the Sears' bathroom, there are two girls at the sink. I don't know them. One girl has her head back and the other is French-braiding her hair.

When they see me, one of the girls reaches up and turns on the hair dryer to shut me out.

I go into a stall and I lean over the bowl, one hand holding onto the toilet paper roll. The other hand turns into a knife and I stab it down into my throat until my stomach starts to shake and my mouth gags open and the pizza rushes back up me and out, splashing in painful lumps down into the bowl.

The hand dryer clicks off. One of the girls says, "Lisa should never wear anything yellow. Have you noticed that? She looks like she's eighty or something when she wears yellow. It's weird."

I fall back against the door of the stall, my head banging against the metal coat hook. My stomach feels thin and flat, empty. I let out a deep breath of air and just for that moment between letting air out and filling myself up again, I feel beautiful—like a puzzle piece sliding in to fit. But, then it's gone and I flush the toilet and come out.

PERFECTLY NORMAL

Lesléa Newman

Lesbians appear to make up a smaller percentage of women with eating disorders than of women in general. Most of the women with eating disorders who are described in the literature are either clearly defined as heterosexual, or their sexual orientation has not been a focus of inquiry. My personal communication with researchers in the areas of eating disorders has also yielded some consensus that lesbians are highly under-represented among bulimic women presenting for treatment or research studies. In the lesbian community, the question has been raised regarding the appropriateness of defining obesity as pathology; consequently, fat lesbians may experience some social or political support (or pressure) for defining their body size and eating styles as normative variations rather than disordered eating styles. Lesbians appear to be over-represented among fat activists, that is, people who define fatness as a normative variation and the stigmatization of fat people as political oppression.

—Laura S. Brown, "Lesbians, Weight, and Eating:
New Analyses and Perspectives"

Nice to meet you, Dr. Polansky. My name is Harriet. Oh, you know that already, of course. I wasn't expecting a woman doctor. Well, life is full of surprises, isn't it? Yes, everything is fine, my room is just lovely. I love the light blue walls—robin's egg blue, they call it. It's the same color as our bedroom at home; isn't that a funny coincidence? Steve and I just painted it ourselves. See that tree outside my window? Just a minute before you came, a bird was singing in the branches—a robin, I think; maybe she thought my walls were her eggs. Just a joke.

I bet you weren't expecting to find someone so cheerful and healthy, were you, Doctor? There's nothing wrong with me; I'm fine really. I'm perfectly normal in every way, as you can see. It wasn't my idea to come here, you know. It was Steve's. He wants me to put on a little weight. I don't think I really need to, but you know husbands—you've got to please them. Anyway, I could use a little rest—who couldn't?

Tell you about my weight? I'm five foot, seven inches and I weigh ninety-seven pounds. I've weighed ninety-seven pounds for three years now, ever since we got married. Was I thin before we got married? Of course—why do you think Steve married me in the first place? Steve would never date a fat girl. Never.

I wasn't always this thin. Before we got married I weighed one hundred and fifteen pounds, and then, once we set the date, I went on a diet so I'd look good for our wedding day. A girl only gets married once in her life—hopefully anyway, you never know these days—so of course I wanted to look my best. I got down to one hundred and seven pounds, and I wore a size three/four wedding dress. It was a beautiful dress—white lace sleeves, a low neckline, little pearl buttons going all the way down the front. Everyone said I looked just like a little doll. I'd wanted to get down to one hundred and give pounds, but somehow I couldn't get rid of those last two pounds.

When I was younger, dieting was easier somehow. I don't know, maybe your metabolism changes as you get older; it's much harder now for me to take off the weight. If it's like this at twenty-seven, imagine what it'll be like when I'm fifty! That's why I work so hard to stay thin. See this roll of flab around my stomach? It used to be much bigger. I know my stomach isn't as flat as it should be. I can't get rid of this roll for love or money. I do three hundred sit-ups every night and I still don't have a flat tummy. I keep trying, though. Never give up; the Lord hates a quitter. That's what I always say.

My relationship with Steve? Oh, he's wonderful. Really. I couldn't ask for a better husband. He lets me do whatever I want, and as long as the house is clean and his dinner's on the table, he doesn't complain. I like cooking for him—he's a real meat and potatoes man. When he comes home from work I sit and watch him eat. Do you know that man can consume a thousand calories in one sitting? Really. A hunk of steak, a baked potato with butter, salad and ice cream for dessert. Men have it so much easier than women. Steve never has to think about his weight, and I can gain five pounds just watching him eat dinner! I never eat with him. Usually I just drink black coffee or diet soda. I don't eat much for supper. A hard boiled egg and a raw carrot sometimes, or steamed spinach with half a cup of cottage cheese. I never eat breakfast or lunch. There's just no time. There's so much to do—I have to clean the house, do the laundry, shop for food and go to my aerobics class, of course. Steve says it's good for me to get out. He's afraid I'll get lonely in the house by myself all day, so I go to aerobics every afternoon. I usually do two or three classes. I know how important it is to stay fit.

Oh, those kind of relations. Well, Steve and I really don't have sex all that much. We did in the beginning of course—everyone does—but I don't know, I don't really think about it. I can't remember the last time Steve and I had sex. I think Steve's afraid he'll crush me or something. Sometimes in the night I'll roll over to hug him, and his hipbones will clank against mine, and it hurts. I think maybe that's why he wanted me to come here, so I'd gain weight and we could have sex again. Eventually we want children, of course, everybody does. I haven't told Steve this, but I haven't got my period in a long time. I don't know why. Maybe you can run some tests, as long as I'm in here anyway.

Sometimes I think Steve goes to a prostitute once in a while. I wouldn't blame him if he did—it's different for men, you know. They have needs, not like women. I just don't care that much about it. Steve would never have an affair or anything, he simply adores me to pieces, but he might go to a prostitute every now and then, you know, to satisfy himself. I don't really mind. It's perfectly normal, that's what those places are for.

He reads *Playboy* and *Penthouse*, you know, men's magazines. He keeps them in the bottom drawer of his dresser. Sometimes when he's at work, I look at them. Pages and pages of gorgeous women, I'd give anything in the world to look like. I still have a lot of potential, you know. I'm not that old, and I have nice features, don't I? My eyes are pretty, everyone says so. You know, I would start eating a little more if you could guarantee that I'd gain weight in all the right places. I know everything would just go right to my stomach, and if there's one thing I cannot stand, it's a flabby belly. Ugh. I wouldn't mind a little padding on my derriere. That's why I'm sitting on this pillow—my bones hurt when I have to sit on a hard chair like this. At home I just sit on the couch or on the bed.

Siblings? Oh yes, I have a sister. Boy, do I have a sister! She's a real problem in our family. I don't talk about her all that much. She lives all the way across the country in San Francisco, so we don't see her very much, which is fine with me. You see, well, I don't tell many people this, but well, you're a doctor, I suppose it's all right to tell you our family secrets. Well, my sister is a lesbian. I know, it's a real tragedy, isn't it? At first I thought about it a lot; I mean, she is my baby sister. We grew up in the same house, and why one of us should turn out perfectly normal and the other one so sick is beyond me.

I think I know what happened, though. I think it's because she's fat. She always was a chubby kid, and then she was pretty big as a teenager, but now she's fat. And I mean fat. She's really let herself go the last couple of years, and I wouldn't be surprised if she weighed close to a hundred fifty pounds by now. She's only five foot three, she takes after my mother's side of the family, so you can just imagine.

Maybe she's slimmed down recently. I doubt it, but you never know. I haven't seen her in three years, not since our wedding. She left home when she was seventeen, and moved to San Francisco. I was twenty at the time, so that was . . . oh, seven years ago. She never came to visit—she said the air fare was too expensive—so I didn't get to see her for four years, not until the night before our wedding.

To tell you the truth, I really didn't want to invite her. I know that's a horrible thing to say about your own sister, but anyone would feel the same way. I mean, how was I going to explain her to Steve's relatives? I had hardly even mentioned her to Steve, but how long could I keep my baby sister a secret? Steve was great about it though. I didn't want to tell him, but finally I got all my courage up, and told him my little sister was gay. And you know what he said? He said, "Oh, that's why you never talk about her," and then he changed the subject. He's so good that way—he never dwells on the bad things in life. He has a real positive attitude—that's one of the things I like about him."

He did look kind of shocked when he finally met my sister though. I guess I should have told him she was fat, but it was hard enough to tell him that she was queer. I was hoping that she's slimmed down some, but I should have known better. She sends my mother pictures every year—my sister's really into photography. For the past few years, she's sent pictures of herself and a woman named Bev, who's her *friend*, if you know what I mean. And get this—Bev is even fatter than my sister is. Thank God the two of them found each other, that's what I say. I mean, who else would have them? Still, I know, it's very sad.

Oh, I tried to help her lose weight when we were growing up, but she never could stay on a diet. I taught her how to add up the calories of her food, how to use smaller plates so her meals would look bigger, how to drink a diet soda before she ate so she would be full before she started—you know, just basic common sense, things that everybody knows. But it never worked. So then I tried to teach her how to dress so at least she could look thinner than she was, even if she couldn't be thinner—you know, dark colors, no horizontal stripes, a necklace or a pretty scarf to draw the eyes away from her hips and up to her face. She really does have a pretty face—it's a shame, a crime really, that she's let herself go like that. She just doesn't seem to care.

I had so much to do before the wedding. I just didn't think about my sister coming until it was time to pick her up at the airport. I volunteered Steve and me to go because I don't really trust my sister—she's not too bright, and she doesn't know when to keep her mouth shut. Steve's brother said he would go, but what if she told him she was gay? I would just die. When she called to tell me she was coming, she said she was sorry but Bev couldn't make it—they couldn't afford two airfares. Thank God for that! Imagine having to explain the two of them.

Anyway, there we were, waiting at the United terminal, and out walks my sister, big as life. I could see all my years of fashion advice had been a complete waste, in one ear and out the other. My sister was wearing—get this—purple pants and a white, button-down blouse with these big purple irises splashed all over it. And, if that wasn't bad enough, she had her blouse tucked in! I could have died. Really, I couldn't believe it. I know Steve was in shock, because, like I said, I didn't warn him, and everyone else in my family is nice and thin, of course. And she had done something really awful to her hair, cut it very short in the front, almost like a boy's and left one piece hanging long in the back and part of it had been bleached. Oh, I tell you, she was a sight. I wanted to get her out of there as quickly as possible—I'm sure people were staring—but she took her own sweet time. She had to introduce us to some girl she had met on the plane and then we had to wait while they exchanged phone numbers and hugged and kissed goodbye like they had known each other for years.

One thing that's strange about my sister is she makes friends wherever she goes. I've never understood it. I think people just feel sorry for her. Women mostly. She doesn't have any men friends, of course—you know why. I don't like women all that much myself. Oh, nothing personal, Doctor. It's just that men are, you know, more interesting. I have one or two girlfriends I go shopping with, but mostly I like being with Steve. When he goes out with the boys, I stay home alone. He goes out, not that much, oh, I don't know, maybe three times a week.

To tell you the truth, I'd rather watch a good TV program and improve my mind than hang out with a bunch of women. Mostly they sit around and gossip, and I'll tell you a little secret—some of them are very jealous of me. I mean Steve's a very handsome guy and we're pretty well off, and I'm about the only one on the block who's kept my figure. All the girls want to know how I stay so thin. It's very easy. Willpower, I tell them, that's all. When you see something you want, you just don't have it. You feel much better about yourself that way. Also, I tell them, try and lose a few extra pounds—that's so you can have a little leeway. I'd like to weigh ninety-five, so I'd have five pounds to play with. That way, if I let myself go, for some reason and gained a pound or two, God forbid! I still wouldn't weigh over a hundred pounds. But it doesn't work that way for everyone, I guess. It seems too simple—I don't know why. I used to think it depended on your type of genes or something, but then how would you explain my sister?

When Steve dropped us off at my parent's house that night, my sister went inside, and I stayed in the car to kiss him goodnight. He took me in his arms and—I'll never forget this—he said, "Promise me one thing." "What?" I asked. "Promise me you'll never get as fat as your sister." I was shocked. "You know I wouldn't," I said to him. "I'd rather die."

After Steve left I went into my old room, the room I shared with my sister when we were growing up. This would be the last night I'd ever sleep in it—the last night I'd sleep anywhere without Steve. Oh, I was so happy! Of course, we'd slept together already; we even had our apartment by then, but we decided to be old-fashioned and not see each other until our wedding day. I think Steve went out with the boys to a strip joint or something. I don't mind. That's just the way men are.

My sister stayed downstairs to talk to my parents for a while and then she came upstairs to go to sleep. I didn't know what to say to her. When we were little we'd talk all night long—brush each other's hair, tell each other stories. She always wanted to be a famous photographer and travel all around the world taking pictures of everything. I wanted to be a ballerina. I took ballet lessons for a while—I still have my pink toeshoes with the satin laces—but then I stopped. I just got too fat. Ballerinas have to be really thin, much thinner than I'll ever be. I always had at least five extra pounds to lose, mostly around my belly, no matter how many sit-ups I do. It's a problem I've had all my life.

My sister still takes pictures though. It's not such a big deal. I mean she doesn't work for *Time* or *Newsweek* or anything. She works on a newspaper for people like her; I forget the name of it. Sometimes she sends pictures home to my mother. She's had some on the front page even, but I don't know, I don't think they're very good.

So there we are in our old bedroom, and my sister just got undressed, like she had nothing to be ashamed of. I couldn't believe it. I tried not to stare at her, but my God, I couldn't exactly ignore her; she took up half the room. And, I have to admit, I wanted to look. Morbid curiosity, I guess. I won't go into the gory details, but take my word for it, Doctor, if you ever get a chance to look at a fat, naked woman, do yourself a favor. One look, and I guarantee, you'll never go off your diet again.

I'll never forget the sight of her as long as I live. Especially her breasts— they were positively vulgar, hanging down from her like, like . . . I don't know, eggplants or something. And her belly was so soft and round—if I didn't know better, I'd have sworn she was pregnant. She looked like she could bounce, she was so soft, like the Pillsbury Dough Boy, for God's sake. Really. You couldn't see a bone anywhere in her entire body.

I felt so bad for my sister, but she didn't seem to mind. She's used to it, I guess. She . . . you'll never believe this, but she sat down on her bed, stark naked, for half an hour, polishing her fingernails and toenails bright red. "Where'd you get the polish?" I asked her. "From Mama," she said. "I'm getting all dressed up for tomorrow." I felt so awful then, I didn't know what to do. I mean, I never dreamed she cared about her appearance at all—you certainly wouldn't know it by looking at her—so, to see her painting her nails as if that would make a difference was just absolutely pathetic.

I wanted to say something to her, you know, to help her. I thought Steve and I could offer to pay for some kind of operation. She could get her stomach stapled or her jaw wired shut or they could take out part of her intestines. Really, there are so many options these days, there's no excuse for anyone to be fat. But I was scared she'd take it the wrong way—you know how sensitive fat people are. So I just kept my mouth shut.

I was dying to ask her how much she weighed, but I couldn't figure out how to fit it into the conversation. I mean you can't just ask someone a thing like that, especially a fat person. It's like asking a woman her age. Some things are too private to talk about, even between sisters.

Later, though, when she went to the bathroom, I did look at the labels in her clothes to see what size they were. She'd folded her pants and her blouse neatly and put them on top of her suitcase. Her shirt was an extra large, can you imagine? And her pants were a fifteen/sixteen. I felt horrible when I saw that. The least she could do was rip out the labels so she wouldn't have to be embarrassed.

Finally I asked her what she was going to wear to the wedding. I should have known not to ask. White pants and a red silk blouse that matched my mother's nail polish. I didn't know what to say. First of all, everyone knows fat people shouldn't wear white. I must have told her that at least a million times. And I could see right away she was planning on tucking her blouse in, which would be a disaster with her stomach and everything. But what could I do? We certainly couldn't take her shopping at eleven o'clock at night. I told her her outfit was very nice with my fingers crossed behind my back. One thing I've learned is that a little white lie to someone who's less fortunate than you isn't such a bad thing if it makes that person feel better.

While she was waiting for the second coat on her nails to dry, I opened the window. To get some fresh air, I told her, but really I was hoping the room would get drafty so she would cover herself up. A person can only take so much. Then I started hoping she would catch a cold and then she wouldn't be able to come to the wedding. I mean, how was I ever going to explain her to Steve's relatives? I know you're thinking that's a horrible thing to say about your own sister, but Doctor, I had spent months getting ready for my wedding. Months. Everything matched perfectly—the flowers, the bridesmaids' dresses, the ushers' tuxedos, and then my sister has to come along and ruin everything. Thank God I had sense enough not to ask her to be a bridesmaid. I mean, can you imagine with her punk hairdo and everything? My mother really wanted me to, but I just put my foot down.

I was hoping the photographer would have enough sense not to get her in any of the pictures, but no such luck. There she is, big as life, smiling all over the place. My sister is not shy, that's for sure. And she does have a beautiful smile—I'll give her that much. I used to be jealous of her smile, but now, well, there's nothing to be jealous of. Sure she seems happy, but everyone knows fat people are always jolly on the outside.

So finally she put on a long T-shirt, thank God. And then she asked me if I wanted to see some of her pictures. I said sure. What the hell, I mean, she probably doesn't have anyone else to show them to and, after all, she is my sister.

Well, first she showed me pictures from the newspaper she works on. They were pretty boring. A lot of them were from some kind of parade for people like her, and none of them knew anything about how to dress, believe me. Then she showed me about a million pictures of her and Bev, her friend, remember? My sister and Bev in their apartment, down at Fisherman's Wharf, on top of some mountain they'd climbed, cross country skiing, paddling a canoe, flying a kite, you name it, they've done it. There was even a picture of them at the beach. In bathing suits yet. They were lying side by side on a big purple towel, leaning up on their elbows, and all I could think about was whales. They looked like two beached whales.

Well, thank God they've found each other, that's all I can say. I mean, who else would have them, and anything is better than being alone. One thing bothered me though. My sister kept referring to Bev as her lover. I don't know why she just couldn't say friend. You see what I mean about not letting her around Steve's relatives. You never know what she's going to say next. What if she started talking about her lover to Steve's mother? I mean, can you imagine? And can you imagine two women having sex together? Two fat women? Ugh.

I asked Steve about it, and he told me they use dildos. He showed me a picture in *Playboy*. One of them straps it on and then climbs on top of the other one. I can't imagine my sister doing that. I used to look at that issue of *Playboy* a lot when Steve wasn't home. On the page after the dildos, they showed two women doing sixty-nine. Really, I know you think I'm making this up, but I can show you. It's so disgusting, I just couldn't get over it. Steve has never put his thing in my mouth. Never. He puts it, you know, right down there where it belongs. And he's never put his mouth down there either. Ugh. We have perfectly normal sex, at least we used to, and I'm sure we will again.

My sister had pictures of other women, too. Her friends. They were all like her, you know, I could just tell, but, thank God, not all of them were fat. There's still hope. She showed me pictures of her last birthday party—there must have been about fifty people there. All women of course. No man would be caught dead near her I'm sure. She says she doesn't like men, that she and Bev are really happy together, but I know she's just saying that. I know she'd give anything to be normal like me. Anyone would.

She asked me if I had any pictures, but all I had was one of Steve that I carry in my wallet. I never let anyone take my picture, everyone knows that camera adds at least ten pounds. And I certainly would never let anyone take a picture of me in a bathing suit. I haven't worn a bathing suit since junior high. Of course I had to let the photographer take pictures of me at the wedding. I learned a trick though, from a woman who went to modeling school. You lift your hands over your head like this, see, and you automatically look five pounds thinner. See how my stomach flattens and my ribs stick out? So that's what I did every time the photographer came near me, I just lifted my hands and pretended I was adjusting my veil.

After we finished looking at the pictures, my sister got kind of sappy. She took my hand and said, "Harriet, are you sure you'll all right?" I could tell she wanted to have one of those heart-to-heart talks with me—she's very emotional, my sister. I told her of course I was all right. She just kept looking at me kind of funny, and then she said, "But Harriet, are you happy?"

"Of course I'm happy," I told her. Who wouldn't be happy the night before their own wedding?

"I'm worried about you," she said. "You've gotten so thin, you've lost so much weight. Have you been sick?"

Well, then, I realized that she was just jealous. I wanted to tell her I was worried about her, she'd *gained* so much weight, but I didn't want to make her feel bad. So I just patted her hand and told her I was perfectly fine, just a little tired.

"You look tired," she said, putting her other hand on top of mine. "Are you sure you're taking care of yourself? Is there anything you want to tell me?"

"Of course I look tired," I told her. "Who wouldn't be tired with all the running around I've been doing lately? A wedding doesn't just happen all by itself. Let's go to bed," I said to her, "tomorrow's going to be a big day." She didn't say anything, but all of a sudden two big tears welled up in her eyes, and I just turned away. It there's one thing I can't stand, it's seeing a fat person cry. As soon as she fell asleep, I got down on the floor and did an extra three hundred sit-ups. I vowed that very night to get thin and to stay thin once and for all.

I didn't see my sister much the next day. Of course we had breakfast together with my parents. I had my usual black coffee and my sister had a piece of toast, an egg, and some orange juice. Funny, I thought she'd eat a lot more, but I guess she's too embarrassed to really eat in front of anyone. I know I would be if I looked like that. I didn't even get a chance to say good-bye to her. There were so many people at the wedding, and of course Steve and I left right afterwards for our honeymoon.

I did catch sight of my sister out of the corner of my eye a few times though. She'd brought along her camera, even though I'd told her not to—we'd hired a professional photographer—but she really seemed to want to, so I said okay. She probably knew no one would talk to her, so at least with her camera she'd have something to do.

She sent me some copies of the pictures she took, but they weren't very good. I wasn't even smiling in any of them. It's almost like she was just lurking around, waiting to catch me at my very worst, and then she'd snap her camera. It's just because she's jealous, that's all. The pictures the photographer took are a hundred times better.

Do I want my sister to come visit me here? You're got to be kidding. Unless you mean to be a patient. Now that I could understand. She could really use a place like this to help her lose weight. Wouldn't that be funny—she'd lose weight and I'd gain. Though I only want to gain a pound or two at the most, and she could stand to lose a good fifty. Maybe if she got thin she could find some man to marry her. I'm sure that Bev would understand. I mean, I wish my sister could just be happy like me and Steve. I know I have a few problems—who doesn't—but at least I'm normal. I really do pity my sister.

Lunch time already? Oh, I never eat lunch. Just black coffee will be fine. I haven't had lunch in years. One thing I did want to ask you though—do you think I could get a VCR for my room? I brought my Jane Fonda workout tape along—I don't want to get flabby while I'm in here. If it's not possible, don't worry, I'll manage. I brought her workout book too, just in case. I put my membership at the aerobics club on hold. I can renew it as soon as I go home.

So I guess I'll get some rest now. It was nice meeting you, Doctor, I'm sure we'll speak again. I hope I didn't talk your ear off, I can be a real chatterbox. But as you can see, there's nothing at all the matter with me. I'll probably stay here a week, ten days at the most. I'm sure Steve misses me already. Of course I miss him terribly, but it's nice to just relax and not have to worry about things for a change.

Will you close the door on your way out, Doctor? I'm just going to do a few exercises, since I won't be going to aerobics this afternoon. I don't like to miss a day—before you know it, one day turns into two, then three, then four, and then it's all downhill from there. I don't want to wind up fat like my sister. Can you imagine me, dressed in horizontal stripes or bright purple pants, like I didn't care about anything, smiling right in front of the camera for all the world to see? Laughing on the outside and crying on the inside? Not me. I've been very lucky. I've got Steve, I've got my health, my looks. I've got . . . well, that's enough, isn't it? I mean, what more could any woman possibly want?

PRIMOS

Connie Porter

Whaddaya mean, only six weeks and already I have a
stomach? You can see it
protruding under my Indian smock and you can
just tell I'm already wearing
maternity pants? Whaddaya mean, already I
have a stomach? Of course I
have a stomach How else am I supposed to eat?
I have borne three children, two of them living, and I
can't quite give them up.
Whaddaya mean, after I have this baby I should do
exercises to get rid of my stomach? What's wrong
with my stomach? It's a perfectly normal healthy
stomach This is the way a post-partum stomach is
supposed to be This is the stomach of a woman who
has borne children This is the stomach of a multipara
This is my red badge of courage.
—Marion Cohen, "This is a Fat-Liberation Poem"

Moraine wanted to break up with Favio the night their windows were shot out.
The shooting was not a personal act. The shooter was like a fisherman casting
a net. Moraine, eight months pregnant, was shocked at how easily she had
fallen from the bed. Like a dolphin diving, cutting through the surface of the
water, she had moved through the dark air, her fall softened by an unexpected
cushion—Favio. She had expected him to be above her, skimming the surface,
looking for a way out for them, running to find her three-year-old, Kati, who
was wailing. It had been Moraine who had to crawl over Favio—he was clutching her, telling her to stay down—to get to Kati who was jumping up and down
in the living room, up and down, like she was being pulled by invisible strings.
Moraine had to grab her by one leg, yanking so hard that the baby's head hit
the cement-tiled floor, sounding like a dropped bowl. But the baby quieted, the
breath knocked out of her. Moraine lay on top of her, listening for more shots,
but there were none. Favio crawled to them and lay on top of Moraine.

"Get up," she said. "You're crushing us." She could feel his penis harden-
ing against her back, and she knew that he was not going to move.

This was a time when she wished she were delicate, one of those women who had to spend the last months of her pregnancy holed up in a bed of down pillows, watching television and eating chocolate-covered cherries. She had read about these women when she was in the checkout line of the Kroger. They were there in women's magazines in those personal stories, the tragedy to triumph ones, that had pictures of the babies that were born of all this pampering. Pink and fat and bald and hearty. She was healthy though, the type of woman who did not get stories written about her. Moraine weighed over 200 pounds. Her weight was 212 on her last visit. The doctor was not concerned though. She weighed 180 at the beginning of the pregnancy. Fueled by beans and bean sauce, plantains fried in lard, bowls of sticky rice, mangos and avocados, her body had grown thick at a young age, fed by her Haitian mother who always cooked for ten, even when it was just her and her husband left at home. Moraine cooked like that for herself, Favio, Kati, and her son Prosper, huge blackened pots filled to their tops with food spiced with red pepper and sazón.

The first time Favio had eaten with them was on New Year's Day. They were at Moraine's parents' apartment in Dorchester and her mother had cooked enough to feed fifty people. Favio had eaten his fill and had drunk three glasses of the anise-flavored liqueur they had for the occasion.

It was on that day Moraine's mother told her she did not like Favio.

"Dominican?" her mother asked, pulling her aside in the kitchen.

Moraine did not answer.

"He is. I can tell, 'Favio.' What kind of name is that? You tell me."

"Favio, Ma. Don't get stared on that Dominican thing, will you." Moraine knew full well how her mother felt about Dominicans. She hated them, hated the Spanish they spoke, hated that they had more than half of the island of Hispaniola, hated that they saw Indian blood as a badge of honor, hated that they looked down on Haitians, hated that they had spoiled everything.

Now that her mother was silent, she felt bolder. "You married an American."

"Don't tell me who I marry. I know. Forty years. He sitting right out there drinking liqueur. I marry him. Your father know him black," she said, poking at a pan of ribs covered in pineapple sauce. "What about your friend?"

Moraine did not say anything. She began filling a plate.

Her mother began, "They think . . ."

". . . they're better than us," Moraine finished.

"They do. My mother always tell me that. You calling your dead grandmother a liar, God rest her soul?"

She did not give Moraine a chance to answer, "We were first free. No slavery for us. We were fighters. Never forget that."

"So free you had to come here to Boston to live, Ma?"

"No."

"Yeah, Ma. You guys were starving back in Haiti."

"What a lie," her mother said, stirring a pot of green pea sauce. "We go hungry, but we never starve. The things they say about us. We starve in Haiti. We make evil voodoo. We start AIDS. Jealous. They're jealous of us. We were first free. We freed them, and how they pay us back?"

"They started a war."

"They did. We had the whole island. One people. They spoil it all. Now what we share with them."

"A handful of nothing," Moraine said. She had heard this all before.

"Never forget that. Ungrateful. That's them. Mulattos. That's them. You know where those Dominicans would be without us?"

"Still in slavery, Ma?"

"There you go. And now we all have nothing. I hope them all happy."

Moraine wanted to tell her then. She was two months pregnant, by a man her mother would like to see still out in the fields with a dirty rag on his head, chopping cane, living off cane juice and mangos, but she had a vision, one of her mother swinging around, a spoon coated with pea sauce raised, coming right at her head.

This fight was old, its roots dug into the mountains of both countries. One island, one people separated into two and brought back together so many times they had broken, their language split as cleanly as a stalk of cane: Spanish, Creole.

The Dominicans were different, more mixed, had Indian blood, white bold. Moraine knew and so did her mother. Her mother had told her that all the Indians on what was to become their side of the island, the west, had been killed before they had had a chance to mix with the Africans. Those who were not killed by disease were killed by overwork. Those who refused to work were killed outright.

Those who did not escape east did have a right to speak, Moraine thought. They had the right to have their voices heard, even centuries later, to speak of their survival through the mouths of black people who called themselves Dominicans.

"Flavio is black as you, but he think he better. He does not love you. He can never love you. You listen to your old mother."

That night Favio was sick. He had diarrhea, and every time he went to the bathroom, he felt like he was on fire. He whined to Moraine. "Did your mother put something in the food?"

"What do you mean, put something in it?"

"I feel so bad," Favio continued.

"You ate too much and you're not used to the spices, all that hot pepper, and that liqueur, who told you to drink so much?"

"You sure she ain't put *something* in the food?"

Moraine caught his meaning that time. She felt a flash of anger rise, a burning in her chest, and she kicked him so hard, he fell out of bed.

"First your mother try to kill me. Now you finishing me off."

Moraine jumped on him. She didn't know what to do. She could have beaten him if she wanted to. She had fifty pounds on him.

But he moaned, "It was only a joke, damn, honey. What's wrong with you? I know your mama ain't worked no voodoo."

"Good because we don't do that! We never did that. Even when my mama was back home, she never did that, and I don't either."

"Shit, with the Bruce Lee killer kick, you don't have to. Did you learn that from your mother?"

Kati began crying. She had wet on herself. The baby Moraine carried was rolling around, probably wondering about what was happening above the surface, in the world of sound and light. Favio was on top of her still, his hands reaching for her breasts, his hip bones winding against her wide behind. Moraine was not going to let herself be trapped between these three. She rose from the floor, dragging all of them into the bedroom and falling onto the bed.

"Give me a cigarette," she said to Favio.

"You promised," he said, pulling away from her. "You want a drink, too?"

"Just shut up, all right, and give me. Just one, that all. For my nerves."

Favio obliged. "What you trying to do to my baby? He going to start choking in there," he said, lighting one for both of them. "Favio, don't cry. It's only your mother smoking."

Moraine watched the bloom of the match light up the faces of Kati and Favio. She saw the wetness, the wildness of their eyes, like fish caught in a net. She blew out the match.

"Favio?"

"What?"

"Where did you come up with that name?" Moraine asked.

"I told you before, from my uncle."

"That's not what I mean, for the baby?"

"I'm just kidding. I don't want him named after me. I was thinking maybe Juan."

"Or, Jean," she said.

So her mother was right. After it was apparent Moraine was pregnant, she told her mother. "Are you happy now?" she asked her mother.

"I am happy now. I'm having no more babies. You are the one. You happy?"

"I'm delirious," she said.

"So, I'm going to have a grandbaby to speak Spanish, no Creole. What can I do about it now?"

"Ma, Favio can't even speak Spanish."

Her mother perked up. "No. A shame, a shame," her mother shook her head. "When the baby come to me I will teach Creole to him. You never wanted to know it."

"That's not true, Ma. When we were in that Catholic school, the nuns used to slap our hands when we spoke it."

"You never tell me that. Why none of your brother and sister ever tell me that?"

"I don't know, Ma."

"A handful of nothing. That's all we have left."

"Can I take a plate home?"

"Take two. I make plenty of food. Take one to Favio."

Moraine glared at her mother.

"What you look at me like that for? Don't let him talk you into giving the baby those Spanish names, especially not his. He's going to want to. They want everything their way."

"That's not true."

"Listen to your old mother. Toussaint, name my grandson that. What a great name. He started it all you know. We were first. Don't ever forget."

"Or maybe John," Favio said. "Maybe we should go all-American."

Moraine changed the subject. "Why didn't you do something? We could have been killed," she said, breathing smoke through her nose. She was trying to sound calm.

"Do what? Jump in front of a bullet?"

"You should have gone to Kati."

"*¡Mira!* She's so little, below the line of the window. I did do something. I pulled you from the bed."

"You did not. I dove on the floor."

"You was sleeping down. I woke up to them shots and I screamed 'shit!' These stupid mother-fucking kids is going to kill us I was thinking, and I rolled right off the bed and pulled you down with me. That's when you tried to jump up—when they was still shooting."

Moraine did not answer. She rose from the bed, carrying her daughter. Her cigarette hung from her lips. She went to the dresser looking for dry underwear for Kati. After only a few drags, she knew she wanted another one and she did not know if she believed Favio. In the confusion of that moment on the floor, anything could have been true.

"It's good Prosper wasn't here. He probably would have got hit," Favio said. He was lying on his back.

"Mmmmm," Moraine had to agree. She feared Prosper was crazy. She could tell, though he was only ten. You could tell these things early on. He had what she thought was an irrational fear of being shot.

Only once before had gunfire hit their apartment, earlier that year when a small caliber bullet came whizzing through Prosper's bedroom while he sat on his bed after a bath. It was a Thursday night and he had bathed early so he could watch "The Cosby Show" and "A Different World," his favorites. Favio had been at work. He worked in a token booth for the T. Moraine could get no sense out of Prosper. All he did was scream and point to the wall. Moraine saw the bullet sticking in the plaster. The window had not shattered, but she could see a hole in the glass, a tiny hole like the kind fishermen cut in ice, neat as if someone had drilled it. She called the police. To her surprise, two cars had come. They were still there when Favio came home.

"They were shooting in your house. Somebody almost shot the boy. Right through that window," the neighbor, Guzmán said, pointing behind him. He was Puerto Rican and a man Favio had argued with before because he accused him of stealing his Sunday *Herald*.

Favio pushed past him and into his first floor apartment. The officers were trying to question Prosper, but the boy had buried his face in his mother's lap.

"I'm his father," Favio said. "Leave my son alone."

The officers looked at him, then at Moraine. She supported his lie. "He is the father." The truth was that she did not know who the boy's father was. She had it narrowed down to two men, both Haitians she had met at a social club, but since she was not sure, she had stopped going to that club and stopped seeing them both.

"I told you. He did not see anything," Moraine said.

The cops left, taking the bullet with them.

Favio went over to Prosper, putting his arms around him he whispered, "It's all right."

"You're my father?" Prosper asked.

"That's right," Favio said. He had been living with Moraine for four months.

"The boy not right in the head," Moraine said.

"You shouldn't say that. If he hear you say that, he's going to believe it."

"How he's going to hear me? He's at camp. And it's the truth," Moraine said, already nearing the end of her cigarette. "He won't even sleep in the bed anymore. Does that make sense?"

Favio laughed, ashes falling onto the bed. "Shit, all I need to do is set the place on fire," he said brushing them away. "After a night like this, you think he crazy? He's got good sense, that boy. It's them damn Jamaicans and them loco Puerto Ricans—that's who's crazy. They running the drugs around here. I bet you somebody was shooting up here at Guzmán's son. I know he deals."

"They could have been shooting at anybody."

"They wasn't shooting at me. I can tell you that. Anyway, Dominicans don't do stuff like that."

"Like what. Shoot at people. I bet no Dominican has shot at anyone ever," Moraine said sarcastically.

"What the hell is that supposed to mean?" Favio asked.

"Can you give me a cigarette?" Moraine asked, shifting Kati to her hip.

"No. What the hell you talking about?"

"It's only those black Jamaicans and those—those Puerto Ricans who kill up people. You Dominicans are the best people on earth. You never did anything to anybody."

"I bet your mother taught you that when she showed you that Bruce Lee kick. *We* ain't the best people on the earth, only in the islands," Favio laughed. "It's in our blood."

Moraine felt the same burning in her chest she felt the night she had kicked him from her bed.

"What's in your blood?" Moraine asked Favio. "I guess you're some kind of damn Indian?"

"No, just part. What's wrong with you. Why does it have to be a 'damn' Indian?"

"Just part? You look all black to me. Don't think you're anything different than me, anything better. Don't you ever think that."

Favio had finished his cigarette. He lit another. "You think I never heard that Dominican/Haitian shit?"

Moraine suddenly became intensely interested in finding dry underwear for Kati. The child had put her head down on Moraine's chest.

"That's what you getting at. I was fed on it in New York, my parents living up in the slums, up in the Bronx. I'm telling you, fucking roaches flying through the house. My father ain't worked a good month of Sundays in twenty-five years, and you know the biggest think he ever did? Do you? I'm talking to you, Moraine."

"I don't want to know," she said. "Let's just get to bed."

Favio continued, "Get the super from renting one of them rat traps to a Haitian family. He tell people that story. He proud of it. I'm sick of it. Tired of it."

"You crazy, and if Prosper is a nut, he got it from you."

The burning Moraine felt moved to her face. Standing there in the dark, she did not know how to go back to the bed. She did not know how to return to Favio.

But he provided a way. "Shit, we probably all cousins," he said. "You probably my cousin. I been screwing my cousin," Favio yelled.

Moraine wanted to laugh. "The neighbors are going to hear you."

"They probably my cousins too. Even Guzmán. Hey, Guzmán, *primo.* You paper stealing bastard."

"I'm telling you," he said dragging on his cigarette, "That whole island could be swallowed up, some damn big fish could jump out the sea and take the whole place down with him, and who would care? A bunch of bean eaters."

Finding a pair of underwear, Moraine turned to go back to the bed, and took in a sharp breath of air.

"What is it, the baby?" Favio asked.

"I stepped on glass." A shard had entered her heel, had gone in deep.

Favio leapt to turn on the light. "Stay right here," he said. "I'm coming to get you." Slipping on a pair of sneakers, he went to her, and picked her up.

"Shit, honey," he groaned. She could feel him sinking under the weight of her, Kati, and the baby. He did manage to get them to the edge of the bed. Taking Kati from Moraine's arms, he lay her on the bed, quickly stripped off her panties and put the dry pair on her.

"I'm taking her back to her bed," he said, lifting the child who was half asleep. When he returned, he was loaded down, towels, band-aids, vaseline.

"There is going to be some blood. I didn't want her to see. She would be scared," Favio said, kneeling next to the bed.

Moraine lay on her back while Favio pulled the glass from her foot. At its widest, it was a half inch thick, and when it was all the way out, he could tell it was shaped like a fish hook. He showed it to her.

"It's going to be all right," he said. "Not too much blood. How you feel?"

Moraine did not answer. She felt like a fool.

"I'll make it better," he said.

"Where's your cigarette?"

"Shit!" It was on the floor. He held it to her mouth for her to take a drag. She could see her blood on his hands. "No," she said.

When she woke the next day, her foot was throbbing, propped up on two pillows. The room was in order. The glass had been cleaned up. The baby was calm. Jean/Juan/John had settled on top of her bladder, content, it seemed, to be under water, in his world of darkness of muted sound.

Favio was there. She could hear him talking to Kati. He worked swing shifts, and this was his day to be on, but she heard him banging around in the kitchen. She looked over at the clock. It was nearly noon. Moraine wanted to call out to them, but as she heard them heading toward the bedroom door, she pretended to be asleep.

"Mama," Kati called. "Wake up."

"You're not sleeping," Favio said. He was carrying a plate of crisp fried green plantain, and on the plate was a bowl of pink beans and rice. Kati had a bowl full of sliced mango.

"I thought you might be hungry," Favio said. "I'll be right back," he said.

Kati climbed on the bed and grabbed a piece of mango. "They're sweet, Mama."

Favio returned, pushing the television on its stand with one hand and carrying a bag in the other.

"I'm going to take a quick look at that foot," he said. "Kati plug in the television."

Favio gently pulled the sock from her foot and unwrapped the bandage. "It ain't that bad really. Too bad you can't look. I'll put a little alcohol on. It's going to hurt some."

Moraine did not flinch when Favio touched her with the cool alcohol-soaked cloth.

"Am I hurting you?" he asked.

"No," Moraine said. She clenched her teeth, biting down on a piece of fleshy mango, welcoming the sweet touch.

THE LANGUAGE OF THE FAT WOMAN
Elana Dykewomon

Unless there is a major support network of language and experiences that is positive, celebratory and confident I don't think "fat women" have a chance in hell of shaping a societal viewpoint. Big women have no voice in our media, in our advertising, in our language or in our present day western culture. Ridicule is the modus operandi, comedy is the venting mechanism. When big women reclaim their language, only then can they claim their aesthetic place in history. . . .

I'll say this time and time again: claim your language, claim your place in history (women in pre-European history celebrated their generous flesh, comparing it to a fertile landscape complete of mountains and valleys). Make it your knowledge base, as no one today uses the past as a prologue to the present.

—Anita Roddick, www.bigfatblog.com

She's as big as a house. She wonders if this means as "big as all outdoors." Fat as a planet. A little planet. Big as a little planet, a bright marble sparkling above amazon campers, rubbing up against the fancies of the night. An orb of delight.

No, that's not what they mean.

Maybe it's as big as a house full of secrets. Yes, that must be it, a house of closets, each closet stuffed with candy wrappers. She listens for the sound of wrappers. A wind comes through the floor boards and sets them rubbing up against each other. Are they dangerous, flammable? A house on fire. She remembers "a house on fire" means ambition. Is she big enough to catch fire, to be a torch on the edge of imagination? You can see her flame for miles, surely her shame is bright enough, anyone can make it flare, but what good is flare when they turn away? If she's going to ignite, she wants to be a beacon.

They cannot mean beacon. They must mean bacon. Fat as a pig. She goes to the county fair. Every year there's a mama pig with her newborns, the sucklings. Men inject pigs with dangerous chemicals to force them to gain weight. Once men forced her to take dangerous chemicals to control her weight. Men mutilate pigs because they're sold by the pound for meat. Much more valuable than she is, especially now that she's "out of control." She's read about pigs. And elephants, hippos, whales. All the great big mammals.

The width of nature. At the county fair, there are prizes for the biggest pig. The fat lady hides in the side show. The fat lady is a freak.

They call her "fat lady." She lies in bed imagining writing a book of conversations with circus fat women. Traveling around the country, interviewing them over tea. She'd write a poem: tea with the fat lady, if she weren't afraid of laughter. The other writers wouldn't respect her anymore. They might not say "freak," but they'd think it. Sideshow: not the main event, just a tangent, at best a frivolous distraction. Freak.

A freak of nature. A freak act. Lightning splits the middle of an oak, earthquake causes the highway to collapse. It seems, then, that freak means: power. The power of an unexpected event to change the course of nature. They react with nervous fear. Now they have a mathematics to explain these rifts, these breaks in the fabric of pattern. They call it the science of chaos, it's in fashion. In fashion not to be taken by surprise. Everyone wants to believe they have control, personal control over destiny.

But freak means even the new technology doesn't explain her size. What can't be controlled must be explained. If there is no hard science, then there must be psychology. Some will to perversity that makes her grow so large. There is no formula yet for chaos of the mind. Perhaps they will find it if they dissect her, label every ounce of fatty tissue around the heart, make it correspond to some unusual curve in the brain. When they notice her, what they see is a specimen. Miss 4 by 4.

"Fatty fatty 4 by 4, can't get in the school room door." Does that mean she's square? She looks in the mirror. Still taller than wide. Fat as a square house? Language puzzles her. She wants to be hip, to be cool, not square. If fat women are, by definition, square, they must have no feel for jazz, poetry or political action. No feel, no feelings, no attraction. 4 by 4, the children try to make their painful words stick.

Everyone knows that schoolchildren are mean. The secret is, we don't grow out of it.

Now 4 by 4 is a kind of truck. They call her that too, a truck, a mac truck. But that's power again. They can't mean to attribute to her the power of lightning or the internal combustion engine. After all, she's just a woman. Just a woman who looks like a truck, a freak, a pig, a beached whale, as big as a house. A house that isn't seen. A truck that doesn't run, a freak behind a curtain, a pig kept off behind the barn, a whale on a deserted beach. The place where women who are not women go.

She knows a lot about the places where women who are not women go. She lives among the lesbians. There is a science for this—what the outcasts do to the most obvious, the ones who call attention to their mis-fit. Among the women who are not women there are pockets of refuge. But in refuge it's her softness, the mother goddess with a low center of gravity. She becomes the refuge she seeks, and the lesbians call her brave. She rarely goes dancing at the bar. Her fat friend said, I can't go there, they'll think I'm as big as a house.

She wants to be as big as a house. As big as a house with a hundred rooms. Lesbians talking, political meetings, a resource center, a library of recipes, a shelf of videos on the rhinoceros, bear, buffalo. She wants to rise out of the sea not like a goddess but like a whale, ringing the world with the slap of her great body on the wave. She wants to be a pig, if by pig she is allowed to mean: a lesbian with appetite, gentle, intelligent and clean. She'd love to be a truck, a 4 by 4, all-wheel drive, going up the side of the mountain, hauling, carrying her house on her own chassis.

A freak. She is what she is. A little freak looking to other freaks for encouragement. In secret, because she is still afraid.

THE MAN I LOVE
Elaine Fowler Palencia

I wish you could see me as I truly am. Instead, when you look at me what you see instead of the me that I am is a catalog of assumptions about fat women which manages to erase me from the situation. This is the experience of living with a spoiled identity.

Have I let myself go? Am I lazy and stupid? Do I sit at home all day eating chocolates and hating myself? Am I not smart enough to understand what good nutrition is? Am I a compulsive eater, out of control, not able to stop myself from gorging on food? All of these assumptions come directly from your head to surround the real person I am. And because I know these assumptions are there, or think that I know, I surround you with my own assumptions.

You will never be trustworthy! You are stupid for believing a cultural propaganda about fat women which is full of such obvious lies. You cannot allow yourself to be sexually attracted to fat women and so I will not risk my own vulnerability and open myself to you in this way. There is something cruel about you; you will always be something less than human to me, since to be human implies a consciousness of other people's pain—some understanding of the oppressions other people suffer from.

Thus you and I are both confronted by false personas as we look at each other. And all of this happens very quickly in the first few moments we see each other. It may be that what we have to give each other could be important: but we will never know this. . . .

At the end of this chain of hatred lies a monster in wait, ready to kill all that is self-loving in me. And the enemy within has so much material from the outside to batter me with. (Fat women in this culture are battered women.) And somewhere always in me is the kernel of pure self which is loving to myself, which appreciates the strength and joy in my body, which tells me I do indeed deserve my presence on this earth, which reminds me this chain of hatred is forged with vicious lies, enemy lies, life-destroying. . . . And so there is a constant war within.
—Martha Courtot, "A Spoiled Identity"

Interviewer: Thank you so much, Miss Susan Callicoat, for agreeing to be interviewed on this historic occasion.

Susan C: You're quite welcome.

Interviewer: I'm referring to your having reached a weight of four hundred and fifty pounds. You are now the fattest person in Moore County.

Susan C: Yes, at last.

Interviewer: You're pleased to be recognized for this accomplishment?

Susan C: I would have preferred to have some recognition eighteen months ago, when I finished reading all the books in the public library. After all, that's not peanuts. But society has its priorities.

Interviewer: Well, in fact, this interview is for our library archives. Our librarian, your cousin Blanche Callicoat Long, has suggested that you might have some words of advice for young people wishing to follow in your footsteps.

Susan C: Wear sensible shoes.

Interviewer: Oh . . . Let's see, was this always a goal of yours, to be the fattest person in Moore County?

Susan C: No, it was not. Actually, I don't have the natural talent for obesity that some people have—Tiny Whitaker, for instance, whom I just passed up. My metabolism is too fast. I have to eat thirty percent more than he does to gain the same amount of weight. It's hard, lonely work, I don't mind telling you.

Interviewer: But you have the desire. The heart of a champion.

Susan C: It's a combination of things. For example, you have to be careful about nerves. Many high school girls nowadays seem to have a great desire to be fat. They spend long hours training on Ho Hos and Doritos, but they're just too nervous to keep the weight on. I see them in the summer wearing those short shorts: little bitty bottoms, no matter what they do. I think of Shakespeare, "There's a divinity that shapes our ends, rough-hew them how we will."

Interviewer: What did you want to be when you were their age? A nurse? A teacher?

Susan C: I wanted to be an alcoholic.

Interviewer: I beg your pardon?

Susan C: However, as you know, Moore County is dry. I was held back in my early, formative years by this environment. By the time I got out in the world, it was too late to acquire the knack.

Interviewer: What makes you think you would have made a good alcoholic?

Susan C: A woman knows these things. I could have been the alcoholic equivalent of a twelve-hundred-pound person if I'd had half a chance.

Interviewer: You sound bitter.

Susan C: I am. Pass me that bag of potato chips.

Interviewer: Here you go. Miss Callicoat, could you recall just when you got the idea of being competitively obese? From these pictures, you were quite thin as a child.

Susan C: And that jar of mayonnaise, please.

Interviewer: Could you tell us something about your years away from Blue Valley? Mrs. Long suggested—

Susan C: That old liar.

Interviewer: I'm just saying, she suggested that—

Susan C: I refuse to discuss my personal life in any way. That was the rule you accepted before I agreed to do this interview.

Interviewer: I'm aware of that. But now I'm not sure how to proceed. . . . What do you think of liquid protein supplements?

Susan C: They're baloney. Reach me that six-pack of Hershey bars.

Interviewer: You're going to eat all of those too?

Susan C: Why? Would you care for one?

Interviewer: Well, maybe just a bite. I didn't have lunch.

Susan C: Sorry, you should have brought yourself a snack. That's the trouble with you amateurs; you never plan ahead. And another thing: amateurs tend to rely on a single taste to take them to glory. Your chocoholics, your peanut butter freaks. They burn out before they can bulk up. My method is to alternate sweet and salty foods, so that I can go on stuffing myself for hours without the taste buds blanking out and boredom ensuing. About a third of a bag of potato chips dipped one by one in mayonnaise, then one Hershey bar, then another round of chips, and so on.

Interviewer: I see. Well, unless you have any more advice, I want to thank you—

Susan C: You're not much of an interviewer, are you?

Interviewer: I'm with the Friends of the Library. Mrs. Long asked me to do this as a personal favor.

Susan C: The coward.

Interviewer: She said you would be difficult.

Susan C: You're not asking any of the right questions.

Interviewer: What am I supposed to ask?

Susan C: Dreams tell a lot about a person. Chew on that.

Interviewer: Dreams?

Susan C: If you had any insight at all, you would ask me what I was dreaming the summer I was twelve years old. My best friend was Maxie Stewart. That was the year we were horses. She was called Wildflower: a black horse, with a white mane and tail. I was a palomino named Silver Star.

Interviewer: Are horses your favorite animal?

Susan C: Not particularly. All twelve-year-old girls are horses. The year before, we'd been dinosaurs; but our brains were too small to adapt to winter and we had died in the first snowfall.

Interviewer: What would be a typical day for you as a horse?

Susan C: There was school to endure, of course. But outside of that, we ran and ran, side by side, all the livelong day. And we climbed trees.

Interviewer: As a horse you climbed trees?

Susan C: This is a dream, you tiny fool.

Interviewer: I'm sorry, excuse me.

Susan C: Mostly we ran along the Trail of the Lonesome Pine. It isn't on any map that adults use. But every neighborhood has another map, the one children carry in their heads. The Trail of the Lonesome Pine connected all the child landmarks in Blue Valley. Every tree along the route was a lookout post, a fortress; a jungle aerie.

Interviewer: Was there, in fact, a Lonesome Pine?

Susan C: So densely needled, with a wide skirt of branches brushing the ground, that you could sit out a thunderstorm against its trunk and stay dry. So tall that one summer night it hooked the crescent moon. From the top you could smell all the suppers of Blue Valley cooking and know when it was time to go home. It was our grandfather. It stood at the edge of the forest.

[*Sound of rustling food wrappers; then Susan C. continues*]

For strangers who may someday hear this, from the top of the Lonesome Pine, the town looks like a medieval fiefdom. The Farnsworth mansion is our castle. The iron picket fence surrounding its city block of grounds is its moat. The town huddles around the fence like a village of serfs and freemen. The hills are the outermost walls of the kingdom, keeping the world—I am tempted to say, the real world—at bay. This is why Blue Valley is the perfect place to be a child. Childhood is medieval, you now. To a child, everything has its place in a great chain of being, and everything is true. Everything: because a child lives by faith. Of course, dark things lurk over the edge of the world, and they are true too.

Interviewer: Excuse me, but aren't you describing the ideal state of childhood? Many children experience a grimmer, a less ordered reality.

Susan C: Then they are not experiencing childhood. They've been robbed.

Interviewer: I used to play in Elliott Creek when I was a child.

Susan C: But we're not interviewing you, are we? Maxie and I loved the forest. The four seasons lived there. In summer the air was green and tasted of mint. In spring it wrapped us in shawls of dogwood and redbud, that streamed out behind us in the wind. In autumn, we wore capes of flame. We were so much a part of the forest that in the winter our hooves left deer tracks in the snow. It belonged to us. No one else ever came there. Then the wrong Edith came to visit.

Interviewer: Who was the wrong Edith?

Susan C: I am now eating fried chicken. You can't neglect your protein. The right Edith was my mother's best friend. Growing up together, they were like Maxie and me, two halves of the same peach. Sometimes I went with my mother to see Edith when we were visiting my grandparents in Indian Springs. Edith had stayed there and married a local boy, Roy. She was plump and pale and sweet and always gave me ginger ale to drink. Roy showed a lot of gold when he grinned. He'd greet my mother and me the same way: "Howya doin', kiddo?" The summer in question, Roy had been dead two years. He'd died of a heart attack right across his desk at the Indian Springs Chevrolet dealership. We hadn't seen Edith since then. She had moved to Chattanooga.

I remember, that is, in my dream, I was sitting up in the maple tree by the front walk one afternoon, when a taxi pulled up.

[*Sound of forceful chewing*]

Interviewer: This was the wrong Edith?

Susan C: If you interrupt me again, I'm going to sit on you. A thin, deeply tanned woman got out of the taxi. She was made up like a magazine ad, wore a bright yellow linen suit, and had orange hair teased up in a stiff bouffant. The right Edith, I should say, had brown hair and no makeup. My mother came running out and they hugged and laughed and then they stepped back and looked each other up and down.

"What happened? This is not the Edith I know!" my mother exclaimed.

Edith squealed, "Oh honey, I got me a new life: hostessing at Howard Johnson's! Yes! And I've been taking dance lessons too!"

I dropped out of the tree and the wrong Edith said, "So this is Susan now. Honey, you'll scramble your insides doing stuff like that."

"I'm not Susan. I'm Silver Star, the famous palomino," I said.

She said, "I used to ride a little horse when we lived up on Sockleg Creek. She wasn't much bigger than you."

"Nobody can ride me! I'm fierce!" I yelled.

"Susan," said my mother.

Edith said, "God, Marge, let's go in the house. I'm dying for a cigarette."

"When did you start smoking?" my mother cried.

"Lord, honey, it keeps you trim," Edith—

Interviewer: My gracious, I can't remember my dreams like this, in such detail!

Susan C: That's it. Give me the microphone.

[*Metallic noises; a gasp*]

There. At dinner they'd talk about the extraordinary things they'd been up to, like eating lunch twice at Francine's Restaurant, which my parents and I did only on Mother's Day. Another day they bought hats. As a rule, my mother only bought one hat a year, at Easter. These butter mints, made by my neighbor Olivia Boggs, are exquisite.

One afternoon my mother went to get her hair done. She never missed her three thirty appointment on Thursdays. Eventually the Bon Ton Beauty Shop gave her a twenty-five-year plaque for perfect attendance. Edith stayed home, saying that there was only one person in the world she trusted her hair to and that was Raoul, in Chattanooga.

I was sprawled on my bed, reading comic books, when she appeared in my doorway. She braced her hands high on either side of the door frame and swayed back and forth, humming "Hernando's Hideaway" and moving her feet in tiny suggestions of dance steps. Sunlight from the hall window shone through her dress and I remember being shocked that she wasn't wearing a slip; I'd gotten the impression you could go to Hell for that.

"Hi," she said. "I hope you know that reading ruins your eyes. It makes you nearsighted and you get crow's-feet before your time." Then she ran her palms approvingly down her sides and said, "I hope you wear a girdle?"

I shook my head.

"I don't know where your mama's mind is at," Edith clucked. "A young girl can't start wearing a girdle too soon. Otherwise your muscles sag right from the beginning. By the time you've grown up, you're already dumpy. The boys won't like you." She left the doorway and in a moment returned holding something behind her back. "Here," she said, tossing it, "from me to you. I've only worn it once since I bought it. I've got plenty. Now scat and put it on. If you do, I'll tell you a secret."

I could feel my muscles sagging like the ropes of molasses. I ran in the bathroom, shucked off my Bermuda shorts, wrestled on the panty girdle, and pulled the shorts back on. The girdle felt like wearing last year's bathing suit, only worse in the crotch.

When I came back Edith said, "See? Now you look and feel better. Here is the secret I promised: even Raoul wears one." She started swirling her hips again. "Of course, Roy loved me no matter what I weighed. Loved me? Listen: the man adored me. He absolutely worshiped the ground I walked on. And do you know what? I still see him sometimes. I'll be watching television at night and I'll feel something, a clamminess in the air, and there he'll be, standing across the den looking at me so sad and mournful with those Asking Eyes. And I know exactly what he wants. Come in the living room a minute."

In the living room I found that Edith had been going through the music in the piano bench. One of my new lesson books, *Gershwin Simplified*, lay open on the music rest.

"Roy wants to hear me sing. Play 'The Man I Love,'" she said around the cigarette she was lighting.

As I stumbled through it, Edith leaned over me, dribbling ash, and said, "One year Roy was in charge of organizing the Lions Club Follies. Nobody in Indiana Springs knew I could sing anything but hymns. But that night I wore a low-cut, stretchy black sweater and a tiger-print skirt tight as Dick's hatband and slit up one side, and—start over, honey, and I'll show you how I sang it."

I started over and Edith sang in a low, husky voice, with cigarette smoke boiling out of her mouth, that someday he'd come along, the man I love, and he'd be big and strong, the man I love. . . .

I was twelve years old and I thought I would faint from the beauty. She lingered on the last note, drawing it out so rich and soft that I could feel it humming all over my skin. When it had died away she said, "I brought down the house. Literally brought it down! And afterwards, Bud Tubbs came up and whispered in my ear, 'Baby, that was smoky.'" She wriggled her shoulders. "It made Roy so mad. He could be insanely jealous. And guess what? Ronnie—that's my teacher at the dance studio—wants to hear me sing too. When I told him about the night I sang at the Follies he said, 'Mrs. DeHart, Sugar, you had the Lions by the tail.' He said that to me when we were mambo-ing. Do you know how to mambo?"

I said I didn't and she said, "Good Lord. Well, I'll teach you. Every woman should know how to type, play bridge, and do the mambo. Otherwise you start life with three strikes against you." She lit another cig-arette and flicked at her hair and her red lacquered nails. Then she said, "Did I tell you that Ronnie and I won second prize in the fox-trot, on Ladies' Night at the Bamboo Room? Of course, we're just good friends, he's work-ing his way through college—he's the cutest thing!—but when we were walking back to the table with our trophy he said, "You are one hot mama, Mrs. D. I'd like to get into your—"

"Edith!" The screen door banged and there stood my mother, looking half scalped in a tight new permanent.

Edith laughed and said, "What's the matter? Kids hear worse than that in school."

"You should be ashamed of yourself! An innocent child!" my mother cried.

"Susan's growing up. She ought to hear how the world really is, and not have to learn the hard way, like I did in that damned hostess job," Edith said.

"Not one more word," my mother snapped.

"Don't tell me what to do!" Edith shrieked, "you smug, fat thing! Sitting in your perfect little house with your stupid husband that won't say two words to me! Roy worshiped me! When I married him, I became queen of the world!"

"He made a pass at me the night before your wedding!" shouted my mother.

"You liar! Shut up!"

"In the church vestibule!"

I ran for the door, the shouts pushing on my back like a big hand.

Outside, a warm summer rain was falling. I ran up the street under low, gray wool clouds, my hooves settling into an even rhythm as I swung onto the Trail of the Lonesome Pine that passed the head of our street. As I ran I anticipated the damp coolness at its base, the smells of wet earth and leaf mold, so much like my own horsy smell. When at last I reached our secret entrance to the forest, I plunged into it, becoming invisible, and took the slippery curving arc of our path. The rain was different in the woods. Cold droplets snaked down my neck like slugs, and wisps of breeze whiled up from the ground, chilling my knees. But I charged on, leaping roots, dodg-ing puddles. In a minute, I knew, I would be safe and calm, inside the Lonesome Pine. Then I saw something that made me stop.

Several yards to the right of the path lay the remains of a fire. A fallen tree trunk had been pulled over for a seat next to it. Beer bottles, an empty cigarette carton, waxed paper littered the ground around it. At first I thought that someone had been having a party there the night before. Then I saw that it was old, maybe several weeks old. Do you understand? People had been there but Maxie and I had never noticed. I walked over to take a closer look. Beside the log lay a twisted sanitary napkin. I stood there a long time, listening. Listening to noises I'd never heard n the forest before. Twigs snapping stealthily. Someone breathing behind me in the underbrush. For the first time, I was afraid of the forest. I was paralyzed. All of a sudden, I woke up. *I woke up,* do you hear? I ran to Maxie's. Not like I used to run, but clumsily. It took forever; I got a stitch in my side. It was the girdle, of course. You can't gallop in a girdle.

I told Maxie what I had seen and made her promise never to go into the woods again. I don't know whether she completely understood me or not. We never spoke of it again, because the forest ceased to be an issue in our lives. I showed her my new girdle, you see. The next day, she had her mother buy her one. Then neither one of us could run worth a lick. Once we slowed down, everything changed. Our friends got girdles too. When Cindy Mauk passed out during geography, the school nurse discovered that she was wearing three of them, one on top of another. Suddenly, all the girls were crazy to have a grown-up shape. I don't need to tell you what that leads to.

[*Long pause*]

Interviewer: I—I'm sorry, but I feel like crying.

Susan C: It would bring tears to the eyes of a potato.

Interviewer: How did you feel about causing this girdle craze?

Susan C: I felt hungry. Night and day. I've been eating ever since. It's the only thing to do. Because in the forest, as I stood contemplating the violated area, I realized that up until that moment everything had been a beautiful dream. Everything: twelve precious years.

Interviewer: Do you miss the woods?

Susan C: I miss the woods every day of my life. But if I eat enough, sometimes I fall into a kind of reverie, in which I am still running there, wild and free, and the Lonesome Pine is still a friend. Do you mind if we bring this to a close? You're keeping me awake.

Interviewer: Of course. Well. Well, this has been most interesting. And I see you still have a whole pecan pie left.

Susan C: It's a gift from an admirer, a thin woman inside of whom is a fat woman, struggling to get out. I'll get to it later this afternoon.

Interviewer: May I ask, in closing, do you feel satisfied with the way your life has turned out?

Susan C: Absolutely. They haven't built the girdle that can hold me now.

Interviewer: Miss Callicoat, you stated some time ago that you planned to weigh five hundred pounds in time for the Fourth of July parade this year. Do you think you'll reach your goal?

Susan C: Piece of cake.

MAGNETIC FORCE

Susan Stinson

Fat is Beautiful. Or, as the name of one fat girl's publication puts it, *I Am So Fucking Beautiful.* What are the effects when fat women begin to say such things? More, important, how do they manage to say such things? Beginning to publish and circulate images valuing the fat female body (or even beginning to value one's own fat female body) in what Eve Kosofsky Sedgwick has called a "fat abhorring world of images," a world in which fat women are charged with "concentrating and representing 'a general sense of the body's offensiveness,'" requires radical confrontation with the representational status quo. It requires undermining the process of abjection that makes fat women's bodies synonymous with the offensive, horrible, or deadly aspects of embodiment. It requires finding a way of representing the self that is not body-neutral or disembodied (and therefore presumptively thin), but intimately connected with the body in a new vision of embodiment that no longer disdains the flesh. This vision of embodiment doesn't obsessively seek the good, thin body (a body good only because it is marked by the self's repeated discipline), but instead redefines the good body and also the good self. By insisting that the body's desires should mark the self as well and that the good self is the self so marked, this new vision of embodiment shifts the relationship between self and body. Shifting the relations of embodiment gives fat women a way to stop living their bodies as the "before" picture and to begin to have a body thought valuable in the present.

—Le'a Kent, "Fighting Abjection: Representing Fat Women"

◇

1.

Every day I walk down the street to the bus stop, and every day people swing around to stare at me. Men in cars have circled parking lots to pass me again. "Scare me, Mama," yelled one guy into my face, his truck blocking the sidewalk in front of me. His passengers laughed. I walked behind the truck, hoping he wouldn't go into reverse. Mostly they just slow down to hoot something out the window. I think they feel safe in their cars: bigger than me, mobile, anonymous, equipped with metal, locks and wheels. My fat body has only clothes to protect it, but it pulls their faces towards me, even through their automotive insulation.

Not all of them are in cars. I was waiting for the bus one day when four boys on bikes rode up the sidewalk. The first one passed me, fast. The next one slowed, turned to his friends, and said, "Watch this, guys." Then he rode very close to me, grabbed at my belly and shouted, "Elephant butt." He didn't quite touch me. The other boys rode past, laughing.

The hardest things to document are the looks. A woman walking with her friend gives me an exaggerated, disbelieving stare. The next person behind her, a woman alone, sucks her breath in disgust. A couple walks behind her. The man glances, nudges the woman he's with, glances again. Maybe she turns to look at me after I pass. This happens everywhere I go. It is almost constant.

My fat is a focus, a magnetic force. The motion of my body pulls people toward me, and they curse and struggle to get away. I don't want their fascination—it wears me down. I don't want to be less of myself, either.

People see me, and they respond, strongly. Sometimes their reactions are masked with politeness More than a few friends have told me, in moments of intimacy, intending a compliment, that they forget that I'm fat. The best that many friends and family members would wish for me is that I become thin. (95-98% of all diets fail over a five year period. This is a failure of the method, not the person.) Short of that, they wish I could live without being seen. They do their best to treat me as if I looked like someone else.

That pretense is never comfortable, and never convincing. It is the gentlest way many people can find to control their panic in the presence of a human body that, in this culture, is shunned.

But *I am seen*.

2.

When I was eight, I took a bus to school. One morning I was waiting at the bus stop with the other kids, and a boy threw a dart at my belly. It hit and stuck. I pulled it out and looked down. There was a spot of blood on my shirt. My fat older sister started crying, but I laughed. I knew what would happen if I seemed weak.

My sister walked me home. My fat mother took me to the doctor. My belly was bleeding a little, and she was worried about tetanus. The doctor raised my shirt, and laughed. He said nothing could hurt me much through all that fat.

When I was in fifth grade, a doctor put me and my mother and sister on a new diet. We didn't eat supper. My mother made hamburger casserole or turkey pie for my father and my two brothers to eat in the evening, but she didn't eat what she had cooked until the next morning. Then the three of us had smaller portions of what was left for breakfast. It was a long time from school lunch to hamburger patties for breakfast the next day.

When I was in my last year of high school, I became sexually active. I went to a clinic for birth control pills. The nurse who examined me said she couldn't find my uterus through all of my fat. Shy in front of my boyfriend, I had shaved the hair that grew on my belly. The nurse was horrified. "You don't go out in public showing *that*."

3.

Most mornings, I wake up and run my hands over my belly. I linger over the texture of stretch marks, but the pervasive feeling is of live smoothness. I slip both hands underneath and hold it. Sometimes it is tender where it folds. It's always warm. My hands are drawn there.

4.

I am in a swimming pool with seventeen fat women. We have our arms around each other's waists and are circling in the center of the pool. We go faster and faster. Our bellies, breasts and arms press together. We lap against each other, screaming and laughing. The water rises around us. When we let go, we're washed against the sides. Sheets of water cross the floor. I'm drenched. My fat spills, as always, over my bones.

This force is real.

THE HERSHEY BAR QUEEN
Elena Diaz Bjorkquist

What Do Fat People Want? We want fat children to grow up safe from ridicule and physical violence. Such hate crimes rob fat children of their self-esteem and their hope for the future. To this end, we want schools, social service agencies, and courts to recognize, and help alleviate, the socially condoned mistreatment of fat children.
—"What Do Fat People Want?"from *FAT! SO?*

Obese children rate their quality of life with scores as low as those of young cancer patients on chemotherapy, a study found, highlighting the physical and emotional toll of being too fat.
—Lindsey Tanner, "Fat Kids Rank Quality of Life Low"

When she was a little girl, Reyna Lara was the same size as other children her age. As they grew up, however, the baby fat melted off the others but Reyna's did not. Instead, she gained more and more weight. At first, it was not her fault. Her parents thought their one and only child was perfect with black sausage curls and cheeks like large ripe peaches. They pinched her cheeks and plied her with *pan dulce*, cookies, and candy. "Sweets for our sweet queen," they would tell her.

By the time she was seven, Reyna was the size of three girls her age and the other children made fun of her, calling her names like "Reyna, the big fat *ballena*." Her only playmates were her cousins and they played with her because they were forced to by their parents. Reyna did not seem to care. Food was her main concern and as she grew bigger and bigger, she had to consume even greater quantities to fuel her immense bulk. She took to visiting her grandmother every evening because Nana served dinner later than her mother. Reyna could eat another full meal there and Nana was liberal with seconds and sometimes thirds. Reyna's four aunts and three uncles also lived nearby and she picked up extra meals and snacks at their homes.

There was an emptiness inside Reyna—a hollow feeling she interpreted as hunger, but no amount of food could fill it, no matter how much she stuffed herself. She ate more than her father; probably more than anyone else in town, except maybe for *Doña* Lupe. The last time that lady was seen outside her house, she could barely squeeze out a door. It was rumored that now she was so enormous, she could not get out of bed. All *Doña* Lupe did was eat, sleep, and read *True Confessions* magazines.

When Reyna was twelve years old, she stood five feet seven inches tall in her bobby socks and weighed 350 pounds. She towered a foot or more over the other girls her age and older. Reyna was taller, not to mention wider, than most women in Morenci, including her mother. Boys her age had not yet undergone growth spurts like the girls, so next to them Reyna was gigantic.

Despite being so large, Reyna was extremely graceful. When she walked, her tiny feet skimmed the earth as if held up by her buoyant body. The other children teased that she looked like a balloon in the Macy's Thanksgiving Day Parade. Their parents thought so, too, but kept it to themselves unless they were chiding their children for eating too much candy. "Quit it or you'll look like a balloon in the Macy's parade!"

The harassment Reyna suffered from schoolmates grew so severe she took to ducking into the Taylor Dunne Mercantile Store every day after school so she would not have to walk home with them. Reyna strolled up and down aisles stacked high with cans and boxes of food. She wandered through the fresh-vegetable section and thought about what *Mamá* and Nana might be preparing for dinner. She envisioned *tacos, enchiladas, mole, chili verde, gorditas, frijoles, calabacita, burritos,* and dozens of other delicious Mexican dishes, and her empty stomach grumbled its complaint. Reyna took a huge sack lunch to school every day, but it was not enough to sustain her until dinner.

When she thought the other children had enough head start, Reyna went to the candy counter. By this time in her life, her parents were concerned about her weight and were afraid she would wind up like *Doña* Lupe, so they limited her intake of sweets. They allowed her to buy only one candy bar each day and Reyna was obedient. Of course her parents did not know about the extra meals she obtained from the relatives.

"What'll it be today, Reyna," asked the clerk. "A plain Hershey or one with almonds?" Reyna always left the pleasure of deciding until the last moment. There was no rhyme or reason as to which one she chose. Some weeks she picked Hersheys with almonds five days in a row and other weeks she alternated them with plain Hersheys every other day. Regardless of which she chose, Reyna always took her chocolate treasure across the large Plaza parking lot to the foot of the grand staircase leading up to the new shopping center. She could have taken the short cut across the footbridge over the road, but avoid it with reason.

When she used to cross the two-way bridge, people coming toward her would have to retreat and wait until she crossed. There was no way that anyone, not even a small toddler could squeeze past Reyna. She filled the passageway from one side to the other. Her girth was such that she could not even turn around on the narrow bridge. One day she attempted it and got wedged in so tight she could not move. The old men who sat in front of the T.D. store buying and selling coupon books rushed to her rescue. They extricated her from this humiliating predicament by tugging and shoving until she popped out like the first pickle in a jar. She landed on the nearest elderly man, who was never the same after that. Meanwhile, the children gathered on both sides of the bridge laughed and taunted her.

"Reyna's a *ballena!*" they yelled.

"She's so big and fat she can't cross the bridge!"

"Reyna's so big, she could be the bridge!"

After that, Reyna never went on the footbridge again.

There was another short cut. It went under the bridge and across the road to a steep staircase behind the Royal Theater, but it was also a problem for Reyna. Nearly a hundred narrow steps led to the top with only one place to rest halfway up. There was no shade where she could stop to eat her Hershey bar. The only time she had gone that route, Reyna thought she would die before she reached the upper level.

So Reyna was forced to take the grand staircase, although it was the longer route to her house. The WPA had built the staircase, during the Depression and it was grand indeed. Two sixty-foot tall cypress trees flanked it at the bottom and the wide stairs meandered uphill as if leading to a mansion. Her grandfather had helped lay the steps and walls enclosing the staircase and Reyna always remembered him when she touched the stones worn smooth by thirty years of use.

Reyna's daily ritual was to sit on the wall shaded by the nearest tree and pull off the Hershey bar's brown outer wrapper. She sniffed it with delight, anticipating the taste of warm chocolate. The candy was usually melted, so she licked it off the foil wrapper. This was the way she liked it best, and since it was the only candy bar she could have, she savored every smidgen of chocolate her tongue lapped off the waxy white lining.

When every trace of chocolate had vanished, she crumbled the wrappers and tossed them under the cypress where they joined an ever-growing pile. Then Reyna commenced to climb the grand staircase, feeling like a queen. She paused now and again to rest on the stone wall and gaze down at the cars in the lot below. Some days, if she were lucky, she spotted one of her uncle's cars and went back down the stairs no matter how far up she was. She sat in the car and waited until its owner came out and drove her home. If she were not so lucky—which was more often the case, she climbed two more sets of stairs behind the post office and a large hill before she reached home.

On the day that would change the course of her life forever, Reyna saw Beto Cisneros sitting on the wall near the top of the stairs. He was sixteen years old and in tenth grade. He would have been in eleventh grade if he had not flunked fifth. Normally, he did not bother glancing her way, much less speak to her, but on this day he surprised Reyna.

"Would you like a Hershey?" Beto asked. He held it out to her but pulled it back when she reached for it. "No. First I want to show you something." He grabbed her hand and pulled her toward the ivy-covered wall next to the power and light building.

Reyna was not sure what was happening so she locked her legs in place and yanked Beto toward her. He bounced off her body and plopped on the ground.

"It's okay, Reyna." Beto got up and offered his hand to her. "I just want to show you my secret hiding place. Come on."

Someone offering to share a secret hiding place, his hand, and a Hershey? No one in Morenci outside her family ever showed such kindness to Reyna. She went with him.

Beto led her up an ivy-covered path alongside the retaining wall. In all the times Reyna passed by here she never noticed the overgrown path. Halfway to the top of the forty-five-foot high wall, Beto stopped.

"Let's go in here." He pushed his way through overhanging ivy onto a four-foot wide ledge jutting out from the wall. Originally intended by the builders as a planter to break the expanse of rock wall, it once contained flowers, but now a jungle of ivy made the ledge invisible to passersby below. A shiver of anticipation went through Reyna as she joined Beto. Two Hersheys in one day!

"Sit." Beto pulled her onto the cushion of cool leaves next to him. "No one can see us here. This is my secret place. Nobody else knows about it so swear you won't tell anyone, not even your mother."

"I swear not to tell." Reyna said. Who would she tell? She had no friends, no one with whom she could share such an important secret.

"You have to do more than swear," Beto said. "You have to seal your oath."

"Seal my oath?" Reyna smelled the chocolate sweetness of the melted candy bar as Beto wafted it under her nose. A Hershey with almonds! Reyna licked her lips and her tongue encountered a smear of chocolate from the candy she had eaten only minutes before. She swiped it off with her tongue and its taste made her hunger for more. She reached out for the Hershey, craving it as if it were the last one on earth.

"No," said Beto. "First we seal the oath. We're going to form a secret club. I'm the leader and you'll do everything I say from now on."

"Okay. Fine," said Reyna. She eyed the Hershey in Beto's hand and hoped he would let her have it before it melted further. Reyna liked it melted on the outside but preferred the inside to be solid enough to get her teeth into it.

"Lay down and close your eyes." Beto pointed to the bed of ivy. Reyna obeyed him, but when she felt her dress slide up, her eyes flew open. "What are you doing?" She struggled to sit up.

"I'm not going to hurt you," Beto said. He nudged her back down. "This is what friends in our club do when they like each other. Close your eyes and relax. You don't have to do anything else."

Friends? Like each other? Not since she was a little girl had anyone offered to be her friend, much less say they liked her. Reyna lay back down— her eyes squeezed shut. She felt Beto slip off her underpants and climb on top of her. Suddenly, something poked her down there in that place her *mamá* had told her not to touch except when she wiped after peeing.

"Oomph!" Reyna's eyes popped open. Something was now inside her pee place and Beto bucked up and down like one of the cowboys Reyna saw riding the bulls at the rodeo.

"Ahh!" Beto grimaced as if something exploded inside him. His body went slack and he lay on her for a few minutes before rolling off and pulling off his jeans.

"That's it," he said. "Your oath is sealed. Here's the Hershey and your *chones*. Remember you can't tell anyone about this place or what we do in our secret club." He crawled through the leafy undergrowth back to the path.

Reyna sat up with her tent-sized panties in one hand and the Hershey in the other. She threw down the panties and ripped open the candy bar. Reyna's teeth scraped the entire gooey mess into her mouth. The delectable chocolate melted on her tongue and oozed down her throat.

There was something strange about what happened with Beto, but Reyna did not know what. It couldn't be wrong, could it? Beto was her friend and he said he liked her. Reyna chomped the almonds and twin streams of chocolate sluiced down either side of her mouth. At the same time, she became aware of a sticky wetness between her legs. She took a hanky out of her pocket and wiped herself. The handkerchief looked like someone with a bad cold had blown his nose in it. There was a tinge of blood running through the mucus. Had Beto broken something down there? Maybe she'd ask her mother when she got home. But no, she couldn't do that. She had promised Beto. Reyna stuffed the hanky in the ivy, put on her panties, and went home.

A couple of days later, Beto was again waiting at the staircase. He flashed the Hershey at her and led the way up the path. Without his help, Reyna found it difficult to maneuver her bulk up the steep slope. By the time she reached the ledge, she was panting.

"Take them off and lay down," Beto said. "I'll give you the Hershey when we're done sealing the oath." He mounted her and repeated what he had done earlier, except he did not take as long. "Remember this is our secret— don't you tell." He handed her the Hershey and left.

Reyna ate the candy with gusto, licking the wrapping and her fingers to get every last bit of chocolate. When she wiped herself this time there was no blood on the handkerchief. She wadded it up and stuck it in the ivy.

Maybe she'd better carry Kleenex. Her mother might get suspicious about too many lost hankies.

For the next month, Reyna counted on getting an extra Hershey two or three times a week. Then one day she found Matt Sandoval instead of Beto waiting for her on the staircase. He flaunted two Hersheys.

"I'm in the club," he said. He turned and went up the ivy-covered trail. Reyna trudged behind him. More chocolate and a new friend!

In the weeks that followed, Sammy García, Tony Moreno, Andres Solano, and Martín Hernández had all joined the club. By the end of the year, Reyna had many more new friends and had gained twenty-five pounds.

By the time she was in eleventh grade, Reyna weighed 439 pounds. The young men in Morenci called her the "Hershey Bar Queen" behind her back. When she was fifteen, her Aunt Tilly, who was seven years older, told her about sex. So now Reyna knew what the boys did to her on the ivy leaves was wrong. Every Saturday, when she dutifully waited in line to confess her sins, she thought about telling Father O'Hara. But how could she betray her friends? The boys were her only friends. The girls hated her. They made snide remarks about her weight and Reyna had had several fights in the girls' bathroom at school. Her bulk was an advantage and each scuffle ended with Reyna sitting on her antagonist. Nowadays no girl dared confront her, but Reyna still heard them whispering about her.

By now Reyna was a mother confessor to most of the boys. They sought her out not just for sex but as someone they entrusted with their joys and tribulations. They called her "Big Reyna" and felt comforted when she hugged them to her mountainous bosom. Reyna was a good listener and only offered advice when they asked for it. She did not condemn or criticize and was quick to offer encouragement. The boys made her feel needed. No, there was no way she could tell the priest about them and the Hershey Club.

Sometimes she felt guilty about holding back something she knew was a sin—especially on Sundays when she received Holy Communion, She was afraid that one day the Host would burn through her tongue as it dissolved. It would be God's way of punishing her for not confessing all her sins. Reyna was not even sure if she were committing a venial sin or a mortal one since the nuns had never mentioned anything about sex in catechism. She prayed it was the lesser one.

Toward the end of the school year, students prepared for the Junior Prom. When Mrs. Ames, the school secretary, posted the nominee list for king and queen on the bulletin board outside the office, Reyna was thrilled to discover her name. Her Hershey boys had come through! She had never been to a dance or even had a date. Now she was not only going to the prom, the biggest formal dance of the year, but the prom committee had nominated her for queen. That was all she could think about day and night in school and at home. In Home Economics, she forgot to take her cake out of the oven and the whole school was evacuated when smoke set off the fire alarm. Homework went unfinished. Teachers' questions she had not heard and could not have answered anyway, interrupted her daydreaming in class.

Her mother sewed all of Reyna's clothes since there were no store-bought dresses in her size. While other young women went to Safford to try on and purchase their gowns, Reyna and *Señora* Lara went to study the designs. In the end, they combined various styles and purchased yards of expensive satin, ribbons, and lace. *Señora* Lara spent hours sewing a gown fit for a queen. Reyna went on a diet, limiting herself to meals at home. She squirreled away Hershey bars from her assignations with the young men. The treasure house of chocolate she was hoarding tempted her to indulge, but Reyna disciplined herself. By the time she figured out she could exchange her favors for the promise of votes for prom queen instead of candy, the collection of Hersheys cached in the ivy was more than adequate for a super binge after the prom.

The night of the prom arrived and Harold Pankovich, who had been nominated for king, came for Reyna in his father's GMC pickup. Harold stood a foot shorter than she did and weighed about 110 pounds in his rented tux and black hightop basketball shoes. He had a reputation for being the most obnoxious person in all of Morenci High School history, but he was Reyna's friend and she overlooked his idiosyncrasies. When Harold saw Reyna in her strapless evening gown, he almost dropped the gardenia corsage he was holding.

"Wow! You look fantastic!" he said. He stood on tiptoes and attempted to pin the corsage on the layers of ruffles adorning her décolletage.

Señora Lara, who had been admiring the product of her handiwork, came to his assistance when she noticed Harold's fumbling fingers brushing the tops of Reyna's breasts. *Señor* Lara brought out his Polaroid camera and took a series of black and white photos of Reyna by herself and with Harold. As it turned out later, he was grateful he had.

Reyna and Harold entered the school gym and stopped to admire the tropical jungle decor. A momentary silence greeted them as everyone turned to stare at them. They walked to the table reserved for the royal nominees, unaware of the snickering and whispering they left behind them. The music started and boy after boy came to Reyna's table to reserve a dance with her. It was a perfect evening as far as Reyna was concerned. Her dance card was full and she basked in all the attention she received. She felt like she was already the prom queen.

During an intermission, Reyna went to the bathroom in the girls' locker room. She was in the large stall at the far end struggling with the unfamiliar garter belt and stockings when she heard a girl in the next stall mention her name.

"Did you see Big Reyna?" asked the girl. Reyna recognized Sharon Martínez's voice. "She looks like a wedding cake in that grotesque dress."

"Yeah, a wedding cake for a giant," said another girl. This one sounded like Priscilla Ayala. Both girls giggled. "It must have taken fifty yards of material to make her gown."

"A strapless gown . . . can you imagine? Every time she went out to dance, I thought her boobs would pop out. They must be the size of watermelons!" said Sharon. "If I were that fat, I'd be too embarrassed to leave my house."

Reyna grappled with the garter belt. Damm! Maybe it was supposed to go on over the panties not under. Yards of satin and lace ruffles impeded her attempts to fasten the stockings. He face flushed. A wedding cake? Watermelon breasts? But Harold said she looked fantastic . . . and the boys had all signed her dance card.

"She has no shame," said Priscilla. "She was flaunting her boobs at all the guys who danced with her."

"What do you expect from someone who's slept with every guy in the school for Hershey bars?" said Sharon.

"She's going to get hers tonight," said Priscilla. "I bet she really believes she's going to get crowned tonight." Both young women laughed and flushed their toilets simultaneously.

"When we counted the votes today, the Hershey Bar Queen had just one vote—hers!" said Sharon. "I can hardly wait to see her face when Sal announces the last runner-up and hands her a Hershey bar in front of the whole school." The girls' laughter echoed off the metal lockers.

Hot tears sprang to Reyna's eyes and mascara flowed down her rouged cheeks. She wiped the tears, smearing her face red and black like the school colors. Wait a minute, how did the girls know about the Hershey Club? The boys had to have told them. Reyna felt a pain in her heart as if a bolt of lightning had ripped through it. How could they? It was supposed to be a secret. All these years, she had kept her promise. Why hadn't they? Out of the hurt, a deep rage exploded. She clenched her fists and plunged out of the stall, ripping the locked door off its hinges.

In the mirror, Sharon and Priscilla glimpsed a bulk of white racing toward them—Reyna snorting like an enraged bull. The young women were so scared, they forgot to run. Reyna grabbed each one by their fancy hairdos and shook them like rag dolls. She flung their bodies into the toilet stalls.

Turning to leave, Reyna saw herself in the mirror. What a mess! Her curls, which had been piled high in an upswept hairdo, tumbled around her head like worms with hairpins stuck in them. Mascara mingled with rouge and flowed down her huge cheeks like lava from a volcano. For the first time in her life, Reyna saw herself as others saw her. Her fist pounded her reflection, splintering the mirror. Blood spurted out of her wounded hand and spilled onto the delicate lace of her dress. Intense hatred overcame her—hatred of the Hershey boys and of herself.

Reyna stormed out of the bathroom and into the gym, pushing aside anyone who got in her way. One shove from Reyna was enough to topple even Buzz Owens, the biggest football player on the team. Harold approached her and Reyna ran right over him like a locomotive. As Reyna made her way to the exit, she pulled down crepe-paper streamers and balloons. The cardboard murals of exotic jungles painted by the art classes crashed to the floor. A path of devastation lay in Reyna's wake. Teachers and students alike were so stunned they didn't even try to stop her.

Anger and hatred fueled Reyna as she tackled the 357 steps that led up from the high school to the plaza. Usually it took her forever to climb this steep staircase because she could not go more than ten or twelve stairs without stopping to rest. But this night, she flew over three and sometimes four steps at a time. At first Reyna did not know where she was going, but when she found herself at the foot of the grand staircase, she knew.

In the darkness, Reyna crawled onto the ivy-covered ledge and dug in the leaves for her cache of Hershey bars. She stuffed candy into her mouth as fast as she could get the wrappers off. Her jaws chewed the mass of hard chocolate—plain Hersheys and Hersheys with almonds—all mixed. Chocolate streamed down her chin and joined the other stains on her ruined gown. Bar after bar went into her cavernous mouth, but none of them brought the comfort she was seeking.

An almond stuck in her throat and Reyna tried to cough. She was choking. Desperate to breathe, she jumped up and the snaps on her garter belt broke. The belt slipped to her ankles, tripping her. Reyna reached out to grab the ivy to steady herself but she was facing the wrong way. Her hands closed on air. The tremendous weight of her upper body plunged her headfirst off the ledge into the ivy leaves below.

The townspeople organized a search party for Reyna that same night, but her body was not found until the next morning. Her parents were in shock. *Señora* Lara took to her bed clutching a tear-streaked snapshot of Reyna in her prom dress. *Señor* Lara was so distraught, his brother had to drive him to the mortuary in Clifton to arrange the funeral. Mr. Morrison informed them there were no caskets large enough for Reyna's body. He hated to do so because the markup on caskets was where he made most of his money. Reluctantly, he told them to ask *Don* Simón to custom-build a coffin. *Don* Simón was the former coffin maker who had been forced to retire when people preferred the fancy manufactured caskets to his wooden ones. It took him four days to build a specially reinforced coffin out of oak. Pine would have splintered under Reyna's immense weight.

On the day of the funeral, Holy Cross Church overflowed with family and parishioners and the entire population of Morenci High School—boys, girls, and teachers. Reyna's uncles had refused to carry the coffin because of their bad backs so *Señor* Lara invited the football team to be pallbearers. It took the whole first string plus one—six on each side—to carry Reyna's coffin down the church's main aisle. Father O'Hara spoke about Reyna and how much she had suffered in her short life but was now finally at peace. Girls sobbed into their hankies, feeling guilty about never having befriended her. Boys had lumps in their throats and felt guilty about having taken advantage of her.

When the funeral mass was over, the football team hoisted the coffin onto their shoulders again and trudged down the aisle. Outside the church, just before the steps, Buzz Owens slipped on what later turned out to be a melted Hershey bar—plain with no almonds. He tried to regain his balance but the coffin weighed him down and he stumbled into Larry Rodríguez, who fell onto Jorge Gutiérrez, who knocked over Salvador Tamayo, the heavy coffin crashing over all of them. It smashed into Beto Cisneros' groin and the blow was such that he was never able to father any children. The coffin slid down the stairs and knocked over several other young men who did not get out of the way fast enough. By the time Reyna's coffin came to a rest at the foot of the stairs, it had managed to injure over twenty young men. Each of the football players had broken something—an arm, a leg, a wrist, an ankle. It was a good thing the football season was over; otherwise Morenci could not have fielded a team that year.

Reyna's funeral turned into a shambles of broken bodies and screaming girls. When her uncles went to put the lid back on the coffin, they noticed Reyna had an angelic smile. It struck them as strange because when Reyna's casket lay open at the Rosary the night before, she was not smiling. With much effort the older men of the parish loaded the huge coffin into the hearse and Reyna was finally laid to rest in the cemetery next to the smelter.

As far as the young men of Morenci were concerned, however, Reyna's spirit was never laid to rest. Those who went past the ivy-covered stone wall, where they had exchanged Hershey bars for Reyna's favors, heard the leaves rustle as if someone were tossing and turning on the ledge above. They caught a faint scent of chocolate as if someone were eating a Hershey bar next to them. Soon they sought other ways to get to the post office, although the grand staircase was the most direct route from the high school. Several years later when T.D. tore down Morenci for the ever-expanding copper mine, men who did not go to school in Morenci and did not know about Reyna had to smash the stone wall. The local young men refused to go near it.

Years later, when dynamite blasts obliterated Morenci and only the rocky levels of the open pit mine marked where the town once stood—workers reported there was a certain spot on a certain level where they heard leaves rustling and smelled chocolate. The young men who had known Reyna shivered every time they heard about it. They were destined never to forget Reyna, the Hershey Bar Queen.

THE STRANGE HISTORY
OF SUZANNE LAFLESHE

Hollis Seamon

Fat women are twice as likely to enjoy sex and to reach orgasm, compared to thin women, according to a survey conducted by Weight Watchers magazine. (A full 85 percent of fat women surveyed said they enjoy sex, compared to only 40 to 45 percent of thin women who said they did. And 70 percent of fat women said they almost always have orgasms, compared to just 29 percent of thin women.) Fat women were also twice as likely to be happy with their partners and their relationships. Three fourths of the fat women surveyed said their partners found them attractive at their present weight.

—Marilyn Wann, *Fat! So? Because You Don't Have to Apologize for Your Size!*

Listen, every day you are being taught to hate and fear your own flesh. You are told that good food—food sweet and rich and whole—will kill you; you are told that good sex—sex rich and whole and sweet—will kill you. You can hardly imagine, anymore, what it is to love your flesh for the pleasures it provides, to honor even fat as bounty and to find joy in plentitude.

Here is a story for you. It may not be strictly true, nor exactly instructive, but it is a real story, and I offer it to you. It didn't come out as I'd planned and I'm not sure yet how it ends but for now, this is it: the strange sad history of me, Suzanne LaFleshe.

The story began last summer. By mid-July I was fat again. Not fat enough, but growing. I could feel the old familiar flesh gathering about my ribs and thighs; my breasts were already straining against the new lace C-cup bra I had bought for them just a few months before. My table glistened with cream and eggs and sugar. I was getting rich, again.

Janet, the woman who had been weighing me in regularly at Weight Watchers, didn't say anything, the first week that the scale went up three pounds. She just smiled and shook her head a bit. The next week—another five pounds up—she looked a little alarmed. "Suzanne," she said, bowing her head over my chart and avoiding my smiling eyes, "is something wrong? I mean, we all backslide at times, after reaching our goals, but don't usually slide back so fast, if you know what I mean." She raised her eyes when I laughed.

"Yeah," I said. "I'm sliding along here like a fiberglass toboggan—whoosh." I drew a steep descent in the air with my hand, pleased at feeling the beginnings of the old jiggle in my upper arm. "Sliding back like a son-of-a-bitch."

Janet stepped back, away from the scale, and looked at my arm. I could actually see the distaste growing on her face. She ran her bony hands down her size-5 navy linen skirt and retucked her sleeveless lemon yellow blouse: not a quiver on those tan arms. Once, she told me, she had weighed 203 pounds; now she held steady at 97. A true transfiguration: I admired her for it. It just wasn't the kind I wanted; I'd learned that it wasn't what I wanted, the way we learn most things in life, after I'd gotten it.

Please understand: I like my flesh. I like the way it moves and bounces; I like to see my breasts floating high, like islands in the bath; I like the sensation of my thighs squeezing together in stockings, caressing each other under one of my favorite full flowered skirts. I like introducing myself to strange men in bars, as Suzanne LaFleshe and seeing if they smile. (If they're too drunk or too stupid to get it, I know I can forget about them, move on, find another.) I like to see the little-boy-lost looks on their faces when they lean over and see, for the first time, the actual scope of my breasts under my white cotton peasant blouse, the kind with the puffy sleeves and deep scoop neck. I like to see that gratitude, the absolute relaxation, the flash of joy when they realize that here, here, is a place they could die, happy.

But I felt a little sorry for Janet. She really had been pleased about my progress, all last winter and spring. She'd sent me a congratulations card for every 10-pound loss. She'd sent flowers when I'd lost 100 and she'd thrown a little party—diet soda and ice milk and sugar-free cookies—at the Weight Watchers center when I'd reached my goal: 145 pounds. "(Hey, I'm tall, 5'11", so 145 really was thin, believe me. Hell, I'd started at 282. And that's where I was heading again, sliding as fast as I could, on runners greased by butter.) So I took her hand, trying not to be scared by its frailty, her bones so hard in my soft palm. Her head barely reached my shoulder.

"Listen, Janet," I said, leading her to a chair in the corner of the room, away from the chattering groups of women lining up for the scales. "Sit down."

She sat, pulling her skirt over her tiny brown knees. Her legs were so small they made me want to weep.

"Listen, it's not your fault. I just want to be fat again. I miss it." I sat down and crossed my legs, listening for that sweet sigh as they slid together. My summer sandal, size 11, special order, showed my toenails, newly painted, a nice clear shade of plum. (Listen, I keep myself clean, polished, shaved, deodorized, shampooed like every else. I'm not some evil-smelling fat woman. Oh, I smell: I smell like your grandmother's kitchen, touched by cinnamon and nutmeg, by yeast and warm bread-dough, rising. I smell like your mother's breasts, before you can really remember them: milky, warm, and solid.) I patted her knee.

Janet folded her hands in her lap, a patient teacher. "Oh, come now, Suzanne," she said. "You're just experiencing a perfectly normal letdown. There's always a little of that after you've reached your goal. A kind of anti-climax, after you've really done it. You know, like the day after Christmas." Janet's eyes, light blue in her tanned face, looked at me with absolute expectation of agreement.

I could see the wrinkles gathering at the corners of her eyes; skin without any fat behind it has nothing to do but fold in on itself—it's inevitable. My face had collapsed, too, but it was reviving. I could feel the fat cells bolstering up my cheeks; like pillows when they're shaken, my cheeks were plumping up nicely. I was always lucky about my face anyway. I had never been one of those fat women who lose their eyes among the rolls and who always look squinty. No, my face just rounded to a certain point and then stopped, full but not piggy. I retained a neck, I acquired no extra chins. I always carried my weight, fortunately, between my shoulders and knees. My ankles stayed trim enough, always, to wear a thin gold anklet: you know, the kind your mother told you were cheap and vulgar and sluttish? Yes, one of those. And your mother was partly right—anklets are sluttish in that men do love them and they do seem to hope for extraordinary sexual adventures with women who wear them. But then, men hope for the same from women who wear hair ribbons and other small adornments, too. I think that men are just always hopeful and they are, so often, let down. I hate to disappoint them, ever. One spring, years and years back, in my college English-major-cum-hippie days when I was a gloriously fat young woman, I even wore a small circlet of silver bells around my left ankle, like a Morris dancer ringing in Spring. The bells jingled, very slightly, whenever I moved my leg. In stuffy college classrooms, those bells brought April in and brought college boys to my dorm room, night after night: boys young and fresh and unthinkingly cruel as April itself. And a few professors came to call, too, bringing their Prufrock poetry and middle-aged sadness. Who could bear to turn them away?

Anyway, I had always kept my youthful ankles and I was one of those fat women that you see on dance floors everywhere, having more fun than anyone else, spinning on slim high heels, moving with the impossible, gravity-defying grace of tops and dreidels. So light on her feet, people say, it's amazing. Grace is always amazing, isn't it? No less so to those of us who have it, believe me.

"No," I said to Janet. "It's not that kind of letdown." I looked at my toes; their painted roundness pleased me. "I lost the weight, I guess, because I was curious to see if I really could. But it didn't make me happy, not at all. I guess I just like being fat better."

"Nonsense." Janet almost snorted out the word. I was glad she could make such a rude noise; it meant there was hope for her, too. "Nonsense," she repeated, more calmly. "No one likes being fat. That's just a common psychological defense mechanism."

I shook my head. What could I say to convince a woman who could take pop psychobabble seriously? I tried: "Janet," I said, "listen. I miss myself—I miss the all-of-me I've always been." She wasn't listening, I could tell; she was preparing her next salvo of common sense. I stared into her dark, frail, wrinkled face. "Listen, Janet," I said. "I miss all the men. Men like to fuck fat women. No: they love to fuck fat women. Remember?"

She went pale, under the surface, and she stood up. "I didn't hear that, Suzanne," she said, lips tight, jaw tight. "I did not hear that." She walked away, navy pumps clicking quickly over the tiled floor. Ass tight.

But I knew that she had heard me and I know that she missed it too, the richness of full-fleshed sex. Janet remembers this, but how can I possibly explain it to you, who haven't known it? I'll try. Listen, it is my own flesh I most love when making love. My flesh moves, wave after wave, all around me. I—the me who lives inside this flesh, feeling—I am like the core, the slim tight core at the center of the storm of sex. The man—and I like tough, thin men although I'm not really picky—the man is the catalyst; he provides the straight hard axis on which I turn. If he's good—and most men are good, really they are—then he joins me, somehow, on the inside of the whirlwind. Together, we set the flesh in motion, with our primitive bumps and grinds and shivering sliding thrusts and pulls, but once begun, it moves us. From my thighs to my breasts, the waves heave and peak, heave and peak. The man is lost; I am lost. He comes once; I lose count.

I'm not saying this quite right, am I? I'm not really capturing it and it sounds like one of the steamier Harlequin romances. Plainly then: pound for pound, my fat multiplies my orgasms. It's really that simple.

Anyway, that day, I left Weight Watchers and went home for lunch. I made a loaf pan of rice pudding, my grandmother's recipe, full of real cream and covered with a rum-laced hard sauce, and ate it all, slowly, rolling each grain of warm plump rice on my tongue. Nothing nourishes like rice pudding.

For the next few weeks, Janet weighed me silently. She noted the growing pounds—6 one week, 8 the next, 9 the next—on my chart, with no comment. But then I guess she broke under the pressure of my mounting flesh and when I went in on a hot August Tuesday, on my lunch hour as always, she met me with a small Weight Watchers delegation. They introduced themselves not by name but by position: one thin woman, the regional manager; and one comfortingly chunky man, the local representative. Jane took us all to a tiny office. I sat in one of the four wooden chairs and deliberately spread myself out. My legs took up most of the floor space and they all had to sit with their feet tucked up under their chairs. They looked very uncomfortable and I relaxed.

The regional manager spoke first. "Well, Suzanne. Or do you prefer Ms. Brown?"

"Suzanne," I said. "Suzanne LaFleshe."

Three faces went blank, then the local rep chuckled. He'd gotten it. I put him down, mentally, as a possibility. I'd already checked his wedding band finger and it was empty, except for the ghost of an old indentation of, maybe, ten years of marriage, awhile back. Definitely a possibility. The regional manager stared him down. "A joke," I said, sweetly. "That's just my fat name. You know, like writers have pen names and actors have stage names? I have a fat name."

No one even smiled, although the local rep looked like he wanted to.

"Ms. Brown will do," I said.

She nodded. "Well, Ms. Brown. Janet tells us that you're upsetting the other clients. That you are deliberately gaining weight, that you undermine her every effort. You bring," she glanced down at a report, typed up, I supposed, by Janet and sent out in triplicate. "You bring recipes to the other women, recipes full of fat and sugar." She shuddered.

The local rep coughed softly into his copy of the report. I really did like him. "Only one recipe," I said. "My grandmother's ice box cake, filled with chocolate custard and iced with whipped cream. I brought it in for Bonnie's little girl's birthday, that's all. She wanted something special, so I . . ."

She held up a slim hand, palm outward, to stop me. "The point is, Ms. Brown, we would like you to stop coming to Weight Watchers," she said. "You are making mock of us."

I appreciated her wording— "making mock" sounds good—but I said, "I've already paid for the next six months. I want to come; I want to keep track of my gain. I want to follow it, see it grow. I want to watch my weight. Isn't that what you people want us to do at Weight Watchers?"

She stared. "We will refund your money," she said.

"No, thank you." I stood up, tall and large and strong. "I prefer to keep coming in." I went to the door, then turned to face them. "I won't bring anymore recipes, though," I said nicely, in order to make a graceful exit. My grandmother, a fine large woman who died in her garden at the age of 97, unslimmed by time or sorrow, taught me that: "Suzanne," she'd say, "always leave a room well. Make them remember you."

And I know for sure that the local rep, whose name turned out to be Chuck, remembered, because he took my home number off my chart and called me that same evening. We spent three nights in a row in my oversized bed, reviving his memories and his spirit (and mine) and his love for his body (and mine), and then I sent him on his way, happy. I don't like to keep men for more than three or four nights, generally; life is too short to waste on repetition. And Chuck, of course, as a Weight Watchers representative, couldn't really afford to take me anywhere or be seen in public with me: me, the embodiment of all that Weight Watchers loathes and profits from. Actually, few men are that brave and I don't expect it. Men are very fragile human beings and it is for that, really, that I love them.

Anyway, after that Tuesday I went in quietly, once a week, and Janet weighed me, quietly, and I felt myself growing richer and richer, in peace. I was up to 200 and still gaining when Janet pulled her rabbit from a hat and defeated me. I admire that woman, really I do. She is far more devious than I'd imagined; many skinny women are. Maybe that's all they have left of their former fat selves—guile. But I think that they too, like you, have been beguiled, charmed into being the serpents in their own gardens.

Because when I went into Weight Watchers one cool September Tuesday at 12:30 as usual, there was a new girl on the scale right in front of me. A girl maybe fourteen or fifteen. A skeletal girl, shivering in a tank top and shorts: arms like matchsticks, legs like a stork. Hair dyed that awful flat black that kids use and sheared off on one side. Skin like the bottom of a dry creek bed, gray and cracked and hopeless. The scale read 83 pounds; I was close enough to read it before she stepped off and pulled on a black sweatshirt, sizes and sizes too big. She walked away and sat down by the long wall mirror, her head bent against her pulled-up knees.

Janet looked at me, triumph shining in her pale eyes. She smiled. "Suzanne," she said, "how are you? Lovely skirt. Hop on the scale, please."

I was suspicious of all the pleasantness but not enough to leave, to just haul myself out into the sunshine and let it go. It took her a long time to adjust the weights on the scale, they'd been moved so far down for that girl.

She fiddled with the weights for a while and then said cheerily, "206," and marked my chart.

I stepped off, smoothing my skirt against my thighs. She put her hand on my arm. I could feel the determination in her fingers. She hated touching me. She was afraid of my flesh. Afraid that her tiny bony little hand would be pulled in, somehow, absorbed and lost. Seduced by Suzanne LaFleshe. But she was tough—she held on, her pink nails making little red crescents in my forearm.

"Perhaps you would like to meet Theresa, our new client?" she said. She leaned closer, standing on her toes, straining to reach my ear, and whispered, "Theresa is a problem case, poor thing, recommended by Social Services. She thinks she's fat. Imagine. Anorexia, of course." She released my arm and I looked at the four moons her nails had left in my flesh. Then she spoke in a normal tone, sure of my attention. "They're hoping we can change her view of food, teach her the benefits of healthy food habits. Perhaps you can help her, Suzanne."

There was still time to leave but I couldn't. I was already walking toward Theresa.

"And, Suzanne," Janet said to my back, "Theresa's been sexually abused, so please be careful what you say to her, okay?"

I turned to see Janet's eyes fixed on my feet, on my cheap and vulgar and sluttish and lovely anklet. "Abused?" I said.

Jane nodded. "By her own father, apparently. Repeatedly. Since she was four or five, the social worker said."

For one moment, I had to picture that: a tiny little girl pinned beneath her heavy father. The sexual proportions all wrong, all backwards: no flesh to protect her. No joy. I felt ill.

Janet smiled. "There are lots of ways to destroy yourself, Suzanne," she said. "You choose to eat; she chooses not to. Go say hello."

Theresa didn't look up at first, while I struggled to put myself on the floor beside her. It wasn't easy for me to get onto a floor but I did it, landing finally in a position where I could lean back on the mirror and stretch my legs out straight. But by the time I'd settled, Theresa was staring, running her eyes over the expanse of my body.

"Hi," I said, holding out my hand. "I'm Suzanne LaFleshe."

For a second she just looked blankly polite, then she giggled. She put her hand, dry and thin as a fallen leaf, in mine. "Hi," she said. "I'm T-Bone."

I laughed. "You certainly are," I said.

That night, I went to a new bar. I liked to change my bars frequently so that I didn't become a regular—the resident loose and easy fatso. I perfumed and shaved and lotioned and shampooed and dressed up carefully, as if for a special occasion. I picked a bar with country/western on the jukebox. They're the simplest, really, with the nicest guys: unpretentious, up-at-5, dance-till-midnight, fuck-till-dawn guys. To me, it didn't much matter if they read books, or wrote them: what I wanted was a poet of the flesh. Lots of men are, more than you'd think from reading Cosmo questionnaires and from listening to thin women gripe. Trust me, lots of men are.

Listen, when you're fat, you learn early how to find nice guys. I learned a lot in high school: the boys in my advanced-level college prep classes wouldn't give me a glance, or if they did, it was just to entertain their friends with fat-girl jokes. (Here's a sample. Question: How do you figure out where to fuck a fat girl? Answer: Roll her in flour and aim for the wet spot. I didn't make this up: who could? Think about that: who could?) So I got a D in fancy-ass advanced algebra my freshman year and, the next year, got placed in dumb-ass plane geometry, the only girl in a class of 25 greaser hoods. It was heaven; those guys were wonderful. I learned a lot about sex and cars simultaneously. I taught some of them to love geometry, its precise angles and its generous truths; they taught me appreciation of my very own physical universe: more than fair bargain. And my geometry teacher, a brusque Korean war vet, took me aside once and said, "I looked up your IQ, Suzanne. It's very high. Did you know that? Did anyone ever tell you exactly how high it is?" "No," I said. "And please don't, okay?" And he, probably because he too was a nice guy and a survivor of a complex life, didn't.

High school geometry served me well my whole life. I could shoot pool with experts, dancing around the table on slim high heels, flashing my anklet, letting my breasts hang over the cue. I moved the cue up and down, deliberately, between my breasts, up and down, then aimed and shot. I'd have a man ready for my bed before the game was half over. It was almost too easy.

Anyway, I chose carefully the night following my lunch with Theresa. His name was Dexter; imagine life as a Dexter. But he hadn't shortened it or resorted to nicknames; I admired that. He was around 45, graying and shy, and he needed the solace of the flesh as much as I did. He chose, from my assortment of condoms—yes, I too had given in to this one form of necessary caution, even though I sorely missed the sensation of skin on skin— my favorite, the deep deep blue. It's funny how that color can make a penis look dangerous, interesting, even a little mysterious, when essentially, as you and I both know, it is not. Dexter stayed until 6 A.M., when he had to go to work. He asked if he could come back for supper. He asked if I'd like to go out dancing. Here was a man not afraid to be seen with me—a find. But I said, no. No thanks to both suggestions. I said goodbye. As I say, it was an occasion.

That day I met Theresa in the park for lunch. I'd brought a lot of food, but it was really just my usual lunch. Theresa sat on the grass, her Q-tip legs folded in front of her. Her eyes got bigger and bigger as I spread out the food on the blue-checked cloth; six pieces of fried chicken, a bowl of potato salad, half a loaf of zucchini bread, and two slices of chocolate pound cake, my grandmother's recipe. I poured milk from my thermos: unskimmed, high fat, real milk.

I leaned back against a tree. September was all around us, rich with smells. I put a napkin on my lap and began to eat. Theresa sat still at my side. I offered her some of everything I ate, chicken, salad, bread, and cake, but she just shook her head. "No, thanks," she said. "I'm not hungry. I had a big breakfast."

I nodded. "That's good. As Janet always says, 'Eat breakfast like a king, lunch like a prince, and supper like a pauper.' Right?" I grinned. I do a pretty fair Janet imitation, even now: lips pursed, throat tense, everything tight.

Theresa giggled. She put a blade of grass between her lips and sucked on it. She looked like an Irish famine victim; I'd read once how they had died with their lips dyed green from eating grass, the only harvest their tired land would produce. Her cheeks were intensely pale and hollow, her eyes a strange dull brown. Her shaved skull glowed through its fringe of dark hair: a black and white girl, all edges, no compromise. My chest actually hurt when I looked at her, as if one of my chicken bones had gone down sideways and lodged there. I felt the dangers of living inside that body, its bones so clear, no padding for any kind of fall.

I didn't press food on her; I just ate it in front of her, sucking on bones, licking chocolate crumbs from my fingers, one by one. Her eyes never strayed from the food. "Janet says," I said, when I was done, every scrap gone. "Janet says you think you're fat. Do you?"

Theresa rolled her eyes. "Janet's a jerk," she said. The piece of grass fell out of her lips and she replaced it with a stick.

"Yeah, well, that is certainly true." I leaned back on the tree with a sigh and let myself spread out over the grass. I folded my hands on my belly and looked down over the field of my flesh. "Now, me, I'm fat," I said. "That's obvious."

She laughed. "Yeah."

I nodded. "So, if I'm fat, what are you?"

She stretched herself out next to me, imitating my position exactly. "I," she said, "am not fat. I am a twig. You're a whole tree."

I laughed; the kid had class.

She looked up into the leaves, just beginning to turn color. "I am T-bone, the twig. I have an official eating disorder, you know." She laughed and I could see her teeth, blackening against receding gums. I looked away, into the leaves. "But I'm not stupid and I'm not crazy." She shut her eyes but kept talking. "It's just that they expect me to say that I think I'm fat because they read that somewhere, you know? They believe what they read in books, like it's real. But I know what I am: I'm T-bone, the girl so skinny nobody wants to touch her. I'm just a twig."

She was quiet for a long while and I didn't say anything. Then, she turned on her side with her back to me, curled up, and went to sleep.

I couldn't move. I'd never had a girl lean against me like that: men, always, children, never. I watched her breathe. With every inhalation her ribs strained, as if they would crack through her skin. I looked up into the leaves and grieved, for all sins against the flesh.

After that, I met Theresa every Monday, Wednesday and Friday for lunch in the park. She didn't eat anything, at first, but gradually she'd accept a scrap or two. I discovered that she was much more likely to take a leftover than a whole piece of food so I began to leave crusts, bones with meat still on them, half-drunk cups of milk. She'd snatch these up, her fingers bent like claws, and push them into her mouth, fast. I always looked away, to let her swallow in private; it was painful to watch her, anyway.

On and off, she told me a little about her life: she lived in a foster home; she went to school when she felt like it; she'd been told she was smart, could make something of herself, if she tried; she had a few friends; she loved Henry, her cat; she'd read all the Bronte novels; she was always cold. I told her a little about my life: I worked in a nice office; I had a nice apartment; I had read all the Pym novels; I liked to cook; I liked to eat; I was always a bit too warm. I didn't mention men and, anyway, there hadn't been anyone after Dexter. I had, for some reason I still don't completely understand, decided to do without, for awhile. It occurred to me that I hadn't treated men as well as I maybe should. I was selfish; I'd used them for my own pleasure. I decided I needed to re-think men, when I had a chance. I mentioned that my landlady liked cats.

On Tuesdays, we weighed in together. I hovered around 210, seemingly stuck there. Theresa gained one pound, then two. Janet smiled on us kindly; if there were fangs and forked tongue slinking behind her lips, she kept them hidden. No need to gloat.

One day in mid-October, when the falling leaves kept burying my lunch, Theresa told me this story: I'll keep it brief because it's really too much to ask you to bear. When Theresa was five, she said, she shared a room with her sister, who was thirteen. The sister, naturally, barely tolerated her; Theresa was a pest, always getting into her sister's things, messing her stuff up. She didn't think her sister liked her at all. They shared a double bed and her sister slept soundly and silently every night, her back turned toward Theresa. She always stayed on the far edge of the mattress, worlds and worlds away. Theresa's father worked the three-to-midnight shift and when he came home, everyone in the house was asleep. He came, a few nights a week, to Theresa's room and he leaned over the bed, right over her sleeping sister, and he lifted Theresa up and carried her, still warm and sleepy, downstairs to the TV room, a room with a lock on the door.

I tried not to think about this too much but sometimes I couldn't help it: into my head would come the picture and I would see an even tinier Theresa, a Theresa just five, in pink feety pajamas. Being carried away by that huge, silent man. And sometimes I could see it all from the point of view of that thirteen-year-old sister in the bed, that sister with her eyes clenched shut, not seeing, not seeing anything. Asleep.

When I was thirteen, I spent a lot of time in bed. The joints in my legs ached all the time and one doctor told my mother I might have some kind of juvenile arthritis and my mother fed me, as recommended, spoonfuls and spoonfuls of cod liver oil, supposedly to lubricate my joints. (I still can't eat an orange, the food she handed to me after the oil, to cut the taste.) Then another doctor, hearing this theory, snorted and said my joints hurt because I was so fat: all that weight was a strain on growing bones. My mother, in disgust with me, I think, gave up and left me alone.

So I remember being thirteen and left blessedly alone, lying on my stomach and letting my new breasts rub against the sheets. I would pull my nightgown up and let all of my naked flesh rest against the roughness of bleached cotton. At thirteen, I learned the pleasures of my own body; I learned that a certain motion, pulling my hips just right along the mattress, caused a weakness and sweetness to rush through me. I learned how to enjoy the weight of breast and thigh and hip pressing themselves down and down into the solid dark. I learned to see, as I can still see now, circles of light behind my eyelids, circles of moving light that tightened and loosened, faster and faster, as I came.

Afterwards I would lie on my back, looking up into the clear clean dark and I could feel myself riding the planet, moving through space. For a year or two, before I forgot how, I could actually perceive, I swear to you, the motions of the spheres. I really could; it's true.

I thought that I'd taught myself all that I would ever need to know about self-love, at thirteen. I knew that I had been blessed—grace, unasked for, sent my way. But I had to reconsider: maybe someone else, somewhere, paid for my grace? Maybe while, somewhere, one girl learns to love her flesh, another learns to loathe hers, to starve it and to punish it? And beside her, her sister wills herself to sleep very very soundly? Maybe.

Anyway, by the first week of November it was too cold to eat in the park, so I asked Theresa if she would come to my house for lunch. She hesitated but she said she'd come and then there she was sitting there in my kitchen, her black raincoat wrapped around her shoulders, held together in front by her two hands, fingers folded like amulets against her chest. She was so dark, a shadow in my yellow kitchen, and here, inside in the warmth of radiators, I could smell her, a bitter strange smell, like dry rot. She'd brought her cat Henry and he was sniffing around the apartment. Henry was an oddly-colored cat, light gray, solid, without a stripe. He was like mist, almost invisible in certain lights.

I'd stayed home from work, especially, to cook our lunch. My hands were warm from stirring saucepans; my face flushed from steam. I'd made all of the things I like best when I'm scared, all the things I think of as nursery foods—creamed chicken, baking powder biscuits, graham cracker cream pie. Everything bland, smooth, almost colorless. Foods that roll down the throat easily, lovingly, without effort.

At first, Theresa stayed huddled in a chair but when I asked her to set the table she got up and did a lovely job, arranging things perfectly even while holding her raincoat shut with one hand. She placed each plate carefully, running a finger around the edges. "You've got pretty dishes," she said.

"Thanks." I didn't look up from dishing out the chicken. "I bought them for myself when I realized I'd probably never get married. Gift from me to me. Here," I said, handing her a saucer of creamed chicken. "Give this to Henry."

She took the saucer in two hands, letting her coat fall open. Under it, she was wearing a heavy gray sweater and a black turtleneck and an old flannel shirt, layer above layer like a bag lady afraid to let go of anything she owns.

She put the saucer down and called Henry. He came right in, sniffed the dish and settled down to eat with intense concentration, tail wrapped tight around his butt.

I laughed. "Well, Henry likes it, anyway," I said. "Let's try it."

We sat down and I filled both our plates. I started to eat and Theresa, looking trapped, picked up her fork. She pushed chunks of chicken around the plate, just barely bringing drops of cream sauce to her lips on the tips of her fork. "It's good," she said politely.

I put my fork down, mid-bite, and looked at her. "Come on, T-bone," I said. "Let's quit bullshitting, okay?"

She put her fork down.

"I've got a deal for you, Theresa. Listen: just look at us. Look." I opened my arms wide, exposing myself and including her. "Look. I'm ridiculously fat and you're ridiculously skinny. Just look at us, Theresa."

She held her arms open, just like mine. She looked at us and then she nodded. "Yeah," she said. "So?"

"So let's swap. Here's the deal. I fill up one plate. Then I take one bite. Then you take one. Then I take one. Then you. Then me. Then you. When the plate's empty, that's it. I'm not allowed to refill it and you're not allowed to go throw up. I get thinner; you get fatter. What do you say? It's the only way I'll ever lose weight."

She looked at Henry, still crouched over his meal. "Can Henry live here?" she asked. "My foster mother hates him."

I nodded. "Okay."

"Can I come every day to see him?"

"If you want to. On Tuesdays, we'll weigh in."

She laughed. "That fucking Janet," she said. "She'll be pleased."

I nodded. "That's okay. She doesn't have much fun in life."

Theresa smiled, her gray, dingy, heartbreaking smile. "Okay," she said, and she opened her mouth like a little bird and waited for me to feed her. I took a bite of chicken first, then while I was still chewing I filled the fork again and lifted it to her waiting mouth. I watched her chew and swallow, my own lips and throat mimicking hers, willing the food into her body. Bite by tiny bite, we ate all the chicken on my plate, soothed by the richness of the cream. I buttered a biscuit and then I broke it with my hands into crumbs. I put a piece on my own tongue and she stuck out hers; I placed the crumbs there and watched her swallow each one. We drank milk from the same cup, in turn.

I've never nursed a baby and I probably never will, but right there I understood how it felt to present the breast and to feel it taken, to nourish a child right from myself: bone of my bone; flesh of my flesh.

Anyway, here it is mid-December and our lunches still take a very long time: they're slow and rich. Theresa still can't eat much at one time and I wait for her to catch up, swallow for swallow. By New Year's, I think she will be able to eat on her own, from her own plate and with her own fork. It will be time to wean her. I will have to buy myself some new year's clothes: smaller.

We've already bought Henry a Christmas present—a red collar with tiny silver bells. Despite the season, it reminds me of spring and it lets us know where that almost-invisible cat has gotten himself to, now that he roams free, inside and out, wherever he pleases.

AFTERWORD

I

If you were to read these stories separately, in the contexts in which they were originally published—simply as individual stories written by particular writers at particular moments in time—they might have an impact on you, might disclose usable insights. But if you read them together, they clearly show that we have the empowering gift of a literary tradition addressing embodiment.

Short stories which take as their focus the theme of woman and fatness have appeared with increased frequency over the last one hundred years. These short stories, however, are not the first in the history of U.S. women's short stories to focus on living as a fat woman, or as a woman who thinks she is too fat, or a woman who someone else thinks is too fat. That literary tradition predates the fat liberation movement. And even the beginnings of the women's literary tradition are preceded by a male-authored story that focuses on a fat *man,* and another story about the tyranny of appearances.

Washington Irving's (1783–1859) 1822 short story "The Stout Gentleman" may be the first work of U.S. literature that plays with how observers think they can "know" someone based on appearance alone.[1] Irving tells the story of a traveler, bored with his stay in a inn but forced to remain because of illness, desperate for diversion, who overhears a waiter referring to a fellow guest in the inn:

> "The stout gentleman in No. 13 wants his breakfast. Tea and bread and butter, with ham and eggs; the eggs not to be too much done."
> . . . "The stout gentleman!"—the very name had something in it of the picturesque. It at once gave me the size; it embodied the personage to my mind's eye, and my fancy did the rest.
> He was stout, or, as some term it, lusty; in all probability, there-

fore, he was advanced in life, some people expanding as they grow old. By his breakfasting rather late, and in his own room, he must be a man accustomed to live at his ease, and above the necessity of early rising; no doubt, a round, rosy, lusty old gentleman.

The story is amusing and still reads well; what is most interesting for our purposes, however, is the fact that the stout gentleman is imagined as a person of influence and success because he is stout. In other words, stoutness, or fatness, is "read" as a cultural "good," a marker of success.

Nathaniel Hawthorne's (1804–1864) 1843 short story "The Birthmark" is an important early story to consider when we think about the relationship between women's bodies and women's lives in short stories by U. S. writers. A small mark on her face, shaped like a hand and considered by most people a beauty mark, is seen as a flaw by Georgina's new and much beloved husband. He becomes fixated on what he considers an imperfection in her physical appearance and loses track of everything else about her. Although at first outraged and insulted by his judgment, she eventually succumbs to it and agrees to undergo a scientifically experimental procedure to get rid of the birthmark.

> "If there be the remotest possibility of it," continued Georgiana, "let the attempt be made at whatever risk. Danger is nothing to me; for life, while this hateful mark makes me the object of your horror and disgust—life is a burden which I would fling down with joy. Either remove this dreadful hand, or take my wretched life!"

The procedure "works;" the birthmark fades and disappears. But the woman dies. What an incredible precursor to liposuction, breast implants, lip-fattening collagen shots, and the various and barbarous bariatric surgeries! And what a heartbreaking introduction to the tradition of women risking their lives to change their appearances for the men they love and the society they live in.

II

One of the earliest fictional references by a U.S. woman writer to a woman's specific body weight occurs in the 1877 book by feminist humorist Marietta Holley (1836–1926), *My Opinions and Betsy Bobbet's: Designed as a Beacon Light to Guide Women to Life, Liberty, and the Pursuit of Happiness, but which may be read by members of the sterner sect without injury to them or the book*. In this first of the Samantha Allen books, Samantha, the narrator of ten books, recalls Josiah Allen's courtship of her:

> I am not the woman to encourage any kind of foolishness. I remember when we was first engaged, he called me "a little angel."

I just looked at him calmly and says I, "I weigh two hundred and 4 pounds," and he didn't call me so again.

With this remark, Samantha begins to enumerate the reasons why women should be granted equality with men on all counts, beginning with suffrage. She inveighs against unrealistic romantic attitudes that diminish women. In her persona as Samantha, Holly advocates for women's suffrage, education, etc., through all of her books. This early statement of her sturdy size answers those who claim that women are too delicate to vote and too fragile to live without the protection of a man. Samantha is the U.S. introduction to the fat woman as political militant.

III

The earliest woman-authored story in which a fat woman (five-foot-ten, and more than two hundred pounds of substantial flesh) sensually glories in her abundant flesh is the 1894 "Juanita" by Kate Chopin (1850-1904), featuring a protagonist who enjoys sex with a man who may or may not be her husband. This story, as is true of most of the widely and well-read Chopin's work, was rooted in French, as well as English and American, literary tradition. "Juanita" introduced into U.S. literature the fat woman as sexually charismatic and sexually active. The story has echoes of the important French naturalist Guy de Maupassant's (1850–1893) story "Boule de Suif" (variously translated as "Ball of Fat" and "Butterball").

"Boule de Suit" was first published in *Les Soirees de Medan*, a collection of stories written by a group of friends visiting at Emile Zola's country home, published in France in 1880. The collection includes two important stories in terms of the history of fat women in literature. Zola included his own "The Attack on the Mill," in which he describes the abundant charms of the heroine of the story, Francoise Merlier:

> Although small as girls went in that region, she was far from being slender; she might not have been able to raise a sack of wheat to her shoulder, but she became quite plump with age and gave promise of becoming eventually as well-rounded and appetizing as a partridge."[2]

But it was no doubt Maupassant's story that had the stronger influence on Chopin. He was her model, she was familiar with his work in the original French (she was bilingual), and she published several English translations of his stories. Many of Maupassant's stories were too sensual for U.S. audiences but after Chopin's collection of stories *Bayou Folk* was published, "Chopin began writing more sensual stories—testing the limits as to what could be published in the United States."[3]

Guy de Maupassant's story "Boule de Suif" centered on a fat woman who was not only sexually desirable but also represents the ideal of patriotism.

> One of those called a coquette, [she] was celebrated for her embonpoint [plumpness; in French, literally, "in good condition"], which had given her the nickname of "Ball-of-Fat." Small, round and fat as lard, with puffy fingers choked at the phalanges, like chaplets of short sausages; with a stretched and shining skin, an enormous bosom which shook under her dress, she was, nevertheless, pleasing and sought after, on account of a certain freshness and breeziness of disposition. Her face was a round apple, a peony bud ready to pop into bloom, and inside that opened two great black eyes, shaded with thick brows that cast a shadow within; and below, a charming mouth, humid for kissing, furnished with shining, microscopic baby teeth. She was, it was said, full of admirable qualities."[4]

In her first biography of Kate Chopin, Emily Toth notes that "'Juanita' was Chopin's first story set in Missouri in three years, and it was inspired by the true experiences of a postmaster's daughter, Annie Venn of Sulphur Springs, whose mother disapproved of everything except the baby."[5]

Although the story is of the genre now called a "short-short story"—only 750 words—it is packed with information contemporary readers would immediately have recognized. The name Juanita would immediately bring to mind an immensely popular romantic song. "Juanita" was written and set to music by Caroline Elizabeth Sarah Norton (née Sheridan) (1808–1877, who was famous throughout the English-speaking Victorian world for her efforts to obtain both child custody and property rights for married women. The song, which was included in most of the song books available in Victorian America (and continues to be included today), would have evoked in readers' minds not only the song itself, a romantic ballad, but also the author's political reputation and the issues she urged civilized governments to adopt. Chopin read Norton's popular poetry and copied her poem about friendship in her schoolgirl diary.[6] Chopin, a careful and deliberate writer, would have chosen the name "Juanita" with full knowledge that it would invoke both the romantic ballad in which a woman by this name is wooed and the women's rights issues for which Norton was equally well-known.

Sulphur Springs, Missouri, the setting of the story, is located about thirty-five miles south of where Chopin lived in St. Louis. This small town on the Mississippi River was mentioned frequently in the diaries and letters of Civil War soldiers on both sides of the conflict as a place they crossed through many times on their ways to war-related sites in Missouri, Iowa, and southern Illinois. It is not unsafe to assume that Juanita's one-legged husband was a Civil War veteran. The "cork leg" that Juanita tried to raise money to buy for her one-legged lover was not a leg made out of cork, but a modern (for that time) prosthetic device that became a well-known item as a result of the Civil War.

Juanita's one-legged lover is described as "puny" while she is LARGE. The same kind of coupling is true of Holley's Samantha and Josiah Allen, and many of the other stories on this theme, including Marjorie Kinnan Rawlings's "Cocks Must Crow" (which I can't get permission to include in this book) and "He Was a Man" by J. California Cooper. A trope if there ever was one! Josiah Allen and Juanita's one-legged lover may be the first F.A.s (Fat Admirers) in American literature.

The tradition of the female lead character embracing from a number of suitors one who is disabled is familiar to readers of Victorian literature and is perhaps most well known through the marriage of Jane Eyre to her beloved Rochester—once he is blind and crippled. There is an extensive feminist historical and literary critical literature examining this pattern and exploring its meanings. The interpretations are always liberatory for the woman involved because the man's "crippling" goes some way toward equalizing their stature in the patriarchy.

The narrator mentions several times Juanita's customary attire: a "soiled Mother Hubbard." This article of clothing was a "class" marker—rural, hard-working, poor, serving as both an everyday work dress and a maternity dress—but it also reflected the late Victorian women's suffrage movement's advocacy of nonconstricting clothing for women that made possible long stride and free and comfortable movement. It is not only a marker of Juanita's position in life and place of residency, but an indication of her freedom-loving, self-determining personality. Had she married one of those wealthy and urban suitors, her new position in life would have required an entirely different mode of dress, one corseted and restricting.[7]

The gender-unspecified teller of this brief tale is a classic unreliable narrator.[8] Does the narrator approve or disapprove of Juanita, admire or feel contempt for her? What can we know, from these 750 words, about the narrator and about the narrator's attitude towards Juanita?

The narrator tells us: "Her face, and, particularly, her mouth has a certain fresh and sensuous beauty, though I would rather not say beauty if I might say anything else." Why would the narrator rather not say "beauty?" We are told that there is no other word for her than beauty. So Juanita is beautiful, at least in the eyes of the narrator. Why does the narrator tell us that Juanita was hard not to see and then tell us of all the ways in which Juanita tried to efface herself, spending time in places where she was difficult to see? And why, if she was so difficult to see, did the narrator see so much of her? "I often saw Juanita that summer, simply because it was so difficult for the poor thing not to be seen. She usually sat in some obscure corner of their small garden, or behind an angle of the house, preparing vegetables for dinner or sorting her mother's flower-seed." How easy was it to see into an obscure corner of Juanita's family's small garden? How easy was it to see behind an angle of their house?

Is the narrator one of Juanita's disappointed suitors? Or if not a suitor, then perhaps a man—or woman—who feels attracted to Juanita, sexually or otherwise, and is ashamed of that attraction? The narrator remains a mystery we cannot solve, but we are left with a clear picture of Juanita, a beautiful big woman pursued by many admirers who made a choice that satisfied her and did not take into account conventional wisdom or bourgeois values, a strong, independent woman who embodies the ideal of the most radical women's rights advocates of Chopin's time.

IV

With the 1897 publication of Octave Thanet's (the nom de plume of Alice French, 1850–1934) short story "The Stout Miss Hopkins's Bicycle," women's dissatisfaction with their bodies becomes a paramount theme.[9] The timing of the publication of this story concurs with the growing interest in "slimming" among those social classes where leisure and disposable income permitted such a form of indulgence. The slimming fads that burgeoned during the last two decades of the nineteenth century—a period when the qualities that garnered admiration and respect began—to move from considerations of character to considerations of appearance[10] accompanied many scientific and technological changes that characterized that period as well as the beginning of the mass exodus from rural to urban life.

This story introduces three important themes that appear in many of the stories that succeeded it. The first is the unmediated (by adults) cruelty of children to children who are "different." We see this retrospectively experienced by both the fat girl and the short boy. The saddest thing about this recurrent theme of childhood cruelties is that regardless of the time period, ethnic culture, geographic region, or economic class of the children, we rarely see adequate adult intervention or the recognition of this teasing bullying, as savage, emotionally-scarring behavior that needs correction.

The dart in the belly of the child in Susan Stinson's "Magnetic Force," the social exclusion of the adolescent in "Goodbye, Old Laura," the cruel exploitation of "The Hershey Bar Queen," the manipulation of the "fat girl" in "Skanks," the humiliation of the teenager in "Bloomingdale's"—all are versions of the big boy who called Miss Hopkins's "Fatty" and "made a kissing noise with his lips just to scare me."

The second theme introduced by this story is the fact that slimming is an activity that takes both money and leisure time to pursue. It is, in fact, a form of conspicuous consumption, a hobby of the wealthy, a marker of social class. In this story we are introduced to weight loss as an expensive leisure-time activity.

In earlier stories, occasional secondary female characters are described with pity, or critically, for being too thin while other female characters are admired for various roundnesses—cheeks, upper arms, or shoulders in particular, dimpled arms, knees, hands, and cheeks, and robustness, a word that implied good health, strength, sturdiness, and fatness.[11] But the size and shapes of their bodies are not significant factors in these women's social lives unless health is an issue. Health is only an issue when a character's appearance suggests a wasting disease, such as consumption (tuberculosis) and a potential marriage is at stake. The history of the debate about whether or not sickly women should (be allowed to) marry is only now being recovered by scholars in disability studies. Sometimes female characters are described in terms of the size of their bodies in order to distinguish them from other female characters, but the distinctions are descriptive rather than predictive or pejorative.

Mrs. Margaret Ellis and Miss Lorania Hopkins try to lose weight by a variety of methods that, by other names, are still being sold as the "answer to weight loss." I imagine that most present day readers will be familiar with the various weight-loss strategies employed by Ellis and Hopkins, although more than likely under different names, since the same strategies have been regularly "discovered" and sold over the decades as new, surefire "cures." Part of the irony in this story, as is revealed in the tone of such sentences as "the two waged a warfare against the flesh, equal to the apostle's in vigor, although so much less deserving of praise" is the evident belief of the author, a fat woman herself, that the weight-loss industry was just another kind of medicine show, one more scam.

> Mrs. Ellis drove her cook to distraction with divers dieting systems, from Banting's and Dr. Salisbury's to the latest exhortations of some unknown newspaper prophet. She bought elaborate gymnastic appliances, and swung dumb-bells and rode imaginary horses and propelled imaginary boats. She ran races with a professional trainer, and she studied the principles of Delsarte, and solemnly whirled on one foot and swayed her body and rolled her heard and hopped and kicked and genuflected in company with eleven other stout and earnest matrons and one slim and giggling girl who almost choked at every lesson. In all these exercises Miss Hopkins faithfully kept her company.

Note that despite their experiments with all the latest fads in diet and exercise, the women do, however, reject the use of the new and dangerous obesity pills.[12]

All the good people in this story have suffered except Mrs. Ellis, whose husband is nowhere to be seen and is never heard from. We know about her only that she "had been married." But the suffering of the wealthy women, Mrs. Ellis and Miss Hopkins, are the two for which the alleviation of there is the greatest expenditure of time, effort, and funds. It isn't until Miss Hopkins has her first "romantic" encounter with little Mr. Winslow that other kinds of suffering enter her universe. She learns that men may be made to suffer from being short and small as women suffer from being tall and fat: "I told him how I had suffered from my figure—he says it can't be what he has suffered from his."[13]

The third pioneering aspect of "The Stout Miss Hopkins's Bicycle" is its status as the first important story to explore the theme of friendship between women who share profound pain about their bodies.[14] There are many examples in the story of the ways in which these two women support each other and are sensitive to each other's feelings. (The wealthier one, Miss Hopkins, matches the charity of Mrs. Ellis, the less wealthy one, to the penny, for instance). Having "come out" to each other about their suffering about their fat bodies, it seems there is nothing they can't share. Their relationship exemplifies Dale Spender's comment on what I call "the ethics of reciprocity:" "The emotional availability of one woman to another is not a visible element in our social arrangements, yet it is often reciprocal and as such, mutually enhancing and immensely rewarding."[15]

Starting with "The Stout Miss Hopkins's Bicycle," the role of women's friendships in stories of women and fatness becomes is a major theme. "The Feeder" is about friendship between two women who might have been enemies almost as easily, whose "problems" with their bodies seem diametrically opposed but are, in fact, not problems with their bodies as much as they are problems with their husbands, and the recognition of this mutuality saves both their lives. "Suzanne LaFleshe" is about another lifesaving friendship between two women, this time across a generation. "He Was a Man" is narrated by the friend of the heroine. "Skanks" is about the perversion of friendship. "The Dream Diet" is about women who are friends.

Like the previous story in this collection, "Juanita," "The Stout Miss Hopkins's Bicycle" is a heterosexual romance. Other stories in this book are also romances: "This Was Meant to Be," "The Food Farm," and, secondarily, "Perfectly Normal." The first is a romantic comedy—a happy ending—and the second a romantic tragedy—they don't get each other. The third includes a lesbian partnership, a romance of long-standing, that seems happy and successful in every aspect. There are many other romance stories, both lesbian and heterosexual, some of them quite passionate and sexually explicit.[16]

V

As literary conventions develop for genres, writers sometimes comment on those conventions in their work in those genres. These comments may take the form of direct address to the reader, but just as frequently, and usually more amusingly, these comments are made through the voices of characters within the work, talking to each other about the genre. Perhaps the earliest incidence, in a short story by a U.S. women writer, of this convention of discussing literary conventions within a piece of conventional literature occurs in the still delectable 1830 story "Cacoethes Scribendi" by Catharine Maria Sedgwick.[17]

Edna Ferber's (1887–1968)1910 story "The Homely Heroine" is part of this women's literary tradition. However, instead of challenging or satirizing the conventions of heterosexual literary romance and the women who wrote them, as Sedgwick did, she challenges the conventions governing the appearance of the characters in that conventional heterosexual literary romance. The story concludes that it's impossible to write a successful romance without a conventionally beautiful heroine. Charlotte Bronte, of course, had defied this convention with her plain Jane Eyre. But Ferber's conclusion has met with astonishingly few challenges in all the time between her own 1910 story and the 1992 "The Language of the Fat Woman" by Elana Dykewomon.

VI

The stories about side show fat women, "Noblesse" and "Even as You and I," are part of the general movement in literature that developed from nineteenth-century literary regionalism. Regionalism refers to the literature exploring human experiences and the relationship of the inhabitants to the particular geography in regions of the United States outside of the major centers of population and social power.[18] Although literary regionalism developed before the Civil War, regional stories became especially popular after the war when people around the newly reuniting United States became curious about people in other parts of the country. Among those people predisposed by their historical faith communities to be suspicious of "pure pleasure," readers could justify their delight in reading fiction, especially short stories, by thinking of this reading as learning—which it might or might not have been, depending on the authenticity of the material and the avoidance of stereotypes. When the stories did not play to the bigoted expectations of some cultural chauvinists. readers did indeed learn about the customs, the dialects, the environments, the economic rigors and opportunities, the social values, and the concerns of people living in various parts of the country. Sometimes the characters and their lives seemed different and strange, but in the best regional literature, in spite of all the differences, they were obviously "just like us."

Along with the popularity of regional literature, which continued into the early twentieth century, a new literature about the increasing numbers of immigrants pouring into the United States began to find willing publishers and eager readers. There were two streams of immigrant literature from the late nineteenth and early twentieth centuries—one by first-generation immigrants and one by American-born members of the dominant immigrant nationalities.

Among the first-generation immigrant writers were Sholem Aleichem (1859–1916), creator of, among other characters, Tevye the Dairyman, whose stories were brought together and repopularized again in the musical *Fiddler on the Roof*, and Anzia Yezierska (1881?–1970), called "Cinderella of the Sweatshops." A recent translation of stories originally written in Yiddish makes available to English language readers stories that have long been lost and that are part of this tradition.[19] A dominant theme and primary metaphor in this literature is hunger: hunger the stalker, hunger the shriveler, hunger the gnawer, hunger the killer. It should come as no surprise that for these writers, born in Eastern European villages plagued by oppression and poverty, America was the land of milk and honey, a place where a person could become fat, which was a good thing, a wonderful thing. Yezierska titled one of her books *Hungry Hearts* and wrote stories called "Hunger" and "The Fat of the Land." As some of these immigrants began to achieve prosperity, they were happy to develop plumpness as outward evidence of well-being, comfort, safety (at least temporary) from hunger, happiness. The now widely familiar song, "If I Were a Rich Man" from the *Fiddler on the Roof*, the dairyman Tevye sings:

> I see my wife, my Golde, looking like a rich man's wife,
> With a proper double chin,
> Supervising meals to her heart's delight.[20]

Among the literature by writers who were born in America to immigrant parents or grandparents, Fannie Hurst's stories of the immigrant Jewish community were perhaps the best loved and most widely read. They are also the most fruitful to plumb for images of women and fatness. Although her stories are most noted for her portrayals of working women, struggling to earn enough to survive in difficult circumstances, many also feature immigrant women who have achieved financial security, and who sport double chins and full bosoms and round waists with pride and deep satisfaction. These women and their husbands take pride in their joyfully, gratefully achieved fatness. But their American-born daughters have begun to learn to hate their own abundant flesh and to seek ways to reduce it. The struggle between the generations of immigrant women and their American-born daughters about food, eating, flesh, and fatness has been one of the primary arenas in which the conflict between Old World and New, European family loyalty and American individualism, and tradition and assimilation has been waged, and class mobility has been gained or lost.[21]

These stories drew on the conventions of regionalism, but their settings were urban rather than rural or small-town. However, there were similarities in their exploration of the conflicts between old and new ways of living and determining values, between loyalties to the needs and expectations of birth families and the call of one's own life choices, and between poverty and exploitation of workers and the assimilationist social-climbing efforts of the financial "winners."

Nevertheless, the public interest in strangers from strange lands plummeted when anti-immigration sentiment began to grow, and erupted during and after World War I, leading to the 1921 Quota Act.[22] The writers of the "ethnic regionalist" literature who had built reputations on their explorations of foreigners struggling to become Americans, such as the popular and successful Hurst, needed new literary subject matter. Some began to explore the ever-compelling interest in the strangers among us—strangers from our own land. These authors began to write about (thinly disguised) celebrities, the very wealthy, and "freaks." Quite often, the "point" of these stories was to prove what Fannie Hurst titled the story included in this collection: "freaks" are people "Even as You and I." "Noblesse" and "Even as You and I" introduce into US literature the fat woman as spectacle.[23]

The first of these new stories was the 1913 "Noblesse" by Mary E. Wilkins Freeman, who was (and continues to be) considered by many to be the genius of nineteenth-century regional literature (and by others as one of the geniuses of U.S. literature in general). In this story about the intersection of class and embodiment, Wilkins Freeman assures readers that fat ladies are ladies just like other ladies when they come from the class of Americans that fosters ladyhood with its quartet of characteristics: piety, purity, submissiveness, and domesticity.[24]

"Even As You and I" assures readers that fat ladies suffer pangs and cherish hopes just like other women, live in communities where people work for a living and struggle with imperfect working conditions, where there are friends, allies, companions—and undesirables, predators, leeches, and deceivers—just as there are in communities where "you and I" live. This 1919 story, written as anti-immigration exclusionary sentiments began to build, is a classic "Other Woman" story, a story in which two women are equally committed to one man who is worthy of neither of them.[25]

Although Hurst writes of her "daring to introduce to you the only under-thirty-years, and over-one-hundred-and-thirty-pounds, heroine in the history of fiction," she more than likely does so not out of ignorance of earlier fat heroines but more in the spirit of the carnival ballyhoo talker. Hurst was well-educated and widely read.[26] She was probably familiar with Maupassant's "Boule de Suif" and, as an aspiring writer who studied the stories published in mass market magazines, she was possibly also familiar with Ferber's "The Homely Heroine."

Neither of the fat lady stories makes any attempt to explain or analyze the women's fatness; the stories simply tell the stories of their lives as fat women. Although both authors detail their central figures' problems living as fat women, neither makes any suggestion that the character's temperament, moral fiber, or personality is defined by the size of her body. Noblesse's unhappiness with her life as a fat lady in a sideshow is a function of her discomfort with being publicly displayed and her distaste for a life shared with people who are not "of her class." The implication of Miss Hoag's tragedy is not simply that it is only among other freaks that she can lead a normal life and be a member of a community that accepts her and recognizes her unique humanity rather than noticing and judging her only by the size of her body. In addition, like many woman, she is vulnerable to romantic disappointments, betrayals, and manipulation.

What neither of these stories tells readers about, however, is the powerful attraction exerted on audiences by these very, very large women (and some men). They seldom lacked for suitors and almost always married, seeming to have had a higher percent of happy marriages than most. The erotic power they radiate made them huge draws, lucrative exhibits whose "keep" was more than compensated for by what they brought to the sideshow coffers.[27]

Reading about Reyna, the "Hershey Bar Queen," who weighs 439 pounds in the eleventh grade, one might imagine a much happier and longer life for her had she left Morenci for a career as a fat lady. In recent years, there has been renewed debate about the safety and economic opportunities for physically anomalous people in sideshows rather than as stigmatized members of the general population whose opportunities for self-sufficiency are limited.[28]

Grace Sartwell Mason's story "Fat" is another "Other Woman" story. In it, a fat woman learns that her husband is cheating on her with a skinny woman whom he plies with sweets and other fattening things, urging her to let him fatten her up. It gives us another take on the interesting term "Sugar Daddy."

VII

In 1946, Cleveland Jewish lesbian Ruth Seid, writing as Jo Sinclair, published *Wasteland* and won the $10,000 Harper First Novel Prize. The main character of the novel was the journalist brother of the lesbian character, a man seriously alienated from his own ethnicity and deeply troubled about many issues. His sister refers him to her own therapist, the doctor who has helped her learn to accept herself and find peace with her lesbian identity. This novel initiated the age of psychoanalytic literature, a literature in which authors took as gospel the doctrine of Freud and often used the fifty-minute hour as the structural skeleton of the work. While *Wasteland* was a bold and rich work in itself, the subsequent trend toward a psychotherapeutic approach to understanding characters seriously narrowed the breadth and depth of characterizations in all genres.

The way this phenomenon affected the literature of fat women was that for more than two decades, almost all stories by women about fat women or women who think they are fat were rooted in psychoanalytic or psychiatric explanations for the fatness. Fatness became only a function of neurosis or psychosis. It made for some very weird stories. There was no such thing as an emotionally healthy or strong fat woman except in young adult (YA) fiction. There were no happy endings for such women and girls other than extreme weight loss—and successful weight loss was accomplished only by the teenaged girls in stories published in magazines directed to that specific market. There were a lot of these stories, and most of them are too redolent of the author's disgust with the fat women, too depressing, and too reductionist to reprint. In all the stories written for adult readers, most especially those written by "literary" writers, the fat woman is seen as an object only, a monster, a freak, a cautionary figure, an embodiment of pathology, mute or meaninglessly garrulous, she is described always by a narrator who is "normal," in language that partakes simultaneously of the rhetoric of the case study and the condescending "objectivity" of the Victorian colonialist anthropologist.

The small burst of stories about fat women published during the 1950s pathologized fatness and introduced an unironic medicalized view of fat as a condition to be "overcome," requiring serious, long-term intervention from professionals. These stories introduce into U.S. literature the fat woman as pathological person in need of professional intervention, or, to put it more simply, the fat woman as mad or sick woman. It is hardly surprising that during this same decade, the American Society of Bariatric Physicians was founded and the first surgery to "treat" obesity was performed on a human being, and the prescribing of diet pills became as common as the advice to take two aspirins and call in the morning.[29]

The most esteemed story of this type was "The Echo and the Nemesis" by Jean Stafford. It was published first in as "The Nemesis" in 1951 in *The New Yorker*, an automatic imprimatur as "high-quality" and "serious" literature. The following year it was included in the *Best American Short Stories* for 1951, and it was published in Stafford's collection *Innocents Abroad*. In the story, the young fat woman is presented as so utterly alien a being that there is no understanding her; there is only describing her, recording her, wondering at her. It is the most thorough "othering" of a fat woman found in all the stories about fat women.

The story of this period included here is "Good-Bye, Old Laura" by Lucile Vaughan Payne. It is among the least disturbing of the stories of this general type, while at the same time being in many ways representative. The story was published in 1955 in *Seventeen*, the most popular and influential magazine for adolescent girls in 1950s.[30] "Good-Bye, Old Laura" is typical of "fat" stories in its assumption that the fatness is pathological, that the social "misfit"-ness of the fat adolescent is not a manifestation of social attitudes, and that psychotherapeutic intervention to "cure" Laura of her fatness is a necessary "good." What is atypical about this story by mid-twentieth-century standards is the characterization of Laura. Laura is not crazy. Laura is a sympathetic, dignified character; she is smart, insightful, energetic, self-respecting, and in control rather than a victim of most of the situations in which she finds herself. She seems to be sane, sensible, rational, and normal.

However, the subgenre of "Good-Bye, Old Laura" is YA (the only example of this literary type in this collection, although there are others that treat these matter in similar ways), and one of the conventions of this subgenre in that period is that the protagonists were relentlessly both healthy-minded and successful problem solvers. The author does a brilliant job of synthesizing the two sets of conventions—young adult as healthy-minded and fat person as pathological.[31]

VIII

Beginning with the frequently reprinted 1967 story "The Food Farm" by Kit Reed,[372] science fiction and fantasy stories began to emerge that took a very different attitude toward fatness: not being able to become or to remain fat is a tragedy, becoming fat is a choice, being fat is attractive, and choosing to be fat is a wise survivalist tactic. I have included only two of these, "The Food Farm" and the 1987 "A Mammoth Undertaking" by Roz Warren, but recommend many others as well. Joanna Russ has written:

> Science fiction is What If literature. All sorts of definitions have been proposed by people in the field, but they all contain both The What If and The Serious Explanation; that is, science fiction shows things not as they characteristically or habitually are but as they might be, and for this "might be" the author must offer a rational, serious, consistent explanation, one that does not (in Samuel Delaney's phrase) offend against what is known to be known. . . If the author offers marvels and does not explain them, or if he (sic) explains them playfully and not seriously, or if the explanation offends against what the author knows to be true, you are dealing with fantasy and not science fiction. . . .Fantasy, says Samuel Delaney, treats what cannot happen, science fiction what has not happened.[33]

Keeping in mind the caution not to offend against what is known to be known, I leave readers to decide if "The Food Farm" and "A Mammoth

Undertaking" are fantasy or science fiction. Both equally figure fatness as an attractive and desirable attribute.

Among the 167 stories I have found on the theme os women and fatness, thirty-six stories fall into one or another of the subgenres of science fiction and fantasy. These include a vampire story, a ghost story, a post–nuclear holocaust story, a climate disaster story, several fairy tales and revenge fantasies, a sword and sorcerer story, and so forth. All of these stories are fat-positive; all postulate a reality in which fatness is an advantage and in which fatness is paired with (other) qualities and characteristics that indicate the general superiority of the fat character(s).[34]

"The Food Farm" is an Abelard and Heloise tragic romance and a table-turning revenge story. It is also a spoof on the elegant, outrageously expensive, and geographically secluded spa/health resort industry which caters to people who want to lose weight, "control" their weight, or are "sentenced" by wealthy parents or partners to weight reduction and body reshaping "retreats."[35]

IX

There are many stories of spoiled girlhoods, stories in which innocent self-esteem is stolen, happiness outlawed, and a self-loving sense of identity destroyed. Only "Bloomingdales" and "The Hershey Bar Queen" focus exclusively on girlhood, and these two stories represent two different ethnicities, different regions, different time periods, and different social classes. However, "The Stout Miss Hopkins' Bicycle," "The Food Farm," "The Man I Love," and "Magnetic Force" need to be remembered and included here, too, although they are only retrospectively "about" girlhood. I have discussed the myriad "well-meaning" ways in which Nelly's parents try to "tame" her body and her appetite in "The Food Farm" will be familiar to many readers. Reed writes:

It was vanity, all vanity, and I hate them most for that. It was not my vanity, for I have always been a simple soul; I reconciled myself early to reinforced chairs and loose garments, to the spattering of remarks. . . .

But they were vain and in their vanity my frail father, my pale, scrawny mother saw me not as an entity but as a reflection on themselves. I flush with shame to remember the excuses they made for me. "She takes after May's side of the family," my father would say, denying any responsibility. "It's only baby fat," my mother would say, jabbing her elbow into my soft flank. "Nelly is big for her age." Then she would jerk furiously, pulling my voluminous smock down to cover my knees. That was when they still consented to be seen with me.

I am certain I am not alone in applauding the comeuppance these parents get—in the form of "just desserts."

In Susan Stinson's "Magnetic Force," we see another fat child tortured, isolated, and made miserable by the sheer meanness of fat oppression. However, we have the pleasure of seeing her metamorphose into a confident, self-loving fat woman who cherishes the company of other fat women. The furious interviewee in Elaine Fowler Palencia's "The Man I Love" is quite clear about—and rages and grieves in no uncertain terms about—the imposition on her child self of perverse adult norms, and her response to those impositions.

In all of these stories, we encounter the fat woman as the bearer of a spoiled identity, the carrier of "stigma" in the sense of the word identified by Erving Goffman in his groundbreaking 1963 book of that title.[36] We often hear movie stars famous for their beauty as much as any other adult attribute tell stories about their sad, lonely childhoods when they were teased for being unattractive in some way—too fat, too skinny, too tall, too acned, too something that made childhood and/or adolescence hell. People listening to these tales often scoff, either not believing that anyone so beautiful could ever have been otherwise, or not believing that the pain and scarring from those early days could have survived to inhibit the beautiful adult's realization of her own beauty.

Is it true that an identity once crushed, stolen, demeaned, devalued, discredited, profaned, abased, humiliated, persecuted can never recover, at least not fully, from the sense of having been spoiled? How does such a self brazen out adulthood if she is never "reconstructed," i.e., never loses weight (or gains weight or gets clear skin or is "caught up to" by the growth spurts of contemporaries)? Or, if she does, will she ever adjust to the "recovery" of a good self? Can she, in fact, recover a "good self?" Is there ever a good enough self after such suffering? In other words, once she loses weight, does the fat girl remain alive inside the "normalized" girl or woman? Is there a fat girl inside of every slender woman, crying to get out? If she has been so stigmatized in her youth, if her sense of self has been so brutalized, does she have a "duty" to "normal" society to "get over it," to "heal," to "get on with her life" now that she, too, has been reshaped to conform? These questions are not just rhetorical, but they can only be investigated through individuals, case by case, and we are provided with the opportunity to think about these questions when we read "The Stout Miss Hopkins' Bicycle," "The Food Farm," "The Man I Love," and "Magnetic Force."

Such are the rules of the game that responsibility for the suffering of fat children and other stigmatized people is attributed to the "stigma bearers" themselves, rather than their tormentors. In *Stigma*, Goffman focuses on how "normals" respond to stigma bearers discredited features and encourage their adoption of a good adjustment:

The good-adjustment line . . . means that the unfairness and pain of having to carry a stigma will never be presented to [normals]; it means that normals will not have to admit to themselves how limited their tactfulness and tolerance is; and it means that normals can remain relatively uncontaminated by intimate contact with the stigmatized, [remain] relatively unthreatened in their [own] identity beliefs. It is just from these meanings, in fact, that the specifications of a good adjustment derive.[37]

Have the women in these stories made "good adjustments?" From a civil rights or social justice perspective, what would a "good adjustment" be? Whose responsibility should it really be to make a "good adjustment?"

X

In this collection, the only mother/daughter story, "This Was Meant to Be," is a lovely romantic story of successful motherly intervention and disruption of an unhappy daughter's misery. The story was originally published in *Woman's Home Companion*, and reached between one and three million readers.[38] Alison Carstair's only slightly "spoiled identity" is restored by her loving (and manipulative—if that term can be used approvingly) mother's clever plan. Olive Carstair, a beautiful, successful, and famous actress, seeks to provide her eighteen-year-old daughter with a "cure" for her unhappiness: "She's still in the awkward age and she has no confidence in herself as a woman. . . . She's not at all pretty," she tells the famous painter Jeffrey Hartshorne, who looks at Alison "with a painter's eye" and agrees: "Her mother has been right in saying she wasn't pretty. She was short and still in the chubby stage. He suspected she was always going to have to worry about plumpness."

After a month of attention from the painter, he sees instead the "gracefully swelling curves" of her "'truly French' figure" and comments on "the line between being chubby and being nicely rounded." He is surprised to find that he has fallen in love with the young woman: "He loved her the way you ought to love the one you want to spend the rest of your life with—loved her stubbornness as well as her honesty, her plumpness as well as her pansy-blue eyes."

However, among the 167 stories, there are some truly heartbreaking and excruciatingly authentic mother/daughter stories, including another one by Kit Reed about two little girls coping with the mood and behavior swings of a mother who is always either on a diet or raging and grieving over her inability to remain on a diet, and one murder mystery story by detective fiction author Sara Paretsky about a mother who uses every trick in the book to encourage her beautiful daughter to become and remain fat so that she won't overshadow and compete with her mother's beauty.[39]

As long as women are judged successful or not in their roles as mothers based on the "outcome" of their product, their children, just so long will mothers be under terrible pressure to force conformity to conventional behavior and appearance standards on their children. It is the rare woman who can withstand the social pressure to enforce "normalcy" on her children. It is often through the agency of the mother, who we think ought to be the source of comfort and safety, that girls are most brutally pummeled "into shape." And, obversely, it is often from the mother's frequently expressed dissatisfaction with her own body that daughters learn the harsh lessons of body hatred. It is with great pleasure that I chose to include "This Was Meant to Be" to open up discussion of the mother/daughter dynamic of the women and fatness theme.

XI

There are five stories in this collection that portray genuine eating disorders: "Perfectly Normal," "Jelly Rolls," "The Feeder," "Skanks," and "The Strange History of Suzanne LaFleshe." Janine, the central character in "Skanks," is an adolescent girl whose home life is so unsatisfactory that she becomes voluntarily homeless and dependent on the (un)kindness of an insincere, manipulative "friend" who uses her as a foil to heighten her own attractiveness. In reclaiming her autonomy, Janine learns to throw up successfully, to binge and purge, to be bulimic. For one moment she feels beautiful and the reader knows the disordered behavior will continue.

Harriet, the narrator in "Perfectly Normal," is an exercise-addicted fatophobic anorectic who is quite likely to die from one of the many life-threatening consequences of this eating disorder.[40] The anorectic wife in "The Feeder" and adolescent girl in "The Strange History of Suzanne LaFleshe" may survive because they are rescued by fat women who become their friends and their healers. This makes three anorectics and one bulimic. The narrator in "Jelly Rolls" may not be eating disordered (yet), but she is certainly psychologically disordered.

Interestingly enough, I haven't found a single case in U.S. women's short fiction of a fat woman who is unhealthy except for the asthmatic writer in "On Ward G," whose fatness may or may not have been exacerbated by treatment with steroids for her asthma, but whose asthma is not caused by her fatness. But there are no stories in which women become ill because they are fat. There is nothing in women's fiction to affirm the calamitous claims of health risks made by the bariatricians, the exercise gurus, and the weight reduction mavens.

In addition to the stories about eating disorders included in this book, there is a vast amateur literature, an immense store of short stories and poems, written by young women with anorexia and bulimia. A great many of these writings are exchanged online among groups of young women who have these eating disorders, and who encourage each other in their disordered eating and share strategies for self-starvation. A quick online search will lead interested readers to these sad and frightening stories.

XII

In *The Beauty Myth*, Naomi Wolf writes, "She wins who calls herself beautiful and challenges the world to change to truly see her." Although heterosexual women and men, both fat men and those men called "fat admirers," have participated in the founding, development, and maintenance of the fat acceptance movement on many fronts,[41] the most radical literature about fat oppression and fat liberation has come from the lesbian feminist fat liberation movement. I have quoted from this literature and other writings as well in choosing the epigraphs to precede the stories included in this collection. My intention is to provide non-fiction statements about the themes addressed in the stories in order to create what I think of as an animated bibliography.

Fat liberation literature is an American literature of pain, protest, and insistence on visibility. We have had many of these literatures in our brief national history; literary conventions have been developed, particular genres have been appropriated, and recognizable patterns have emerged. Literatures of pain, protest, and insistence on visibility are written by those in pain, not about those in pain. The literatures of African American civil rights, women's liberation, gay liberation, disability rights, American Indian rights, and all the movements for freedom of other oppressed groups are all literatures of pain, protest, and insistence on visibility. So, for instance, abolitionist literature, although a civil rights literature, is not a literature of pain, protest, and insistence of visibility, while slave narratives are. Prison reform advocates have not crafted one of these literatures, but those who have been imprisoned have. Weight loss books are not one of these literatures, but the voices quoted in the epigraphs in this book, as well as many of the stories it contains, certainly are.

The literature of fat liberation (or size acceptance, or the fat civil rights movement) is a bravura literature ranging in tenor from pugnacious to lyrical, ironic to heartbroken, furious to comical. It includes the genres anticipated in such a literature: moving memoirs, heartbreaking confessions, declarations of love and alliance for those like the writer, white-jawed rants, murderous tirades, well-reasoned arguments, angry manifestos, three point sermons—and poetry that reflects all of these sentiments and more. As a body of literature, it is relatively new, seeming to begin with writing by the Fat Liberation Underground in 1974 in the genres I have mentioned above. But short stories espousing the principles and purposes of the fat liberation movement are the most recent.

As is true with all the literatures of pain, protest, and insistence on visibility, the order in which the voices of fat liberation begin to make themselves heard starts with personal essays or poems, memoirs, rants, and tirades, all "confessional" materials. They represent the earliest efforts to put words to pain, to give our chosen names to the suffering and the outrage, to make those choices of language by the oppressed rather than the oppressors. Next come more formal genres—formal essays, carefully reasoned arguments, declarations of intentions and principles, analyses of the contexts in which the oppression thrives. These materials are developed in a variety of situations, from the most radical and separatist underground to the most seemingly objective and professional settings. Then novels and short stories begin to appear. Once one of these genres begins to appear, it continues to appear: the poems don't stop when the manifestos come, the memoirs don't cease to be written when the short stories appear.

The history of the fat liberation movement has been documented in a number of places. That documentation is, of course, part of the literature itself.[42] *Shadow on a Tightrope: Writing by Women on Fat Oppression,* coedited by Lisa Schoenfielder and Barb Wieser, with a foreward by Vivian Mayer, is the first, and truly groundbreaking, "collection of articles, personal stories, and poems by fat women, about their lives and the fat-hating society in which they live." In this book, the writings from the Fat Underground of the early 1970s are collected and contextualized. The first attempt to publish this material was made in unsuccessfully in 1976 by Vivian Mayer and Sharonah Robinson (formerly known as Sharon bas Hannah), and it wasn't until 1983 that Aunt Lute Books brought the book out.

One of the original cofounders of the Fat Underground, Fat Chance, the fat women's dance troupe, and the Fat Lip Readers Theater, Judy Freespirit, represented in this collection with "On Ward G," talks about the early days of the fat liberation movement in a 1994 interview with Andrea Hernandez. offers a clear perspective on the early relationship between this movement and NAAFA (which now means the National Association to Advance Fat Americans), an even earlier group dedicated to ameliorating the situation in society of fat people.[43]

In the winter of 1985, the feminist periodical *Sinister Wisdom* brought out an issue with a special focus on "Fat-Body Image-Eating-Food." That same year saw the publication of what appears to be the first fat liberation short story published in the United States: "The Feeder" by Maria Bruno appeared in the *Women's Studies Newsletter* of the Women's Studies Department at Michigan State University, a small publication with a small audience, in the spring of 1985.

Earlier, in 1978 and 1981 respectively, Susie Orbach's *Fat is a Feminist Issue: A Self-Help Guide for Compulsive Eaters* and Kim Chernin's *The Obsession: Reflections on the Tyranny of Slenderness* appeared in mass market editions from publishers. The first book grew out of the experiences of Orbach in a 1970 group of women meeting under the guidance of Carol Munter to deal with body image issues, and she believes it was the first such feminist group. The second is "about the suffering we experience in our obsession with weight, the size of our body, and our longing for food." Both of these books brought broad attention to the issues of fat women, but neither suggested that it was all right to be fat, to stay fat, to like being fat, to pay no particular attention to the fact of one's fatness.

After these early publications, there has been a steadily increasing river of books—both nonfiction books and novels and story collections[44]—as well as numerous articles and even new periodicals addressing women and fatness. That more and more of these publications were feminist and represent something truly new in literature—that is, the voice of the fat woman herself, the fat woman as agent rather than object—is a consequence of many factors.

Foremost among the factors contributing to the almost exponential proliferation of these stories in the last thirty years are the feminist literary periodicals[45] and fat acceptance and fat liberation periodicals founded during that time. The creators of these publications have created a welcoming home for this brand new kind of story.

During the last three decades, fat people have begun to find our authentic literary voices and used them to portray and protest our outsider role in society, to question the science used to condemn us, and to assert our determination to define ourselves and live on our own terms. During the same period of years, eating disorders, including anorexia, bulimia, exercise addiction, binge eating, and compulsive overeating, seem to occur with greater frequency and the attention focused on these conditions has increased. These conditions, too, have been treated in short stories. And in some stories, we see both fat acceptance and eating disorders addressed, as in Maria Bruno's "The Feeder," Lesléa Newman's "Perfectly Normal," and Hollis Seamon's "The Strange History of Suzanne LaFleshe" in which the distinction between being fat and having an eating disorder is clearly made.

Beginning in the late 1960s and early 1970s, we see a coming together of the oppressed, a recognition of their sisterhood, a mutual development of an analysis—a kind of fat consciousness-raising—followed by a celebration of being fat women. In the 1980s we begin to see stories in which the connection is made between fat women and women who were trying to starve themselves. The 1990s saw a small explosion of short stories about fat women who are brave and smart and strong and heroic and seductive and beautiful and voluptuous and successful and desired. I hope that this book will contribute to the stimuli to inspire more such stories, more celebrations of being themselves, ourselves, of being fat women.

XIII

Fatness and thinness are rarely central issues in short stories and novels by African American women. For the most part in these works, the fatness of a woman is a secondary characteristic. It is clearly not an issue over which African American women in short stories are driven to despair, shame, self-abuse, or suicide, although some fat women do express a measure of unease or dissatisfaction with their fatness in some stories. The stories I have included in this collection—J. California Cooper's "He Was a Man," Wanda Coleman's "Fat Lena," and Connie Porter's "Primos"—portray two African American and one Afro-Caribbean-American fat women, each in the midst of her life, each aware of her fatness but not obsessed with it, each in possession of an intact identity, each chosen by a partner she loves, each getting on with her life.

Cooper's "He Was a Man! (But He Did Himself Wrong)" presents one of the classic heterosexual fat woman story patterns: the big woman and the small man. We see that combination of lovers in the Samantha and Josiah Allen pairing by Marietta Holley, in the coming together of Miss Hopkins and Mr. Winslow in Octave Thanet's story, and in the story "Cocks Must Crow" by Marjorie Kinnan Rawlings (omitted here for lack of permission).

In Connie Porter's "Primos," Moraine outweighed Favio by fifty pounds before the thirty-two pound weight gain by her eighth month of pregnancy. We can assume that Coleman's Lena is fatter than her new husband because she is repeatedly described as fat and he is not.

Is there anything of particular interest in this pattern? Yes. We see that heterosexual fat women are not necessarily bereft of male lovers. We see that some of the men are respectful, loving, and sexually aroused by the bodies of these fat women they love—as are some of the men who are paired with slender women. We see fat women in these short stories who like themselves just as they are. We see fat women getting on with their lives as if they were normal people and not body outlaws deserving of punishment, both self-inflicted and socially imposed.

On the other hand, the figuring of fat and/or skinny black female bodies in both short and long fiction by African American women writers is not insignificant. For example, we see the cycle of domestic violence being justified by the abusers on the basis of their preference for one kind of female body over another—although in an interesting twist, it is thinness that is punished. In Zora Neale Hurston's 1926 story "Sweat," Syke is determined to murder his hardworking, skinny wife, Delia Jones, because "He's allus been crazy 'bout fat women." The wife-murderer in Alice Walker's 1970 novel *The Third Life of Grange Copeland* justifies killing her based on her weight loss: "He liked plump women. That was the end-all of his moral debates. Ergo, he had murdered his wife because she had become skinny and had not, with much irritation to him, reverted, even when well-fed, to her former plumpness He was not a fool to ask himself whether there was logic in his nerves. He knew what he liked."[46]

However, I do not mean to imply that in "real" as opposed to "fictional" life, particularly contemporary urban life, African American women are immune from the pressure to be thin or from the cruelties of childhood bullies.[47] Margaret Bass's essay "On Being a Fat Black Girl in a Fat-Hating Culture" tells a familiar story about fat-baiting schoolmates, a perpetually dieting mother, and a lifelong struggle with her own weight. She exposes the lie that the various African American cultures are affectionate toward and accepting of fat female bodies. Her pain—"No one prepared me for living life as a fat person"—is complicated by the fact that she was carefully, tenderly, and skillfully prepared for life as a black person in a racist society.[48]

There ample evidence that African-American women experience pressure to be thin, from articles and diets in targeted periodicals to conference presentations in various disciplines that encourage African American women to pay attention to their diets and to exercise. Part of this trend is a reflection of the dominant culture's ideals about bodies and beauty and a function of upward social class mobility. But the adoption of those values is further complicated by the rejection of the "Black Mamm" stereotype, the woman whose fatness desexualizes her. Although little of this trend has found its way into fiction, Alice Walker succinctly captures it in the 1973 "Everyday Use," her famous, often anthologized mother/daughter short story, as Mama contemplates the impending visit home by her daughter Dee, the daughter who has "made it." She describes herself: "In real life I am a large, big-boned woman with rough man-working hands. In winter I wear flannel nightgowns to bed and overalls during the day. I can kill and clean a hog as mercilessly as a man. My fat keeps me hot in zero weather. . . . [In my television fantasy] I am the way my daughter would want me to be: a hundred pounds lighter."

Walker explores fatness in many of her stories and novels, from "Her Sweet Jerome" and "1955" to *The Color Purple*, but the explorations are always, at best, secondary, and, more often, tertiary concerns of her characters.

In the 1998 novel *Nothing But the Rent* by psychologist Sharon Mitchell, four young African American women who formed a friendship as undergraduates at a predominantly white college in Minnesota renew their friendship eight years after graduation. One of the women, Cynthia, is fat and feels that her chances to find "true love" are compromised by her fatness. By the end of the book, she realizes that she is worthy of love as she is. But in the second novel in this series, the 2002 *Near Perfect*, Cynthia is still alone, still seeking love.

In the work of African American lesbian writer Audre Lorde, fat female bodies function as a "turn-on." In her biomythography *Zami: A New Spelling of My Name* she identifies herself as a fat black lesbian and falls in love with a woman whose beautifully fat knees make her swoon.

Conversely, the young lesbian's rejection of the heterosexual adult world takes, in part, the form of rejection of fat female bodies she associates with adult female heterosexuality in Becky Birtha's 1987 story "Johnnieruth:"

> All the grown women around my way look just the same. They all big—stout. They got bosoms and big hips and fat legs, and they always wearing runover house shoes and them shapeless, flowered numbers with the buttons down the front. 'Cept on Sunday. Sunday morning they all turn into glamour girls, in them big hats and long gloves, with they skinny high hells and they skinny selves in them tight girdles—wouldn't nobody ever know what they look like the rest of the time.
>
> When I was a little kid, I didn't want to grow up, 'cause I never wanted to look like them ladies. I heard Miz Jenkins down the street one time say she don't find being fat 'cause that way her husband don't get so jealous. She say it's more than one way to keep a man. Me, I don't have no intentions of keeping no man. I never understood why they was in so much demand anyway.[49]

Yet the frequently quoted, the forever-forwarded on the internet words of African American poets Lucille Clifton's "Homage to My Hips"and Maya Angelou's "Phenomenal Woman," celebrating their big bodies, are among the most beloved "anthems" of the size acceptance movement.

The theme of women and fatness in African American culture is an immensely conflicted, historically inflected issue that is being addressed with increasing frequency by creative writers and scholars from a variety of disciplines. One of the generative articles in the field, Becky Wangsgaard Thompson's "A Way Outa No Way: Eating Problems Among African-American, Latina, and White Women,"[50] is one of the most frequently assigned articles in courses ranging from Black Women's Studies to Sociology of the Body to Psychology of Women to Images of Women in Cultural Studies courses. In it, Thompson asserts the fact that eating disorders are hardly the possession of white women only and talks about food as the drug of choice for many women of color. In Deborah E. McDowell's "Recovery Missions: Imaging the Body Ideals" she moves from a discussion of her own envy of Tina Turner's body to talk about the metamorphosis of Joe Tex's female body preferences from his rejection of the woman with "Skinny Legs and All" to his declaration that "I Ain't Gonna Bump No More with No Big Fat Woman" to a discussion of Oprah Winfrey's more than two decades of public yo-yo dieting and fat loathing and the varying responses of the members of her enormous audience to Oprah at different sizes.[51]

XIV

Five of these stories in this book are by writers whom I know to be Jewish women, whether or not the characters in the stories are (recognizably) Jewish. In some of them, the characters are definitely not Jewish. The writers are Edna Ferber, Fannie Hurst, Jyl Lynn Felman, Lesléa Newman, and Elena Dykewomon. Jewish women have been particularly prolific in addressing the subject of women's embodiment in both fiction and nonfiction and as activists in the size acceptance movement. I believe that this activism is peculiarly tied to Jewish history, although Jewish women have not been the exclusive pioneers in this work, nor is Jewish history the only ethnic history with important ties to this issue.

Many of the ethnic groups who immigrated en masse to this country were motivated by hunger: Eastern European Jews, the Irish, Southern Italians, others. There were of course, other driving forces as well, such as escaping the dangers of pogroms, seeking educational opportunities, the desire for work when none was available, escape from played out agricultural fields, and so forth. But all of these other motivations were joined to and included *hunger*. And when these hungry people arrived at the end of their difficult and dangerous journeys their hunger was often not assuaged but continued to plague them.

When these starving people finally began to get enough food, enough wasn't enough. It wasn't enough often for several generations—especially if the Great Depression of the 1930s or the even greater depression of the 1890s intervened in the achievement of the American Dream, the Americanization process. Food—the getting, the preparing, the eating, the sharing of recipes, the arguing about recipes, the remembering what has been eaten, the remembering of meals that others have eaten and told you about—these things become important as events, memories, subjects of conversation. When women are starving, they have these conversations.[52] And when they are no longer starving, they buy the food, prepare, serve, and eat those meals.

None of the stories in which these dynamics are played out is represented in this collection, because in none of these stories are these issues central. Rather, the issues of food, hunger, and fatness permeate the stories in the way that oxygen permeates our atmosphere. These stories also tend to be very long—too long to include here, when they deal with issues of fatness only indirectly. But to leave out mention of them would be to ignore a major component of the empowering gift of this previously overlooked literary tradition addressing women's embodiment.

The cadenced cries of hunger reverberate through the stories of Anzia Yezierska with such passion and heartbreak that no matter what or how recently you have eaten your fill, your body will ache with the emptiness that tortures her hungry characters. And considering the joy they take in food— if not eating it, then dreaming about eating it, remembering having eaten it, describing the feasts of people who have enough money not to live on "potato peelings and crusts of bread"—it is no wonder that these people would welcome flesh to fill out and fatten their bodies when finally they can afford it. In Yezierska's "The Fat of the Land," one character declares:

> "Do you know Mrs. Melker ordered fifty pounds of chickens for her daughter's wedding? And such chickens! Shining like gold! My heart melted in me just looking at the flowing fatness of those chickens. . . . In Savel, Mrs. Melker used to get shriveled up from hunger. She and her children used to live on potato-peelings and crusts of dry bread picked out from the barrels; and in America she lives to eat chicken and apple shtrudels soaking in fat."[53]

Fannie Hurst, too, talks endlessly about food, hunger, and fatness—although again, it was almost never the central issue of her stories. And when it was, as in "Even You and I" and two others, those are not stories about Jewish characters, but gentile characters rooted in the Ohio world Hurst knew from spending her summers on the farm of her mother's parents.[54] Almost all of her stories about immigrants mention these issues, but "The Gold in Fish" offers especially vivid equations of thinness with assimilation, and fatness with ethnicity. Maurice Fish, nee Morris Goldfish, the adult son of immigrants, is quite successful in his drive to assimilate, which depends in large part on his "Jewishness." His wife, Irma, who shared his values and out-Americaned everyone else in the extended family, "weighed one hundred and fourteen pounds and attended Lyman Wastrel's Stretching Classes for weight reduction." But his sister, Birdie, actively rebelled against the assimilation that would have led to upward mobility. Birdie takes frank enjoyment in cooking and eating fattening traditional foods, and she couldn't have "passed" even if she had wanted to:

> Somewhere imbedded in Birdie's face was a certain squab-young prettiness. A one-hundred-seventy-six-pound prettiness. If Birdie's ankles in their too sheer flesh stocking lopped over her blond leather pumps her foot itself was absurdly small. So were her wrists before the heaviness of arm set in."[55]

The close cultural connection between Jewish women and food continues to be manifest in the writings of many Jewish women today. For instance, the many novels by Marge Piercy are rich with luscious meals lovingly prepared and shared, bonded over and remembered. Many of her female characters confront sizeism, both internalized and external, and part of their healthy development often includes learning to accept and to love their own bodies despite the fact that those bodies resemble more closely the plump softnesses of their grandmothers than the models they see in advertisements.

XV

Criticism of a girl or woman's body by those whom she trusts most, with whom she is most intimate, and to whom she is most vulnerable is not only one of many kinds of domestic abuse, it is one of the most common. As Dorothy Taber, a rehabilitation counselor working with persons with psychological and physiological disabilities, has commented, "Over the many years that I have worked as a counselor of women, every female client I have worked with over a period of time, of months, regarding partner abuse, has commented about the trauma caused by negative remarks concerning their body by their abusers, adding to the basic shame that most women apparently have about their bodies. One would expect for persons with disfiguring conditions to have negative bodily images. But this isn't necessarily so. Many people with average, healthy, 'normal,' and often beautiful physicality believe they are ugly, homely, and misshapen."[52]

The criticism can be couched in any number of ways, and whether it is presented "lovingly" as "for your own good" or brutally as "you deserve to be punished for what you have done to yourself," it is always experienced as painful. Whether the words come from a husband, a domestic partner, a lover, a parent, or a sibling, they always wound. The earlier the criticism begins in the life of a person, the more permanent and long-term the damage can be. And when the criticism begins after or in conjunction with some highly stressful event (and a stressful event can be a welcome event, such as pregnancy or childbirth, as well as a catastrophe, such as illness or the loss of a loved one), the person being criticized is even more vulnerable than at other times. Insulting remarks about a person's natural appearance delivered by those who are supposed to love you are toxic. Being told you are *too* anything—too fat, too thin, too tall, too short, too dark, underdeveloped, overdeveloped—not only is a blow to self-esteem and the natural sense of communion with one's own body, but also undermines the ability to trust in the safety of anyone's love.

One kind of abuse or another is significant in the lives of many of the fat women in the 167 stories on the theme. The kind of social abuse and sexual exploitation experienced by Reyna in "The Hershey Bar Queen" appears in several stories not included in the collection, and in one of them[56] this abuse leads to a suicide attempt —which leads to time in a mental institution, which leads to weight loss—but the sexually abused fat girl remains palpably alive to the now slenderized girl, haunting her. In the section on spoiled girlhoods, I talk about the emotional and sometimes physical abuse, bullying, intimidating, humiliating, that fat girls often experience from their peers, in public settings such as school or playgrounds. But seven of the stories in this book involve one or more kinds of both blatant and relatively subtle and intensely damaging intimate abuse I have discussed above. Some of these stories explore abuse in adult heterosexual relationships and some in families of origin; they are as much about abuse as they are about women's embodiment.

In Fannie Hurst's "Even As You and I," we learn at the end that Will Jastrow has been physically abusive to his wife, Sidonia Sabrina, and that his (mis)treatment of Miss Hoag is a function of his treatment of and attitude towards other human beings in general, rather than a consequence of his attitude toward Teenie's great size. Whether Jastrow's abusiveness is a function of psychopathy or alcoholism or both is not discernible, but that he was abusive is unquestionable.

The neglect and emotional withholding by Payt Tierney in "Fat" is a kind of abuse often not identified as abuse because of its passive-aggressive character ("for years he had been comfortably indifferent"), but it is clear that Mrs. Tierney is little more than an old, used, passé possession of his and that he has no qualms about going in search of a new possession. Mrs. Tierney muses, "a man never does a thing to keep his figure—eats and eats—but if a woman gets the least little bit plump—the things he says! Bulgy—he called me bulgy—. . . .resentment, like a thin bitter rain, dropped down upon her spirits. . . .a man ought not to be rude to his wife. He ought not to tell her she bulged. Not with a certain kind of smile." The shared poverty and hunger of their early marriage has been supplanted by the wealth and luxury of their later years, but it has driven them apart, too. The loneliness and isolation of her life has lulled Mrs. Tierny into the kind of existence-in-waiting that inevitably leads to a severing of the vital sense of being a part of the world. With no comfort but food, no companionship but that she can pay for, and nothing to anticipate except the next culinary delight, Mrs. Tierny has nevertheless decided to forgo all of these flimsy supports that make up her lonely life in an attempt to reduce her flesh, to change herself under the sting of her husband's criticism. And then she discovers, in the midst of her efforts, that there is another woman in his life—a tall, thin, young woman who is deliberately trying to gain weight to please this same man who criticizes his wife's bulges.

The catalogue of abusive behaviors of the parents of Nelly in Kit Reed's "Food Farm" is frighteningly familiar to the many fat girls and fat young women put through the routine of shaming, blaming, depriving, and distancing common to the parents with means and determination to govern the bodies of their fat youngsters for their own good:

> In time I was too much for them and they stopped taking me out; they made no more attempts to explain. Instead they tried to think of ways to make me look better; the doctors tried the fool's poor battery of pills; they tried to make me join a club. For a while my mother and I did exercises. . . . For a while after that they tried locking up the food. Then they began to cut into my meals.

That was the cruelest time. They would refuse me bread, they would plead and cry, plying me with lettuce and telling me it was all for my own good. My own good.

Nelly's vengeance is, of course, the stuff of fantasy, but it is a fantasy I am certain many force-dieted, pilled, pummeled, fat-camped young women share with glee.

Smitty's insufferably cruel behavior towards Della in "He Was a Man! (But He Done Himself Wrong)" is also familiar to many women in abusive relationships:

"I am the man! You gon have to do what I say! I ain't taking no shit!" . . . Della's hell was that every once in awhile, Smitty hit her, abused her. It hurt and it didn't hurt! But it seemed to do so much for him, being so small and all, hitting a woman so large, she never tried to hit him back. . . . He whipped his woman, all 207 pounds of her! . . . "I hate you, you big, fat, ugly bear! You ape! A gorilla! You ain't no woman!" . . . . but he done stopped crying now and was really talking mean to her, calling her all kinds of names, sloppy fat bitches and things like that! It was untrue and it hurt her. You could almost see her drawing up, shrinking, every time a word struck her. Seemed like the words were razor blades cutting her to ribbons.

In "The Feeder" Maria Bruno portrays two abusive husbands, each trying to control the lives and appearances of their wives. It isn't clear whether the men are dissatisfied with their wives' bodies at a personal level or if they are just desperate to have their wives conform to current beauty ideals because their wives' appearances reflect on them in the corporate world they inhabit. No doubt the men couldn't make the distinction between their own personal preferences and their career ambitions themselves. The pioneering story of the friendship between Sylvia and Alma is the first story in which wife abuse, women's friendships, and women's embodiment issues are brought together. Literary scholar Linda Wagner-Martin has written eloquently about this story:

The devastating portraits of the power-hungry husbands. . . make the story an explicit account of women's friendship in the face of macho sexual and economic force that is clearly malignant. As Alma and Sylvia grope their way toward a language that will express the inexpressible—even the unthinkable—the reader is drawn into the seemingly comic yet simultaneously angry narrative. Characterized by their fat and too-lean bodies, as if their selves and souls were imaged only by their fatty tissues, Bruno's women find both identity and power in their friendships.[58]

Steve, the young husband-to-be in Lesléa Newman's "Perfectly Normal," shares his fiancée's horror of female flesh. "When Steve dropped us off at my parent's house that night, my sister went inside, and I stayed in the car to kiss him goodnight. He took me in his arms and—I'll never forget this—he said, "Promise me one thing." "What?" I asked. "Promise me you'll never get as fat as your sister." I was shocked. "You know I wouldn't," I said to him. "I'd rather die." After their marriage, together they conspire in her increasing emaciation. He prefers her skeletal to sexual.

The final story in which domestic violence plays a dramatic role is "Skanks." Rennie Sparks's spare prose gives us only the voice of Janine so there is no exposition to nudge us towards connections between the world of domestic violence that has been Janine's homelife: "My step-dad is better than my real dad anyway and I shouldn't have pissed him off. My real dad broke my mom's jaw against the bathroom sink. My step-dad just slaps her without a fist and it doesn't look like it hurts much." And she is prepared to be a victim in the adolescent social world to which she escapes from that home. Having witnessed the abuse of her mother by her father and stepfather has prepared her for the victim role in her own life. The idea that her stepfather is "better than" her real dad because his battery of her mother is less damaging sets her up to choose the apparently less-damaging abuse by her false friend Dawn over what has seemed like the more damaging behavior of her parents. It is no surprise that she would, at least temporarily, succumb to sexual abuse, misuse, and exploitation by the adolescent boys in her world. It all seems to be of a piece. And so it should also be no surprise that with all of this abuse going on around her, she takes control over it all and becomes her own chief abuser. She "learns" to be eating disordered.[59]

In these stories, as in the world at large, the abuse of fat women remains, for many, a secret, surrounded by fear, shame, and self-blame. And like abused women in general, many fat women are likely to go on suffering in silence unless the larger truths are told, and blame is placed where it belongs—on the abusers, and on the culture that produces them. In a society with a general penchant for punishing difference, and an excessively high regard for bodily appearances as cultural markers, it makes perfect sense that fat bodies will be abused in a variety of ways. In fact, it often does not matter if a woman is really fat; if she lives in a fat-fearing, fat-hating culture and she is in an intimate relationship with an abuser, she is likely to be will be told she is fat, scolded and punished for being fat. This abuse is perhaps only the most literal expression of the punishment our culture imposes on bodies that dare to transgress from the socially prescribed norms.

XVI

Throughout this essay I have referred to stories I did not include in this collection. Some are missing because I couldn't get permission to include them. Others are by an author who has another story here, and it has been my policy for many years to include only one story per author in a collection. Some stories are simply too pathological in their "take" on women and fatness, too "driven" by outdated psychological theories to bother with today. Some were left out with great regret because I didn't want to overrepresent a particular sub-genre or a particular approach to the theme of women and fatness. There is an additional group of stories I have not only left out of the book, but not included in my own list of 167 stories about women and fatness. These stories are just plain bad literature. They are stories in which a stereotype of a fat woman or an anorectic woman is used as a foil or a joke or a piece of literary furniture, but the caricature hasn't a shred of believable humanity.

Other than the 1932 "Fat" by Grace Sartwell Mason, the only stories about women and fatness from the Great Depression of 1929 through the early 1940s are two from 1939: "Cocks Must Crow" by Marjorie Kinnan Rawlings (which, as I have already mentioned, we were unable to get permission to reprint), a story heavy with southern rural dialect representing a return to local color/regionalism, and Dorothy Parker's "Big Blonde."

I didn't include Parker's story because none of those I consulted with about the stories seemed to "get" that it is about women and fatness. Throughout "Big Blonde," Hazel, a woman of "easy virtue," keeps getting fatter and fatter and fatter. And the fatter she gets the lower the class of men she attracts. They are increasingly crude, rude, and penurious. And increasingly she has to "entertain" more and more of them to get by financially. But most people don't think of it as a story in which fatness figures in a central way, which I think is interesting since the title is not just "Blonde," but "*Big* Blonde." The story is available in many publications and easily accessible. Read it and let me know what you think about it. Is it a story about women and fatness?

Other than these three, there seem to have been no stories published about women and fatness during the years of national financial panic, homelessness, and hunger. I am inclined to assume that whether or not such stories were written, they were not published for reasons similar to those that explain why no stories explicitly addressing and portraying domestic violence were published during World Wars I and II: There was no sympathy, no readers' eyes yearning, for such stories in either case. Nevertheless, fat ladies in freak shows, sideshows, carnivals, and circuses seem to have thrived during the Depression: One sideshow fat woman, Ruth Pontico, "at her peak . . . made close to 300 dollars a day during the Depression."[60]

There are also no explicitly sexual stories in this collection. A great many such stories exist on the internet, and they are easy to find. Whether they are erotic or pornographic is a decision I will leave to each individual who seeks them out and reads them. I do include the eighteen stories in *Zaftig: Well Rounded Erotica,* edited by Hanne Blank and published by Cleis Press in 2001, in my list of 167 stories, but I do not include any of the internet stories in that figure.

And, as I mention earlier, I have included no "pro-ana," or pro-anorexia stories, although the brilliantly written "Skanks" comes dangerously close and needs to be read very carefully. Despite being clearly amateur efforts, some of the online pro-ana stories are well written, and few resort to caricature or stereotypes. Over the years, I have heard many people, most particularly young women, suffering from the pressure to be, to become, or to remain slender express wistful longings to "learn how" to be either bulimic or anorectic. They think it is a condition they can control at will, one they can "use" as a diet instead of a form of suicide. But because of the general misunderstanding of the danger of these often fatal eating disorders, I will not include "how-to" literature.

XVI

In "Magnetic Force," Susan Stinson presents a memorable image: "I am in a swimming pool with seventeen fat women. We have our arms around each other's waists and are circling in the center of the pool. We go faster and faster. Our bellies, breasts and arms press together. We lap against each other, screaming and laughing."

When thinking about the emotionally overloaded subject of women and fatness, it is important to remember that what is most valued in our current culture is actually an exaggerated version of one ethnicity and class: the upper-class Anglo-Saxon. Every embrace of that exaggerated and, for most of us, impossible "ideal," represents a rejection of the body types representative of all the other groups who are part of our polyglot American society. Furthermore, the current and unhealthy overvaluing of slenderness, of what some refer to as "heroin chic," is a fashion of the moment, one rooted in, among many other factors, the culture of a class with both abundance and leisure, luxuries available to only a few in our society. The standards of that class are imposed on everyone. Those who fail to "measure up" are subjected to harsh judgment. It is an historical aberration, but one that, nonetheless, causes some of us living in this historical moment who do not or cannot conform to "body fashion/fascism" intense anguish, shame, guilt, and despair. Others of us feel internal rage. Still others of us are outraged and spurred to political activism.

A fat woman may be a radical fat liberationist, fat and proud and defiant and bound and determined to claim her rightful share of joy, to have her say, to take up space on the dance floors of life, to look you in the eye and say, "Fat! So?"[53] She may be a size acceptance advocate, who believes passionately in the all-rightness, the normalcy, the beauty of women of all shapes and sizes. Or she may be still in hiding, still wearing that black raincoat in summer, who hasn't been swimming in decades, who spends her days and nights waiting for her life to begin once she "does something about hersel." All of these women are telling their stories, writing poems and essays and manifestos and novels and short stories that say, "This is how it is for *me!*" We are grateful for their stories.

NOTES

1. Henry James's 1892 story "The Real Thing," which explores how an artist's drawings are affected by his perceptions of his models, is perhaps the most well-known story by a U.S. writer that plays with this theme, but it was by no means the first.

2. From *Great Short Stories*, Vol. 3, *Romance & Adventure*, edited by William Patten, New York: P.F. Collier & Son, 1906, 7–8.

3. Emily Toth, *Kate Chopin: A Life of the Author of The Awakening* (New York: Morrow, 1990) 272.

4. From *Selected Tales of Guy De Maupassant*, edited by Saxe Commins (New York: Random House, 1945), 310–344

5. Toth, 232.

6. This information is available in Kate Chopin's Private Papers, edited by Emily Toth, Per Seyersted, and Cheyenne Bonnell (Bloomington: Indiana University Press, 1998).

7. See Department of Textile and Apparel Management, University of Missouri, Exhibit: "Exploring Our Vernacular Past: Everyday Clothing in Missouri, 1870-1910." Information found at www.missouri.edu

8. This is a narrator who is not objective and whose version of the story reflects personal attitudes and judgments that the reader can't trust. The narrator's distorted point of view can reflect emotional instability, arrogance, lack of sophistication, or prejudice. Usually, the bias is inadvertent, creating dramatic irony. According to the "Glossary of Literary Terms" in *World Literature: An Anthology of Great Short Stories, Drama, and Poetry*, edited by Donna Rosenberg, (Lincolnwood, IL: National Textbook Co., 1992).

9. Mrs. Margaret Ellis and her personal trainer Shuey Cardigan appears in an earlier story by Thanet, "Harry Lossing," *Scribner's Magazine*, 13:2 (February, 1893), included in her 1893 collection *Stories of a Western Town*. However, Mrs. Ellis' obsession with physical training and weight loss is a "tag" for the narrator to hang this secondary character on; her obsession is played for humor. As did many literary regionalists, Thanet used some of her characters over and over, in roles of various prominence in her stories.

10. Several books trace this evolution. See especially *The Body Project: An Intimate History of American Girls* by Joan Jacobs Brumberg (New York: Random House, 1997). "The fact that American girls now make the body their central project is not an accident or a curiosity," writes Brumberg, "it is a symptom of historical changes that are only now beginning to be understood" (xxv). Brumberg draws on diary excerpts and media images from 1830 to the present . . .exposing the shift from the Victorian concern with character to our modern focus

on appearance—in particular, the desire to be model-thin and sexy" (Paperback back cover).

11. Typical of the judgments recorded in stories up until the latter decade of the nineteenth century is the following: "He would not, at any rate, extend his self-elected office of chorus so far as to include her. He felt a dislike toward her. She was too thin, he thought." From "Osgood's Predicament" by Elizabeth D. B. Stoddard. Originally published in *Harper's Magazine*, June, 1869; included in *Library of American Fiction*, Vol. 8 (The Success Company, 1884, 1904), p 197.

12. The Harvey-Banting Diet (otherwise known as the "Banting Diet" or "Harvey Banting Diet") was one of the first low-carb diets to be documented, first published by the Englishman William Banting in 1863. See www.low-carb-diet-plans.com. The Salisbury Diet was, basically, another low-carb, high protein diet. A brief history of Dr. Salisbury can be found online at www.bones.med.ohio-state.edu. The diet pills of the time commonly contained the poisons strychnine and arsenic.

13. In "The Stout Miss Hopkins's Bicycle" the dynamics of class play a role similar to that of size. Mr. Winslow's shortness places him, in a sense, on a par with the stout Miss Hopkins. Likewise, Mr. Winslow and his mother are beneath the two ladies because they don't have as much money as they do, but their credentials of descent are as good as theirs. So, since he has made money and can become president of the bank even though he is short, he is a worthy contender for her heart and hand—and with her money he can actually afford enough stock to be president of the bank.

14. For a more thorough discussion of women's friendships in U.S. women's short stories, see *Women's Friendships: A Collection of Stories*, edited by Susan Koppelman. (Norman: The University of Oklahoma Press, 1991).

15. Dale Spender, *Women of Ideas (and What Men Have Done to Them)*. (London: Routledge & Kegan Paul, 1982), 2.

26 Susan Stinson's "Crease," a lesbian love story which is also an homage to Gertrude Stein's famous "Lifting Belly," is one of these. However, I use only one story by a writer in each of my collections. See also *Zaftig: Well Rounded Erotica* edited by Hanne Blank (San Francisco: Cleis Press, 2001).

17. "Cacoethes Scribendi," *Atlantic Souvenir* (Philadelphia), 1830, 17–38, reprinted in *Stories of American Life*, edited by Mary Russell Mitford III (London, 1830), 162–186, and in Sedgwick's *Tales and Sketches*, series one (Philadelphia 1835), 65–181. Also included in the most recent edition of the *Norton Anthology of American Literature*, vol. 1 (1998) and in Judith Fetterley's *Provisions: A Reader from Nineteenth-Century American Women* (Bloomington: Indiana University Press, 1985). In this story, Sedgwick satirizes the sources of material of female authors of popular short stories. "The most kind hearted of women, Mrs. Courland's interests came to be so at varience *(sic)* with the prosperity of the little community of H. that a sudden calamity, a death, a funeral, were fortunate events to her. To do her justice, she felt them in a two-fold capacity. She wept as a woman, and exulted as an author." *Tales and Sketches*, p. 175.

18. "The political reality is that the writing of New England and the Atlantic coastal area has often been considered mainstream, while the writing of other parts of the country has been marginalized by being called regional." Linda Wagner, "Regionalism," in *The Oxford Companion to Women's Writing in the United States* edited by Cathy N. Davidson and Linda Wagner-Martin (New York: Oxford University Press, 1995), 752.

19. *Found Treasures: Stories by Yiddish Women Writers*, edited by Frieda Forman, Ethel Raicus, Sarah Siberstein Swartz, and Margie Wolfe (Toronto: University of Toronto Press, 1994).

20. From the Musical "Fiddler On The Roof," lyrics by Sheldon Harnick and music by Jerry Block (premier September 22, 1964).

21. For more on this theme in Jewish women's writing, see section XIV of this afterword. For an exploration of this and other food-related themes in Italian American women's writing, see *The Milk of Almonds: Italian Women Writers on Food and Culture*, edited by Louise DeSalvo and Edvige Giunta (New York: Feminist Press at CUNY, 2002).

22. This act limited annual European immigration to 3 percent of the number of a nationality group in the United States in 1910. Continuing intolerance toward immigrants from southern and eastern Europe culminated in the Immigration Act of 1924, which placed a numerical cap on immigration and instituted a deliberately discriminatory system of national quotas.

23. See "Exuberant Proportions" by Wilson Barber in *Dimensions*, November, 1994, and at www.geocities.com/wilsonbarbers/sideshow for a discussion of circus, carnival, and sideshow fat ladies that provides a succinct history of the public careers of very fat women from Victorian times through Jerry Springer. Note the provocative emphasis on the erotic appeal of these performers.

24. Barbara Welter. "The Cult of True Womanhood: 1820-1860," in *American Quarterly* 18 (1966). 151–74.

25. For a much more thorough exploration of the theme of the "Other Woman" in U.S. women's short stories, see *The Other Woman: Stories of Two Women and a Man*, edited by Susan Koppelman, (New York: Feminist Press at CUNY, 1984)

26. See my article "The Educations of Fannie Hurst" in Women's Studies International Forum, Vol. 10, No. 5, Oct., 1987.

27. In "Exhuberant Proportions," Wilson Baker writes of the erotic appeal of the "fat lady": "Unfashionable, politically suspect, the image of the sideshow fat woman hovers over many a fat admirer. What straight male FA has not come upon this vision and marveled? For many of us, the fat lady is our first contact with the provocative power of size. Behind the exploitation, the cynical mockery that so often surrounded the sideshow lies a sexual attraction that has made the fat lady such an enduring icon."
As sideshow attractions go, the fat lady (and man) are relative newcomers. Where dwarves, for example, were a staple of Renaissance imagery, the first major public displays of supersized women and men didn't catch on until the eighteenth century. It didn't take long for them to become a standard sideshow feature, and part of this can surely be linked to their erotic appeal to unknowing male admirers caught by what one Italian writer called "those representatives of the gentle sex with particularly exuberant proportions and floridity." That the fat lady could do this, hampered by disparaging stage names ("Dolly Dimples," "Dainty Doris," "Baby Ruth Pontico") and outfits that burlesqued girlishness, says much for their power.

28. See Sharon Mazer, "She's so fat . . . : Facing the fat Lady at Coney Island's Sideshows by the Seashore," in *Bodies Out of Bounds: Fatness and Transgression*, edited by Jana Evans Braziel and Kathleen LeBesco (Berkeley: University of California Press, 2001), 257–276.

29. Bariatric physicians are those "with special interest in the study and treatment of obesity." This professional society was founded in 1950. According to the section on the history of bariatric surgery on the webpage of the American Society for Bariatric Surgery, the first took place in 1954. Diet pills were mainly amphetamine derivatives (speed). They were prescribed as appetite suppressants, caused increased heart rate and many other short-term and long-term health problems and were highly addictive.

30. *Seventeen* magazine has been an icon since 1944, pioneered the young women's magazine market, and is still the leader with the 12–24 age group, and a dominant force in the culture.

31. Another story in this genre that might be fruitfully compared with "Goodbye, Old Laura" is "Emily" by June S. Strader published in *Everygirls Companion*, edited by A. L. Furman (New York: Lantern Publishers, 1966).

32. "The Food Farm" has been published in two different translations with two different titles in French, and in Spanish, Dutch, German, and Japanese, as well as in almost a dozen anthologies in English.

33. Joanna Russ, "The Image of Women in Science Fiction" in *Images of Women in Fiction: Feminist Perspectives* (Popular Press, 1972), 79–80.

34. For those interested in reading more stories in these subgenres of short fiction, I heartily recommend *Such a Pretty Face* edited by Lee Martindale (Atlanta: Meisha Merlin Publishing Co., 2000; contact PO Box 7, Decatur, GA 30031 or www.MeishaMerlin.com) and Martindale's own collection of stories, *The Folly of Assumption: The Collected Fat Fantasies of Lee Martindale*, a chapbook of five size-positive short stories (available from Amazon.Com or—and even better—directly from the publisher, www.yarddogpress.com). I regret being unable to get permission to reprint any of these fine stories.

35. The hot springs and spa industry has flourished for millennia all over the world, including the United States with its famous spa resorts in the nineteenth century at Hot Springs, Arkansas, Eureka Springs, Missouri, Saratoga Springs, New York, and so forth. The kind of spa being spoofed in "The Food Farm," those that advertise their dedication to wellness and wholeness of the mind, body, and spirit but are really dedicated to weight loss, began with the founding of the Golden Door in Escondido, California, in 1958, and eventually included Canyon Ranch and Mirival in Tucson and dozens of other such facilities around the country in some of the most beautiful settings on the continent. The industry has expanded the services offered and now includes in its programs drug and alcohol rehabilitation, recovery from "nervous exhaustion," and a host of other problems you have to be very, very wealthy to heal from in such places. As weight loss facilities, the combination of luxury and deprivation makes these places ripe for satire.

36. The term "stigma" is used in the sense crafted by Erving Goffman in his groundbreaking book *Stigma. Notes on the Management of Spoiled Identity* by (Englewood Cliffs, NJ: Prentice-Hall, 1963). His work has been embraced by disability studies scholars and his conceptual "inventions" have been among the germinal ideas in this field. By "stigma" he meant any characteristic or attribute that rendered a person unable to conform to social norms. He posited three categories of stigma: body abnormalities or abominations, character blemishes or deviancies, and membership in discredited categories, such as certain races or ethnicities, when the membership can't be hidden by passing or assimilation. He was particularly interested in exploring how stigmatized persons felt about them-

selves, their strategies for dealing with rejection, and the interactions between stigmatized individuals and "normals."

37. Erving Goffman, *Stigma*, quoted in "Celebrating Erving Goffman," by Eliot Freidson, in *Contemporary Sociology*, 12:4 (July 1983), 359–62.

38. By 1900, the number of American monthlies had expanded to about 1,800, reaching nearly 1 million families. Magazines for women came to dominate magazine circulation. The most important of these were the *Ladies' Home Journal* (1883–), the *Woman's Home Companion* (1873–1955), *McCall's Magazine* (1870–2001) and *Vogue* (1892–). (See the "Special Interest Magazines" section on Encyclopedia.com for more details.) The importance of women's magazines in developing and supporting writers cannot be overstated. Nor can the stories published in these magazines be dismissed as "not literary" or "not important." The stories are important for understanding the mass reading public—what was intriguing enough to be worth the price of the subscription to the magazine, the time it took to read them, and the ideas about women contained within them. As for literary quality—that is such a political topic, so rife with controversy, that I do not have time or space to begin exploring it here—except to say that I never anthologize a story I think is lacking in literary quality. *Women's Home Companion* blossomed under the thirty-year editorship of newspaperwoman Gertrude Battles Lane, who began in 1911 to include two serials and four or five stories per issue. Willa Cather, Ellen Glasgow, and Mary Wilkins Freeman were all published in *Women's Home Companion*, which was reputed to offer as much as $85,000 in the 1920s for serial rights to a novel by Sophie Kerr, Dorothy Canfield Fisher, or Edna Ferber. By 1927, the *Companion* enjoyed a circulation of two million and reached over 170 pages in length." See the introduction to *Breaking the Ties that Bind: Popular Stories of the New Woman, 1915–1930*, edited by Maureen Honey (Norman: University of Oklahoma Press, 1992), 6. Honey's discussion of Women's Home Companion is based on Frank Luther Mott's *A History of American Magazines, 1885–1905*, vol. 4 (Cambridge: Harvard University Press, 1957) 766–72. A brief glance through the tables of contents of various issues of *Women's Home Companion* reveals it to have been the first place of publication of John Steinbeck's *The Pearl*, of the column by Eleanor Roosevelt that evolved into the famous "My Day," and of stories by F. Scott Fitzgerald. It was also the source for the 1927 story "Fat" by Grace Sartwell Mason.

39. See "Mommy" by Kit Reed in *Scare Care*, edited by Graham Masterton (1990) and "A Taste of Life" by Sara Paretsky in *"A Taste of Life" and Other Stories* (1990).

40. Edward Cumella, Ph.D., Director of Research, Education, and Quality at Remuda Ranch in Arizona, a respected inpatient facility that treats about seven hundred women with eating disorders each year, states the following: "It's absurd to assert that feminists have inflated the mortality rate of anorexia. The mortality rate is based on scientific research published in peer-reviewed journals. Mortality for anorexia was 10 to 1 percent in the past, but since 1990 studies have shown a decrease, most likely due to improved treatment methods. The mortality rate for females with anorexia now stands at 5.7 percent. That number is a meta-analytic average of more than 150 peer-reviewed studies on mortality in eating disorders. The mortality rate for females with bulimia is 1 percent, also a fairly reliable meta-analytic average.

Moving from mortality rates to actual numbers of deaths per year is more difficult. Many times people die from anorexia but anorexia is not the cause listed on their death certificate. The cause is listed instead as heart failure, heart attack, etc.—one of the medical complications of anorexia. So the data from death certificates—which incidentally are what the detractors are using to say that mortality from anorexia is much lower—cannot be relied on. It is necessary instead to combine the known mortality rate with prevalence data. And, of course, prevalence data are less reliable, since good population studies of disease are expensive and rare in the U.S., and especially unreliable for the less common illnesses like anorexia—it's hard to find the needle in the haystack. So my recommendation for you is that you stick with the mortality rate of 6 percent for anorexia and 1 percent for bulimia." (Personal communication, September 2003)

Dr. Cumella has also made the following important point: "Anorexia is more fatal than depression and its concomitant suicidality. Anorexia is truly the MOST fatal mental illness. It affects many fewer people than depression, so the raw numbers of deaths are smaller, but the percentage of deaths is higher. Anorexia is associated with extraordinary self-hatred; it is driven by our culture; it affects mostly women and gay men; it is compelling evidence to me of women's continuing oppression in our culture." (Personal communication, September 2003)

41. Another term for men who prefer fat partners is "chubby chasers." This term is disrespectful of both parties to the relationships, while "fat admirers" is an attempt to simply name in a neutral manner a group of people whose only similarity is a particular kind of preference in their choice of romantic or sexual partner. The most interesting thing to notice about these terms is the absence of similar terms for those who prefer very slender partners, such as the husbands in Maria Bruno's 1985 story "The Feeder" and Lesléa Newman's 1990 story "Perfectly Normal." There are terms for heterosexual men whose sexual preferences reveal fixations on particular female body parts, such as "leg men," "butt men," and "breast men" (and yes, these terms refer to sexual preferences rather than culinary preferences!), but there simply are no terms for men whose preferences are for women whose bodies approach the current cultural ideal--except, maybe, "trophy wife."

42. See "Fat Feminist Herstory, 1969–1993: A Personal Memoir" by Karen W. Stimson," *Expository Magazine* 1:1 2001–02. This piece can be accessed at www.expositorymagazine.net/fatfemherstory.

43. The interview with Judy Freespirit can be accessed at www.lustydevil.com/fatgirl/judyfree.

44. Among the novels and volumes of short stories are several published by women who have short stories included in this volume. See Elana Dykewomon's *Riverfinger Women* 1974, reprinted by Naiad Press in 1992, and *Moon Creek Road*, Spinsters Ink 2003; Susan Stinson's *Fat Girl Dances With Rocks*, Spinsters Ink 1994 and *Martha Moody*, Spinsters Ink 1995; Lesléa Newman's *Good Enough to Eat: A Novel*, Firebrand Books 1986, *Eating Our Hearts Out: Personal Accounts of Women's Relationship to Food* (an edited multigeneric anthology), Crossing Press 1993, and *Fat Chance* (a young adult novel), 1999.

45. Among the feminist periodicals see especially Conditions, Sinister Wisdom, Hurricane Alice, Sing, Heavenly Muse and 13th Moon.

46. Alice Walker, New York and London: Harcourt Brace Jovanovich, 1970, 161.

47. Susan Bordo writers, in *Unbearable Weight: Feminism, Western Culture, and the Body* (Berkeley: University of California Press, 1993): "It has been argued that certain ethnic and racial conceptions of female beauty, often associated with different cultural attitudes toward female power and sexuality, may provide resistance to normalizing images and ideologies.

This has been offered as an explanation, for example, as to why eating disorders have been less common among blacks than whites. Without disputing the significance of such arguments, we should be cautious about assuming too much 'difference' here. The equation of slenderness and success in this culture continually undermines the preservation of alternative ideals of beauty. A legacy of reverence for the zaftig body has not protected Jewish women from eating disorders; the possibility of greater upward mobility is now having a similar effect on young African American women, as the numerous diet and exercise features appearing in *Essence* magazine make clear. To imagine that African American women are immune to the standards of slenderness that reign today is, moreover, to come very close to the racist notion that the art and glamour—the culture—of femininity belong to the white woman alone. The black woman, by contrast, is woman in her earthy, 'natural,' state, uncorseted by civilization. 'Fat is a black woman's issue, too,' insisted the author of a 1990 *Essence* article, bitterly criticizing the high-school guidance counselor who had told her she did not have to worry about managing her weight because 'black women aren't seen as sex objects but as women. So really, you're lucky because you can go beyond the stereotypes of woman as sex object. . . . Also, fat [women] are more acceptable in the black community.' Apparently, as the author notes, the guidance counselor had herself not 'gone beyond stereotypes of the maternal, desexualized Mammy as the prototype of black womanhood.' Saddled with these projected racial notions, the young woman, who had struggled with compulsive eating and yo-yo dieting for years, was left alone to deal with an eating disorder that she wasn't 'supposed' to have." (63)

48. See Margaret K. Bass's moving essay "On Being a Fat Black Girl in a Fat-Hating Culture" in *Recovering the Black Female Body: Self-Representations by African American Women*, edited by Michael Bennett and Vanessa D. Dickerson (New Brunswick, NJ: Rutgers University Press, 2001), 219–230.

49. "Johnnieruth" by Becky Birtha in *The Unforgetting Heart: An Anthology of Short Stories by African American Women, 1859-1993* edited by Asha Kanwar (San Francisco: Aunt Lute Books, 1993),. 223; Originally in *Lover's Choice* by Becky Birtha (Seattle: Seal Press, 1987).

50. Becky Wangsgaard Thompson, "A Way Outa No Way: Eating Problems Among African-American, Latina, and White Women from *Gender and Society* 6:4 (1992), 546–61.

51. In Bennett and Dickerson, eds., *Recovering the Black Female Body*, 296–317.

52. For a detailed and powerful account of this behavior under the most extreme circumstances, see "Food Talk: Gendered Responses to Hunger in the Concentration Camps" by Myrna Goldenberg. In *Experience and Expression: Women, the Nazis, and the Holocaust* edited by Elizabeth R. Baer and Myrna Goldenberg (Detroit: Wayne State University Press, 2003), 161–79.

53. From Yezierska's "The Fat of the Land," first published in *The Century*, August, 1919; included in *The Best Short Stories of 1919*, edited by Edward J. O'Brien (New York: Small, Maynard, and Co., 1920) and in Hurst's 1923 collection of short stories *Children of Loneliness*.

54. The two other Hurst stories are "Sob Sister," first published in *Metropolitan Magazine* 43:4 (February 1916); included in Hurst's *Every Soul Hath Its Song* (New York: Harper & Bros., 1916); reprinted in *Famous Story Magazine*, October 1925; and "Song of Life," first published in *Cosmopolitan*, September 1926; included in *Song of Life* (New York: Knopf, 1927).

55. "The Gold in Fish," first published in *Cosmopolitan*, August, 1925; collected in *Song Of Life*; filmed as *The Younger Generation*, directed by Frank Capra with a screen play by Sonya Levien (Columbia Pictures Corp., 75 minutes, premier March 4, 1929).

56. Amanda Davis, "Faith, or, Tips for the Successful Young Lady," from *Circling the Drain* (New York: Morrow, 2000).

57. An exploration of the overlap between disability issues and fat issues is beyond the scope of this essay, but I do want to mention here one particularly poignant characteristic in the childhood histories of people born with disabilities or chronic illnesses, those who become disabled or chronically ill as children, and fat children: they all tend to be anomalous, "others," in their families of origin. The grown-ups in the worlds of these children—parents and professionals alike—who do not share the condition of these children, whatever it is, are the ones who set the standards, establish the goals, and make the determinations about "what is to be done" for the "poor" child. The similarities between the experiences of childhood recorded in the autobiographies and memoirs of fat children and disabled or chronically ill children are unmistakable.

58. In Koppelman, *Women's Friendships*, 243–44.

59. For a more thorough exploration of domestic violence as a theme in short stories by American women, see *Women in the Trees: Stories of Battering and Resistance, 1839–1996*, edited by Susan Koppelman (Boston: Beacon Press, 1996; revised edition forthcoming from the Feminist Press in late 2004).

60. See Barber, "Exuberant Proportions."

61. *FAT! SO?* is the title of both the periodical and the book published by Marilyn Wann. The full book title is *FAT! SO? Because you DON'T have to APOLOGIZE for your SIZE!* (Berkeley: Ten Speed Press, 1998).

BIBLIOGRAPHY

BOOKS

Angelou, Maya. *Phenomenal Woman: Four Poems Celebrating Women.* New York: Random House, 1978.

Antin, Mary. "Malinka's Atonement" in *American and I: Short Stories by American Jewish Women Writers,* edited and with an introduction by Joyce Antler. Boston: Beacon Press, 1991.

Allegra, Donna. "Fat Dancer" in *Journeys to Self-Acceptance: Fat Women Speak,* edited by Carol Wiley. Freedom, CA: Crossing Press, 1994.

Bass, Margaret K. "On Being a Fat Black Girl in a Fat-Hating Culture" in *Recovering the Black Female Body: Self-Representations by African American Women,* edited by Michael Bennett and Vanessa D. Dickerson. New Brunswick, NJ: Rutgers University Press, 2001.

Baum, Charlotte, Paula Hyman, and Sonya Michel. *The Jewish Woman in America.* New York: Doubleday, 1976.

Beller, Anne Scott. *Fat and Thin: A Natural History of Obesity.* New York: Farrar, Straus & Giroux, 1977.

Birtha, Becky. "Johnnieruth" in *The Unforgetting Heart: An Anthology of Short Stories by African American Women, 1859–1993,* edited by Asha Kanwar. San Francisco, Aunt Lute Books, 1993. Originally published in *Lover's Choice.* Seattle: Seal Press, 1987.

Blank, Hanne, ed. *Zaftig: Well Rounded Erotica.* San Francisco: Cleis Press, 2001.

Bordo, Susan. *Unbearable Weight: Feminism, Western Culture, and the Body.* Berkeley: University of California Press, 1993.

Boston Women's Health Book Collective. *Our Bodies, Ourselves,* 2nd ed. Chapter One. New York: Simon & Schuster, 1976.

Braziel, Jana Evans and Kathleen Le Besco, eds. *Bodies Out of Bounds: Fatness and Transgression.* Berkeley: University of California Press, 2001.

Brown, Laura S. "Lesbians, Weight, and Eating: New Analyses and Perspective" in *Lesbian Psychologies: Explorations & Challenges,* edited by the Boston Lesbian Psychologies Collective. Urbana and Chicago: University of Illinois Press, 1987.

Brumberg, Joan Jacobs. *The Body Project : An Intimate History of American Girls.* New York: Random House, 1997.

Butler, Sandra. "Backwards and Forwards in America" in *Celebrating the Lives of Jewish*

Women: Patterns in a Feminist Sampler, edited by Rachel Josefowitz Siegel and Ellen Cole. Binghamton, NY: The Harrington Park Press, 1997.

Calcagno, Ann. "Story of My Weight" in *Pray for Yourself and Other Stories*. Evanston, IL: Northwestern University Press, 1993. Reprinted as "Let Them Eat Cake" in *The Milk of Almonds: Italian American Women Writers on Food and Culture*, edited by Louise DeSalvo and Edvige Giunta. New York: The Feminist Press at CUNY, 2002.

Caputi, Jane. "Tabooing the Ugly Woman," in *Forbidden Fruits: Taboos and Tabooism in Culture*, edited by Ray B. Browne. Bowling Green, Ohio:Popular Press, 1984.

Chernin, Kim. *The Obsession: Reflections on the Tyranny of Slenderness*. New York: Harper-Collins, 1981; reprint 1994.

Clifton, Lucille, "Homage to my Hips" in *Good Woman: Poems and a Memoir*. New York: BOA Editions, 1987.

Cooke, Kaz. *Real Gorgeous: The Truth About Body and Beauty*. New York: W.W. Norton, 1996.

Courtot, Martha. "A Spoiled Identity" in *Shadow on a Tightrope: Writing by Women on Fat Oppression*, edited by Lisa Schoenfielder and Barb Wieser. San Francisco: Aunt Lute Books, 1983. Originally published in *Sinister Wisdom* 20 (1982).

Davis, Amanda. "Faith, or, Tips for the Successful Young Lady" in *Circling the Drain*. New York: Morrow, 2000.

Dennet, Andrea Stulman. "The Dime Freak Show Reconfigured" in *Freakery: Cultural Spectacles of the Extraordinary Body*, edited by Rosemarie Garland Thomson. New York: NYU Press, 1996.

Dykewomon, Elana. *Riverfinger Women*. Originally published 1974; reprint Tallahassee, FL: Naiad Press, 1992.

———. *Moon Creek Road*. Denver: Spinsters Ink, 2003

Edison, Laurie Toby, photographs and Debbie Notkin, text. *Women En Large: Images of Fat Nudes*. San Francisco: Books in Focus, 1994.

Forman, Frieda, Ethel Raicus, Sarah Swartz, Margie Wolfe, and Sarah Silberstein-Swartz, eds. *Hidden Treasures: Stories by Yiddish Women Writers*. Toronto: University of Toronto Press, 1994.

Frye, Marilyn. "Oppression," in *The Politics of Reality: Essays in Feminist Theory* by Marilyn Frye. Trumansburg, NY: Crossing Press, 1983.

Garland Thomson, Rosemarie. "Introduction: From Wonder to Error: A Genealogy of Freak Discourse in Modernity" in *Freakery: Cultural Spectacles of the Extraordinary Body*, edited by Rosemarie Garland Thomson. New York: NYU Press, 1996.

Goffman, Erving. *Stigma: Notes on the Management of Spoiled Identity* Englewood Cliffs, NJ: Prentice-Hall, 1963.

Goldenberg, Myrna. "Food Talk: Gendered Responses to Hunger in the Concentration Camps" in *Experience and Expression: Women, the Nazis, and the Holocaust*, edited by Elizabeth R. Baer and Myrna Goldenberg. Detroit: Wayne State University Press, 2003.

Hawthorne, Nathaniel. "The Birthmark." 1843. Included in *Selected Tales and Sketches*. New York: Penguin, 1987.

Holley, Marietta. *My Opinions and Betsy Bobbet's: Designed as a Beacon Light to Guide Women to Life, Liberty, and the Pursuit of Happiness, but which may be read by members of the sterner sect without injury to them or the book*. 1877.

Honey, Maureen, ed. *Breaking the Ties that Bind: Popular Stories of the New Woman, 1915–1930*. Norman: University of Oklahoma Press, 1992.

Huff, Joyce. "A 'Horror of Corpulence:' Interrogating Bantingism and Mid-Nineteenth-Century fat-Phobia" in *Bodies Out of Bounds: Fatness and Transgression*, edited by Jana Evans Braziel and Kathleen LeBesco. Berkeley, University of California Press, 2001.

Hurst, Fannie. "The Gold in Fish." *Cosmopolitan*, August 1925. Collected in *Song of Life*. New York: Knopf, 1927.

——. "Sob Sister," *Metropolitan Magazine* 43:4 (February 1916). Included in *Every Soul Hath Its Song*. New York: Harper & Bros., 1916.

Hurston, Zora Neale. "Sweat." 1926. Included in *The Complete Tales of Zora Neale Hurston*. New York: HarperCollins, 1996. Also included in *"Women in the Trees:" U.S. Women's Short Stories about Battering and Resistance, 1839–1994*, edited by Susan Koppelman.

Irving, Washington. "The Stout Gentleman." 1822. Included in *The Complete Tales of Washington Irving*, edited by Charles Nieder. New York: DaCapo Press, 1998.

James, Henry. "The Real Thing" 1892. Included in *The Complete Short Stories, 1892–1898*, edited by John Hollander and David Bromwich. New York: Library of America, 1996.

Kaye/Kantrowitz, Melanie. "Jewish Food, Jewish Children" in *The Tribe of Dina: A Jewish Women's Anthology*, 2nd ed., edited by Melanie Kaye/Kantrowitz and Irena Klepfisz. Boston: Beacon Press, 1989.

Kelly. "The Goddess is Fat" in *Shadow on a Tightrope: Writing by Women on Fat Oppression* edited by Lisa Schoenfielder and Barb Wieser. San Francisco: Aunt Lute Books, 1983.

Kent, Le'a. "Fighting Abjection: Representing Fat Women" in *Bodies Out of Bounds: Fatness and Transgression*, edited by Jana Evans Braziel and Kathleen LeBesco. Berkeley: University of California Press, 2001.

Koppelman, Susan, ed. *The Other Woman: Stories of Two Women and a Man*. New York: The Feminist Press at CUNY, 1984.

——, ed. *Women in the Trees: Stories of Battering and Resistance, 1839–1996*. Boston: Beacon Press, 1996; rev. ed. forthcoming, New York: Feminist Press at CUNY, 2004.

——, ed. *Women's Friendships: A Collection of Stories*. Norman: University of Oklahoma Press, 1991.

Lorde, Audre, *Zami: A New Spelling of My Name* Trumansburg, NY: Crossing Press, 1983.

Manheim, Camryn. *Wake Up, I'm Fat!* New York: Broadway Books, 1999.

Martindale, Lee, ed. *Such a Pretty Face*. Atlanta: Meisha Merlin Publishing, 2000.

——. *The Folly of Assumption: The Collected Fat Fantasies of Lee Martindale*. Alma, AR: Yard Dog Press, 1999.

Maupassant, Guy De. "Boule de Suit" in *Selected Tales of Guy De Maupassant*, edited by Saxe Commins. New York: Random House, 1945.

Mazer, Sharon. "She's so fat. . . . ,: Facing the fat Lady at Coney Island's Sideshows by the Seashore" in *Bodies Out of Bounds: Fatness and Transgression*, edited by Jana Evans Braziel and Kathleen LeBesco. Berkeley: University of California Press, 2001.

McDowell, Deborah E. "Recovery Missions: Imaging the Body Ideals" in *Recovering the Black Female Body: Self-Representations by African American Women*, edited by Michael Bennett and Vanessa D. Dickerson. Mew Brunswick, NJ: Rutgers University Press, 2001.

Millman, Marcia, with photographs by Naomi Bushman. *Such a Pretty Face: Being Fat in America*. New York: W. W. Norton, 1980.

Mitchell, Sharon. *Near Perfect.*, New York: Signet, 2002.

——. *Nothing But the Rent*. New York: Dutton, 1998.

Newman, Lesléa. *Good Enough to Eat: A Novel*. Ithaca, NY: Firebrand Books, 1986.

——, ed. *Eating Our Hearts Out: Personal Accounts of Women's Relationship to Food*. Freedom, CA: Crossing Press, 1993.

——. *Fat Chance*. New York: Putnam, 1999.

Orbach, Susie. *Fat is a Feminist Issue: A Self-Help Guide for Compulsive Eaters*. New York: Berkeley Books, 1978.

Paretsky, Sara. *"A Taste of Life" and Other Stories*. New York: Penguin 1995.

Reed, Kit. "Mommy" in *Scare Care,* edited by Graham Masterson. New York: Tor Books, 1990.

Russ, Joanna. "The Image of Women in Science Fiction" in *Images of Women in Fiction: Feminist Perspectives,* edited by Susan Koppelman Cornillon. Bowling Green State University, Ohio: Popular Press, 1972.

Schoenfielder, Lisa and Barb Wieser, editors. *Shadow on a Tightrope: Writing by Women on Fat Oppression.* Foreward by Vivian Mayer. San Francisco: Aunt Lute Books, 1983.

Schwartz, Hillel *Never Satisfied: A Cultural History of Diets, Fantasies & Fat,* The Free Press, 1986.

Sedgwick, Catharine Maria. "Cacoethes Scribendi." *Norton Anthology of American Literature,* vol. 1. New York: W.W. Norton, 1995.

Seid, Roberta Pollack. *Never Too Thin: Why Women Are At War With Their Bodies.* Englewood Cliffs, NJ: Prentice Hall, 1989.

Simmons, Rachel. *Odd Girl Out: The Hidden Culture of Aggression in Girls.* Orlando, FL: Harcourt, 2002.

Sinclair, Jo. *Wasteland.* New York: Harper, 1946.

Spender, Dale. *Women of Ideas (and What Men Have Done to Them).* London: Routledge & Kegan Paul, 1982.

Stafford, Jean. "The Echo and the Nemesis." 1950. Included in *Collected Stories of Jean Stafford.* Farrar, Straus & Giroux, 1992.

Stinson, Susan. *Fat Girl Dances With Rocks,* Denver: Spinsters, Ink 1994.

———. *Martha Moody,* Denver: Spinsters, Ink, 1995

Stoddard, Elizabeth D. B. "Osgood's Predicament." Originally published in *Harper's Magazine,* June 1869. Included in *Library of American Fiction,* vol. 8. New York: The Success Company, 1884, 1904.

Thanet, Octave. "Harry Lossing." Originally published in *Scribner's Magazine* 13: 2 (February, 1893). Included in *Stories of a Western Town* by Octave Thanet, 1893.

Toth, Emily. *Kate Chopin: A Life of the Author of The Awakening.* New York: William Morrow, 1990.

———, Per Seyersted, and Cheyenne Bonnell, eds. *Kate Chopin's Private Papers.* Bloomington: Indiana University Press, 1998.

Wagner, Linda. "Regionalism" in *The Oxford Companion to Women's Writing in the United States,* edited by Cathy N. Davidson and Linda Wagner-Martin. New York: Oxford University Press, 1997.

Walker, Alice. *The Color Purple.* New York: Harcourt, Brace, Jovanovich, 1982.

———. *Everyday Use.* New Brunswick, NJ: Rutgers University Press, 1994.

———. *The Third Life of Grange Copeland.* New York: Harcourt Brace Jovanovich, 1970.

———. *The Way Forward is with a Broken Heart.* New York: Ballantine Books, 2000.

Wolf, Naomi. *The Beauty Myth: How Images of Beauty Are Used Against Women.* New York: Doubleday, 1991.

Wann, Marilyn. *Fat! So? Because You Don't Have to Apologize for Your Size.* Berkeley, CA: Ten Speed Press, 1998.

Yezierska, Anzia. "The Fat of the Land." Originally published in *The Century,* August 1919. Included in *The Best Short Stories of 1919,* edited by Edward J. O'Brien. Small, Maynard, and Co., 1920. Also included in *Children of Loneliness* by Anzia Yezierska. 1923.

Zola. Emile. "The Attack on the Mill" in *Great Short Stories,* vol. 3: Romance and Adventure, edited by William Patten. New York: P.F. Collier & Son, 1906.

ARTICLES

Barber, Wilson. "Exuberant Proportions." *Dimensions,* November 1994; online at www.geocities.com/wilsonbarbers/sideshow.

Bray, Rosemary. "Heavy Burden." *Essence,* January 1992.

Brown, Roxanne. "Full-Figured Women Fight Back: Resistance Grows to Society's Demand for Slim Bodies." *Ebony,* March 1990.

Brownell, Kelly and Judith Rodin. "Medical, Metabolic and Psychological Effects of Weight Cycling." *Arch Intern Med* 154:1325–1330 (1994).

Ceja, Diane M. "Mothers and Daughters: Healing the Patterns of Generations." *Radiance: The Magazine for Large Women,* Fall 1992.

Cohen, Marion. "This is a Fat Liberation Poem." *Mothering Magazine* 113 (July/August 2002).

Feltz, Vanessa. "Who Says Fat Isn't Sexy?" *Redbook,* 1993.

Freespirit, Judy. Interview. Online at www.lustydevil.com/fatgirl/judyfree.

Freidson, Eliot. "Celebrating Erving Goffman" in *Contemporary Sociology* 12:4 (July 1983).

Klass, Perri. "What Really Shapes a Girl's Self-image: A pediatrician speaks out about how parents can boost—or burst—their daughters' confidence." *Family Life Magazine,* March 2001.

Koppelman, Susan. "The Educations of Fannie Hurst" in *Women's Studies International Forum* 10:5 (October 1987).

Lieberman, Janice S., Ph.D. "On Looking and Being Looked At." *The Round Robin,* Newsletter of Section I, Psychologist-Psychoanalyst Practitioners, Division of Psychoanalysis (39), American Psychological Association, 43:1 (Spring 2003).

Mabel-Lois, Lynn. "Position Paper: Humor." *The Fat Underground, A Fat Liberation Collective.* Online at www.largesse.net.

Margolis, David. "Glorious Food." *Jerusalem Post,* July 23, 1995

Reynolds, Elaine. "Racing with a Butterfly." *Radiance,* Spring 1999.

Stimson, Karen W. "Fat Feminist Herstory, 1969–1993: A Personal Memoir." *Expository Magazine* 1:1 (2001–02); online at www.expositorymagazine.net/fatfemherstory.

Thonpson, Becky Wangsgaard "A Way Outa No Way: Eating Problems Among African-American, Latina, and White Women." *Gender and Society* 6:4 (1992).

Welter, Barbara. "The Cult of True Womanhood: 1820–1860." *American Quarterly* 18 (1966).

ONLINE RESOURCES

A list of web sites and listservs dealing with women and fatness, fat acceptance, and related topics appears on the web site of the Feminist Press at the City University of New York. Go to *www.feministpress.org* and click on Special Projects. This is meant to be an interactive and expanding resource for readers interested in these topics. Readers are encouraged to email their suggestions for additions to the list to *MelodyMoskwitz@msn.com.*

CREDITS

OPENING EPIGRAPHS

W. Charisse Goodman. *The Invisible Woman: Confronting Weight Prejudice in America.* Carlsbad, CA: Gurze Books, 1995.

Allan F. Johnson. *Privilege, Power, and Difference.* Mountainview, CA: Mayfield Publishing Company, 2001.

Miss Piggy. *Miss Piggy's Guide to Life* by Henry Beard. New York: Knopf, 1981.

Rosemarie Garland Thomson. *Extraordinary Bodies: Figuring Physical Disability in American Culture and Literature.* New York: Columbia University Press, 1997.

George Carlin. *Brain Droppings.* New York: Hyperion, 1997.

Tracy Wheeler, *The Modesto Bee,* Modesto, CA, July 23, 2003; see www.modbee.com.

Rachel Simmons. *Odd Girl Out: The Hidden Culture of Aggression in Girls.* Orlando, FL: Harcourt, 2002.

Emily Toth. *Ms. Mentor's Impeccable Advice for Academic Women.* Philadel-phia: University of Pennsylvania Press, 1997.

STORIES AND STORY EPIGRAPHS

JUANITA: Kate Chopin. First published with "The Night Came Slowly" under the title "A Scrap and a Sketch" in *Moods* (July 1895). Included in *The Complete Works of Kate Chopin,* vol. 1. Ed. Per Seyersted. Baton Rouge, LA: Louisiana State University Press, 1969. Also included in *A Vocation and a Voice.* Ed. Emily Toth. New York: Penguin, 1991. EPIGRAPH: Anne Scott Beller. *Fat and Thin: A Natural History of Obesity.* New York: Farrar, Straus & Giroux, 1977.

THE STOUT MISS HOPKINS'S BICYCLE: Octave Thanet. First published in *Harper's Monthly.* (February 1897). Included in *Different Girls: Harper's Novelettes.* Ed. William Dean Howells and Henry Mills Alden. Harper & Brothers Publishers, 1906. EPIGRAPHS: Hillel Schwartz. *Never Satisfied: A Cultural History of Diets, Fantasies & Fat.* New York: Free Press, 1986. Elaine Reynolds. "Racing with a Butterfly." *Radiance: The Magazine for Large Women* (Spring 1999).

THE HOMELY HEROINE: Edna Ferber. *Everybody's Magazine* 23, no. 5 (November 1910).

EPIGRAPH: Jane E. Caputi. "Beauty Secrets: Tabooing the Ugly Woman." *Forbidden Fruits: Taboos and Tabooism in Culture.* Ed. Ray B. Browne. Bowling Green, Ohio: Popular Press, 1984.

NOBLESSE: Mary E. Wilkins Freeman. First published in *The Copy-Cat & Other Stories.* Harper & Brothers Publishers, 1913. Included in *The Best Stories of Mary E. Wilkins Freeman.* Harper & Brothers Publishers, 1927, reprint Scholar's Press, Inc., 1971. EPIGRAPHS: Rosemarie Garland Thomson. "Introduction: From Wonder to Error: A Genealogy of Freak Discourse in Modernity." *Freakery: Cultural Spectacles of the Extraordinary Body.* Ed. Rosemarie Garland Thomson. New York: New York University Press, 1996. Andrea Stulman Dennet. "The Dime Freak Show Reconfigured." *Freakery: Cultural Spectacles of the Extraordinary Body.* Ed. Rosemarie Garland Thomson. New York: New York University Press, 1996. 323.

EVEN AS YOU AND I: Fannie Hurst. First published in *Cosmopolitan* 66:5 (April 1919). Included in *Humoresque: A Laugh on Life with a Tear Behind It.* New York: Harper Bros., 1919. EPIGRAPH: Gordon Allport, *The Nature of Prejudice.* Boston: Addison Wesley, 1954.

FAT: Grace Sartwell Mason. First published as "Sweet Tooth" in the *Woman's Home Companion* (May 1927). Included in *Women Are Queer* (Ayer Company Publishers, 1932). Reprinted by permission of the publisher. EPIGRAPH: The Boston Women's Health Book Collective. *Our Bodies, Ourselves,* 2nd ed. New York: Simon & Schuster, 1976.

THIS WAS MEANT TO BE: Alberta Hughes Wahl. First published in *Woman's Home Companion* (February 1946). Included in *A Diamond of Years: The Best of the Woman's Home Companion.* Ed. Helen Otis Lamont. Doubleday and Company, 1961. EPIGRAPH: Kelly. "The Goddess is Fat." From *Shadow on a Tightrope: Writing by Women on Fat Oppression.* ©1983. Ed. Lisa Schoenfielder and Barb Wieser. Reprinted by permission of Aunt Lute Books.

GOOD-BYE, OLD LAURA: Lucile Vaughan Payne. First published in *Seventeen* (June/July 1965). Included in *The Boy Upstairs: and Other Stories.* Follett Publishing Company, 1965. EPIGRAPH: Lynn Mabel-Lois. "Position Paper: Humor." Originally published in 1974 by The Fat Underground. Available at www.largesse.net/ Archives/FU/humor.html.

THE FOOD FARM: Kit Reed. First published in *Orbit 2: Brand New Science Fiction of the Year* (1967). Included in *The Attack of the Giant Baby.* New York: Berkley Books, 1981. Copyright © 1974 by Kit Reed. Reprinted by permission of the author. EPIGRAPH: The National Association to Advance Fat Acceptance, from NAAFA Policy—Fat Admirers www.naafa.org/documents/policies/fat_admirers.html.

JELLY ROLLS: Jyl Lynn Felman. First published in *Penumbra* 1, no. 2. (1979). Included in *Hot Chicken Wings.* San Francisco: Aunt Lute Books, 1995. Copyright © 1979 by Jyl Lynn Felman. Reprinted by permission of the author. EPIGRAPH: Marcia Millman. *Such a Pretty Face: Being Fat in America.* New York: W. W. Norton, 1980.

HE WAS A MAN! (BUT HE DID HIMSELF WRONG): From *A Piece of Mine* by J. California Cooper, copyright © 1984 by J. California Cooper. 1984; reprint. New York: Anchor Doubleday, 1992. Used by permission of Doubleday, a division of Random House, Inc. EPIGRAPH: Rosemary Bray. "Heavy Burden." *Essence* (January 1992).

THE FEEDER: Maria Bruno. First published in *The Women's Studies Newsletter* (Michigan State University, Spring 1985). Copyright © 1985 by Maria Bruno. Reprinted by permission of the author. EPIGRAPHS: Roxanne Brown. "Full-Figured Women Fight Back: Resistance Grows to Society's Demand for Slim Bodies." *Ebony* (March 1990). 28, 30. Vanessa Feltz. "Who Says Fat Isn't Sexy?" *Redbook* 1993.

BLOOMINGDALE'S: Perri Klass. *I Am Having An Adventure: Stories* (Putnam Publishing Group, 1986). Copyright © 1986 by Perri Klass. Reprinted by permission of the author. EPIGRAPH: Perri Klass. "What Really Shapes a Girl's Self-image: A Pediatrician Speaks Out about How Parents can Boost — or Burst — Their Daughters' Confidence." *Family Life Magazine* (March 2001).

THE DREAM DIET: Susan Dyer. *Redbook* (January 1986). EPIGRAPH: Largesse, the Network for Size Esteem, "10 Good Reasons Not to Diet," www.largesse.net/reasons.html.

A MAMMOTH UNDERTAKING: Roz Warren. *Backbone* 4 (1987). Copyright © 1987 by Roz Warren. Reprinted by permission of the author. EPIGRAPH: Catherine Beecher, quoted in *Never Too Thin: Why Women Are At War With Their Bodies*. Roberta Pollack Seid. Englewood, NJ: Prentice Hall, 1989.

FAT LENA: Wanda Coleman. First published in *A War Of Eyes And Other Stories*. Santa Rosa, CA: Black Sparrow Press, 1988. Recorded on *High Priestess of Word*. BarKubCo/ New Alliance Records, 1991. Copyright © 1988 by Wanda Coleman. Reprinted by permission of the author. EPIGRAPH: Donna Allegra. "Fat Dancer." *Journeys to Self-Acceptance: Fat Women Speak*. Ed. Carol Wiley. Berkeley, CA: The Crossing Press, 1994.

ON WARD G: Judy Freespirit. *Sinister Wisdom 39: On Disability* (Winter 1989–1990). Copyright © 1989 by Judy Freespirit. Reprinted by permission of the publisher. EPIGRAPHS: Fatima Parker. "Shedding Light on Fat Discrimination." http://size-accept-ance.org/arab_nations/index.html. Cheryl Olsen (cheryl@midmo.net). Debbie Notkin. *Women En Large: Images of Fat Nudes*. San Francisco, CA: Books in Focus, 1994.

SKANKS: Rennie Sparks. First published in *North American Review* 275 (1990). Included in *Tyranny of the Normal: An Anthology*. Ed. Carol Donley and Sheryl Buckley. Kent, OH: Kent State University Press, 1993. Copyright © 1990 by Rennie Sparks. Reprinted by permission of the author. EPIGRAPHS: Joan Jacobs Brumberg. *The Body Project: An Intimate History of American Girls*. New York: Random House, Inc., 1997. Rachel Simmons. *Odd Girl Out: The Hidden Culture of Aggression in Girls*. Orlando, FL: Harcourt, 2002.

PERFECTLY NORMAL: Lesléa Newman. *Secrets: Short Stories*. Norwich, VT: New Victoria Publishers, Inc., 1990. Copyright © 1990 by Lesléa Newman. Reprinted by permission of the author. EPIGRAPH: Laura S. Brown. "Lesbians, Weight, and Eating: New Analyses and Perspectives." *Lesbian Psychologies: Explorations & Challenges*. Ed. Boston Lesbian Psychologies Collective. Champion, IL: University of Illinois Press, 1987.

PRIMOS: Connie Porter. *The Bilingual Review/Editorial Bilingüe*, Vol. XVII, No. 2 (May/August 1992). Copyright © 1992 by Connie Porter. Reprinted by permission of the publisher. EPIGRAPH: Marion Cohen. "This is a Fat Liberation Poem." *Mothering Magazine* 113 (July/August 2002).

THE LANGUAGE OF THE FAT WOMON: Elana Dykewomon. *Amazones D'hier/Lesbiennes D'aujourd'hui*, "La Grosseur: Obsession? Opppression!" 23 (December 1992). Copyright © 1992 by Elana Dykewomon. Reprinted by permission of the author. EPIGRAPH: Anita Roddick, founder of The Body Shop, from an interview at www.bigfatblog.com/inter-views/roddick.php

THE MAN I LOVE: Elaine Fowler Palencia. First published in *Sing, Heavenly Muse*. Reprinted from *Small Caucasian Woman: Stories*. Elaine Fowler Palencia. Columbia: University of Missouri Press, 1993. Reprinted by permission of the University of Missouri Press. Copyright © 1993 by Elaine Fowler Palencia. EPIGRAPH: Martha Courtot. "A Spoiled Identity." From *Shadow on a Tightrope: Writing by Women on Fat*